Praise for Ac...

"Everything I hope for in a suspenseful read—chilling, complex, and intense. Millar's riveting novel, with its frightening premise and twists and turns, kept me frantically turning pages late into the night."

—Heather Gudenkauf, *New York Times* bestselling author of *The Weight of Silence*

"Taut, chilling, and utterly brilliant—my thriller of the year."

—Lisa Jewell, internationally bestselling author of *The House We Grew Up In*

"As Millar makes truth elusive and builds suspense, she is establishing herself in the top tier of writers of psychological thrillers."

—*Booklist* (starred review)

"Compelling . . . a heady page-turner that should appeal to fans of Kate Atkinson's Jackson Brodie series."

—*Publishers Weekly* (starred review)

"A deliciously disturbing read, with paranoia seeping from every page."

—Alex Marwood, author of *The Wicked Girls*

"[A] chilling psychological thriller . . . Fans of Gillian Flynn and Joy Fielding will welcome this story. It's an emotional journey readers won't want to miss."

—Susan Wiggs, author of The Lakeshore Chronicles series and *The Apple Orchard*

"A brainy thriller lodged satisfyingly in the contemporary moment."

—Holly Goddard Jones, author of *The Next Time You See Me*

"Millar is the new master of domestic suspense. *Playdate* showed the world what an exceptional writer Millar is, *Accidents Happen* cements it."

—*Cayocosta Book Reviews*

"A suspenseful tale featuring surprising twists."

—*Library Journal*

"A fantastically compelling thriller with a dark mystery at its core."

—*Cleveland Plain Dealer*

FICTION

Praise for *The Playdate*

"Engrossing . . . a gripping psychological thriller."
—Publishers Weekly (starred review)

"Taut, page-turning, and surprising."   —Cleveland Plain Dealer

"A supremely accomplished debut thriller."   —Booklist (starred review)

"Unputdownable."   —Marie Claire (UK)

"A must-read that will tap into every mother's primal fears."
—Sophie Hannah

"Thought-provoking, taut, and suspenseful."   —Easy Living (UK)

"Gripping."   —People

"When you put this book down, you'll wish there were more."
—Ann Bauer, author of *The Forever Marriage*

"A disturbing psychological thriller."   —New York Times Book Review

"This gripping tale will strike a chord."   —Time Out (UK)

"A taut chiller."   —The Mystery Gazette

"Compelling . . . creepy and unsettling."   —The Guardian (UK)

"Louise Millar's novel sucks the reader in like quicksand to the surprising ending. I did not want to miss a page!"
—Lee Woodruff, New York Times bestselling authors of *Those We Love Most*

"A well-paced psychological thriller with more than a hint of Minette Walters about it."   —Sunday Express (UK)

"Quietly creepy and expertly crafted."   —Stylist Magazine

"Clever and scary. Millar plays with the darkness beneath apparently normal lives."   —Irish Examiner

The
Hidden
Girl

The Hidden Girl

* *A Novel* *

LOUISE MILLAR

EMILY BESTLER BOOKS
—
ATRIA

New York   London   Toronto   Sydney   New Delhi

ATRIA PAPERBACK
A Division of Simon & Schuster, Inc.
1230 Avenue of the Americas
New York, NY 10020

Copyright © 2014 by Louise Millar

First Emily Bestler Books/Atria Paperback edition August 2014

EMILY BESTLER BOOKS / ATRIA PAPERBACK and colophons are trademarks of Simon & Schuster, Inc.

For information about special discounts for bulk purchases, please contact Simon & Schuster Special Sales at 1-866-506-1949 or business@simonandschuster.com.

The Simon & Schuster Speakers Bureau can bring authors to your live event. For more information or to book an event contact the Simon & Schuster Speakers Bureau at 1-866-248-3049 or visit our website at www.simonspeakers.com.

Cover design by Rodrigo Corral
Cover image by Valentin Casarsa/Getty Images

Manufactured in the United States of America

10   9   8   7   6   5   4   3   2   1

Library of Congress Cataloging-in-Publication Data has been applied for.

ISBN 978-1-4767-6009-4
ISBN 978-1-4767-6012-4 (ebook)

For Molly

The
Hidden
Girl

Prologue

They are coming.
They are on their way.
I can taste them in the air like sand in sea wind.
Starlings flit, a handful of stones thrown at the sky.
A plane swims through the clouds towards Ipswich.

"The apples fall down one by one
And with a crack they hit the ground
And with one chop, a head falls free
Under the rotten apple tree"

I lie on the floor and wait.
I stretch my arms above my head, and push my feet far away.
I try to push them all the way to China.

"The apples fall down two by two
And roll under my leather shoe
And with one chop, a head falls free
Under the rotten apple tree"

If I could touch both sides of this room, I would be a giant.
I know what a giant would do.
A giant would wait till they came.
Then it would lift up its feet and do this . . .
STAMP! STAMP! STAMP!

1

"Where the hell are we?"

Will and Hannah's car slammed to a halt at a crossroads, forcing the moving van to brake sharply behind them.

Hannah looked up from the map and peered ahead. No signposts, for the fifth time today. She made an apologetic gesture out the window to the driver, and ducked back before he could lock eyes with her.

"Weren't we here a minute ago?" Will said, grabbing the map from her.

"The driver looks like his head is going to blow off," she said.

"Screw him." Will's hair fell forward, obscuring his face, as he checked the map. "Why isn't it on the GPS? What's the point of having a fucking GPS if it doesn't have tiny places on it?"

She said nothing. Instead she tried to spot landmarks to help him. It was difficult. The bare branches of the trees that lined this tiny sliver of Suffolk lane clasped in the middle like witches' nails, blocking out much of the late-afternoon March light. It didn't help, either, that through the gaps the land beyond was featureless. Flat mud, spreading aimlessly. She recalled their last visit, nearly six months ago. The sky had been chalk-blue. Heavy green boughs waving in the late-summer breeze. A pale golden shimmer across the fields.

How long was it again till summer? She counted the months.

Will tapped the dashboard. "Right, so we came left from Thurrup, right at Snadesdon and . . ."

Hannah kept her mouth shut. Half an hour ago, old, childish Will had appeared. She would wait for grown-up Will to return. She'd told Barbara about this tactic when they'd had to describe how they resolved their arguments. Barbara had declared herself impressed by Hannah's strategy.

Will threw the map back on her lap. "Let's try right."

"Didn't we do that last time?"

He banged the steering wheel. "What do you want me to do, Han?"

Just stop stressing out, and hurry up, she wanted to say, but didn't.

This time, however, for no obvious reason, turning right and then left worked. Ten minutes and two more pin-narrow Suffolk lanes later, a faded sign saying TORNLEY appeared out of the dusk, shortly before a terrace of three traditional pink cottages.

Will shot Hannah a conciliatory smile, but she was too excited to respond. This was it.

Bending forward, she tried to catch glimpses through the bare branches as Will took the last bend—although, if the countryside looked this different in winter, what on earth would the house look like?

She steeled herself.

A snatch of chimney appeared first, through bristles of hedge. Then a redbrick Victorian gable. And then it was rushing towards them. Tornley Hall, standing side-on to the road as if it had been abandoned for so long it had given up waiting for new owners and had turned away to stare wistfully at something in the distance.

Hannah fell very still.

Actually, it did look a bit different.

She tried to refocus her mind on a sight that was both familiar and unexpected. She realized, surprised, that the facade of the house had altered dramatically in her head during the long wait to exchange contracts since their last viewing: it had widened and softened and become more beautiful. The reality was thinner and taller. Shabbier, too. The windows were filthy from the long winter, and there was a rash of moss across the roof tiles, two of which were missing.

Quickly she reminded herself of the surveyor's report. "Tornley Hall is a solid house in need of a lot of love." As long as it looked presentable to Barbara in two weeks' time—or, more precisely, thirteen and a half days—that's all that mattered.

Will pulled over by the wooden five-bar gate.

The lane behind was empty.

"Where are they?" Hannah asked.

"Probably stuck behind that lad in the tractor who pulled out after us."

"Oh, God, they hate us."

Will banged the steering wheel again, but more softly. "I used to know these fucking roads like the back of my hand. . . ."

His Salford accent always returned when he was tired. *Fookin' roads.* On days like these, being responsible and dependable in a crisis always seemed to drain every ounce of energy Will had.

She knew a hug would revive him. So she did her best and grasped his left hand in her lap.

"What?" Will said.

"Go on then."

"What?"

"Describe the back of your hand."

Will made an unamused face at her, and she replaced his hand firmly on the wheel. To be sure it stayed there, she opened her door. "I'll get the gate."

"Don't go far. We might need your hostile-environment training when they get here."

She held up her fists like a boxer, then jumped out, relieved. Grown-up Will was back, making jokes to ease the tension.

She shivered. It must be five degrees colder in Suffolk than it had been in London this morning. Hugging her coat to her, she peered over the gate. The garden was pretty unrecognizable, too. The grand oak trees that lined the driveway on their previous visits now appeared naked and undignified, as if someone had stolen their bath towels. Their leaves lay long discarded on the gravel in rotting heaps. Up ahead, the freshly trimmed side lawn from last summer was a sea of weeds.

An acrid smell drifted into Hannah's nostrils. Below her lay something tiny and dead, its guts claret-red and bursting out. A mouse or a bird. She kicked it into the bushes, then wiped her boot on the grass.

OK. Well, this was unexpected. She hadn't even thought about the garden. Would two weeks be enough to get Tornley Hall ready, inside and out?

Hannah lifted the gate catch.

As she walked forward, the gate rebounded, trapping her hand.

"Ow!"

The wood was swollen and threaded with tiny cracks. Instead of sanding and fixing it, someone had clearly sloshed tarry black paint over it. Now it was warped. It no longer fit in the space between the posts.

There was a roar behind her and the moving van shot round the bend, coming to an abrupt halt, bumper-to-bumper with Will.

Hannah's own patience slipped. She had waited too long. The gate was one obstacle too many today.

She kicked the bottom, hard. The gate battered into the bushes. She waved both vehicles through, avoiding the van driver's glare, then shut the gate and forced the latch down.

Suddenly, she realized she was still standing in the road.

"Han?" a shout came. Will had got out of their car and was retrieving the keys his cousin Laurie had left under the plant pot by the front door. "What are you doing?"

A thought came to her from nowhere. Will looked ridiculous out here. In his red skinny T-shirt and jeans, his curly musician hair and leather wristband, he looked more like a member of an indie band on his way to Latitude Festival, not the owner of this big country house.

Hannah lifted the latch again, wondering why she'd shut the gate before entering. Then, as she closed it behind her, she knew.

She had dreamed about Tornley Hall every night for eight months. The dream had kept her going. The minute she crossed the threshold, reality would be waiting to pounce again.

•   •   •

Three minutes later Hannah's next impressions of Tornley Hall did nothing to reassure her. The implications of buying a house that had stood empty for two and a half years were becoming quickly apparent. After its third winter unoccupied, and with the previous owners' furniture removed just yesterday, the inner hall was as unrecognizable as the garden. There was a strange odor, too: an unpalatable mixture of antiseptic, a sickly chemical flower scent, and, most unpleasant of all, foot rot.

"Kitchen's in the back, thanks," Hannah said to the moving men, averting her eyes from the ghostly picture-frame marks and hairline plaster cracks that crisscrossed the walls. Now that the Horseborrows' vast Oriental tapestry had been removed, the absence of a yard-long chunk of picture rail had been revealed.

Grown-up Will had disappeared again. Childish Will was back with a vengeance and appeared to have gone into shock. The last few days had been so hectic, with working late in the studio, and packing up and cleaning the London flat, that he hadn't shaved. The three-day stubble made his naturally tan skin look sallow.

"We knew it would look like crap when everything was gone," she said.

Will's pissed-off expression told her that was an understatement.

She tried again. "Remember when we moved into the flat and there was that massive burn hole in the carpet that they'd hidden with a rug?"

No reaction.

Giving up, she tried the sitting-room door. Houses always looked bad when you moved in. There was no time to sulk. They had too much to do.

The handle rattled uselessly in her hand.

"This is locked. Will, can you see a key?"

They checked on the windowsills, in the understairs toilet,

and in the side alcove with the stained glass window at the back of the hall.

No key.

Will tried the door opposite. "Study's locked, too."

"That's annoying."

"Where do you want this?" asked a moving man, heaving a sofa through the front door with his partner.

"Just here, please, for the moment." Hannah waited till the men had dumped it—a little unceremoniously, she thought—then whispered to Will, "If we don't find the keys, they'll leave everything in the hall."

That cheered him up.

Hannah peered through the sitting-room keyhole and saw nothing but black. She tried to look in from the garden, but the shutters were tightly closed on the three tall picture windows.

"Dining room?"

"I'll go," Will said, grit in his voice.

"I'll try the kitchen," she said, trying to create the illusion of teamwork between the two of them—for herself, as much as for the smirking moving men.

The kitchen stopped her in her tracks.

This room had taken center stage in her dreams since last summer. It ran along the back of the house, and also had picture windows overlooking the small back garden. On their previous visits, rails of shiny French copper pans had hung from the ceiling, and a grand pine dresser decorated with bright crockery had added cheer to the room. Flower watercolors and landscape oils had hung on the walls, gingham curtains at the windows. Cleared of these homely charms, the dank, bottle-green walls emerged like ghouls.

"God, they really took everything," she said.

Will walked in. "Clue's in the name."

"Hmm?"

"House clearance."

"Funny. No luck?"

"Nope."

When the search around the old, built-in cupboards proved fruitless, too, they tried the little scullery at the far end.

"Oh, good. They remembered to leave it," Hannah said, opening a tall, old-fashioned fridge. "And look what Laurie's left. That's nice," she said, unconvinced. On a shelf was a bowl of bright-green apples, a pint of milk, cheese, a sliced loaf, spread, a large tray of pasta bake bobbled with black olives, and a bottle of cava.

"Coffee table?" came a shout.

"Hall . . ." Will called back curtly. Hannah shot him a look. ". . . *Please.*"

"I'll see if I can catch Brian."

Their estate agent's phone, predictably, went to voice mail. Having managed to offload the keys onto Laurie on his way to the airport this morning, he'd be halfway to his brother's wedding in Italy by now. She turned and saw Will staring at the high Victorian wall ten yards behind the kitchen window. His hands were clasped behind his head.

"What?" Hannah asked, not really wanting an answer.

"Nothing."

She tried to think of something to humor him, then gave up. This was not the time. The balance between them was too off-kilter, like the old brass scales that had sat on the counter here on their previous house viewings with Brian. There would be plenty of time to fix things later. What mattered was that they were finally in.

The countdown had started.

Two weeks—or thirteen and a half days—to go.

Hannah pulled an A4 whiteboard and a red marker from her bag. *Two-week Countdown!* was written at the top. Underneath was a list.

Day 14: Saturday, MOVING DAY, the first entry said.

She crossed it out. That was one done, at least. She considered the entry for tomorrow. Day 13: Sunday, PAINT SITTING ROOM.

Not without the keys, they couldn't.

Hannah crossed out SITTING ROOM and replaced it with KITCHEN. They had to be practical. She scanned the putrid walls and wondered if needing only one day was optimistic. A quick glance through the list of everything else they had to do told her it would have to suffice. They didn't have a choice. They'd just have to do the best job they could. She started to turn.

"OK, Will? So I was thinking that we should start on the kitch—"

She stopped.

Will had left the room so quietly she hadn't heard him go.

•   •   •

Forty-five minutes later, gravel shot up as the moving men hurtled back to London, clearly eager to escape this rural hellhole with its tight horse-cart lanes and slow tractor drivers.

"Right," Hannah said, shutting the front door. The hall was packed with the sitting-room and study furniture, including their sofas, four sets of Will's record shelves, and forty boxes of his vinyl. "Shall we get the bed made up first, and put up the bedroom curtains?"

Will surveyed their pile of belongings, faint menace in his eyes.

She knew if she put her arms round him he would soften; lean into her, and cheer up.

Instead, she picked up a rogue box of clothes to take upstairs.

Will took his jacket from the banister. "When I get back."

"From where?"

"Snadesdon. I'm going to get some beer and milk, before the shop shuts."

"But Laurie's left us a pint—and some cava."

Will opened the door. "We'll need more milk for tomorrow. You have the cava—I fancy a beer."

Beer. She said nothing. Tonight wasn't the night to argue about it. "Want me to come?"

His expression softened a little. "No. Why don't you see if the oven works, and put on that food that Laurie left? I won't be long."

"OK."

Will leaned towards her. The movement was so unexpected Hannah recoiled.

"It was just a kiss, Han."

She touched his arm. "Sorry. I know. I'm just tired."

"OK. Right. I'll be back in half an hour. If . . ."

". . . you don't get lost."

"Yup."

"Good luck." She waited for him to smile, but he didn't.

Will went to the car. Music pounded as the engine started, and he drove away.

Hannah wandered out to the garden, wincing at the pot of saccharine-sweet pink polyanthus that Laurie had left on the doorstep. They'd have to keep them, to be polite.

Will's red rear lights streaked along the hedge, then disappeared up the lane. Why couldn't he just be patient?

Hannah sniffed. The air was so fresh.

She took a deep breath, not quite believing they were finally here.

Phase one completed. Phase two to begin tomorrow.

Tall weeds dipped and danced in the breeze along the edge of the front lawn before disappearing into the black night. How on earth would they cut these back in time for Barbara's visit?

Hannah inhaled again, smelling rotting leaves and damp earth nurturing the first blossoms of spring. She stretched her arms up, to ease off the ache from moving boxes.

The temperature was dropping again, but the breeze was pleasant. She felt it reviving her after their long day. Hannah looked around. The depth of the darkness was astounding. It was that thick, berry blackness that you didn't see in the city. Through the bare trees that bordered the far end of the garden she saw the distant glow of half a dozen houses and farms in Tornley. To her left she made out the slope-roofed garage that would become Will's studio one day.

His mood had been difficult today. She reminded herself that he had worked all week and was exhausted. He was probably dreading the commute back to London on Monday, too. At least one of them didn't have to worry about work anymore. She could manage the decoration of Tornley Hall and just give him jobs to do in the evenings. That should take some pressure off.

Hannah decided to take Will over to the garage after dinner. It might encourage him to look beyond the cracks—to the future, and what this house would bring to their lives.

She let her head fall back and shut her eyes. This was idyllic. No sirens or buses; no voices from the fried-chicken shop on the corner; no drum and bass from passing cars, or taxi engines running outside the pub.

She swayed a little, and picked out the distant bray of an animal and a soft hiss, and wondered fancifully if it might come from the sea, across the marshes.

To her left, there was a rustle in the bushes.

Hannah opened her eyes.

There was a second rustle, this time farther away.

"Hello?" she said, feeling silly. The nearest property must be fifty yards behind the high wall at the rear of the kitchen.

Hannah scanned the darkness. The rustling stopped. A rabbit, or a fox, probably. That would be part of the joy of this place. Nature right on their doorstep.

A stronger, colder wind buffeted the tall weeds. She picked one and ran its spiky stem through her fingers. Their schedule for Barbara coming was already tight. Only thirteen days from tomorrow to finish the whole house. Tidying the garden would steal at least one of those days, now.

Hannah imagined seeing this scruffy lawn through Barbara's eyes.

You've taken on an awful lot here, Hannah. Maybe we should wait another few months?

She felt a flutter of panic and shook her head.

No. Not a single month more. She couldn't bear it.

Hannah stamped her feet to shake off the day's fatigue. Thinking about it, Day 14 wasn't actually over yet.

She returned inside, picked up her marker, thought for a moment, then rewrote the first entry. Day 14: Saturday, MOVING DAY/START KITCHEN.

She found a box in the hall, and went to rip it open.

Just before she did so, however, she rattled the sitting-room door handle again, in case it was just stiff. Nothing happened.

This was so annoying. She put her nose to the keyhole and sniffed.

That was weird. She could swear she smelled petrol.

2

On his way out of Tornley, Will sped along the narrow Suffolk lane, turning the music up louder than he knew Hannah could bear. He opened the window, feeling as if he'd taken off a too-tight sweater, and let the pounding bass escape.

Yet another T-junction without signposts appeared ahead. His headlights illuminated a bald hedge beyond it. Cursing, he looked left, then right. Which way?

There was a crooked iron gate to the left, with a red rope tied to it. Something drifted into his memory about that gate, then out again. A flash of smooth thigh. Lights on a pickup truck. Music. To his right was just darkness. Already he was lost, five minutes from the house. How? It wasn't as if anything round here ever changed.

He tried turning right, but a mile later the black silhouettes of the trees and hedges vanished into a navy sky, suggesting that he was nearly at the sea. After a six-point turn that nearly reversed him into a ditch, and five more miles of pitch-black roads, his headlights finally picked out a sign on the verge that said SNADESDON.

"Thank you," he muttered.

A terrace of pink nineteenth-century cottages appeared next, as if conjured by magic and, suddenly, Will knew where he was. He swung into the village green, passed the shop, which—as he had guessed—had shut two hours ago, and parked by the Fox & Hounds. An old lad walking a Yorkshire terrier frowned at him. Nan Riley entered his thoughts. He turned the music down and gave the man a reassuring nod, receiving a raised walking stick in return. It wasn't his fault, after all.

Will turned off the engine and surveyed Snadesdon.

Saturday night, and the place was already dead.

The uneasy feeling he'd had since this morning persisted.

He dropped his head onto the steering wheel.

What the fuck had he done?

The car clock changed: 7:11 P.M.

Forcing himself out of the car, Will ducked under the low doorway of the thatched pub. It must have been eighteen years since he'd been in here, but the smell was depressingly familiar: horse leather and wood smoke. A fire roared at the far end, and a few faces looked up. The only noticeable change was the introduction of a blackboard, which offered "red" or "white" wine.

A woman turned round at the bar and held out a half pint of lager. "Thought I was going to have to send out a search party."

He hugged her through layers of fleece, and took the lager. "Cheers."

He still never recognized her straightaway. It was the extra weight, the glasses, and the short back and sides, which he suspected was the village hairdresser's idea of a bob. Even though

it was only eight months since Nan Riley's funeral, he still expected to see teenage Laurie, with her long, shiny hair, skin-
tight black jeans, and coatings of purple eyeliner.

"Some signposts would help."

"Yeah, then the place would be full of your lot. Bloody Londoners."

A barman handed Laurie her change and gave Will a curious
look.

"Chris!" Laurie said. "Meet Will, my cousin—your new reg-
ular. He's just moved into Tornley Hall."

"Have you now? Hello!" Chris said, shaking Will's hand.
"That explains it. My wife, Gemma, does your mail. She was
wondering why there were lights on in the old place."

Laurie frowned at Will and shook her head. "No, they just
moved in today, Chris."

"Is that right? Oh, don't tell Gemma that—she'll think she's
seeing ghosts!" He laughed.

"That'll just be the estate agent getting it ready," Laurie said.
"Getting the electric back on and stuff, won't it, Will?"

Will sipped his beer. It tasted good. "Maybe."

He didn't know and he didn't care.

·   ·   ·

He and Laurie found a booth by the window. Will clinked his
cousin's glass. "Cheers for sorting out the keys this morning,
missus."

"You're welcome. So?" She bounced on her seat. "Did you
get my text?"

He had. He'd read it in the service station on the way here,
while Hannah was in the loo. "Yeah. What's the big thing?"

"I've been there before!" Laurie squealed. "We both have!"

"Where?"

"Tornley Hall!"

Will sipped his beer. It was definitely taking the edge off. He shook his head. "I haven't."

"You have!" she said, her eyes widening behind her square black glasses. "I remembered as soon as I walked in. That massive hall with the black-and-white tiles. And the stained glass window. Nan took us there!" She waited for him to react. "We were about six or seven? Nan was probably collecting something for the WI. Do you remember that we used to go round to people's houses with her, around the villages, and get cookies and juice?"

"I don't know what you're talking about."

"Will, you wet your pants in the hall."

"Fuck off, Lor."

She giggled. "You did."

To his surprise, a vague memory did return of warm pee running down his leg onto a red rug, and him looking to Nan, ashamed. And someone—a woman—giving him a toffee and telling him not to cry.

Laurie watched him closely. "Do you remember?"

"I don't know. I remember Nan taking me into this freezing old toilet and wiping my leg . . . and you being there, being a pain in the arse. No idea where it was, though."

Laurie banged his arm. "Oh, my God, you're right! It was there—I remember that. An old toilet covered in blue flowers? I couldn't reach the handle. Is it still there?"

"I don't know." Tornley Hall could have six toilets covered in blue flowers. He hadn't noticed.

"Isn't that weird?" Laurie babbled on. "Anyway, I can't believe you've bought that place. I didn't even know it was there.

Can you imagine Nan's face? She was always boasting about you at the post office: 'My boy, up in London, mixing with the stars, you know. . . .' She'd have had a field day with this. And God, the garden's amazing! I couldn't get the kids out of it this morning. I'll warn you, they're going to ask you if they can have a trampoline on the lawn. We haven't got room, and . . ."

Will waited for Laurie to remember. One, two, three . . .

". . . and . . . anyway. So." On cue, Laurie's cheerful expression disappeared. "So, no Hannah, then? Did she not fancy a drink?"

She watched him with the unabashed affection that had made him uncomfortable as a teenager, but now made him grateful every time he saw her.

He waited to feel guilty about not being honest with Hannah about where he was right now, but didn't. She never stopped talking about that bloody house. He needed a break.

"No. She wanted to get sorted. But she says hi. And thanks for the food."

"That's a shame," Laurie said unconvincingly. Will had seen his cousin watching Hannah by his side at Nan Riley's funeral: suspicious, a cat guarding her owner's garden.

"But, yes. What an amazing house," she said, subdued.

Will sipped his half pint, wanting a proper one. He also wanted to tell her that Tornley Hall was a complete shit hole, and he'd known the minute they arrived that he should never have let Hannah talk him into either the house or coming back here.

"You don't want to know how much the mortgage is, Lor. Needs a lot of work, too."

She nudged him. "You should get Ian over with his power spray. He cleans everything with it. Fences, walls, bins, kids, me . . ."

Will knocked back his half pint, checking the bar clock and wondering how long he could push it to, before he had to go back.

Laurie scratched her nose under her glasses. He saw the words teetering on her lips.

"No," he said, putting her out of her misery.

"No, what?"

"We haven't heard anything."

"Oh, OK. And how's Hannah?"

Where would he start? "You know," he said. "Got her plans."

"Well, tell her if she needs any help . . ."

He wondered, if Laurie did actually spend time with Hannah, on her own, how long she'd be able to act polite.

"How are the kids?" Will asked before he said something about Hannah that he'd regret.

He saw the relief on Laurie's face that she could now mention them without worrying. He forced himself to smile as she reeled off the recent achievements and funny things said by Daniel, Caitlin, and Sam. Then he did what he had done his whole life and summoned a song into his head, to drown it all out.

3

In the end Will stayed for one more drink, ignoring Laurie's glance of disapproval as he ordered a full pint alongside her half. Later he found his way more easily along the dark lanes back to the bald hedge and the crooked gate with the red rope, and turned right.

The Tornley sign appeared, and he bore right again, past the terrace of three cottages. That was better. He knew where he was now.

Will slowed down, scrabbling around in the side pocket to find chewing gum to disguise the alcohol on his breath.

Something moved to his right.

He braked, tensing for a thud.

A tall, lumbering figure ran towards him from the direction of Tornley Hall at a clumsy half trot, wearing a black hoodie and tracksuit trousers, head bent forward.

He waited for the person to look up into his headlights and wave an acknowledgment that they'd seen each other, but the runner just kept going, diving into the long beam of the car's headlights, then onto the verge, before disappearing.

Wanker. He'd get hit out here, wearing that at night.

Will turned the last bend. The illuminated gables of the old house appeared through the bare hedge. The ridiculousness of what he'd let Hannah do—buying this run-down old dump—hit him again.

He drove up the drive, parked, and entered the house.

A pile of cracked air fresheners lay on the hall floor, as if they'd been chucked from upstairs. Behind their collective stink, he detected a new smell.

She must be joking.

Picking his way through all the crap in the hall, Will found Hannah up a ladder in the kitchen. She was running the roller over the dark-green walls, pushing white emulsion into cracks and over cobwebs.

"What are you doing?"

Her strokes traveled in all directions—out to the side, diagonally, then straight—as she covered the surface as fast as she could. She had found the radio in a box and had turned it up. It wasn't even music she liked, just generic shit. There was a burned smell. A dried-up tray of pasta sat on the burner, pitted with the carcasses of olives.

"Why did you take so long?" she shouted over the music.

"Shop was shut—I had to drive to Thurrup," he lied, holding out the beers he'd persuaded the guy at the Fox to sell him. "Bumped into Laurie."

"How's she?"

"Good."

"Where's the milk?"

"They'd run out."

"Of milk? Really?" She took a brush and sloshed paint around the yellowed light switch. It dripped onto a hastily laid dust sheet below. "I've put the decorating schedule for next week on the worktop. Do you want to check it? I've tried to divide it up, so you can finish off the high bits like the ceilings in the evenings, and lift the heavy things into the rooms with me."

And, in that second, Will saw that this was never going to end.

This house was not going to fix things, as she had promised. It was just going to fuel her obsession.

"It's eight thirty," he said wearily.

"I know, but it just looks so bad, with all the Horseborrows' furniture gone. And I didn't even think about the garden—that's going to add at least a day. We've only got thirteen days now, so I thought I might as well . . ." Her words trailed off as she stretched to cover a missed patch.

Will found a plate, and pointed at the burnt pasta.

"Is this Lor's?"

"Yeah. It's all right, if you take the top off."

His stomach rumbled through the gas of the beer. He sat down and surveyed this monstrous kitchen that he now owned. It must be as big as Mum's whole flat in Salford. Their table looked like an island in an ocean of flagstone. He opened his third beer of the evening, promising himself it was a one-off, and excavated the pasta with a fork until he found some edible sauce.

Hannah was wiping paint from her nose. She was so close to the bare bulb that it made her skin look wrung out, like a wet sheet, and her pale hair a harsh reddish pink. She'd scraped it back. She turned to him, and Will waited for the sharp edge of her cheekbones to soften, as they always used to from the front, but the hardness remained. Her upper lip was pulled in tight with concentration. He wondered when she had started to look like this.

"Listen, I don't want to stress you out," she said, "but I think, if you're going back to work on Monday, we need to start now."

Will froze, a fork in his mouth. "You want me to start painting? Now?"

"If you take over the ceiling, I could do the walls, and we could maybe get half of the kitchen done tonight. That would claw back a half day later on, for the garden."

He chewed and the cold pasta sank down inside him.

He saw Hannah thinking of ways to reword her request, to make him do what she wanted. She did it a lot these days, as if now that she wasn't using her negotiating skills at work, she needed to use them on him.

"I know you're tired. I am, too. And I know it's not on the schedule, but I thought we could go over to the garage later and talk about the studio."

Ah, the sweetener. She always finished with a sweetener.

Hannah leaned down and rubbed Will's head. He felt the rare touch of her skin on his and wanted it, but he also knew it would disappear as quickly as it had come, as she pretended to need to scratch her nose or pick up a boiling pot. Every day he had to stop himself from grabbing her and hoping that, if he held her for long enough, she would relax and stop moving. That she would listen to him when he told her to stop doing this, and believe him that it would all be OK.

Yet Hannah's hand had already gone. She was climbing off the ladder and walking towards the kettle.

Will watched her go, knowing he was losing the ability to believe he could make anything right for her anymore. After all, he'd told her it would all be OK once before, and he'd been wrong.

"Let me eat this," he said.

Hannah's schedule sat on the table. Fierce red capitals filled the cramped spaces, crossed out and struck through. A window into Hannah's head. A place he was no longer invited to go.

Will sipped his third beer, and eyed up the fourth. It was less than two days till he was back in London. He realized he was already looking forward to it.

In the meantime he would continue to do what he'd done for the last eight months, and do what she asked, just to get through.

4

For the rest of the weekend Hannah remained glued to her paintbrush.

Thank God, Will had stopped protesting. After dinner on Saturday night he'd begun painting the kitchen ceiling with fast, wide strokes, and then taken over the walls, while she transformed the kitchen cupboards with a cheap version of a posh gray eggshell that she'd had color-matched in a DIY store. She didn't bother with the greasy, scuffed insides. Barbara would never look in there.

They finished at 2:00 A.M. and started again at 8:00 A.M. on Sunday. By Sunday afternoon they had applied a second coat in the kitchen and scullery, and then, when there was still no answer from Brian about the missing sitting-room keys, they moved upstairs to the smallest of the five bedrooms. Will had continued with the roller, moving quickly over the elderly, porous wallpaper with its faded pink roses, covering yellowed patches and rips and nail holes. He played the music so loud that they couldn't talk, but she didn't care. Whenever Hannah suspected he was lagging, she brought coffee and sandwiches.

For much of the time she followed behind, her strokes growing less and less dainty as she pushed her rapidly splaying brush into the rotten window frame, which the surveyor had warned needed "attention," and over the picture rail, skirting boards and original fitted wardrobes. When the dark hairs of the exhausted brush began to escape, she painted over them.

Up close, she knew it was a mess. It would have to be re-done, but for now it looked fresh and clean at first glance, and that's all that mattered.

At some point that evening Hannah went to make yet an-other coffee.

In the hall outside their own bedroom, she noticed a new pile of boxes Will had found on his last trip downstairs. She saw as she descended that he'd taken them from the pile by the stained glass window. The pattern on the window was becom-ing exposed.

She picked her way through to look. She loved this win-dow. Next to the grand, silver fireplace in the locked sitting room, it was the most beautiful Victorian feature in the house: a turquoise glass peacock, wrapped in intricate strands of ruby roses. That first time they'd walked into Tornley Hall last sum-mer with Brian, it was the first thing they'd seen. The sun had just hit the side of the house and was blasting through. It had felt like a beacon of hope. A sign that Tornley Hall would make things right again.

And here they were.

Something on the window caught Hannah's eye.

Was that a stain?

She leaned over some boxes to check the glass. It was.

The stain was quite big, almost the size of a football. It ran from the turquoise belly of the peacock down the gray background glass towards the windowsill.

She sighed. Was everything in Tornley Hall going to have to be fixed?

Hannah licked her finger and reached out to rub it, hoping it was dust.

The stain moved.

"Oh!" Startled, Hannah tripped backwards. She fell over a box and landed awkwardly on the arm of the sofa, deflecting onto the floor with a thud.

What was that?

She pulled herself up and ran her finger over the same spot on the window. She was not imagining it—the stain had completely disappeared.

How weird. Curious, Hannah flung open the front door, ran into the dark night, crossed in front of the shuttered sitting room, and turned right onto the overgrown side lawn that ran down to the lane.

She arrived at the odd six-foot square exterior alcove that nestled between the protruding back walls of the front sitting room and the rear scullery. Its sole architectural purpose appeared to be to allow extra light through side windows into both rooms, and through the peacock window into the central hall.

Hannah checked the peacock's belly again.

No stain here, either.

She touched the glass to check for liquid or dust, but her finger returned with the normal oily residue of unwashed windows.

"Han?"

She jumped. Will stood behind her. "What happened?"

"Oh, nothing, I just tripped. I thought I saw a stain on the window, and . . ."

His shoulders dropped, and she knew it had been a mistake. "It must have been a shadow. A cat or something . . ."

If Will's momentum was broken, he might not start again. And there were only twelve days from tomorrow.

Will leaned towards the peacock window, releasing the scent of sweet perspiration and white spirit. Automatically she sidestepped him, willing him to return upstairs.

"Right," Will said. "I'm done."

"But it's only about half nine."

"Han! It's eleven."

Was it? She checked her watch, amazed at how fast time had flown.

He sniffed under one arm. "I'm going to have a shower and look for some clothes."

"I'll find them," she conceded, forcing herself to remember his 7:30 A.M. train. Back in the house, she washed out the paintbrushes and tidied around, as Will locked up and headed for the shower. Upstairs, in the hall, she opened the boxes marked CLOTHES and took out items for Will.

One box caught her eye as she was sifting through them.

SECOND BEDROOM, it said in red marker pen.

That's all.

Second bedroom.

Hannah opened the door of the bedroom next to theirs, kicked the box inside it, and slammed the door shut.

She didn't want to think about that right now.

There was whistling from the shower down the hall, then it turned off.

Damn.

Hannah bashed into the wall in her haste to run into their bedroom. There she flung Will's clothes on the chair, stripped off, and climbed into bed without cleaning her teeth. It was surprisingly cold. She wrapped the duvet around her and turned over. A minute later, Will came in. She heard him sorting through his clothes, and lay still.

The duvet was pulled back and Will climbed in. He smelled of lemon shower gel, and she could tell from the brush of cotton on her leg that he'd found pajama trousers. She knew her naked skin must smell sour and clammy from the day's exertions, and her hair hadn't been washed.

That was fine.

Anything that kept him away.

Will exhaled heavily as he settled himself in the bed and turned off the lamp.

"Bloody hell, it's cold," he said.

She stayed still as he turned over, gave a long yawn, and laid his freezing hand on her back, as he always did. She tensed, unable to move away in bed.

His fingers rested in the gaps between her vertebrae. They flexed a little, checking for a response—a twitch of her muscles, or a deeper breath.

She sighed inwardly. He never gave up.

After a second, Will tapped her spine gently, playing back, she suspected, the track inside his head he was working on with Jeremiah. The rhythm changed and she guessed that he'd reached the bridge of the song.

Her eyes tightly shut, Hannah transported herself, as she did every night, to her world of paint swatches and curtains and rugs and table lamps and furniture layouts. She propped up the schedule mentally in her mind and trod the well-worn path of visualizing the decoration of each room in Tornley Hall.

She imagined Barbara's response to each one when it was finished, and then to the whole house.

Perfect! A perfect family home, Hannah!

The tapping on her back slowed. Will's hand grew heavier. A small snore came from behind.

She breathed deeper, knowing that, with the motion of her rising ribs, Will's hand would gradually slip away.

When it did, she turned about-face and smelled toothpaste on his breath, and coffee on her own. She brushed his hair softly from his face, so as not to wake him. Her finger halted at what she thought was a gray hair, then realized it was white paint. Would they ever become parents before one of them really did turn gray?

Cold air blew into the small gap between their bodies, and she shivered. Will had started the boiler, but the bedroom was still freezing. What would the bills be like on a house this big? It was a concern now that she wasn't working—and a subject they should probably avoid when talking to Barbara.

Hannah turned and backed into the length of Will's body to find warmth.

She reestablished her decorating schedule in her mind and ran through it till sleep came, as it always did, and stole her away from the unimaginable fear that she could never face— that all of this could yet be for nothing.

5

When Hannah woke on Monday morning, the pocket of chill in the bed had returned. Will's space was empty, just the crease in his pillow left.

She peered at the clock.

9:54 A.M.

What?

Hannah sat upright. Why hadn't he set the alarm? A muscle in her shoulder twinged and she rubbed it. That action, in turn, stung her forefinger. An angry paintbrush blister had appeared on the end. Sucking it, she went to throw off the duvet—then stopped.

If Will wasn't here, there was no need to jump out of bed.

She could stay in the warm bed for a few minutes, without him hoping it was going to lead to something. She stretched out her stiff arms and surveyed the cracked Victorian ceiling rose above her.

Now that she'd thrown out the sickly air fresheners she suspected Brian had brought to disguise the weird smell in the house, there was a faint scent of old-fashioned perfume in this room. Lavender? Lilac? She tried to recall the previous layout of the room. Her eyes roamed from wall to wall. There had definitely been a high, single bed on this side, which had seemed odd for an adult. An elegant green velvet chaise longue opposite. A kidney-bean-shaped dressing table in the bay window, with a gilt hairbrush-and-mirror set. It had clearly been the elderly sister's bedroom. The one next door was surely the brother's, with its extendable metal bed and drip stand, presumably abandoned when he was taken to the nursing home.

Who had died first, Hannah wondered, Peter or Olive Horseborrow?

Had Olive died in this room?

She yawned, checking whether Will had left her one of his notes to say "Bye x."

His bedside table was empty, as was the dressing table. Thinking about it, there hadn't been a note for a while.

With a shove, she threw back the covers.

"Oh!" Hannah exclaimed.

Her skin felt as if it had been doused in iced water. Jumping up, she ran to the door, grabbed Will's bathrobe, and flung it on. She touched the radiator and found surly cold metal. Why was the heating not on?

In the bathroom across the hall she switched on the shower and stood shivering, hand out, surveying the plain white suite and walls. According to Brian, all the plumbing and electrics had been redone ten years ago. This was one room then, at least, that would do as it was for Barbara's visit.

She waited, but the water didn't heat up.

Not the boiler, on top of everything else, please.

Holding the robe around her, Hannah went downstairs, checked another unresponsive radiator in the hall, and was turning towards the kitchen when there was a soft thud at the window.

Shocked, she walked towards it.

No way.

It was early March, and the garden of Tornley Hall was completely white. Thick snow fell heavily from an opaque sky. Apart from a few stubborn brown patches in the flower beds and gravel, the garden was nearly covered.

This could not be happening.

Hannah rushed to the kitchen and turned on the radio to a news channel.

"High pressure over Scandinavia and cold winds from Russia have clashed with weather systems from the Atlantic, leading to snow overnight in many parts of Britain . . ." said a voice of doom.

No! Snow would ruin everything.

Fighting back panic, Hannah opened the boiler cover. A light flickered. She pressed one button, then another. There was a rumble and the boiler burst back into life. At least that was working.

She grabbed her mobile from the worktop and rang Will's number.

"Have you seen this?" she said when Will picked up.

A pause. "What?"

"Snow!"

A longer pause. "Yeah. It was starting when I got to Woodbridge."

It was only just after 10:00 A.M. and yet already he sounded tired. She felt guilty about the four-hour-plus daily round commute he was now going to have to do, in order for them to be far enough out of London to afford a house like this. It would only be for a year, she reminded herself, till the studio was built and Will could work from home.

"Really? You don't sound worried. You realize if this goes on, it's going to mess everything up?"

Another pause. A chair creaking. "How?"

"Because I won't be able to do stuff! I won't be able to cut the grass and get rid of the weeds. Or get to Ipswich if I need more paint. Can you come back? This afternoon?"

"Er, no." Will sounded bemused at the thought.

"Will!"

"Han. It's a stupid question. . . ."

He drifted off again. She knew he'd be adjusting some tiny piece of reverb on the Mac, his phone jammed against his shoulder. She knew it was a stupid question. They needed the money from Jeremiah's record company to pay for the increased mortgage payments for the next few months.

A guitar strummed in the background. She heard Will's studio assistant, Matt, chatting in his goofball, mockney voice to someone she guessed was Jeremiah. A mobile rang. Familiar London sounds. Life sounds.

Hannah walked to the window. The high Victorian wall rose steeply behind the small rear garden. Snow was forming a soft ridge along the top. How far away was the nearest human being right now?

There was a crackle. Will's voice started to break up.

"I'll try to . . . back earlier this evening . . . not this afternoon. Listen . . . going . . . a session now, so . . . talk later."

"OK, but when you say earlier, can you at least make it . . ."

Hannah started. She knew what he was like: when he became immersed in a song, he could work all night and lose track of time.

The phone died. She checked. One bar of signal. Then nothing. Cursing, she returned to the table, where it strengthened to two bars, and tried again. Will's phone went straight to voice mail.

"Will!" she said, knowing it was too late. When he turned off his phone, that meant he'd be working for hours now.

She put down her phone. If she wasn't bringing in a salary anymore, she could hardly argue.

Back in the two-bar zone, Hannah's phone beeped.

Two voice messages arrived in her in-box. The first was an unfamiliar voice.

"Hello, Mrs. Riley. I'm very sorry, but our engineer will not be able to get to you today, due to poor road conditions on the A12. We'll arrange another appointment when we know more."

The engineer! With all the decorating this weekend, she'd completely forgotten that they'd arranged the broadband installation for today. Now there'd be no landline, or Wi-Fi or TV, for another day at least. Hannah told herself to remain positive. She could manage. The second message was from the estate agent.

"Hi, Mrs. Riley, this is Janet. Sorry, I've had no luck getting hold of Brian about those keys. We're expecting him back from Italy today, though, if the airport isn't closed, so I'll ring you as soon as we hear. Apologies again. All the best."

Hannah examined her schedule, forcing herself to think practically.

Day 12: Monday, SITTING ROOM, she'd rewritten optimistically last night. If they still couldn't unlock the door, she'd just have to paint another guest bedroom today.

She went to cross out SITTING ROOM. Before she could write a word, however, there was a loud cranking noise.

.   .   .

The boiler had definitely died this time. You didn't have to be a plumber to tell that. The dials had settled at zero, and the pilot light was out. Hannah jabbed uselessly at the button as before and then, when that didn't work, at all the others.

The intense cold crept quickly inside Will's bathrobe.

Hannah grabbed her marker pen.

EMERGENCY PLUMBER, she wrote at the top of her schedule. PRIORITY.

She'd just have to get on with it. It was that or a panic attack.

With no phone book evident in the house, she sat in the two-bar-signal area of the kitchen and typed "Emergency plumber, Thurrup" into her phone's search engine. The Internet symbol ticked round interminably, then froze. Then the phone signal disappeared altogether, forcing her to move again. This would take all day. For a second she had the brilliant idea of asking Laurie and Ian for a plumber in Thurrup.

Then she remembered.

Laurie's number was on Will's mobile, not hers.

"Bloody hell!" Hannah shouted. She texted Will asking for Laurie's number, wondering how long it would be before he saw the message. She watched the snow drift across the garden, starting to realize how cut off she was out here. She hadn't even considered this type of scenario when they visited in late summer. At home in Shepherd's Bush the snow would have little effect on anything. She'd just pop round to a phone box or the Internet café. Here, she was a quarter of a mile from Tornley, five miles from Snadesdon, and nine from Thurrup. And even then she wouldn't risk cycling in this weather.

Hannah gulped her tea and made herself imagine this was a press trip abroad. If a bunch of journalists was relying on her to fix the situation, what would she do?

"Right," she said, standing up. Enough moaning. First thing she needed was a stronger phone signal—or, even better, a neighbor with a phone book and a landline.

Hannah jogged upstairs and threw on some warm clothes, followed by Will's big sweater and his gray beanie. Her winter boots were packed in a box somewhere, so she pulled on the green wellies she'd bought for Will as a joke, when he'd been invited to a pheasant shoot by a rich client who owned a Scottish castle. They were covered in neon-lime frogs. At size eleven, they looked ridiculous on her size-five feet, but would do for now. Nobody would care what she looked like here, anyway.

Insulated against the cold and snow, Hannah stomped out of the house into a garden that had transformed since yesterday.

It was so cold it hurt her lungs to breathe.

The falling snow had stopped, at least. The lawn was bathed in hush, as if the animals and insects had burrowed away to sleep it off. The ice-topped weeds looked strangely pretty, too, like a field of giant snowdrops. Holding her phone in front to check for a signal, Hannah headed down the driveway, her footsteps echoing on the snowy gravel like gunshots.

When the signal did not improve, she turned right out of the driveway towards the high electronic gate next door. There was an intercom, with no name. She pressed it and scanned the eerily quiet lane behind and the white marshes that led to the sea. They were so far from the nearest B-road you couldn't even hear traffic.

There was no reply.

Trying not to feel defeated, she turned back up the lane towards Tornley, checking her phone intermittently. When two bars finally turned to three, she tried Will again and left a voice message about the boiler and another request for Laurie's number.

The signal died again. She fought back her frustration and kept going.

The snow was pristine, untouched by car tracks. The only sign of life was the odd set of triangular bird footprints. It was beautiful. She'd never seen snow like this in London. As soon as it fell there, it was turned into snowballs, kicked away by sledders fighting for space on the city's few slopes, and melted by the traffic fumes and the hurried breath of eight million people. She'd seen snow like this as a child, though. A random memory returned of Dad pulling her sled up on the Downs in Kent, with her in her red anorak.

Before she could stop herself, Hannah allowed herself to imagine the future here: her and Will, and a small figure in a red coat on a sled on this lane.

No, she told herself.

Don't do it. *Do not tempt fate.*

Shaking away the image, Hannah continued up past Tornley Hall and around the bend, checking her phone repeatedly. There was a cough, and she glanced up to see an elderly man.

The sight was so unexpected that Hannah stopped dead.

The man was entering a field with a golden retriever. If he was surprised to see her, he didn't show it. He was small—her height—and wore a hat with earflaps. His head looked too large for his shoulders. Thick lines were beaten into his face, and his cheeks were purple and veined.

"Hello," she said, lifting a hand. The man regarded her impassively. "Hi, sorry, do you live here?"

His eyes were watery and blue, set in pink creased burrows. "I do."

"Hi. I'm Hannah," she said. "We just moved in, up the road."

That might have been a nod, she wasn't sure.

"Sorry, but our boiler's just broken and I don't have a landline. I'm trying to find someone who might have a number for a plumber."

The expression on the man's face was so blank that she stopped short of asking to use his own landline.

"Dax," the man said, pointing behind him.

"Dax?"

"That's your man. Dax. In the cottages."

"Oh, really? He's a plumber, is he? Or do you mean he's got a phone book?"

The old man whistled. "Henny! Damn dog. Dax, that's who you want." And with that, he entered the field and walked away.

"Oh. OK. Thanks," Hannah called uncertainly.

She carried on. The snow was even thicker here in the dip of the road. She lifted her feet high, to stop it trickling inside Will's boots. A scarlet-and-blue pheasant dived out of a hedge and disappeared into another. A faint engine noise filled the air. She passed the Tornley sign, and arrived beside the terrace of three pink cottages.

The engine noise came from behind. Hoping she wasn't trespassing, Hannah walked up the side of the cottages. A garage came into sight. A man in a blue boiler suit was bent over a motorbike, gloves on, twisting something with a wrench. He turned and regarded her. He had a prominent, straight nose and dark-blue eyes, with wild, oil-dark curly hair and thick eyelashes and brows. There was a challenge in his expression. He looks like a Fagin's boy grown up, she thought.

"Hi," Hannah said, raising a hand in greeting in case she'd alarmed him. "Sorry. Are you Dax?"

The man turned off the motorbike and gave her a once-over. "Don't know—am I?"

"Oh, a man up the road said . . ."

"Who's that then?" He rubbed his nose on his sleeve.

"Oh. I don't know. Wearing a hat. Had a dog. My height." She lifted her hand to her head. "In his seventies, maybe?"

"Bill?"

"Might have been."

"He won't like you saying he's in his seventies."

She hesitated. "Oh, OK. Anyway, listen, I'm sorry, but I've just arrived from London and our boiler's broken, and I need to find an emergency plumber, and the man—Bill—said that 'Dax' might be able to help?"

The man in the blue boiler suit exhaled heavily, as if she were asking something very difficult. "This is your house in London you're talking about, is it?"

Hannah blinked. "No. My new house, up the road." She pointed towards Tornley Hall.

"Right," the man said, "well, that's why I'm asking, because I wouldn't know, would I?"

"No . . ."

"And it's important to know, because otherwise I might come and fix your boiler in London, mightn't I?"

Was he joking?

She tried to remain polite. "OK, good point. So would you be able to come?"

The man returned to the motorbike. "I'm busy right now."

Hannah moved from foot to foot, cold air attacking every inch of her exposed skin.

"Oh. Right. It's just that we haven't got any heating. And it's snowing."

"It's snowing, is it?" the man repeated, as if she'd made a good joke. His teeth shone white in his grease-streaked face. As he said it, a light smattering of snow started again.

"I mean, is there any way you might be able to come today?"

"Is there any *way*?" he repeated. Was he mocking her? "Got a million quid?"

"Er, no."

The man cleared his throat. "Have to be tomorrow, then."

"Really?"

She checked her phone. It was only ten thirty. "OK. Well, if you could do it tomorrow, that would be better than . . ." She stopped, waiting for him to say he was winding her up.

"Right you are," he said. He turned his back on her and waved with his wrench.

"OK," she continued. "So I'll see you tomorrow."

She turned hesitantly.

"Bye, Janice," he called.

"Oh. It's Hannah, actually."

"That's good, or I might have gone to Janice's house."

She stared, not comprehending.

He kept his back to her. "Where do you live, Hannah?"

"Oh, I see, sorry—up the road. Tornley . . ." The next word sounded wrong in her mouth. ". . . Hall. I just assumed that—"

"That we're all talking about you? Londoners moving in?"

"No!" she said, flustered. These cottages were similar to her childhood home in Kent. Tornley Hall had cost only thirty thousand pounds more than the tiny two-bed London flat she and Will had almost bankrupted themselves to buy in their late twenties and had then, to their astonishment, watched rocket in value. In Tornley, she now saw, that random financial luck had elevated her to a social position that made her uncomfortable. She'd have to order a new house sign; get rid of the "Hall." Barbara might find it odd, too, as if she had misjudged who Hannah and Will had told her they were; what their values were, regarding work and money. "Tornley Studios" sounded like a business venture, no different from a farm, or a riding school. "Tornley Hall," on the other hand, might be interpreted as vacuous social aspiration.

The man stood up abruptly. He stared at her feet, shook his head, then headed down the garden path towards the middle of the three terraced cottages, before Hannah could think of a better answer.

• • •

The snow fell more heavily as Hannah retraced her steps to Tornley Hall. Dax was clearly going to be no help. She tried Will again, and left another voice message suggesting that if he couldn't get hold of Laurie to ask for a plumber's number this afternoon, he should stop at the pub in Snadesdon on the way home tonight and ask for one.

As she continued up the lane, snow blew into Hannah's eyes so heavily that she could hardly see, so it was only when she was halfway back up the driveway of Tornley Hall, under the bare oak trees, that she noticed the footprints.

A second set, parallel to her earlier ones.

The same size as the ones she'd made in Will's boots.

Hannah slowed and surveyed the empty front doorstep up

ahead, trying to think if she'd passed fresh vehicle tracks that might belong to a car or postal van. She couldn't remember.

As she emerged from under the half cover of the bare trees, both sets of footprints were already vanishing in the fresh snow-fall. The second set tapered off completely by the side lawn.

Maybe the next-door neighbor had answered the intercom too late and had come round to say hello.

It was freezing. Hannah marched on, desperate to get inside. She opened the front door and bashed the snow from Will's wellies. There was no mail on the mat. She threw off her wet coat, her teeth chattering. It was hardly any warmer in here. She lifted up a foot to remove one of Will's wellies, and tripped backwards over a coffee table.

"Oh, for God's sake!"

This was ridiculous. They needed to get inside that sitting room.

Hannah peered through the keyhole again. It was still dark. Even in the daytime there was nothing to see.

The action, however, detonated a memory about locks.

The attic!

Brian had unlocked it on their first visit. She remembered now. It had been stiflingly hot and packed to the rafters with broken furniture, old carpets, and boxes.

Maybe he'd left the inner house keys in the attic door?

Hannah ran up to the wooden stairs beside the upstairs bath-room. They creaked heavily under her weight. To her disappoint-ment, the attic door was ajar. There were no keys in the lock.

She peered round the door. "Wow," she said out loud.

The house-clearance people had taken everything, and the space left behind was enormous, even with the sloping eaves.

She turned on a light and walked in. This was exciting. They could easily convert this, maybe into an office for her, if she decided to freelance later on. Or even a play—

Hannah stopped herself for the second time today.

Don't tempt fate.

Curious, she noticed a skylight at the rear that must have been covered before by boxes. Carefully she stepped across the rafters and undid it. Snow fell onto the roof tiles below as it creaked open.

Hannah stuck her head out and found herself looking right over the Victorian wall into the property next door.

Up until now she'd only seen part of its red roof from the rear-bedroom window. The rest was obscured by conifers. Now she understood what Brian meant when he said that their neighbor's house had been built in the former walled garden of Tornley Hall.

The property comprised about an acre of land and was surrounded on all four sides by the high Victorian wall. But the house wasn't the cosy little cottage Hannah had envisaged. It was a functional-looking, tidy 1970s-style bungalow, which sat in the middle of a homestead. The garden was packed with rows of polytunnels and greenhouses. It looked closed up for the winter. The curtains were pulled, the driveway empty. Blue tarpaulins were draped over large objects on the front terrace and held in place by stones.

Hannah shut the skylight. So if the new footprints on the driveway didn't belong to her next-door neighbor, where had they come from?

Maybe Bill was more neighborly than he had appeared? Maybe he had stopped in after his dog walk to check she was OK and that she'd found Dax?

Hannah headed downstairs, cross with herself.

This morning's events were distracting her from her goal. It was a pain about the boiler, and about the sitting-room keys, but it was not the end of the world. One would be fixed, and the other would be found.

She'd lost an hour of decorating time this morning already, and there were only eleven and a half days now till Barbara came. She needed to focus.

There would be plenty of time later to find out more about the tiny hamlet of Tornley, and the people who lived here.

6

At 6:00 P.M. in London, after what had turned out to be a long day, Will exchanged looks with his assistant Matt and rapped on the vocal booth, where Jeremiah, his latest client, was strumming his guitar.

"Nice one," Will said into the mic. "Let's take a break, Jem."

The track was a bloody mess.

They'd been working on it since 11:00 A.M., but the lad's Gothic tale about a girl called Carrie who went into the woods and was never seen again still sounded flat and monotone. It was nowhere close to the wrenching, stark quality that Jeremiah's record company wanted Will to inject into their new YouTube find.

"Going for a smoke, man," Jeremiah said, appearing and rubbing his blond beard. Will avoided Matt's eye. Jeremiah was wearing a nineteenth-century-style American woodsman's hat. The fact that his real name was Paul and he came from Stevenage and his dad was a bank manager, had no bearing on his determination to live out his artistic calling. That also included smoking a clay pipe.

Jeremiah headed off through the maze of rental rooms that comprised Smart Yak Studios.

"Fu-uck me," Matt whispered. "The thing is . . . I'm not too hot on that idea . . . man," Matt drawled, mocking Jeremiah's sensitive whine.

Will folded his arms.

"So, what now?" Matt said.

"Hard to tell them anything at that age," Will said. "I was the same. Pain in the bloody arse. What is he—nineteen? He hears some alternative American folk band and wants the sound, but he doesn't know the genesis of it."

"So . . ."

"So . . ." Will made a clueless face. "We work the magic."

Matt stood up. "Want a beer to help you with that magic, sir?"

Will did want a beer, but the old habit of drinking in the studio was creeping back recently. "Coffee, if you're going, mate. Cheers."

As he tried to think of how to stop Jeremiah sounding like a pastiche of an Appalachian folk singer, he realized that Matt was holding the door open, talking. A woman's coat was visible. It was Clare, the lighting designer, who rented the smallest of the Smart Yak studios.

Matt popped his head back in. "Clare says they're canceling trains."

"What?"

Will jumped up and headed to the corridor. "Is it that bad?" He wiped the window and saw a white blizzard below. Dark figures hurried through Shepherd's Bush. There were no cars anywhere.

"Where's it you've moved, Will?" Clare said, placing a fake-fur Cossack hat on her head.

"Suffolk," he said, distracted.

She grimaced. "God, well, good luck. Jamie's stuck in Brighton at his dad's. Just as well his school's closed."

"Do you want to head off?" Will asked Matt.

"Might do, actually. What about you?"

"I'll crash here, I suppose. Jem might be up for another session, anyway."

"Well, good luck," Clare repeated, heading downstairs.

They waved good-bye to her, and returned to the studio.

"I didn't know they'd split," Will said, sitting back at the desk. "Wasn't he in the pub, at Christmas?"

"Broke up on New Year's Eve." Matt pulled on his jacket. "You need to spend more time in the kitchen. Right. Sure I can go?"

"Yep. Let me know if you can't get in tomorrow."

"Will do."

"Cheers."

As soon as Matt left, Will turned on his mobile. Hannah was going to go mental. Excellent.

The message sign was lit. He counted. One, two . . . five. All from Hannah.

The first voice mail cut out almost as soon as she spoke, leaving him none the wiser. The rest weren't much better, both garbled and intermittent. Even so, he could make out that irritating hyper-quality in her voice. Something about the broadband engineer canceling, and . . . a . . . broken boiler? Will swore. A boiler would cost a grand, plus. This house was going to eat every penny he made for the next ten years. At this rate he'd never be able to build the studio. He'd be on that bloody train from Woodbridge for the rest of his life.

There was a soft knock on the door, and Clare came in. She held out a six-pack of beer.

"Forgot my gloves—your lovely Matt asked me to bring this up from the shop."

"Did he?" Will said, surprised, taking them from her. "Thanks."

"You want to hang on to him," she said, pulling on a black leather glove.

"You're telling me." He scratched his upper arm and saw her eyes flicker to his tattoo, then away again.

"Long night then?" Clare said, nodding at the battered leather sofa that Hannah's parents had given him when they'd sold up to move to Spain. "That looks comfy."

It wasn't, but a bad back was starting to sound preferable to another evening of Hannah's insane decorating schedule.

"It's all right. I need to catch up anyway, so . . . Where are you off to?" He realized he knew nothing about her.

"Oh. Me and Jamie have just moved round the corner." She paused as if this might be something Matt had told Will. He nodded, clueless. "So getting home without falling on my arse again is pretty much the plan for tonight." She turned and pointed to a wet patch on her backside. "Wish me luck!"

He grinned. "Good luck."

Clare pulled on her other glove. "By the way, he's very sweet, your little guy out there, with his pipe. Though he keeps getting snow in it."

Will laughed, and she waved good-bye again.

What was different about her? he thought, opening a new file on the Mac. Her hair color or something. In the six months or so she'd rented a studio here, she'd always walked down the corridor with a shut-off look about her; friendly enough, but self-contained, like she had something on her mind. Talking of which . . . Reluctantly he dialed Hannah, and waited for the bollocking he knew was coming.

•　　•　　•

Five minutes later Will sat in the same spot, staring at the wall. His conversation with Hannah had broken up so many times, due to the crap signal, that he hadn't heard most of it. The few words he did hear were seared into his head.

"Why did you get . . . the bloody train if . . . snowing? I can't do . . . all . . . my own. We've only . . . eleven . . . now . . . a bit."

In the end she'd disappeared altogether while talking about plumbing and, annoyed, Will had pressed "End call" instead of waiting for the signal to cut back in.

If she said "bit" one more bloody time . . .

The door opened again. Jeremiah walked in. "All right, man?"

"Yup, all good," Will said. "Listen, Jem, you up for another session tonight?"

"Yeah, no problem, man." Jeremiah blew on his cold hands, as if he'd just jumped off an American railroad car.

"There's something I want to play you," Will said, reaching up for an old Delta blues record. Twenty-four hours suddenly stretched ahead, of doing what he wanted, when he wanted, without hearing the words "Barbara" or "Tornley-sodding-Hall" or hearing Hannah cutting days up into fussy, stupid little "bits."

And with that feeling came the old impulse. Will reached forward and took a beer.

No, maybe the snow wasn't a bad thing. He needed this. Twenty-four hours away from Hannah and her bloody schedule.

He turned off his phone.

7

Hannah stayed up painting the rear guest room till well after midnight. Eventually she climbed down the ladder and appraised the walls. Like the smallest bedroom, it now looked fresh again. A few prints on the wall, a vase of fresh flowers . . . Hannah practiced her speech for Barbara next Friday out loud. "Yes, so this is the spare room, where my parents and Will's mum are going to stay when they visit. It's going to be fantastic having all this space for our families, and they're excited about coming to stay and being part of—"

She hesitated.

It was becoming more difficult to stop herself imagining the future, now she was here. More difficult not to tempt fate.

Now she'd stopped painting, the biting cold gripped her again. She could swear snow was seeping through the walls of Tornley Hall. The oven and gas burners helped to warm the kitchen, if she kept the door shut, and the electric wall heater was on full blast in the bathroom, but the rest of the house was now a series of freezing, inhospitable no-go areas.

Shivering, Hannah washed her paintbrush, forced herself to do her teeth, and jumped into bed fully clothed, too cold to undress. It reminded her of those press trips she ran to precarious places, when social niceties quickly disappeared among the journalists she looked after, as they lived in hot tents or ramshackle hotels, in pursuit of a story.

Hannah watched the snow outside the window. Was it only eight months since she'd stopped doing the press trips? It felt like eight years.

She suspected the skills she'd needed to run a foreign press trip under pressure were already out of date, her hard-earned network of contacts quickly fading. How long would it be before she forgot the basics? Would she still know the best time during a period of political unrest to shift up to armored transport, or how to track down and protect locals who wanted to speak to the foreign press, or when—and when not—to bribe police when they were stopped on the road? Would she remember all the little tricks she'd learned from Jane about how to secure a dodgy hotel door with a triangle of wood, and when to produce a bottle of whisky for her group after a tough day?

The reward had been to read their travel stories in the newspapers back home and know that she'd helped to make it possible.

It had been the best job of her life.

Now it was gone.

Without even the low murmur of a radiator, the bedroom was completely silent, apart from the soft thud of snow on glass. In fact, now Hannah thought about it, she'd hardly heard a sound all day—not a car, or even a plane—and apart from Dax and Bill in Tornley, she hadn't seen another soul.

The setting was idyllic here, but the isolation was going to take some getting used to.

Hannah picked up her phone, suddenly wanting to hear another voice. The clock said 1:08 A.M. She listened to the messages she'd received earlier, from Mum and Dad in Johannesburg, wanting to know how the house move had gone. She heard the concern in their voices that they were not there to help her and Will. She wished they were here, too. She'd had a bad feeling from the start that the endless delay in closing on their London flat would cause the move to clash with her parents' annual trip to visit her brother in South Africa.

There was another quick call from Jane, who was at a conference in New York, checking she was OK and telling her they were all missing her, back at the TSO office.

Nothing, however, from Brian about the keys, or from Will.

Hannah rolled over, hoping the studio sofa wouldn't do Will's back in again. She needed him fit for decorating. She imagined him right now, lost in one of his late-night sessions, that intense concentration on his face as he listened to playback, his long tanned arm pushing the faders up and down. Will never looked as at home anywhere as he did in that studio. She thought about how far he'd come. How proud she was of him.

Snow flew faster past the bedroom window. She didn't want to think what would happen if he couldn't get home tomorrow, either.

Yawning, Hannah went to shut the curtains, then stopped. Walking along the lane today in thick snow had reminded her how it felt when nature took charge, when there was no option to travel underground, regardless of the storms or blizzards above. Here, nature ruled your days, and it had felt strangely restful, handing over that responsibility.

Hannah burrowed into the warm. No, Mother Nature and she had not been on good terms for a long time. It would be a relief to make peace again—to fall back into the rhythms of the seasons and the natural cycle of the day. And to start with, tonight, she would sleep with the curtains open, now that there was no light pollution to keep her awake. It would be nice to wake gently with the dawn, instead of being rudely prodded by the alarm.

Turning over, Hannah summoned the decorating schedule to lull her to sleep. She was just dropping off when a noise exploded into the bedroom. Her eyes flew open.

The bedroom fell silent again.

She waited.

What was that—the boiler?

Nothing happened.

She exhaled. It must have been a dream.

Uneasy, Hannah shut her eyes.

The noise burst into the room again, forcing her upright.

It was horrible. An agonized honking.

Then she knew.

An animal.

It was the braying she'd heard when they arrived on Saturday, but much, much louder.

Hannah wrapped the duvet around her and shuffled to the window. The noise came from the field to the left, behind the garage. She traced her finger down the condensation, swaying as her eyes closed again.

Maybe it would stop in a minute.

The insistent roar blasted into the room again. Then again. Every minute or so.

No one could sleep with that. She remembered a story Ian

told them at Nan Riley's funeral about weekending Londoners asking Suffolk locals to stop their cockerels crowing at dawn. She'd laughed at the time, but this wasn't funny. This was the middle of the night. Cursing, she padded downstairs, turning on lights, and pulled on a coat, gloves, and Will's wet frog wellies. She took a flashlight from the toolbox, placed the door on the latch, and stepped outside into the freezing night.

Screwing up her eyes against the snow, she followed the bellowing towards the garage, her lips and fingers turning numb. Spitting snowflakes from her mouth, she shone the flashlight on the fence behind the garage and saw a space, just a few feet wide.

She sighed. This was ridiculous.

With no choice, she squeezed into the gap and sidled along the farmer's fence. Weeds brushed against her clothes, soaking her further. There was another deafening bray, much louder now. A second later her beam caught the end of a long nose lifting up through the snow on the other side. There was a trembling of nostrils and then another honk.

A *donkey?*

Hannah approached carefully, trying not to frighten it.

"Hello," she called softly. The donkey looked young. It was small—its back as high as her chest—and was wearing a thin waterproof jacket inside a makeshift wooden shelter. The shelter was hardly bigger than its body, and left its hindquarters and nose exposed.

This was appalling. The animal was clearly distressed.

The donkey brayed again, showing teeth. Hannah sheltered her eyes from the snow, and tried to see where the donkey had come from. Two dim lights shone through the flurry across the field. Both could belong to farms, but it would be impossible to know which one owned the donkey.

It brayed again, so loudly that she put her hands over her ears.

Snow drifted into gaps in her clothes and she felt her body temperature falling. Both farms must be a ten-minute walk across the exposed field. It wasn't safe to set off in this weather. Nobody even knew she was out here.

Hannah shone her flashlight on a gate farther down the field and headed for it. "OK, boy. Hang on."

Balancing on a bumpy crop track, she slipped and stumbled her way up to the donkey and, with the flashlight in her mouth, fumbled to unknot the rope.

"Come on, boy," she said, desperate to get back inside.

She tugged and, to her relief, the donkey came meekly through the gate to the garage. Opening the doors and switching on the bare bulb, Hannah saw the animal was pale gray and skinny, with sweet, sorry-looking eyes.

"Who did this to you, hmm?" she asked, rubbing its nose. Its fur was tufty, like Will's hair when he got fed up with it and sheared it short. Some patches were bare.

Hannah looked around. The garage was a mess. It looked as if the house-clearance people hadn't touched it. There were oil patches and dried mud on the floor and old smears of paint, and that same strong smell of petrol or diesel. The moving men had piled up their gardening tools and bikes in the corner.

Hannah tied the donkey to a wall hook and removed the soaking jacket, watching out for its back legs.

Something red fluttered above her. It was the corner of a blanket hanging from under the roof. It seemed to be on a shelf. Curious, Hannah spotted a ladder nailed to the wall. Testing it first, she climbed up. At the top there was a large storage shelf that stretched the width of the garage, just three feet under the

arched roof. On it lay a dusty red blanket, some empty veg-
etable crates, a bucket, a deflated bicycle tire, three unopened
packets of crisps, and a scattering of grain. This was useful. Will
might be able to store equipment up here.

She took the blanket and bucket back down, tied the blanket
on the donkey with their gardening twine from London, then
washed out and filled the bucket with snow. The donkey's thin
ears shot up momentarily.

"Now, listen," she said, patting its neck and untying it,
"you've got to be quiet, or your owner will notice you're gone
and tell the police I've stolen you. And that would be bad, before I get a chance to explain, OK?"

She shut the garage doors behind her, and ran back to the
house with the wet blanket, desperate to get warm.

Hannah pushed the front door.

It wouldn't budge.

She stood back, shocked. "What the . . . ?"

It was locked.

She pushed again, uselessly. If she was stuck outside in the
snow, she was in trouble.

The snow plowed into her, coating her eyelashes and filling
her nostrils. She felt her internal temperature dropping further.

Think!

There was nothing else for it. Hannah found a rock in
the flower border, wrapped her hand in her coat sleeve, and
smashed the window.

She cleared the glass and leaned through.

The latch was down. How had that happened—had it
slipped?

Back in the freezing hall, she threw off her wet coat and
boots and regarded the broken window.

Great. Now the front door was not safe tonight, and there was another problem to fix before Barbara came.

Muttering crossly, Hannah searched in a box and found the triangular wooden doorstop that she used when traveling. She jammed it under the bottom of the front door for extra security, wishing Will and her parents were here. She'd had enough today.

She hung the blanket up to dry on the upper banister, then went to her bedroom. Her teeth were no longer just chattering, but slamming together now. Remembering her emergency training at work, she stripped off her wet clothes and wrapped herself, naked, in the soft wool blanket from the guest room. She climbed back under the duvet. Long shudders racked her body.

She lay, listening.

There was one—less noisy—bray from the garage. Then another.

Just when Hannah had resigned herself to a very long night, finally it stopped.

She should have felt relief, but she didn't.

This was a disaster. First the boiler, then the window, and now she'd been forced to abduct a donkey.

As her shaking decreased, Hannah turned over, trying to sleep. Yet an uncomfortable thought kept her awake. Eight months ago, if she'd found an animal in those conditions, she would have rung the RSPCA in the middle of the night and waited with the donkey till they arrived.

She wouldn't have worried about talking to the neighbor first, or about the consequences for herself.

Hannah shut her eyes more tightly and summoned her decorating schedule.

8

Will woke in the Smart Yak studio that Tuesday morning with his first hangover in years. He stretched out his back on the lumpy sofa, feeling the old familiar parched mouth and the tightness in his temples. It was worth it, though. He and Jeremiah had cracked "Carrie" last night. In fact, he hadn't felt this good about a track for ages—probably because he hadn't been able to concentrate for so long, thanks to Hannah's obsession with the move out of London.

Around 1:00 A.M. Jeremiah had had the brilliant idea—without realizing he'd been led there by Will's two-hour listening session—of singing his Gothic tale of a girl lost in the Arkansas forest in his Stevenage accent. Immediately, the track had a new resonance. Carrie was no longer an imaginary redneck girl, but a girl from sixth-form college in Stevenage, who'd run into the forest to escape Internet bullies and was never seen again.

"Carrie" was starting to sound interesting.

Will stood up stiffly, found the spare clothes and toothbrush he kept for late sessions, and went to the shower room, yawning.

Smart Yak was unusually quiet. He checked out the window. The weather was even worse than yesterday. Two people below pushed a snow-covered car back into a parking space, as the driver spun the wheels uselessly.

The reception area downstairs was deserted. It was only when he returned from the shower that Will heard a sound. Coming up the stairs was the top of a Cossack hat.

"Morning," he called.

Clare glanced up. "Oh, hi. You stayed then?" She reached the top. "Listen, I wasn't sure if Matt would make it in." She held out a polystyrene cup and a brown packet. "I got this for you, in case. It's all they had."

Will opened the packet. Inside was a croissant. "Oh. Thanks."

"You're welcome. Though I don't know how fresh it is. . . ."

"No, it's good." Will tried to think of something to say to be polite and realized he didn't know much about her. "So did your son make it back from Surrey?"

Clare was removing her hat. Ice fell onto her hair. He was right; it definitely looked blonder than it used to. He'd also assumed she was his age, midthirties, but close-up now, he suspected she was younger.

"Sussex, no. God, Will, have you not seen the news?"

"What?"

"The airports are shut, and the motorways. They're saying maybe Friday for the trains to start again."

For reasons Will didn't want to think about too deeply, he felt nothing but relief.

"So, no, Jamie's still in Brighton." Clare's nose was pink. She wiped it with a tissue. "I can't remember; do you have kids?"

That question.

"No."

Before Clare could inquire further, he turned the handle of his studio door. "Right, thanks very much, missus. I owe you."

"I'll hold you to that." She smiled.

He'd never seen Clare smile before. She had a nice smile. Sunny. It reminded him of the nurse who'd looked after him when he'd had his tonsils out as a kid, around the time the old man left home. The nurse had brought him ice-cold water for his throat in the night, and had smiled as she tucked him back in. His memory was that it lit up the dark.

Clare walked to the end of the corridor and opened her studio door. There was an explosion of color as the silk rolls and glass that she used for her floor lights burst into view.

With her back to him, she pulled off her winter coat, revealing a fitted denim dress that sat tight into her waist. Too late, Will caught himself imagining his hands there. He opened his own door and slammed it behind him. What the hell was that? He'd never thought about Clare in that way.

Wondering what was up with him, he counted back. It must be three months since he and Hannah had had sex. That was probably it. And even then, that last time had been crap, with her lying there, tense, looking like a martyr, and him hating it, but not wanting to stop because, God, it had been so fucking long.

He sat down and picked up his phone. One new message from Hannah.

He knew he should ring back to check she was all right in the snow, but something stopped him. Hannah had survived in worse places.

He sipped his coffee.

No, the break was doing him good. After last night he was starting to realize how much Hannah's obsession with Barbara and moving house had been distracting him from work.

She could get on with her manic decorating.

It was her idea, anyway, not his.

He'd ring later.

9

Hannah spent the first few moments of Tuesday morning standing by the bathroom sink, recalling last night's bizarre episode with the donkey. The electric heater on the wall burned her head. Every time it became unbearable, she moved into the sub-zero chill for a few seconds of relief, then back. In between she washed her body in hot water that she'd poured from the kettle.

Then she returned under the duvet and piled on her own clothes, and another dry sweater from Will's box. When she could bear it, she made a run through a blast of ice-air from the broken hall window to the kitchen, where she turned on the oven and burners and stood for another full five minutes, with a cup of tea in her frozen hands, unable to move.

God. How was she going to stand another day of this? She looked out of the window. The soft ridge of snow on the wall was twice its previous height. She prayed Will would find a way home tonight. She couldn't get the house ready all by herself.

To stop herself panicking she ticked off yesterday's entry

from the schedule, then walked around the kitchen to find a phone signal.

There was still no message from Brian, or from Will. To her relief there was, however, a new message from Laurie, asking if she was all right in the snow. Apparently she and Ian were cut off, too, over in Thurrup. There was no plumber's number on the message—either Laurie had forgotten or Will hadn't asked her yet. Hannah sighed. If Thurrup was cut off, then a plumber wouldn't make it out here anyway.

No. The snow would go eventually. She'd just have to be practical.

Hannah picked up her marker pen. Today's reworked entry on the schedule, written last night before bed, had been optimistic. Day 11: Tuesday, PAINT SITTING ROOM. She struggled to think straight about what to replace it with. In the end, she replaced SITTING ROOM with DINING ROOM.

First, however, she had to deal with the donkey.

After another cup of tea for heat, she grabbed an apple, dressed for outside, and forced herself into the freezing garden.

The air was thick with icy fog, and her feet crunched on a shell of newly formed hoarfrost towards the garage.

Inside, the little donkey looked up at her hopefully.

The red blanket was gone. The loosened twine lay on the floor. "Where's your . . . ?" she said, looking around. He hadn't eaten it, had he? She held out the carrot. The donkey plucked it from her with yellow teeth and ate it, as she mucked out into the field, looking around for the blanket. Had he kicked it somewhere?

She checked her watch: 8:30 A.M. This had to be sorted out. If she went now, she could start painting at nine, latest.

Pulling her coat close, Hannah returned to the field. Through the fog she saw that one light from last night belonged to a gray farmhouse, about a quarter of a mile away. The other belonged to a grain shed of some kind. There was no doubt then. The donkey's owner lived in the farmhouse.

As she passed by its shelter, she saw that it was even more pathetic than she'd realized last night: a few pieces of wood hammered onto badly erected gateposts. They'd clearly done it in a hurry, to move the donkey—and its snow-protest honking, presumably—away from their own bedrooms.

The old sense of injustice sizzled inside her. How could people behave like this?

Hannah wrapped her scarf around her mouth and stomped across the field. Yet ten minutes later, to her surprise, she still hadn't reached the farm, and her legs were tired with the effort of balancing on the narrow crop tracks. Thank goodness she hadn't attempted this last night. Distance was difficult to judge in this flat Suffolk landscape.

A few minutes later she reached a scruffy farmyard. Snow-covered machinery was parked around it. The house was built of ugly gray stone and was exposed to the elements. There were no trees or hedges, just fields and barbed-wire fences. Looking back, Hannah saw that the Horseborrows must have planted trees around their property when they moved in, a hundred years ago. Only the roof and two bedroom windows were visible through the bare branches of the tall oaks and ashes around it. In summer, she suspected, Tornley Hall would be completely obscured.

Hannah knocked on the front door. A cacophony of barking started up.

"Who is it?" a gruff voice shouted.

"Hannah, from . . . across the field."

There was a pause. The door scraped open, and an unsmiling woman stood in the doorway. Instinctively Hannah stepped back. She was enormous. Over six foot tall, with broad shoulders, like a cage-fighter. She was dressed in men's cords, a man's checked shirt, and an insulated waistcoat. Her face was red and sore looking. Dry skin flaked around her nose. Dark-gray hair was pulled back in a tight bun. In one hand she had a piece of toast; in the other, a rifle.

"Hi," Hannah said in the friendliest tone she could muster. "I'm Hannah. I've just moved in across the field—at Tornley Hall?"

"H'llo." If the farmer was interested in her new neighbor, she wasn't showing it. Two large hunting dogs pushed behind her. One barked, and the other joined in.

"Shut uppp!" the farmer yelled. She split the toast and threw it on the ground. The dogs pounced.

Hannah tried to ignore the gun. "Listen, I'm sorry, but do you own a donkey?"

It sounded so ridiculous she almost laughed.

The woman glanced over to the field. "Escaped, has he?"

"No. No, it's just that last night I found him outside, in the field."

"Got out of his shelter."

It was presented as a statement, not a question. Hannah held her nerve.

"Yeah. No. Sorry—no, he didn't escape. He was braying really loudly last night, and it woke me up. I found him outside, with a lot of snow on him. I was a bit worried, so I put him in our garage overnight. I wasn't sure if there'd been a mix-up and no one knew he was outside, or something."

The woman squinted at the distant field. The dogs pushed behind her, brushing Hannah's legs. "Where is he?"

"In my garage," Hannah repeated, wishing the woman

would put down the rifle. "At Tornley Hall—the thing is . . . I've worked in hot countries, and I'm pretty sure that donkeys aren't very good in cold weather. I think they need shelter. I just wanted to check that someone knew, and that, um . . ."

How much more bloody diplomatic could she be? To her dismay, Hannah heard the farmer swearing under her breath.

"Sorry?"

The woman pointed the rifle downwards. "You can't walk onto farmland and take animals. The police'll have you for that."

Damn. This was exactly what she didn't want.

"Oh. No. I'm sorry. I didn't mean to do anything to upset anyone. I just—it was late, and cold, and I didn't know what else to do."

She couldn't believe the words she was hearing come out of her own mouth.

The woman softened a tiny amount. "It's all right. Just put him back, please."

Hannah bit her tongue. So much for her negotiation-skills training. This woman was walking all over her.

The farmer watched Hannah with expressionless pale-blue eyes lost in pockets of loose skin.

Hannah forced herself to remember Barbara, and why they'd come to Tornley. She couldn't damage their chances for this. She pointed to a barn. "I mean, could he go in there, maybe—till the snow's gone?"

The woman banged her gun down. Hannah jumped.

"That shelter's fine. My sons built it. And, as I say, you don't just walk onto land and take livestock, or tell people what to do with theirs."

"No. No, I didn't mean to. . . . Sorry, I've just come from London, so . . ." She knew she sounded pathetic.

The farmer stood her ground, unflinching.

"OK. I'll put him back," Hannah said. "No problem—you're probably right."

She waved good-bye, but the woman didn't react.

Disgusted with herself, Hannah returned to the field. If Jane and her other TSO colleagues could see her now, they'd never speak to her again. She put her head down as a fresh flurry started, and climbed back onto the crop ridges.

Behind her came a shout. "Take the road, please, not my field!"

The thought of Jane and her uncompromising brown eyes finally galvanized Hannah. She kept her head down and pretended she hadn't heard; partly because she wasn't used to giving in to bullies, and partly because if she tried to navigate her way back to Tornley Hall by the unsignposted roads, she knew she'd end up in Ipswich.

Hoping the farmer wasn't allowed to shoot her for trespassing, she continued the way she'd come.

Midway across the field she allowed herself a glance back, and saw a second tall figure in a dark jacket, boots, and a woollen hat arriving beside the farmer. Her son? The farmer was pointing towards Hannah.

Hannah quickened her step. She'd have to stay away from them. It was too risky. The last thing they wanted Barbara to discover next Friday was that Will and Hannah had fallen out with the gun-wielding madwoman next door, and that Hannah had been arrested for donkey rustling.

She pulled out her phone to tell Will what was going on.

When he didn't answer she left another message.

This was becoming annoying. Where was he?

. . .

Back at Tornley Hall, Hannah fetched the donkey's coat, took it out to the garage, then led it shamefully back to its pitiful shelter. The donkey fixed its woeful eyes beyond her, and blinked with long lashes as the snow fell into them, as if accepting its fate.

"I'm sorry," she whispered, rubbing the donkey's head. "I just can't get involved right now, but I promise that when this is all over, I'll have your back, OK?"

Her mobile buzzed.

Brian's name popped up on the screen.

"Yes!" Hannah hissed. A text appeared.

> H/clearance ppl shd have put keys back in cupboard under scullery sink. Brian.

• • •

Hannah ran back to the house, trying to put the donkey out of her mind. Under the scullery sink was a cupboard they'd checked previously. She now saw, however, that inside it was a small box, painted the same green as the walls, with no handle. They'd missed it. She pried it open with her fingernails.

Two silver keys appeared, along with a bunch of old-fashioned brown ones, one of which she guessed belonged to the attic.

She took them to the sitting room. The first silver key turned in the lock straightaway.

Yes!

Hannah's mind flew to her schedule. This was fantastic. She could start painting the sitting room today after all, with the duck-egg-blue. She opened the door, fired up again.

The room lay in shadow. The diesel smell was even stronger inside. The only light came through an old cream blind on the square rear window that led out to the side alcove.

Hannah opened the first of the three sets of wooden shutters on the grand picture windows. Blue-tinged light rushed in, along with the great view of the lawn. Exhilarated, she turned to take in the dramatic effect.

Her eyes flew to the shelves on either side of the fireplace.

No!

There were books. Everywhere. The house-clearance people hadn't taken them.

"Oh, for God's sake!" Hannah yelled. Her plans were being thwarted at every turn. Every space on every shelf was packed, right to the ceiling, with volumes piled horizontally on top of upright ones.

Ironically, in the gloom she could already see that the rest of this room was in better condition than the others, with smooth, papered walls, that stunning Victorian silver fireplace, and the polished wooden floor. But it would take her hours to clear all these books before she could paint.

Over by the side window there was also a pile of black rubbish bags that the house-clearance people had left.

Frustrated, she started to open the second set of shutters.

In her peripheral vision a black bin bag moved.

At first it was a rustle of plastic, like a spider or a mouse, then all the bags seemed to rise up right on top of each other.

Hannah's heart dropped through her stomach.

Someone was in here.

Forcing her legs to move, she ran to the door, almost horizontal in her attempt to stop the intruder catching her. Breathless with fear, she swung round into the hall and slammed the sitting-room door shut so hard behind her that the handle nearly came off. Fumbling, she turned the key back in the lock.

Hannah jammed her feet into Will's trainers by the front door and ran out into the snowy garden. The driveway looked a mile long.

Was he behind her?

She stumbled through the snow blizzard towards the lane.

How did he get in there?

She reached the oak trees and kept going. Panicked thoughts flew at her.

If I hide in the bushes, he'll see my footprints in the snow and find me.

The house next door's shut up.

No cars come down this lane.

Tornley's a quarter of a mile away.

If he comes for me, I can't get away.

Hannah tripped, steadied herself, and kept going, trying to remember what to do.

First rule in a dangerous situation: alert someone.

She grabbed for her phone as she reached the gate.

A growling noise came out of nowhere.

With a gasp, she jumped sideways into the bushes, waiting for a hand on her back.

Then she realized it was a car. After forty-eight hours of near-silence, the engine cut through the garden like a chainsaw.

A red pickup truck with huge, broad tires swung through the gate and skidded to a stop, sending snow and gravel into her legs.

The door flew open.

A man jumped out.

• • •

Hannah was so shocked, it took her a second to recognize him. Dax.

He was still wearing an oily boiler suit and black gloves. If he was cold, he didn't show it.

"Aye-aye. Bit chilly for gardening, in't it?" He had that bemused expression on his face.

Hannah stood up and walked out of the bush. Her knee stung. It was bleeding.

"Right," Dax said, marching away. "Let's see this boiler."

She found her voice. "No! Don't! There's someone in there. In the house."

He halted.

"They've broken in. There's someone in the sitting room."

Dax gave her a quizzical look.

"Please, it's not funny," she said, brushing off snow. "I just unlocked the sitting room and there was someone in there."

"Who's that then?"

"I didn't see. He was lying on the floor under bin bags, and when I walked in he stood up, and I ran."

Dax glanced down at Will's size-eleven trainers and back at her face. He shrugged. "Vagrant, most like."

"A vagrant?"

He marched towards the house. "Get 'em, round here. Pain in the bloody arse. Where is he?"

"No!" Hannah called, following him. "No, Dax. Please. I locked him in. We need to call the police."

Dax snorted. "You'll be waiting all day then. Police don't waste time on that lot. Too many of 'em." He turned sharp left through the front door and, to Hannah's horror, unlocked the sitting-room door with the key she'd left in the lock, and walked straight in.

How did he even know where the sitting room was?

She crept behind him, trying to focus in the half gloom.

To her astonishment, the sitting room was empty. Dax was already pushing back the rest of the shutters. On the floor was what she now saw was just one black bin bag, and a brown blanket. There was an apple core and two empty chips packets, and a dusty black T-shirt and some rolled-up socks. With a fright she saw the red blanket by the window. She spun around.

Where was the man?

"Yup. Vagrant." Dax nodded, poking his finger at the side window. To her shock, the cream blind had been pulled up. The window opened straight out into the exterior alcove. There was no catch on it. A thought hit her and she felt sick. Had the man been in the house last night while she slept?

"Came through here," Dax said, pointing.

"Seriously?" she said, trying to gather her thoughts. "Oh, my God. When you say vagrant, you mean a homeless person? Isn't that a bit weird—I mean, in the middle of nowhere?"

Too late she realized how rude it was to call Tornley—Dax's home—"nowhere."

"No. Foreigner most like; come yesterday morning, get a head start on the seasonal work. They come around now, the early ones—get the land ready for planting. Bet he wasn't expecting snow, though!" Dax chortled. He pulled a hammer out of his tool belt, then a nail.

Hannah picked up the chips packets and dirty socks, trying not to breathe. "But don't the farmers give them accommodation?"

He nodded. "If they come here legal with the agency, they do. They got RVs for 'em. Some don't want to pay rent, though. Or they's illegal. Old Samuel had two in his tire shed, summer gone. Buggers had a bloody gas stove and all. Could've gone up."

Hannah looked at the red blanket and recalled the chips packets in the garage. Had farmworkers been sleeping in there, too? Before she realized what Dax was doing, he nailed the window shut.

"Oh . . ." Hannah started. But it was too late. Dax pulled out another nail and did the other side, then stood back.

She tempered her dismay at the nail holes in the original Victorian wood with the knowledge that at least the intruder was locked out.

"Thank you," she said. "Actually that might explain it—there was stuff in the garage, too."

Dax nodded. "That'll be it. House's been empty two . . . three years, right? Probably been a few of them 'ere. This one won't be back. Knows you're 'ere now. Probably gave him the fright of his bloody life!"

"Really?"

"Oh, yeah. That type don't want trouble with the police." Dax put his hammer back in his belt. "Right." He clapped his hands together. "Boiler." He marched off towards the kitchen, as if it was completely normal to find someone in your house, and he now had better things to do.

"Dax, do you know Tornley Hall?" Hannah called. Nervously she peeked into the dining room and the understairs toilet.

Dax ignored her. In the kitchen he opened the boiler, twiddled a knob, and pulled his overall sleeves up to his elbows. He had those big, solid forearms of men who work with their hands, not at a computer, like the men she knew in London. Dax stood back.

"Can you fix it?"

He made a face. "If I was a plumber, I might."

"Oh. You're not?"

Dax ignored her and stalked off again, with that full-power energy of a man who works outdoors.

She traipsed behind, to see his big boots disappear out the front door, leaving a trail of muddy prints behind.

"Put the kettle on, then," he shouted. "Milk, two sugars."

Knowing that, right now, she'd do just about anything to be reassured that the intruder wasn't coming back, and to be warm again, Hannah did what he so graciously asked. As she waited for the kettle to boil, she rang Will to tell him what had happened.

His phone went straight to voice mail again.

He must have woken early in the studio and started work. She prayed he'd find a way to return this afternoon.

Hannah looked at the phone, wondering if she should ring the police, despite what Dax said.

Barbara came to mind again. What would Barbara say if she knew Will and Hannah had a break-in, three days after moving in? It wasn't exactly the safe, perfect family-home environment she was expecting.

She put down the phone.

If she reported it as a crime, would Barbara stumble on the police report if she did a home check on Tornley Hall in the next few weeks? Would it be concealment if Hannah didn't tell her? Hannah turned to make tea, frustrated. In fifteen years in London she'd never seen a gun or had a break-in. Here, she'd experienced both within three days.

The front door banged. She took the tea to the hall. Dax held an armful of logs.

"Oh, OK," she said.

Ignoring her again, he walked off into the sitting room.

This man was making her head spin.

Dax threw down the logs by the fireplace, peered up the chimney, banged it with a big fist, then chucked twigs onto the empty grate, followed by four logs.

As with the window, he wasn't even asking her if it was OK.

"Sorry, Dax, that chimney's not been swept. It might go up . . ."

Dax pulled a grubby can from his boiler suit and poured a liberal amount of murky liquid onto the logs. He threw on a lighted match.

"Listen, I don't think—"

Fire exploded in the grand old Victorian fireplace. It was so startling to see a warm glow in this cold, bleak house that Hannah shut up. Even from twenty feet away she could feel heat pricking faintly at her frozen hands and face. The dank cream walls turned a pale, warm orange.

For the first time since they arrived Tornley Hall suddenly looked homely and welcoming again.

She leaned against the door. Dax kicked the logs with a hefty boot.

"Thank you; that looks—"

"Right!" He cut across her.

He marched past with more logs and set a second fire in the small fireplace in the hall. It, too, exploded into life, adding a warmth to the heart of the house. Hannah shoved Will's boxes of vinyl away, then crouched by it, transfixed.

Dax took his tea from the mantelpiece. His eyes flashed in the firelight. With his tangle of dark curls, he reminded her of some creature: a wild horse off the marshes. She was so used to office workers in the city being groomed and clean, to make themselves acceptable in others' cramped company, that there was something strangely appealing about Dax's honest work grime.

Suddenly his eyes creased up, pushing the oil on his face into his crow's feet.

"What the hell do you call that?" he roared, spitting out his tea.

"Oh, sorry, it's the only sugar I could find. It's muscovado. . . ."

Dax frowned. Before she could offer him something else, he tried the study door handle and, when it wouldn't open, looked over and grabbed the key ring from the sitting-room door. Without asking, he unlocked the study and walked in, cup in hand.

This was her house.

"You need to fill them cracks," he said, surveying the walls.

"Yeah, I know," she said, walking in behind him. Thankfully the study was both intruder-free and as well maintained as the sitting room. It was cosy and small, with that window seat that she planned to cover in a remnant of material for Barbara's visit. "I will. But right now I'm just trying to paint it quickly, so I can get these up when my husband gets home." She pointed to the four record shelf units clogging up the hall.

Dax glanced sideways at them, as if he were eyeing up a secondhand car. He gulped his tea. "Where's he, then?"

"Stuck in London, in the snow."

Dax shook his head with a scathing grin, as if London was the most ridiculous place on earth anyone could choose to go.

"Right. Come on then," he said, marching out the front door.

What now? She was starting to feel as if Dax owned Tornley Hall, not her.

He booted the snow out of his way as he headed past the study windows, down the right-hand side of the house, and stopped at a wooden door.

He yanked it open, revealing a stack of logs.

"Oh," Hannah said. "Great!" This wasn't what she needed, but it would help.

Dax felt the wood. "Should be dry. If not, stick that on." He pulled out the can and shoved it at her. "Go up like a rocket."

The can was sticky. "What is it?"

"Sump oil—from the bike."

"Isn't that dangerous?"

He looked astonished, as if she'd said something both stupid and funny, threw back the last of his tea, and turned on his heel.

She sniffed the can's strong oily odor, wondering if this was why the sitting room smelled of fuel. Had Olive and Peter used sump oil to start fires, too? Was that what people did here?

"Right, then. Jim at Thurrup, he's the plumber—won't get down till the snow's gone. His car's a piece of shit." Dax stuck the cup in her hand, as if she was his servant. "Thank you very much." And he walked off again.

"Oh. Right. So, Dax, sorry, do I owe you for the logs you brought?"

He waved back. "We'll sort it out."

What did that mean? Was that a country thing?

She followed him to the truck.

"So you really don't think he'll come back, then—the farm-worker?"

"No. He'll be halfway to Norfolk now, thinking the coppers is after him. But . . ." He reached into his truck, scribbled a number on a cigarette packet. "You have any bother, you ring." He thrust it into her hand. "Me and Bill will be round. Sort him out."

The offer was so unexpected that Hannah forgave him his awkward manner. Dax jumped in his truck and revved off, without giving her the chance to thank him. He drove like he walked—no time wasted.

She scanned the garden nervously, in case the vagrant was watching. The bare hedges and branches left nowhere to hide. She went round the side alcove, double-checked the sitting-room window Dax had nailed shut, and the big square one opposite it, into the scullery. Both were secure. Just in case, she locked the garage doors, too.

Back inside, Hannah checked the upstairs rooms, the attic, and the windows and doors, then made herself a sugary cup of tea for the shock and walked towards the sitting-room fire.

She needed to pull herself together. This was all distracting her from getting the house ready today. Dax was local. He must know what he was talking about. The man had run away, probably as scared as she was.

She was just sitting down when there was a creak, then a sudden loud bang behind her.

"Oh!" Hannah exclaimed, jumping back up.

The hall beyond the doorway had fallen into gloom, with just the faint glow from the fire licking at the shadows.

Her heart thumped hard for the second time today. That hall light had been on a second ago.

Hannah tiptoed over, reached into the hall, and found the switch. She pressed it and nothing happened. Swearing under her breath, she crossed to the study. That light worked, as did the one in the dining room. She examined the hall fitting in the dull mid-morning light from outside and saw misted glass.

"For God's sake, calm down," she said out loud. The light-bulb had blown. That's all.

Relieved, she fetched a new one from the kitchen and stood on a chair to replace it. Light once again flooded the center of the house. She was about to turn off the study lamp, then hesitated. The more rooms that looked as if they were occupied, even during the daytime, the less likely any more transient farmworkers would be to mistake the house for an empty property.

Trying to relax, she returned to the sitting-room fire and sat down. What a weird bloody morning. Clearly she'd been naive, thinking everything out here would be idyllic.

Behind her there was another creak, this time farther away.

"Oh, for God's sake," Hannah muttered, jumping up to peer out the hall door.

The door into the kitchen was open, as she had left it. She checked round the hall once again, her eyes stopping at the little fire in the corner. Didn't heat make houses expand? She wrapped the blanket more firmly round herself and returned to chuck another log on the sitting-room fire, then picked up her phone to tell Will what had happened.

Hannah's finger froze over the keypad.

Was that a good idea? What would he do? Worry that she was out here on her own with a madman on the loose, and ring the police?

They couldn't mess this up with Barbara. She couldn't let her nerves spoil everything they'd dreamed about.

She had to trust Dax, and believe the man was long gone.

Hannah put down the phone and shifted a burning log with their old poker from London. It was a much grander, bigger fireplace than their little Edwardian one in the flat. A pleasant pine smell drifted off the wood, masking the lingering petrol smell in the room.

Dax was probably right. And if, by some remote chance, the vagrant did come back tonight, her new neighbors had promised to come straight round.

Hannah lowered her phone. She'd tell Will after Barbara had been. Once this was over. She was so behind now with the schedule that, when Will did finally get back, she'd need him focused on preparing for Barbara's visit and nothing else.

Hannah looked up at the Horseborrows' dusty old library to

distract herself. What, for instance, were they going to do with this lot?

The books were crammed along wooden shelves that ran up to the high ceiling. She stood up and trailed a finger along one.

On the right side of the fireplace, underneath a large collection of dry-looking history and military tomes, was a row of old children's books. She took one out and opened it. "To Olive Horseborrow, For Diligence, Fifth Year, 1934," the inscription said, in copperplate writing. How amazing. And how sad that she and Peter had no family to pass these books on to.

On the left side of the fireplace there were mainly old travel books. *Walking Through Inner Mongolia*. *A Vagabond Abroad*. Hannah opened *Swaziland on a Horse*, her fingers immediately darkening with dust. She leafed through the wafer-thin pages, fascinated by the old maps and old-fashioned fonts. Dried flowers and old postcards fell out, and a handwritten receipt dated 1956, from an Ipswich bookshop.

Is that what Olive and Peter did? Worked abroad in far-off lands, and brought their wonderful tapestries and antiques back to this rural part of Suffolk? What work had they done?

Hannah sat down again, not wanting to leave the heat.

Suddenly there was a longer, much louder creak outside.

She spun round. What the hell was going on?

Picking up the poker in one hand and her phone in the other, she found Dax's number and tiptoed out into the hall.

Once again, it was empty.

She waited, then kept going quietly, glancing into the dining room and then into the kitchen.

The old fridge door, from where she'd taken out the milk, had fallen open.

Shutting it firmly, she checked the kitchen clock. Right. Enough. There was no more time for shredded nerves. The man was gone. She had to get started. Hannah picked up her schedule for today. And then, from nowhere, she had the strangest feeling she was being watched.

She turned.

The scullery behind her was empty apart from the sink, the old fridge, wall shelves, and their own washing machine.

This was ridiculous. She had to calm down.

The doors were locked, the sitting-room window was nailed shut, and the vagrant knew the house was occupied now. He was hardly going to stand outside in the freezing snow all day, waiting to steal back in. For all he knew, Dax was her husband—and she might be waiting right now for the police to arrive.

No, she had to focus.

She opened the fridge in the scullery and took out the last green apple for her breakfast.

As she did so, there was another creak beside her on the floor.

She looked down at the old linoleum, relieved. That creak had happened right in front of her, and there was clearly no one here. That's all it was—the heat, waking up the chilly old house, and the wooden floors contracting.

Hannah bit into the apple.

Vaguely she noticed an odd taste, but ignored it.

She went to fetch the paint roller.

10

By four o'clock that afternoon, Will's hangover had been replaced by fatigue and hunger. He threw on his jacket and walked out of the studios into the snow to find food. There was a light on in the King's Head. That would do.

To his surprise, the pub was full. Will found himself ordering a pint again, and decided not to think about it. It had been an odd week. Stressful.

At the next table was a group of fashion students. One, a Japanese girl, was wearing what looked like a slit white cushion on her head. He smiled, then recalled the Fox & Hounds with its huddle of desiccated faces.

Resentment gripped him that he'd had to leave London. Resentment at Hannah.

He turned on his phone and saw two more messages from her. They were broken and difficult to hear again. Something about a donkey she'd found in the snow, and how she wanted to call the RSPCA but was worried that, if the police became involved, Barbara might find out.

He deleted the message, annoyed. What was up with her? That wasn't like Hannah. The first time he'd visited her flat in Holloway, he'd found her and her flatmate confronting the wanker next door who'd been hitting his wife. The guy was telling them to fuck off, while his wife hid inside. The atmosphere had changed when Will arrived, but he'd suspected Hannah didn't need his help. She was fearless.

It's what he'd liked about her from the start. She looked after herself. She wasn't like his mum, a bottomless pit of neediness. Or the clingy girls who'd followed him and the lads around shit gigs in Camden pubs, pandering to them, even when they acted like the coked-up arses they were back then.

No. The Hannah from that time wouldn't have thought twice about calling the RSPCA on some knob.

The pub door opened, with a blast of cold air. In the mirror, Will saw Clare shaking snow from her hat. To his surprise, she was with two Smart Yak producers. She must have started coming to the pub more since she'd split up from her boyfriend.

Hannah's second message came to an abrupt halt in his ear: ". . . so can you . . . please, Will. My phone hardly . . . out here, and—"

Will saw Clare sit down with the producers, and decided to ring Hannah back later.

Right now, he wanted to go over there. Not because of the unexpected whisper of suggestion when Clare had taken off her coat earlier. He didn't know where that had come from. He just wanted to sit and enjoy a rare afternoon pint in the pub before he returned to work, without Hannah controlling his every move.

He turned off his phone, waited to feel bad—and didn't.

It was her idea to decorate the whole house in two weeks, not his. He'd told her that Barbara didn't care what color the walls were, but that had just caused more "discussions" about him "being ridiculously naive and not being realistic about what they needed to do."

His stomach rumbled. He'd forgotten to order any food. He checked the menu on the wall. Clare and the producers saw him and waved him over.

Exhaustion and hunger, and the need for easygoing company, propelled Will towards them, and pushed Hannah from his thoughts in a way that would not have been possible eight months ago.

He told himself it wasn't serious.

. . .

All along, Will's intention had been to return to work after he'd eaten.

It just didn't work out that way.

His afternoon in the King's Head started with one pint. By five o'clock, however, he was on his second, and locked in a conversation with more Smart Yak people, as they, too, gave up work for the day, having lost clients and bosses and assistants to the snow. There was a party atmosphere in the pub. Plates of steak pies and chips were ordered. Someone started a pool tournament.

Clare seemed to know quite a few people. "You're not on that sofa again tonight, are you?" she shouted to Will, across the noisy table.

He gave her a wry smile. The truth was that he'd hardy slept for an hour at a time last night and needed to find a hotel, or his back would go completely.

There was something animated about Clare tonight. That lightness in her face again. She leaned over a producer Will didn't like, a young cokehead called Neil with a beer belly, who made bad dance music. "Listen, Will. You know, if Jamie's stuck in Brighton, you should use his room. You're more than welcome."

"Wahey! There's an offer, mate," Neil exclaimed.

"And you'd know, because your world's just full of offers, isn't it, Neil?" Clare cut across him.

Neil blushed, attempting a cocky smirk.

Will smiled. She was feistier than he had given her credit for. "Cheers," he said, "but I'll probably work through."

"Sure?"

He raised his glass. "But thanks."

"Tell you what," Clare said. She fished in her bag and handed him keys. "Those are Jamie's. I'm out tonight," she said, glowering at Neil. "But if you change your mind, use them. Really. It's 42C Arndale Road—two up on the right towards the Tube." She pushed them into his hand.

"Well, listen, I probably won't, but cheers," he said.

"Up to you—you're welcome." She put on her Cossack hat, said her good-byes, and disappeared into the whiteout.

Will ignored Neil's attempt to recover from Clare's putdown—now that she was gone—with a more confident version of the smirk. It's not that Hannah would care if he stayed at Clare's. That was another thing he'd loved about her when they met. She'd never been even vaguely bothered when he went out for the night, or off on writing trips abroad with female musicians or press officers. She was more likely just to be pissed off that Clare had made it easier for him not to make an effort to return to Suffolk tonight. He put her keys in his pocket.

"Will—you're on!" came a call from the pool table.

Before he knew it he'd played three games, and drunk another pint. He felt more relaxed than he had for months.

Eight months, precisely.

It was a relief just to hang out, without Hannah obsessing about Tornley Hall and Barbara all the time.

He hit the ball hard. It bounced off the green and hit a yellow.

He'd gone along with her plan, because she'd promised it would make everything right again. But Will was starting to realize he didn't believe her anymore.

Resentment grew for what he'd had to leave behind. She wasn't the only one last summer had happened to.

Will stood back to let his opponent play.

Someone shouted his name from the bar, and motioned a drink. He raised his thumb.

One more pint, then he'd go and work on Jeremiah's track. The sofa would be fine tonight. He'd find a hotel tomorrow.

His opponent missed and Will stepped forward, sizing up his shot.

Clare's keys crushed into his hip as he leaned across the table.

11

That same evening, Hannah stood back and examined her handiwork. Following the intruder episode, she had decided to paint the study rather than the dining room. That way she could unclutter the hall into the study when the paint was dry.

In the end, it had only taken seven hours. She saved decorating time by leaving four large areas of nasty brown wallpaper where the record shelves would stand.

At 8:00 P.M. she washed out her brushes and poured the last, flat glass of Laurie's cava, and ate the last of the cheese. Will's job had been to do a supermarket shop on Monday night on the way home. If he didn't make it back tomorrow, either, she'd start to run out of food soon.

Today, however, had at least ended better than it had started. One more room done.

After the unnerving events of the past twenty-four hours, Hannah felt her focus return.

Ten and a bit more days till Barbara came, and nothing was going to stop her.

Not Will being stuck in London.

Not vagrants.

Not broken boilers.

Nothing.

Also, she hadn't heard the donkey all day and was starting to feel hopeful that her "word" with the unfriendly farmer had actually done the trick.

She stoked up the little fire in the hall and sat on the hall stairs, sipping her cava, wondering what Barbara's initial impression would be when she walked in next week. Would she see what Hannah wanted her to see: a welcoming, happy family home?

Her mind drifted back to the first time Barbara had visited the London flat, more than two years ago. It was immediately clear that they'd struck it lucky. Barbara was intuitive and kind, with a warm laugh. She'd handled Will's initial reticence to talk about his difficult childhood with sensitivity and patience. They'd begun to trust her, to become used to her in-depth questions about their families, their life experiences, and their own relationship. They realized that Barbara liked them.

Yet Hannah was not stupid. Behind Barbara's warm manner lay a sharp, professional eye. It was her responsibility to check that Hannah and Will were telling the truth, that they were trustworthy.

Hannah surveyed the cracks on the ceiling and the stained floor tiles.

If for a moment Barbara thought they were deceiving her, Hannah knew that everything would change.

•   •   •

Nighttime was so unrelentingly dark out here. Despite the log fires, the cold crept through the drafty windows and loose doors. Shivering, Hannah nailed a piece of wood to the small, broken hall window, and double-checked the doors and other windows before heading upstairs.

She was on the second step when the donkey's agonized honk entered the house again.

"Oh, for God's sake!" She sat on the stairs, head in her hands.

The plaintive bray reached through the windows, once, then twice more, tugging at her conscience. It was back out in the snow. What was wrong with that farmer?

Hannah threw on her coat, grabbed her keys and, as an afterthought, her phone. If she couldn't report the farmer right now, she could at least collect some evidence.

She entered the dark, snowy garden and walked to the field. The shelter from last night had gone. When the bray came again, she followed her flashlight beam down the field and saw the donkey thirty yards farther along the fence. To her anger, she saw that the farmer and her sons had simply moved its crap shelter farther away from Tornley Hall, yet still far enough from the farm that the noise wouldn't disturb them. Bastards.

"Poor boy," she said. Shielding the flash from view of the farm, she took five photos of the scene on her phone from different angles.

Checking no one was nearby, she set off towards the donkey. "Come on," she said, untying its rope and returning it to the garage for the night. Back in the house, five minutes later, she stripped off her wet clothes for what felt like the tenth time this week.

Hannah wrapped herself in her duvet and sat in front of the sitting-room fire, checking the photos on her phone. This is what she'd have to do: help the donkey when she could, and keep collating the evidence.

Even as she thought it, however, she knew she was trying to make herself feel better for not ringing the RSPCA right now.

To distract herself, she tried Will one last time. To her surprise, he answered.

"Hi, where are you?" she asked. "Are you going to make it home?"

"Hi, Han." The sound of his voice made her want him there now, inside this duvet, so much it hurt. She missed him so much that she wanted to have sex with him, even though she knew that, when it came to it, she wouldn't.

"No. I'm still here. Sorry, I've been working . . . on the track . . . day."

"Oh, OK. Don't worry. Listen, the signal's crap. You're cutting out, and I want to talk to you. Did you get my messages?"

This time Will's words cut out straightaway.

"Will?"

She thought she heard music down the phone. Then a shout. A woman's voice.

"Will?"

"Hello?" He sounded distracted.

"Where are you?"

"In the studio . . . just back . . . the pub—Jem and his girlfriend are here . . . late session."

"OK," she said uncertainly. "Well, look, I really need to speak to you. There's been some weird stuff going on here. Will you ring me tomorrow?"

"OK."

She waited for him to ask her how she was.

The phone crackled.

"I'm really missing you," she said, pushing the phone into her cheek. "You didn't leave me a note."

The crackling stopped. The call had finally cut out.

She sat on the floor, the phone still at her ear, even though Will was gone.

12

Back in London, Will listened to Hannah's voice. "I'm really missing you. You didn't leave me . . ."

Quietly he pressed the "end call" button. He put the phone on Jamie's bed.

"Coffee?" Clare shouted from her living room.

.   .   .

Will's plan to return to the studio had not materialized. At half past nine tonight he was still in the King's Head. It had just felt too good to be out, talking music with a few mates and having a few more pints.

In fact he'd probably still be in the King's Head now, if he hadn't stumbled into a wall outside the toilet and realized he'd overdone it.

At that point he'd tried to work out how much he'd drunk, but gave up. Instead he'd left the King's Head to a wall of cheers. At some point—he wasn't sure when—he'd decided to take

Clare up on her offer. Hotels were probably shut anyway because of the snow. And he was cold.

That studio was freezing at night.

The street was a practical whiteout, but being London, life went on. Girls in club gear of dresses and high heels were having a snowball fight. One threw a snowball at him flirtatiously, and he threw one back, grinning. A black cab crawled through the snow with its yellow FOR HIRE light on. A gig was going on at the Brazilian bar opposite, people salsa dancing in the window.

Will hugged his jacket and walked unsteadily onwards.

He loved this city. The energy never stopped.

Why the hell had he let Hannah make him leave it?

He brushed snow off each street sign until he found Arndale Road. He veered into it at an angle, feeling the freezing air sobering him up already. Number 42 was the entrance to a small block of ex-council flats. It reminded him of Hannah's Holloway flat.

He walked up to the second-floor balcony, unlocked door C with Clare's key, and stumbled inside, hoping she wasn't there. That way he could crash out, without having to make awkward conservation.

The flat was tiny. It was feminine, like her studio. There were fake-fur rugs and silk draped around, and two of her floor lamps, dripping with glass beads and silver leaves. It looked as if she'd used this house move to remove every trace of her ex-boyfriend.

Will took off his coat, thinking of the long, dark corridors and huge kitchen at Tornley Hall. Nobody needed that much room. He liked this place. This was all you needed. If this were his, he'd fill it with vinyl and books and a sofa.

He peered into a rear bedroom and saw a Victorian bedstead, piled with clothes. Next door was a child's room.

He threw his coat onto that bed, listing to the right. Would Clare mind if he made coffee? In the kitchen he searched through a pile of herbal-tea boxes until he found a jar of instant. On the fridge there was a photo of Clare, altered on an app to look obese. She had giant cheeks and a triple chin. "Fat mum," it said in childlike writing underneath it. On the fridge door was a small banner that spelled "Love" out in glitter. A sheet of house rules was next to it, starting with "1. Mum is always right." "Mum" had been crossed out and replaced with "Jamie," which in turn had been replaced with "Mum" again, and then with "The Cat."

Will smiled. This is what he wanted with his kid.

A sense of loss hit him, and he rubbed his face.

He took his coffee into the sitting room. The flat kept reminding him of Hannah when he'd met her, eight years ago, when kids hadn't even crossed their minds. When he'd go round for dinner and find people from countries he'd never heard of squashed at her pull-out table, eating food he'd never eaten before, talking politics—Hannah in the middle of it all, pouring wine, jousting with her boss, Jane, touching his foot with hers when no one was looking. Hannah's world had been big and bold then, and she'd raced across it.

A sadness crawled through him for what had gone, and then for what had never been.

He recalled Hannah last summer, on the floor of their flat in Shepherd's Bush, rocking. A ripped photocopy of a photo on the floor. Lost. He'd have done anything to make it right for her.

So when she'd pushed for this move to Suffolk, he'd agreed.

He'd just wanted her back.

But the longer he was away from her, the more he saw the truth. The move wasn't fixing things. It was ripping their world further apart. The earth was opening up beneath them, shifting them out of each other's reach.

He had lied to Hannah on the phone tonight.

When Clare had walked into the flat and shouted "Hello," he'd said it was Jeremiah's girlfriend, then pretended that the phone signal had died.

He didn't want to think why.

•   •   •

"Will, do you want coffee?" Clare shouted again.

He couldn't ignore her. It would be rude.

"Hi," he said, opening the bedroom door.

"Hey! You came—excellent."

"Yeah, I thought the hotels might be closed. So, thanks." He tried not to slur. It felt like trying to control a skidding car.

"Oh, you're really welcome." Her nose was pink again, and ice dripped off her hat. Perhaps because he was pissed, she reminded him—with her silvery eyes—of the penny arcades in Great Yarmouth that Nan took him and Laurie to on summer nights.

He touched the sofa, trying to stay steady.

"So you got in OK?" she asked, removing her coat. He averted his eyes from her dress.

"Yeah," he said, not knowing where to put himself in the tiny sitting room. It felt awkward. She seemed different here, among her own things. More confident. Her hair was tied back in a loose bun. She picked up a tartan blanket and threw it over her shoulders, and gave a big comedy shiver.

"Sorry—it's freezing in here."

"No. It's good," he said, wondering whether he should sit down.

"So was that your wife you were speaking to?" She motioned towards Jamie's room.

The word "wife" still sounded strange to him. Another thing he'd done for Hannah, because she thought it would improve their chances with Barbara—even though previously she'd been no more bothered about marriage than him.

"Yes."

"How's she managing in the snow?" Clare sat on a sofa that was covered in lace and cushions. She motioned to an old leather chair, and he sat unsteadily. "Matt said your new house is in the middle of nowhere?"

"Yeah, um . . ."

Jesus. Talk, man. If he didn't start acting normal soon, she'd worry about having him in the flat. "Hannah's not . . . She doesn't spook easily."

Clare tucked her long legs under her denim dress. "Matt said she used to have an amazing job—traveling to war zones, or something?"

Used to have.

"No, not quite; she traveled to some dangerous places, but she is—well, she was—a press officer for a human-rights charity that campaigns for educators, so she used to take journalists to countries where people were jailed by governments for writing the wrong textbook or teaching the 'wrong' thing—organizing a union, that kind of thing. Yeah, so . . ."

"Wow." She watched him carefully. "But not anymore?"

"No."

"So, do you, um . . ." she tried.

He saw concern in her eyes.

"Clare," he said. "Look. I'm sorry, but I'm wasted. I stayed in the pub."

Her expression immediately relaxed. "I knew it! You bunch of piss-heads."

He grinned, relieved.

"Right, you've got no excuse then," she said, unwrapping herself. "You have to keep me company. They only drink tea and sherry at my sewing group—it's all very vintage, you know."

She went to fetch whisky, two glasses, and a packet of cookies.

"Jamie's—don't tell him. Do you want to put some music on?"

"Yeah."

He was so pissed he grabbed the first thing—a Mazzy Star CD—and Clare lit candles and poured out the whisky. Slow, dreamlike music filled the room. Will sat back, starting to feel relaxed, which was weird, because he hardly knew Clare.

He lifted his glass. "Well, cheers. Thanks very much."

"You're welcome," Clare said, winking. "I'm going to spinning class in the morning, so I reckon I'm allowed."

"Spinning class?"

She made a face. "Only since I split up with Dave. Got to get back out there."

"Oh, right, yeah—sorry."

"Oh, don't worry. It was coming for a while," she said, biting a cookie. "Between you and me, Jamie was an accident actually, and then we stuck it out for about—oh—ten years longer than we should have."

"How old is Jamie?"

"Ten."

They both laughed. Will eased back in his chair. This was OK. She was nice, the flat was nice. The whisky took the edge off thinking about Hannah. For once there was no schedule, no painting, no long, serious discussions. And he could go to bed without watching Hannah turn her back on him.

"But no, it's fine," Clare said. "I've been wanting to get the business moving for ages, and now I can. Dave always wanted to live in Brighton, and he's met someone, so . . ." She shrugged. "Jamie loves it there, too, so it's OK."

Clare casually pulled the tie from her bun. Her hair tumbled onto her chest and Will examined the bottom of his glass.

"So I meant to ask you: why the move to Suffolk?"

He sighed inwardly. It was a subject too close to home tonight.

"Uh . . . it's a long story, but we went there when my gran died, for the funeral. And I was showing Hannah where I used to hang out in the summer, and we got lost."

Clare's eyes widened. "No!"

"Yeah, in a place called Tornley, down a dead end. We did a U-turn outside this old house with a FOR SALE sign, and Hannah wanted to see inside."

"Seriously, just like that?"

"Yeah. We rang the estate agent and he showed us round the next day. It had been empty for years, so we put in a stupid offer, thinking there was no way they'd take it."

"And they did?"

"Yup. Then it all just happened."

Clare sipped her whisky. "Wow. But you like it, right?"

Will chose his words carefully. "Well, it's got an acre of land and a place to build a studio, so . . ."

"Oh. So you'll stop renting at Smart Yak?"

For a second he thought he sensed disappointment in her voice, and put it down to the drink. "Well, I spend part of my fee on studio rent, so I might as well invest it in my own place. And Hannah's idea is to section off a guest area in the house, where clients can stay."

"Sounds great. Big life change, huh?"

"Yup."

Her felt her sparkly eyes on him. "So . . ."

"So . . ."

"So . . . sorry!" She smiled. "Why don't you sound convinced?"

It was strange. His head was clearing despite the whisky. "What do you mean?"

"Well, if your wife loves the house, and you want a studio—well, you didn't exactly seem upset about not going back yesterday."

He swirled the drink in his glass.

In this cosy flat, with whisky on his tongue, he nearly told Clare. Then he reminded himself he was drunk, and it was late, and they were here alone.

He wasn't stupid. He knew how these things could go.

"Yeah, well that's house moves, for you. You know yourself." He gestured at her flat. "Takes a while."

"Tell me about it."

He put down his glass, and saw her glancing at his faded Celtic-band tattoo again. This time she didn't look away.

"I was eighteen," he offered. "We all got one. I can't even remember why."

"You and your mates?"

He nodded. Clare flung back her blanket and unbuttoned the top of her denim dress. She pulled away one side, and a tangle of blond hair, to reveal a small blue dolphin diving under a lacy bra strap. "Me, too! First year at art college."

An unexpected sexual volt charged through Will. He shook himself. *Grow up.*

"Nice," he said politely. "Anyway, listen." He stood up, holding the arm of the chair. "Thanks for the whisky. And for the bed. I'm going to leave you in peace now."

She twisted a lock of hair. "No, I'm glad you took me up on staying. There's a towel under the sink."

"Cheers."

"Night. Sleep well."

"Night."

As he headed for the bedroom, an image came back to him of Hannah meeting him at the door of her Holloway flat with a soft kiss, bare feet, cheeks flushed with cooking, smelling of spice and garlic.

Then he knew what was different about Clare recently.

She seemed happy in her own skin, like Hannah used to be.

Will shut the door, and sat down on Jamie's bed. He realized he wasn't just unhappy that Hannah had forced him to move out of London.

He was just unhappy.

13

That night Hannah put out the sitting-room fire in Tornley Hall, thinking about her conversation with Will. Was it the phone signal, or was he drunk? Without her around, Matt and the studio boys had probably talked him into four or five pints.

Well, good for them. Matt had only ever known grown-up Will. Grown-up Will, who was responsible for other people's careers and mortgages. He'd never met childish Will. He'd be out of a job in a month, if he did.

It didn't matter. Will would be home tomorrow, hopefully.

As Hannah stood up, she spotted the vagrant's red blanket, still lying in the corner by the window. Wrinkling her nose, she picked it up with the poker to throw it out the back door.

The corner of a green leather-bound book appeared underneath it.

What was that?

Hannah dropped the blanket and knelt down. The rest of the book was stuck in a narrow gap under the lowest bookshelf.

She pulled it out. "Photographs," it said on the front in gold letters.

Ooh! This was interesting.

Behind it, she saw the edge of another green album. She dragged it out. There was a third behind that one.

Intrigued, Hannah kept pulling. Four, five . . . She continued until there were seven photograph albums lying on the wooden floor. This was exciting. Three of the covers were more battered than the others and had a faint white coating, as if they'd been stored somewhere damp. Lots of pages were stuck together. She opened the first clean album. The spine was stiff and came apart with a creak. Black-and-white photos appeared on the page. They were inserted into little cardboard frames, with soft, off-white tissue nestled between each page.

Hannah flicked, fascinated. This page showed Tornley Hall!

What were these: the Horseborrow family photographs?

She found more photographs of people in the garden and around the house, at the beach and on the lanes. This was amazing. If Brian was right, and the Horseborrows had been the only residents of Tornley Hall since it was built in 1902, these photographs would provide an invaluable history of the house.

With the fire now dead, the temperature plummeted. Hannah grabbed three of the better albums, locked up the inner doors, and ran to her freezing bedroom.

When she'd warmed up under the duvet, she examined them in more detail. The first collection appeared to be from the 1920s. Tornley Hall looked much grander than it did today. The front lawn was manicured, with elegant paths and rose beds, and a posh car in the driveway. There were two Irish wolfhounds in a few of the photos. One image was taken at the front of the house.

In it, a nipped-mouthed elderly woman in a hat and muffler sat in a wheelchair. Behind her was a girl with the vacant look of a bored servant. Could the woman be Olive and Peter's mother, Mrs. Horseborrow, the original owner of the house? Hannah peered closer. The front door was ajar.

Was that . . . was that . . . ?

It *was*. In the shadows was the Oriental tapestry that had hung here till last week.

She sat back. This was incredible. Will had to see this.

In the second album the photos were from a little later, perhaps the 1940s, and appeared to have been taken inside the original walled garden. One set was of a party. Cheerful young men wore slicked-back hair and baggy wool trousers; the women were dressed in tea dresses, their hair set in waves. Some played croquet. All were smiling for the camera. The same two faces appeared on every page: a woman with a pleasant, round face and brown plaits, tied Austrian-style on top of her head; and a man with jolly apple cheeks, round glasses, and a tubby tummy, encased in a suit—like Santa Claus without the beard.

Olive and Peter?

Hannah laid the album on her chest. Fresh snow drifted against the window. How strange for a brother and sister to live in one house their whole lives, even if they had traveled the world in between. She thought of the other photo albums downstairs. It would be fascinating to see photos of those travels, especially if they'd been to countries that she'd visited for work.

She yawned. She'd look at more tomorrow. Right now, she needed sleep. It had been a very long, strange day.

Hannah shut the albums and turned off the light, wondering where the vagrant was sleeping tonight. He'd completely terrified her, but for his sake she hoped it was somewhere warm.

• • •

One minute Hannah was lulling herself to sleep with her plans for tomorrow, the next she was examining the stained glass window again.

Yet now the peacock wasn't a peacock. It was a tall bird, brown and plain, with flat feathers. Its legs were twitching as if they were trapped, and the stain was there again on its belly, wriggling, but not moving away.

Then Hannah's face was being pushed towards the glass and she couldn't stop it. To her horror she realized the stain was, in fact, a mass of maggots, dripping onto the windowsill. Her face touched it, and it was warm and sticky, and she was screaming, knowing the glass was going to break.

Hannah sat up in bed, clutching her stomach.

A wave of nausea hit her.

Throwing back the duvet, she ran to the ice-cold bathroom, knelt on the cold tiles, and vomited.

How could this be happening? Every single thing was going wrong.

She retched again, then leaned her head miserably on the toilet bowl. In the freezing cold of the night, she couldn't help wondering if this was someone telling her it was just not meant to be.

• • •

The nausea passed around 2:00 A.M.

Clutching a blanket around her, Hannah struggled downstairs to find water. As she reached the middle step, she stopped.

There was a faint light on in the kitchen. Befuddled by lack of sleep and disoriented by the sickness, she tried to remember if she had left it on.

Suddenly she heard a thump, then a click, from below.

Her stomach jolted.

She touched the wall, then eased herself downstairs quietly, her legs starting to shake, to grab her phone from the hall table, checking that the windows and doors behind her were still shut. Praying, she checked that she had a signal and found Dax's number. Would he come in the middle of the night? He'd be here quicker than the police. She checked the time: 2:04 A.M. She better be sure, before she rang him.

She took a deep breath and boldly turned on the hallway light.

"Yes," she shouted. "I've just rung the police. When will you and Bill get here, Dax? Two minutes? Great, see you then."

She waited, her finger poised on Dax's number, trembling. When there was no further noise, she crept towards the kitchen. At the doorway, she peered in cautiously.

The light came from the scullery. The fridge door was lying open again.

From inside came a very loud thump. Then a click, click, click.

The old-fashioned noisy fridge motor was adjusting itself to the temperature outside the door.

Exhaling with relief, she walked over to shut it. The sight of the last bits of food turned her stomach, and she slammed the door. God, her nerves were frayed.

Knowing she wouldn't sleep again, Hannah drank some water and folded a piece of junk mail, to jam under the fridge door. She'd spent years traveling in politically volatile countries, but two days on her own here had creeped her out more than anywhere she'd ever been.

Needing to hear another voice, she turned on Radio 4, then walked round the house, switching on lights, double-checking windows and doors. If any passing vagrants were still in any doubt as to whether Tornley House was occupied, they bloody wouldn't be now. She glanced at the stained glass window—remembering her nightmare. The thought of the maggots brought a hand to her mouth.

Back in the kitchen, Hannah sat down and checked her schedule.

Day 10: Wednesday, DINING ROOM.

She had to stay strong. Just ten days, and it would be over.

She rubbed her stomach. Had she eaten something bad?

She glanced at the paintbrushes and rollers in the scullery, and back at the clock.

If she couldn't sleep, she might as well do something. She could even claw back a half day for the garden next week.

When she was sure her nausea had settled, she turned on the stove again for heat and went to change into her painting clothes. Then she went to fetch the white paint from the study.

She stopped in the doorway, not believing what she was seeing.

The white paint had tipped over. The lid was off, and there was a thick streak of dried paint on the wooden floor.

"Idiot!" she shouted. How could she have been so stupid?

She'd have to cover it with a rug.

Annoyingly there was also now a thick rubbery layer across the top of the paint in the tin.

Avoiding the temptation to burst into tears, she carried it into the rust-colored dining room that they would use to host Will's clients one day. The color in this room was as dense as the bottle-green in the kitchen. It would need three coats probably. Three coats of lumpy paint.

Hannah began to concentrate so hard on painting, that the sense of being watched crept up on her slowly.

She turned to the window, and saw a figure.

She gasped.

Only then did she realize that it was her reflection.

Maybe it was fatigue, and the sickness, and the disorientation of the hour, but with it came a vision of herself here in the future, alone.

An old woman, looking out the window onto a bleak garden full of weeds. The towering wall beyond only added to the sense of being buried alive.

Hannah shook herself. This was stupid. She was just worn out.

She climbed up and tied some dust sheets to cover the window, then changed the radio to an urban-music-and-chat channel that reminded her of London.

Yet, even with the window covered, she still felt the same strange sensation of being watched. She pushed on, ignoring her nerves and grumbling stomach, trying to keep her morale up.

Somewhere, out there, right now, a child might be waiting for her and Will. A child who needed them as much as they needed him or her.

She had to keep going.

She could do this.

"I'm coming," she whispered to a child who might or might not exist.

She tried to imagine his or her face but it was hidden in the shadows.

14

The next morning, in London, Will stayed in Jamie's bed till he was sure Clare had left for her spinning class.

His sleep had been broken. He'd woken intermittently, feeling dehydrated, but had stayed in bed, not wanting to scare Clare by wandering around in the middle of the night to get water.

Instead, he'd lain awake for an hour at a time. Through the wall he'd heard a creak, and suspected she was awake, too. Her bed, he recalled, was on the other side of the wall.

She was lying, a foot away, through the thin plasterboard.

Now, at eight thirty, once he was certain Clare had gone, he stretched out his back and went for a shower. Hanging on the door was a plastic bag, with a note: "*TV says trains not running again! Help yourself—and feel free to shower / eat / stay tonight, etc! C*." ☺

That was nice of her. The bag contained men's clothes. Dave's, presumably.

The bathroom was small. He pulled back the shower curtain. Two bras hung on a clothes drier in the bath, alongside underwear and T-shirts. He lifted it out, awkwardly. One bra was purple with lace, the other darker with pink ribbon. This was definitely not like Hannah's underwear. In fact, that first Christmas they'd gone out she'd cried with laughter when he'd presented her with lingerie in some misguided attempt to be a "proper" boyfriend for the first time in his life. To tease him, she'd worn the red lacy bra outside her clothes, stuffed with toilet roll, and called him "optimistic."

Will showered, then pulled on the donated underwear and T-shirt. They were big. He remembered Clare's boyfriend now from the Smart Yak Christmas drink. Spiky hair and a pink polo shirt, talking about sailing a boat to France. A florid face, and a rugby player's bulky size. Not the kind of guy he'd imagine an arty girl like Clare choosing.

Will pulled the front door shut behind him and walked to Smart Yak. It was still snowing. Another day's reprieve from Hannah and the house.

He ordered coffee at the café and decided it would be polite to buy Clare a drink back. He picked chamomile tea, hoping it was right.

To his surprise, he found Matt in the reception area of Smart Yak, shaking snow from his coat. "You made it?"

"Yeah, I walked to Victoria, and the Tube was running, so . . ." Matt said, beaming at Will's approval. He saw the second cup. "Is that for me—cheers."

Before Will could stop him taking it, the kitchen door opened and Clare exited, holding a steaming mug. Her cheeks were pink, presumably from her spinning class.

"Hey!" she said to Will. "Did you find everything?"

He saw Matt's face twitch.

"Yeah, cheers for that," he said.

Clare looked at his chest. "And it fits?"

"Uh, yeah . . ."

He pulled the T-shirt out from the stomach, and a handful of excess cotton came with it. Matt's eyes swerved between them.

"Oh, poor Dave." Clare giggled. "His pre–Weight Watchers T-shirt. It was all that comfort eating, from the stress of having to live with me."

Matt took the top off the second cup. His expression turned to confusion when he saw the chamomile tea.

"Ah, no, this one . . ." Will said, swapping it for the coffee.

It was too late. The herbal fragrance filled the corridor.

"They gave me the wrong one. I'll go and change it," Will said.

Clare smiled. "Right. See you later."

He went outside, and poured the hot chamomile tea onto the pavement. A dark patch appeared in the white snow.

Now that the lies had started, he didn't seem to be able to stop.

• • •

Hannah finished painting the dining room at around six o'clock on Wednesday morning.

The nausea had not returned, so she'd managed tea and dry toast, around 5:30 A.M.

It was as she was watching the navy sky brighten into day, waiting for the kettle to boil, that she remembered the donkey. Steeling herself, she walked out into the icy new morning and unlocked the garage.

"Hello, boy." She scratched the donkey's head. "Come on outside before Farmer Nasty catches us."

But the little donkey was wise now. An obstinate glare entered its eyes. When she pulled on the rope, it refused to budge. She cajoled it for a few minutes, gave up, mucked it out, found some grass under the snow to feed it with, went back, cajoled it again and pulled, but the donkey wouldn't move.

"Oh, come on!" Hannah snapped, exhausted. The few wasted minutes had allowed the sky to lighten into gray-violet. On the horizon sat a new shot of washed-out orange. "Quick. Or someone will see us."

By the time she managed to drag the donkey back to its pathetic shelter, the new day was already up, yawning a pale gray. Hannah gave the animal a pat, then scurried away.

There was a movement to her right.

Startled, she ducked behind a bush.

There was someone at the distant edge of the farmer's field.

It looked like a farmworker or maybe the farmer's son, tall and bulky, dressed in a hooded top, carrying a heavy bag on bowed shoulders along the fence. He disappeared behind the barn. Hannah stayed still in the bushes, snowy branches soaking her head, till she was sure no one had spotted her.

Then she crept back to the house, fighting the urge to go and complain once again to the farmer. That woman couldn't get away with this.

Even as Hannah said it to herself, however, she knew that wasn't strictly true.

Thanks to her doing nothing, that's exactly what was happening.

•   •   •

She didn't mean to fall asleep when she returned to Tornley Hall. One minute she was warming up by the little fire she'd made in the hall; the next, she was falling off the sofa with a jerk.

Bang, bang, bang.

Hannah woke shivering. The fire had died.

What time was it?

Bang, bang, bang.

Someone was at the front door.

She sat up. Oh no. Had the farmer or her son seen her with the donkey?

Stumbling up, Hannah went to the hall window.

Dax's red pickup truck was outside.

Relieved, she opened the door.

Dax stood on the doorstep, holding a pane of glass and a plastic bag. "Aye-aye. What you been up to?"

"Nothing." She pushed hair out of her face. "I was sick. I'm fine. Gosh, is that glass for the window? Thanks."

"That's all right." Dax rested the glass against the wall and handed her the plastic bag. "Your fella didn't come back then?"

"Oh. No," she said, opening the bag. Inside was milk and white sugar. She took it out, amused. "He still can't get home. . . . Thanks for this."

Dax marched past her and bent to test the weight of a shelf unit.

"Go on then—kettle on!"

She turned. What was he doing?

Dax lifted the shelves upright, experimentally. Then, with a groan, he lifted them a few inches off the floor.

"Oh, Dax—right. No, you don't have to . . ."

But he was already shuffling one of the shelf units through the study doorway. If Will tried that, he'd put his back out.

"Here?"

"Thanks."

With a grunt, Dax placed the shelf unit against one of the four brown patches.

A welcome space appeared on the hall floor.

"Oh, OK. Thanks," Hannah said.

Dax came back and tested the weight of the next unit.

She yawned, too tired to argue.

Leaving him to it, she put on the kettle and leaned wearily against the worktop, trying to wake up.

She heard Dax grunting, and wondered if this was a neighborly favor or whether he expected payment.

Right now, she didn't care. Her stomach was sore, her shoulders and neck ached, her blister stung, and she couldn't get warm. She didn't want to see another paintbrush or roller as long as she lived, and Will still wasn't back. Talking of which . . .

"Have you heard how long this snow is going on for, Dax?"

"Friday," he called back.

She made the tea and took it through. In the hall she found Dax carrying the third shelf unit into the study, his forearms straining. The improvement in the hall was already dramatic. A large space had appeared between the boxes, finally exposing the black-and-white tiled floor. Perking up, she followed him into the study. Dax dragged the third unit beside the second. Too late she realized he'd scraped the wooden floor.

She decided not to argue. There was a big dried patch of white paint on it anyway now. They'd stick a rug on it for the moment. And without Will here, she needed all the help she could get.

Dax looked as though he had hardly broken a sweat. He raised his eyebrows as he took the tea. "You keeping all them books in there?" He nodded to the sitting room.

"No," she said, sipping her own. The hot, sugary liquid

helped her dry throat. "The Horseborrows' solicitor rang this morning—apparently they accidentally hired a house-clearance firm that doesn't take books. They're going to arrange a specialist bookshop clearance when the snow's gone."

"Worth anything?"

"Some of them look like they might be. But it all goes to the Horseborrows' estate, and they've left the whole thing to some seafaring charity, so . . ." Hannah put down her tea and went to restart the fire in the hall. "Did you know them, Dax?"

"Horseborrows?" He pronounced it "Horse-bras." Everything Dax said sounded sarcastic, as if she was asking him a ridiculous question. "Oh, yeah. Since I were a kid. Kept an eye on the house for 'em, after my dad died. My granddad was the gardener here. Then my dad."

"Oh, really?" Hannah poured some sump oil onto the fire, thoughtfully. No wonder Dax treated Tornley Hall as if it was his house. His family had clearly been custodians of it for decades— the old village tradition of working-class families serving the rich ones. "What were they like?" Hannah asked, lighting a match. The fire exploded in the grate. "The Horseborrows." She caught herself saying "Horse-bras," as Dax had—an old habit from traveling abroad, to make herself understood.

Dax emerged from the study, took another gulp of tea, then lifted the fourth unit and began maneuvering it in. "What you on about now?"

"Well, what kind of personalities did they have?"

From his expression, it was obviously another stupid question. "They were all right. Olive was Olive, Peter was Peter." He grunted as he moved the last unit. She followed him and saw the final patch of brown wallpaper disappear. "So, giving it all to charity, are they?"

Hannah wasn't listening. The study was transformed. White walls, new cream curtains, white shelves waiting for records. On impulse, she searched in a box for the remnant of cherry silk that she'd bought and wrapped the window-seat cushion in it.

She stood back, pleased. The room looked good.

Dax pointed at Will's boxes of records. "Right. These going in now, too?"

"Oh, yeah, but I can do that." Will hated anyone touching his vinyl. He'd even brought it from London in the car, because he didn't trust the moving men.

But Dax was already lifting the first box and carrying it through. He banged it down and Hannah cringed.

"Actually, it's funny," she said, lifting the second one gently, to demonstrate how careful they needed to be. "I actually found some old photos of the house. I haven't had a proper look yet, but you should—there might be photos of your granddad and your dad in there."

Silence fell in the study.

She looked up, to see Dax peering out.

"Where d'you find them?"

"Under the bookshelves."

Dax glanced at the sitting-room door, then at her again. He pointed at her box. "You should keep them boxes to pack books."

"Actually that's a good idea."

"Actually!" Dax snorted, as if he'd never heard such a stupid word.

Hannah flushed, too tired to think of a rejoinder. She was also starting to notice that she really did need a shower. She placed her box carefully next to Dax's. "They're quite fragile, these," she said. Dax walked off to fetch more records, ignoring her. "OK. I'll be back in a sec," she said, giving up. How much harm could he do?

Reluctantly Hannah left the warm hall and ran upstairs with the recently boiled kettle to wash and change into fresh clothes in the bathroom. When she returned, her spirits lifted at the sight of the space in the hall. To her delight, she saw that Dax had also stuck the new pane of glass in the window with putty. At this rate, she might be able to paint and finish the hall to-morrow, if Dax would help her move the furniture into the sitting room.

When she arrived downstairs, however, the study was empty.

There was a creak in the sitting room.

Dax stood, his back to her, flicking through the books.

"Hundreds, in't there?" he said, without turning.

"Yes," she replied uncertainly.

They were going to have to have a chat sometime about the way Dax walked around her and Will's house. Clearly he'd been used to doing it his whole life. But right now, like everything else, it could wait till later.

Till after Barbara.

• • •

Without discussing it, Dax did stay, for another two hours. First he carried the rest of the record boxes into the study—rolling his eyes when Hannah hinted again that the boxes needed to be lifted more carefully—then he helped Hannah shift the furniture into the sitting room. Every half hour he barked orders for more tea. As she still didn't know whether Dax expected pay-ment, or was just being a helpful neighbor, she bit her tongue and brought it. When the hall was finally cleared—the last few

boxes stored in the newly painted dining room—to her surprise Dax took the filler and trowel from Hannah's decorating
box and began to plaster the cracks in the hall ceiling and walls.

"Oh, I wasn't going to . . ." she started.

"I've just seen the bloody mess you've made in there." He
gestured at the dining room.

He had a point. In the morning light it looked as if a child
had painted it last night. She'd have to open the door quickly,
then shut it, when Barbara came. Hannah started to unpack the
records onto the shelves, relieved to find none were broken, as
Dax filled in the cracks.

They worked in silence. It didn't feel uncomfortable. Dax
clearly wasn't interested in small talk, and she was tired.

"So when's your mate, Madonna, coming then?" Dax called
eventually, from up the ladder.

"Sorry?"

"Oh, they're all on about it, over at the Fox. A record producer, your bloke, is he? Gemma's got herself all worked up.
Thinks she's going to be delivering mail to rock stars."

Hannah stopped filing the records. How did everyone know
about Will's job? Had Laurie been gossiping, or Brian?

"Er, no—he doesn't do Madonna. His clients are more likely
to come on the train, actually. Or borrow their mum's car."

She smiled at her own joke, but if Dax thought it was funny,
he didn't respond.

"Where's he going to do it—in the garage?"

"Yeah. He's got to convert it first, though."

"Jonno over in Snadesdon—he's the builder."

"Well, we're a bit of a way off that yet, but . . ."

Hannah started on a box of blues vinyl. She knew Will would
reshelve it later in some anal order, but for now it would do.

Dax gave a heavy sigh. "Right."

The ladder creaked.

"Couple of hours." He appeared in the doorway, and handed her sandpaper. "Then give it a bit of that."

"Thanks."

"And make sure you do it." He opened the front door. "You can keep that sugar."

"Oh. That's very kind of you," Hannah said, biting back a laugh.

She surveyed Dax's work in the hall. Delicate white spider-webs of filler crisscrossed the walls and ceiling. If she and Will had done it, it would have taken all night. The task ahead suddenly felt less daunting than it had in the depths of last night.

"Honestly, Dax, this is brilliant," she said. "Thanks."

"Honestly," Dax repeated, with another snort.

She watched him, disconcerted. He reminded her of men she'd known as a child down at the docks with Dad. Straightforward, direct. Living in a city, she realized, had filled her own sentences with clarifying clauses. "I mean, honestly, actually, I have to say," and so on, as she tried—along with everyone else—to squeeze past other people in a crowded city, apologizing, checking she'd been understood, wanting things done, not wanting to give offense by accident.

Out here, language was clear-cut, practical, and used to get things done.

"So. Tomorrow," Dax said, walking out.

Tomorrow? Why tomorrow? She was too exhausted to ask.

"Oh, OK. Great. Thanks." She waved him off and shut the door. Two hours ago the hall had been a mess. Now, miraculously, it was clear and the walls were prepared for painting, and the tiles ready to be cleaned.

Filled with renewed energy, Hannah decided to go and hang curtains in the guest room while the filler was drying.

.   .   .

She was up the ladder at the window when she heard the donkey. Someone had untied it, and it was ambling miserably through the snow, halfway between Tornley Hall and the farm.

She dropped the curtains. The poor little thing looked hungry. This was her fault. If she'd rung the RSPCA, it would be somewhere warm now, being properly looked after.

Frustrated, Hannah fetched her phone and switched it to video mode. At least she could keep gathering evidence. But when she tried to film it, snow drifted onto the windowpane, obscuring her view. Checking that no one on the farm was around, she lifted the catch and banged the rotten old frame open, showering new paint flakes into the garden below. Leaning out, Hannah refocused the phone. She filmed the field, to show the donkey walking in the snow, then zoomed in on its wet blanket and its shoddy shelter.

Suddenly, a figure walked into the background of the shot.

Shocked, Hannah dived down and waited a second, before peering back over the windowsill.

The person was still there—a large, bulky figure walking fast along the far end of the field. Hannah lifted her camera carefully and zoomed in. It was Farmer Nasty, wearing that same cap and waistcoat, despite the snow. Ahead of her Hannah now saw the figure in the hooded jacket from this morning, just behind the hedge. Her son, or perhaps a farmworker?

To her shock, Farmer Nasty picked up speed and began to run at the other person, her hands flying in the air. Her head was bobbing, as if she was shouting. Hannah took her eye from the viewfinder and tried to listen.

Nothing. It was too far away.

She carried on filming. The woman pushed the man hard. He nearly fell over. Her hands flew in the air, gesticulating.

This was bad. Farmer Nasty was clearly abusive, and not just to animals.

Then, without warning, the farmer swung round. Hannah found herself looking right at the woman's face through the viewfinder.

She dived to the floor. Had she seen her?

The guest room window lay wide open. To her annoyance, Hannah realized she had seen this same window from Farmer Nasty's farmyard. That meant the farmer could see it now, lying open in the snow, even if she couldn't see Hannah's face or the phone.

Hannah sat on the floor and ran back the footage. And there it was: the farmer swiveling round to glare at Tornley Hall, her face a featureless blob.

Hannah peered. There was something about her hands. One was clenched like a fist. The other was . . .

Hannah squinted. Was that a middle finger?

15

That Wednesday afternoon, in London, Will and Matt continued working on "Carrie."

Matt miraculously managed to find two session players in West London who could walk though the snow to lay down the strings. They were concentrating on that for so long it took Will a while to realize that his normally cheerful assistant was subdued.

"What's up?" he said around six o'clock, as he waved off the session players.

Matt shook his head. "Nothing." He eased back in his chair, avoiding Will's eye. "So, are you staying at Clare's again tonight then?"

Will paused. "Why?"

"Nothing," Matt said. "Just wondered if you were going to the pub later."

Matt was the most promising assistant Will had had, but right now he was stepping over the line between studio banter with his boss and sticking his nose into Will's personal life.

"Yup, just heading off now," Will said, standing up, despite not having thought about it until a second ago. "Do want to finish the strings and lock up?"

Matt nodded, registering that he was not invited. "Yeah. Yeah, of course," he said uncertainly.

"Good. See you tomorrow."

Will walked out. Shame. But Matt would be dealing with bigger egos than his in the future, and with far more "creative" personal lives. He needed to learn.

He pulled on his jacket, glancing at Clare's studio door. He hadn't even thought about tonight. All he knew was that, right now, he needed some air.

Outside the snow was still falling, and evening was starting to fall. Will saw lights on in the King's Head and felt the old familiar pull of a pint.

He forced himself to walk past, and pulled his jacket collar up against the cold.

Without knowing where he was going, he headed along Grayson Road and turned right, up the hill past the cheap Moroccan restaurant that he and Hannah used to eat at on Fridays.

The snow came thicker and faster.

He kept his head down and plowed on. Without planning to, he turned left and, three minutes later, stopped opposite a terraced Edwardian house.

A SOLD sign stood in the garden, the l and the d obscured by snow.

Through the flurry, Will saw a lamp on inside their old garden flat. Someone had lit the fire. There were new blinds at the windows, and new books on the shelves he'd built.

The snow drifted into his eyes and mouth and pressed his hair onto his face.

His resentment grew. He'd loved living in this flat. They could have made it work here with a child.

Why hadn't he stopped Hannah from making them leave?

The snow swirled and tumbled around him and, before Will knew it, he was caught in a whiteout. For a few seconds he was invisible to the world. And in that secret place, where there was no one to answer to, Will allowed one unspoken, forbidden thought to enter his head.

If Hannah had been able to have children naturally, like Clare, none of this would ever have happened. They'd still be here.

A man appeared at the window of the flat and shut the blind.

Will walked away, wanting to go home and realizing that he didn't know where that was anymore.

16

Back in Suffolk, Hannah sanded and painted the hall until nightfall, then went in search of food, her appetite having finally returned. The fridge shelf was nearly empty.

This was not funny anymore. She needed Will back with food.

She retuned the radio to find a weather report: "Snowfall due to continue till Thursday, possibly Friday."

Dax was right.

Friday? Today was only Wednesday.

She checked the supplies of dried food they'd brought from London: two cans of soup and a packet of oatcakes, spices and herbs, some rice, pasta, chutney, cooking oil, and sweet corn.

Hannah was opening the oatcakes when her mobile rang in the hallway.

The clock said ten thirty. Yes! Only Will would ring this late.

She rushed to pick it up. Maybe he was even on his way home. Outside, the donkey brayed again.

Hannah peered into the dark garden, furious with the farmer. The donkey would have to wait for a few minutes. She answered the call.

"Where the hell are you?" she barked into the phone.

There was a little laugh, then she heard a female voice with a familiar, faint Jamaican accent. "Hannah?"

Hannah's mouth dropped open.

"Barbara!" she said, in a tone so high-pitched it was almost a squeak. "Hi! How are you?"

She heard herself adopt what Will called her "Barbara voice"—the one that made him pull faces like the queen and dance around with flappy hands—whenever she spoke to Barbara on the phone. He was probably right, but she didn't care. With Barbara, Hannah had one goal: to transmit that all was well. "We are calm, unshakable, steady, reliable, collected, patient, and pleasant!" the voice said. "We are ready!"

"Oh, I'm fine. I'm sorry to ring so late, Hannah. I've got to be in court tomorrow, and I wanted to catch you about the visit next week. How's it all going?" Barbara's voice was warm and friendly.

"It's brilliant, thanks!" Hannah tried to think how sharp she'd sounded when she'd answered. "Sorry about that, by the way. I was just waiting for Will to ring."

"Oh, don't worry. Now listen, I won't keep you on, but how's the house?"

"Oh, it's fantastic, thanks. We love it," Hannah said cheerfully. The donkey brayed, and she walked into the kitchen to escape it. "The space is incredible. And we've met a few neighbors—Bill and Dax, and the local farmer—so it's really friendly. And quiet. And Will's cousin Laurie—you know, our family-support person—has been over with the kids, so . . ."

Translation: we have created the perfect family setting.

She checked if there was anything she'd forgotten that might tick a box on the list she imagined Barbara carried around with her.

"Oh . . . so glad. I'm dying to . . . But listen, Hannah. Oh, it's . . . bad line. Do you . . . a landline yet?"

Hannah froze. The signal was going. She rushed around to find a better one.

"Sorry, Barbara. No. The engineer's booked for this week," she lied.

Translation: I'm organized, committed, ready.

Then Hannah bit her lip. No, he wasn't. What if Barbara rang again next week and there was still no landline? What was she getting herself into here?

"Well, listen, don't worry. It was two things . . . wanted . . . a detail on Will's form. Is he there—he's not stuck . . . in the snow . . . he?"

The signal was going again. Panic erupted in Hannah's chest. She hadn't expected to speak to Barbara till next week. Her mind flailed around, trying to form the story Barbara would want to hear, without her having to lie again. If Hannah said Will was stuck in London, what did that say? That Hannah was stranded in Tornley with no food or car? Barbara might question how remote the new house was.

She screwed up her face. "Barbara, actually he's not. I'm sorry. He's, um, popped over to see Laurie, his cousin, and the kids. . . ."

Translation: because he loves kids.

". . . in Thurrup. He won't be back till a bit later. Sorry. Is it important?"

"Oh, that's good he's there. I thought he might be stuck in London in this terrible snow."

A flush started on Hannah's neck.

"No! No, he thought it might be bad . . ."

Translation: Will's such a responsible, caring husband.

". . . so he decided to work from home this week because of the snow. That's the great thing about being self-employed: he can do some stuff from here on the laptop, so no. It's all fine."

There was a pause. "Oh, OK, well, that's great, Hannah. . . . So . . . got Internet? So if I . . . to e-mail you something?"

Hannah grabbed her hair and squeezed it. There'd be no Internet without a landline.

"Um, no. No. He's just working on his laptop. Without the Internet. So, I'm . . ."

Shut up before you say something even more stupid!

"Listen, Hannah, you're breaking . . . bit. Don't worry. I just . . . on . . . form. I'll text him. Could you just . . . Will to text . . ."

"Yes, of course." Hannah squeaked, not trusting herself to say any more. The donkey brayed and she shut the kitchen door.

Barbara cut out, then returned.

". . . other thing, I'll . . . come on Thursday next week now, not Friday. Staff training's . . . moved. . . . OK for you . . . Will? Otherwise we'll have to . . . at another day and . . ."

No!

Hannah leaned her forehead against the lumpy white wall. A whole day gone out of her decorating schedule. One day less to find someone to fix the boiler, too.

"Sure," she forced herself to say. "That'll be fine."

"Great!" Barbara's voice became more distorted. Then, in the middle of it, Hannah heard three words. "Hopefully, might . . . news."

She drew breath. "Sorry, what was that, Barbara?"

There was a crackling, a groan, then silence.

"No!" Hannah shouted.

She rang Barbara straight back and the call went right to voice mail. She tried once more, then stopped. More than two missed messages on Barbara's phone at this time of night might look strange.

Desperate.

Then Hannah went cold—what if Barbara had given up on Hannah's crap phone signal and was, right this minute, ringing Will?

• • •

Will! Urgent—do not answer phone till u speak 2 me!!!

She tapped the message frantically into her phone and searched the house for a signal strong enough to send it.

Hopefully, might . . . news.

What did that mean? Was this it?

And now she'd told Barbara a stupid lie. Why?

The donkey was braying repeatedly outside again, as it had been on Monday night.

"Oh, for God's sake." Hannah grabbed her coat, lowered her head into the snow, and strode towards the field.

Idiot! She'd lied to Barbara for no good reason. If Barbara found out, it could ruin everything.

The donkey was once again standing miserably in its pathetic shelter. Hannah remembered the farmer's aggressive behavior in the field earlier today and checked that no one was around before she led it away.

Quickly she took it back to the garage, realizing she had no carrots.

"Hang on."

She went to the main lawn and reached with her bare hands into the freezing snow, cursing Farmer Nasty, till she found two handfuls of stubby winter grass and ripped it out by the roots. Why was Will not answering his bloody phone? She must have left six messages this week that he hadn't replied to.

As Hannah stood up, a tall shape loomed behind her.

"Oh!" she gasped, spinning around.

It was a tall pillar, around four feet high.

She stood back. What the hell was that?

At first she thought it was a small tree or rogue gatepost covered in snow, yet as she shone the flashlight up and down, she saw that it was smooth. Even odder, at the bottom of the pillar were two mounds.

Hannah stood back. It was so smooth it looked handmade. Could snow fall in this way? She searched the darkness.

Nothing moved.

She shone the flashlight, again right from the bottom to the top.

Then she saw a ridge. A thick line circling the pillar, about six inches from the top. Snow bulged above it. The flat top itself, she now realized, was slightly curved. Lying across it was a black twig. It looked as if it had been carefully placed. Almost like a . . .

Hannah stepped back with the flashlight and surveyed the whole shape. From the round balls at the bottom to the tip of what she now saw might not be a pillar, but a shaft.

"Oh, my God!" She half-laughed, bewildered. "You are not serious?" she shouted towards Farmer Nasty's field.

17

Will! Urgent—do not answer phone till u speak 2 me!!!

Will sat at the top of the snow-covered stairs up to Clare's second-floor flat, reading Hannah's message. A light was on inside the flat.

He hadn't yet decided whether to go inside.

His walk earlier had taken him through the snow blizzard from their old flat back to the King's Head. The pull of a pint had proved too strong. He'd added in a whisky chaser for the cold. There had been no one there this afternoon, so he'd dried off by the fire and read a paper, chatted to the barman for a while, made a phone call to the record company about Jeremiah, eaten, and watched the news on the pub's television. He'd meant to have one pint. Somehow it had crept up to six again. Or seven, maybe. He wasn't sure.

He hadn't even meant to come back to Clare's. He'd just walked back out into the freezing cold and realized that, despite sitting by the fire, his jeans and coat were still slightly damp and he wanted to go somewhere warm. Somewhere comfortable and easy.

And then Hannah's text message had arrived and he'd sat down, not caring that the step was wet.

Urgent.

He didn't want to speak to her. He didn't want to speak to her, because he didn't know what he wanted to say. It looked as if something had happened, though. Something bad.

Drunkenly he fumbled her mobile number.

"What's up?" he said when she answered.

"Oh, thank God. Is that you? Hang on," Hannah replied. The line was bad again. He heard a door open, then a crunching sound. "I'm just walking down to the end of the lane to see if I can get a better signal."

That new hyper tone that he couldn't stand was in her voice again. He had to stop himself ending the call. There were more footsteps.

"Can you hear me better?" she said after a second.

"A bit. What's up?"

She hesitated. "You sound pissed. You're slurring."

"No, I'm not."

"Yes, you are. Has Barbara rung?"

From the balcony, Will watched the distant lights of central London. Days without speaking properly, and the first thing Hannah wanted to talk about was Barbara.

"No," he said wearily.

He heard her breathing deepen as she walked down the lane.

"Well, listen to me—it's important, if she does ring, you've got to lie."

"About what?"

More crunching.

"Can you hear me better now? I'm in the lane heading towards the village—in case I'm never seen again." She laughed, but he didn't want to join in.

"It's OK."

"Right, listen," she continued. "I've cocked up. She just rang, and I said that you were over at Laurie's in Thurrup."

This new lack of integrity in Hannah's words itched at him like a wool sweater on skin. "Why? What was the point in saying that?"

The signal went again. Crackling. Hannah reappeared. "Lost you there—what?"

When had she become so small-minded? He felt a pang of loss for the Hannah who had been so passionate about exposing the truth. Whose world used to be big and bold, and who used to race across it.

"Why did you tell her that, Han?"

"Because I didn't want her to think that you were stuck in London."

"I am stuck in London."

"I know, but I don't want her to think that we've moved somewhere really cut off, and that I couldn't get food or to the hospital if we had an emergency."

He clenched his fist and put it behind his head to stop himself punching the wall. "Han, half the fucking country's cut off. Barbara's probably cut off. You've got to stop this."

"Stop what?"

His words flew. He couldn't stop them. "Trying to make out to her that we're something we're not. She likes us. She approved us. But she's not stupid. Start lying to her, and she's going to think there's something wrong with you."

"Oh, shut up, Will," she retorted. "That's so naive. And annoying. One of the reasons she rang was because you messed up on some bloody form. What does that say about us? 'They're a bit unreliable. Maybe they don't want to do this enough.' And I don't need you to shout at me—I know it was stupid. But I've done it now, so you've got to turn your phone off in case she rings."

What he wanted to do was throw his phone off the fucking balcony. Instead he bit back his anger. "I won't answer it."

"No! You've got to turn it off. If her phone connects with your phone, she might find out that your signal is coming from London."

He laughed in disbelief. "How exactly would she do that?"

"I don't know. People can track phone signals."

"Who can?"

"Just people."

"Maybe if they're in fucking MI6. Han!"

"You don't know," she pleaded. "Please. Just do it. For me."

He held his phone four inches from the wall, imagining smashing it.

"When are you coming back?" she asked after a second. He heard her trying to get a grip, to sound more reasonable, to get what she wanted from him again. "You know there's hardly any food or any heating? And Barbara's coming on Thursday now, so can you tell Laurie? And I'll need help with the decorating. Oh, and she says she might have news."

He leaned against the wall unsteadily. "What news?"

"I don't know. She just said 'news.'"

He sighed. This was going to send Hannah over the edge.

"Well, it's probably nothing."

"*Will!*" The attempt to sound reasonable was short-lived.

"She said 'news.' So please, just do what I'm asking. I need you to get back and help me sort out the boiler and the painting, and to cut the garden and—"

He couldn't deal with this.

A helicopter droned loudly into the sky. Will thought his head would explode. He didn't mean to do it, but he cut across her. "No."

A pause.

"No, what?" she asked. "What are you talking about? I'm doing everything by myself here, and you're swanning round getting pissed, by the sound of it. Which is good, because that always works well for you, doesn't it, Will?"

Sirens appeared on the road below. Will walked to the railing and watched police and ambulances driving slowly along the snowy road, lights flashing. The helicopter followed them.

"I said 'No.'"

"What do you mean, 'No?'"

He tried to think through the fug of alcohol about what he was doing.

"Will? Talk to me! I'm standing in the freezing cold in the middle of nowhere."

He took a deep breath. "I think . . ."

"What?"

Then, finally, he said it. "I'm just wondering if we should be doing this right now."

Silence.

"What?" Hannah asked uncertainly.

Ice dripped from the balcony above onto Will's shoulders. "Whether we should be carrying on with this."

Silence.

He rubbed his face. "Han, I don't know what's going on

with you. The more I think about it, I can't believe you gave up your job like that—Jane can't, either. And the flat. For that dump?"

A catch in her voice. "You bought this house, too, Will. You're not a child. You could have said no."

"No, I couldn't, because you said you needed it. You said it would make things better, but it's not going to, is it? And now I'm starting to wonder if we should even be bringing a kid into this . . ."

Her voice splintered. "Into what?"

He searched for the word. ". . . Uncertainty."

The sirens and helicopter disappeared over to the west.

Will swayed, and pushed his back against the wall.

"Are you there?" he asked.

Nothing.

"Han, come on, what are we doing? You don't even want to have sex anymore; but I bet, if Barbara asked you, you'd say we were. All this lying—and this obsessive fucking decorating to try and create this home that's not ours—it's doing my head in."

More silence.

He knew he was saying things he wouldn't say if he was sober, but fuck it. They had to be said.

"Han . . ."

When her voice returned the anger had gone. "Well, maybe that's the difference between us, Will."

"What?"

"You can have kids, and I can't. You have a choice, and I don't."

His girl, who once took on the world, sounded beaten.

In that moment Will felt his heart break—for all that should have been between them, but had never happened.

"No. That's not what I'm—"

There was a click.

"Han?"

He fumbled to ring her back.

Her phone went to voice mail. It was a general message, but one that he knew was designed for Barbara—and Barbara alone. A bright, cheerful voice communicating that all was well with the world.

"Hi! This is Hannah, please leave me a message and I'll get straight back to you!"

·   ·   ·

Will sat on the staircase on Arndale Road, mobile in hand.

There was a click to his right. Clare's flat door opened.

She was wearing a low-cut long black dress, with a thin green cardigan draped around it, her hair tied up again. He could tell by her face that she'd heard every word. Behind her he saw candles.

"Drink?" she asked.

He stood up unsteadily. "Nah. I'd better go."

Clare shot him one of those sunny smiles. "Come on."

For a second, he nearly walked away. Then he hesitated. He was so pissed, and so cold, and feeling so shit. Will turned and followed Clare into the warm. Inside the sitting room he let her pull his jacket off. She motioned to the sofa, and he sat.

"Sorry. Did you hear all that?"

She touched his arm. "You're soaking. Hang on."

She returned with a towel and rubbed his hair unselfconsciously. He let her. After eight months of Hannah not touching him the way she used to, it felt pathetically good.

A man's sweater, some tracksuit trousers, and another T-shirt appeared.

"Here you go. More from Dave's plus-size period."

He forced a smile. She left him to strip off and dress in the dry clothes, then returned with wine, two glasses, and a little tin.

"Do you mind?"

He shook his head. Quiet music played. She sat beside him on the sofa, poured the wine, and opened the tin. He watched her roll a spliff between long fingernails, her silver rings flashing in the candlelight.

"We're waiting to adopt," he said.

Clare lifted her delicate feet under her and lit the spliff. She gazed at him through the candlelight as she took a long toke.

"Wow. My friend Rachel did that last year. Not easy, huh?"

She held out the spliff.

He regarded it. It had been years. Eight years.

He imagined Hannah's face. Her voice, furiously reminding him about questions on the adoption form about recreational drug use.

He took it and put it to his lips. The smoke burned into his lungs. The forgotten swell inside his chest pushed him like an invisible hand back against the sofa. He exhaled, feeling the blood pumping round his body.

"Have you been waiting long?" Clare asked. She let her hair down again and made herself comfortable.

Will took another toke and felt his head space out a little. He nodded. "Eighteen months."

"Eighteen months? That's insane."

He passed it back. The perfumed smoke hung in the air between them. He averted his eyes from the swell of her cleavage as she leaned forward to take it.

She's taken off her cardigan, his brain told him. *She took it off in the kitchen.*

Clare regarded him gently. "So I gather it's not going that well. . . ."

He let his head fall back. He heard each guitar string perfectly in isolation from the others. The singer's notes as pure as piano keys.

He opened his eyes and felt dizzy. He sat up again and sighed.

"Last summer our social worker put us up for this kid. A little boy. But there was another couple in the running, too, and his social workers chose them and not us." He took the spliff back from her. "Hannah had her heart set on him and it's caused a bit of a . . . situation."

Clare bit her lip softly. "Oh, no. Can they do that?"

He shrugged. "They've got to find the right family for the kid—which is the way it should be—but Han . . . Well, we'd been waiting nearly a year already and so"—he drew in the smoke, then exhaled—"it was hard."

He looked for an ashtray.

"I'll get one," Clare said. When she sat back down she was closer to him. He felt her leg touching his. He was too wasted to move it.

"God, Will, that must have been awful."

The image of Hannah curled on the floor appeared in his head, more vivid than usual.

"Yeah," he said, passing it back to her, "and it was worse because the other couple were on holiday, so we had to wait a month after we saw his photo for everyone to meet each other and make the decision, so . . ."

Clare tapped the ash. "Can I ask you something?"

"Hmm."

"I've always wondered. The first time I saw Jamie I felt this—God!—overwhelming love, straightaway. When you see the photo of a child you might adopt, does it feel the same?"

Will tried to think how to describe it. "It shouldn't, because he's not your kid yet, but you've been waiting a long time, and then you see his face and it's difficult not to, you know . . ." He stopped. His head was buzzing.

"So why do you think they didn't choose you?"

She picked up her wine and passed him the spliff. Her bare arm brushed his. He thought how easy it would be.

"Hannah thought it was our fault."

"Why?"

He blew smoke at the ceiling. "Well, when his social workers came to meet us, Hannah turned up late."

"Oh . . ." Clare tucked a long strand of hair behind her ear. He saw a small emerald earring in the upper part.

"Yeah, she was in the States at a work conference and her plane got delayed because of a storm, so she got home on the Monday instead of the Sunday."

He didn't tell her the worst bit. That Hannah was so jet-lagged she had confused the time. That she had burst into the flat from the airport with a bag of flowers, shouting, "I need vases, Will! Quick, they'll be here in ten minutes," while the child's social workers sat in the kitchen, where they'd been chatting to Will for nearly an hour. Or that, after they'd gone, she'd screamed at him for not putting the toilet drain cleaner away in the bathroom, as if there was already a child in the flat.

"What, and you think that mattered?"

"No. I don't think they cared. I think social workers know you're trying to be perfect, and they know that's not possible. They know you've got lives and jobs. They just want to know you're safe, reliable people who can be trusted with a child. I don't think they care if you have flowers in your house."

"But Hannah does?"

He shrugged. Who knew what Hannah thought anymore?

"Well, she convinced herself it was because the other woman didn't work, and the guy worked from home. And they had a big house with a garden. In Essex."

Clare nodded. "Which is what you've got now? That explains it. I did think you were the last person I could imagine moving out to the sticks."

Will passed the spliff to her, surprised that she'd formed any impression of him at all, before this week. His head felt heavy, as if it were falling off his neck. He tried to keep it upright, like a football on a stick.

"But it's not what you want?"

"I don't know."

His limbs felt leaden, too. The sofa seemed to sink below him. It would be very easy just to sink down and stay on this sofa all night.

"So what about you? How did you feel, when it didn't happen?"

Will scratched his head. Hannah had never asked him that. "I don't know. You imagine it happening and then, when you see their photo and there's a chance, it feels real."

Clare touched his arm. "That must be hard."

He sipped his wine, knowing where this was going and wondering why he was not stopping it.

"Can I ask why you can't have kids?" Clare said.

It wasn't a secret. All their friends and family knew. "Hannah. It was unexplained."

Clare's eyes narrowed through the smoke. "Really? Poor her. I just can't imagine. I always wondered if that was difficult, as a couple, you know—if one of you could, and one of you couldn't—how you make that work?"

He felt a twinge of protectiveness towards the couple he and Hannah had been.

"It's not really like that. It creeps up. You try, and nothing happens. Then you have tests and nothing's wrong, then you start treatment and it doesn't work, but they say there's still a chance. And the next thing it's IVF, and then another IVF, and then another one; and by that time it's been a couple of years and you've spent fifteen grand. So, by the time you realize it's not going to happen, it's a relief. We both liked the idea of giving a home to a kid that needed it, so . . . it wasn't a big deal." He didn't add that not passing on his old man's genes was no loss to anyone.

Clare stroked his arm. "God—sorry. It sounds like you've been through it."

He turned and found her face close to his. There was a ring of green pencil around her silvery eyes. He saw her eyebrows were drawn on with a brown pencil. A flick at the end had gone astray.

He should have stopped it there—gone to the toilet, or leaned forwards to get his drink, but he didn't.

She kept stroking his arm, and he shut his eyes.

He let the music drown everything out.

A heady perfume close to him.

He drifted off, and then Clare's hair brushed his ear, and he drifted off again. Then her hand was in his hair, and her eyes and lips were close to his. When she kissed him, he didn't stop it.

Strangely, her lips didn't feel unfamiliar. They were soft, and tasted like weed and toothpaste, and although his brain was dragging through mud, he knew that she had brushed her teeth while he was putting on the T-shirt, and that this was planned.

Even then, he didn't stop her. Her lips didn't push him away like Hannah's. He kissed her back, because he could, wondering how it could be so easy to do this after eight years with Hannah.

Her breasts pushed into him.

And then . . .

. . . spinning. It came out of nowhere.

Will opened his eyes and blew out his cheeks. "Whoa."

Clare's cheeks were flushed, a metallic glint in her eyes. "What?" There was a new tone in her voice, too. A hint of angst.

"Oh . . ." He sat up and tried to focus. "Sorry. I need to go."

"You don't."

"I do."

The brightness in her smile extinguished.

He stood up and pulled away. Grabbing his wet jacket, he lurched out of the front door.

The ice-cold air hit Will like a shovel in the chest. He found his way to the top of the stairs, stumbled down two flights to the pavement, and threw up in the snow.

18

After her phone call with Will, Hannah marched back up the pitch-black lane towards Tornley Hall, her arms out for balance, trying not to slip on the frozen ice under the snow.

Will's words raged in her head. *I'm just wondering if we should be doing this right now.*

She turned into the driveway, furious.

Uncertainty? After all they had been through together.

"You fucker, Will!" she shouted into the night.

As she approached the house she saw that the garage doors were ajar. Her mouth fell open in astonishment. They had been here. Right under her nose. The donkey was gone. Farmer Nasty had come and taken him.

For some reason that, more than anything, made Hannah cry. Tears spilled down her face. With a yell of frustration, she picked up the spade and ran at the snow penis. She smashed it to pieces, sending shards of ice flying into the darkness.

Furiously wiping away tears, she then ran inside the house and up to the second bedroom and flung open the door.

The unopened box sat in the empty room.

With a strangled sob she opened it and took out the pristine packs of child-safe cupboard locks, doorstops, and electrical covers that she'd bought eight months ago and never used. She chucked them on the floor.

At the bottom, she found a blue denim elephant.

"I saw this in the village fete—I couldn't help it," her mum had said five years ago, when Hannah had stupidly confided that she and Will had started trying for a baby, when they were still full of naive optimism. "Sorry, I know I shouldn't have, but it's so gorgeous. Keep it for later."

It had sat on a shelf in the spare bedroom in their London flat for two years. Then it had gone into a cupboard, and a year later into a box.

She thought of the little boy who had nearly been hers last summer. If she hadn't been so bloody pigheaded and stupid and committed. If she'd just told Jane she wasn't taking that trip to the States, she would have been there that Monday morning to meet his social workers with Will—calm and ready. Not rushing in like a loon, waving flowers, yelling about the time.

The little boy would be here now, and none of this would be happening. This blue denim elephant would be his.

Hannah cried into its head.

19

Next day Will woke with a hangover for the second time that week, on the sofa in the studio. This time, however, his head felt as if it were in a clamp. He groaned as he shifted his back, and tried to remember how he'd ended up here.

Unable to move without a searing pain shooting through his temples, he checked his watch. Nine fifty-five.

What day was it—Thursday?

He tried to sit up and couldn't.

Shit. Matt would be here any minute.

Will ran his hands over his three-day stubble. A taste lingered in his mouth. Of the weed, and the wine, and . . . Clare. He sat up, grimacing as his back pulled.

Fuck.

The memory of kissing her came back. And then of the phone conversation with Hannah on the balcony.

He stretched his arms ahead of him to loosen the muscles, trying to recall what he'd said. He'd been angry with Hannah. Angry-after-six-pints angry. Just like his old man.

He tried to stand up, knowing he'd done something bad. Whatever he'd said, he shouldn't have said it drunk.

A wave of nausea hit him.

He grabbed the bin just as the door opened and Matt walked into the studio.

• • •

Hannah sat, later that same morning, in the kitchen with the duvet wrapped around her. She'd woken on the floor of the second bedroom in the middle of the night, shivering, with the blue denim elephant under her head.

Her breath in the bone-cold kitchen danced with the rising steam from the tea. She held the hot china in her palms till it was almost unbearable. She watched the Victorian wall outside.

The ridge of snow at the top was smaller. The snow was melting. Iced water dripped from the ivy.

Tap-tap-tap.

She regarded the schedule in front of her, took the board scrubber, and wiped it clean.

• • •

After a while she stood up. A green six o'clock shadow glowed through the hastily painted white kitchen walls.

Holding the duvet around her, she set off aimlessly through the downstairs rooms. *You're trying to create this home that's not ours.* She saw the cracks, and holes, and lumps, hidden by paint. Was she?

One thing she did know: Tornley Hall was starting to feel like a tomb.

She had to get out of here. Go for a walk, and think.

• • •

As Hannah pulled on her coat and boots, she saw her phone charging on the hall table. She hadn't even turned it back on last night to check if Will had rung back. She couldn't deal with it right now.

Leaving it on the table, she turned left out of Tornley Hall and went up the lane.

Dark patches of tarmac were already appearing on the road, and a few brown cat's tails and green stalks of sea grass had emerged from the snow-covered marsh. A magpie with brilliant blue feathers flew past.

Hannah searched for a path across the marsh.

Uncertainty.

Will's words came at her like a dog attack.

How did you go through IVF, and all the challenges of the adoption process with someone, and then feel uncertain?

As she approached the bend, a familiar engine roar came from up ahead. Knowing the way Dax drove, she dived into the side, her left boot dipping into a ditch of icy water. His red truck zoomed precariously round the bend and skidded to a halt. The window came down. A radio blared.

"No painting today?" Dax yelled cheerfully, turning the radio down.

Hannah dragged herself out of the ditch, surprised at how grateful she was to see him. How lonely she felt.

"No, I'm going for a walk, down to the sea." She went to say "actually" and stopped.

"Why's that?" Dax asked, apparently flummoxed at this idea.

"Why?" Hannah replied. "I want to go for a walk. Which way is it, Dax? Is there a path?"

Dax's head ducked down. The passenger door flew open, nearly banging her into the ditch again.

She approached, expecting him to produce a map. Instead he swung upright again and took the handbrake off. "Come on then." He motioned her in.

"But I'm—"

"Come on!"

She sighed. What was it with him? She couldn't seem to say no. Dax was clearly wasted out here—he'd do great things somewhere in government.

She climbed into the truck.

"Dax," she said, shutting the door. "Do you ever ask anybody if they actually want to do something, or do you just make them do it?"

"Ha!" Dax roared. "Ha!"

For the first time in a while, Hannah smiled. "OK, but if you could just show me the path, that would be great."

He turned the radio back up and raced off, not waiting for her to buckle up. When it became apparent there was no seat belt, she clung to the door with one hand and to the seat with the other.

His truck reminded her of Dad's van, full of newspapers and rags and tools, but less tidy. There were old tracksuit trousers rolled in a ball in the footwell; a cup with a dirty ring mark in the drink holder; and food wrappers. It smelled of diesel and dogs.

Dax raced along the narrow roads, whacking his gear stick in and out.

Loud pop music played on the radio, the soundtrack to his crazy driving. It made talking impossible, but right now that suited her fine.

Will's words came at her in the cold light of day.

All this lying.

I can't believe you gave up your job like that.

Jane can't, either.

That one had hurt as much as anything; that Jane—who'd given Hannah her first desk job at TSO, then fired up her passion for human rights and sent her abroad at age twenty-four to do things she wouldn't have dreamed she was capable of—was disappointed in her.

Dax braked as they met a car head-on. With no self-consciousness whatsoever, he placed his arm behind Hannah and reversed at speed back into a lay-by. The other car passed. A gruff wave. And on again.

Around the next bend Dax swerved sharp right onto an un-paved road so narrow that Hannah knew she'd never attempt it in a car. She wasn't even sure if it was a road—more like a cycle lane lined by high verges of grass. A small sign in the bushes up ahead said GRAYSEA.

"Oh, no. Dax, listen!" she shouted over the music. "I just wanted to find the path, so I could walk there."

"You want me to show you the way or not?"

"Yeah, but . . ."

She gave up and sat back.

As the truck bumped along, with the marsh on one side, hedges on the other, strangely it reminded her of a TSO trip. Of bombing along in a hired minibus or Land Rover, in blasting heat, in crazy, beeping traffic; kids sitting in the back of trucks, cows on the road, the local driver she'd hired double-overtaking on hills; Hannah reassuring the journalists in the back that it was all fine, when in truth she was wondering if any of them—including her—would ever get home.

She'd never felt so alive.

Will said he was upset that she'd given it up.

She felt a burst of anger towards him. How could he say that, after what had happened last summer? She'd ruined it for both of them, because of her job. Did he have no idea how hard it had been to leave TSO? How hard it had been to give up such a huge part of who she was? Did he not realize what a sacrifice it had been for her?

Dax drove, one hand on the wheel, the other resting on the windowsill. She glanced at him. She couldn't imagine Dax bowing down to anyone. If ever there was someone who knew who he was, and where he came from, she suspected it was Dax.

His head was thrust forward. His eyes darted left and right.

A second later she knew why.

Dax slammed on the brakes and his arm flew across her chest as she jerked forward.

A pheasant scurried across the road.

"Shit!" she said.

"Come on, fella, or we'll have you for dinner," Dax said, removing his arm, and accelerating at speed again. "Hold on!" His arm shot out again.

Hannah grabbed her seat as the truck hit a short upward slope and burst out with a little skip onto an area of high grass.

The grass parted like theater curtains and the sky opened up—and there was the sea.

"Wow," Hannah said as the truck came to a halt.

She'd never seen a beach in the snow. It stretched, a white arc, into the distance, bordered by a gray line of shingle, melted at the water's edge. The sea was flat and salty-gray; dirty packs of ice and flotsam surfed the current.

"I didn't realize it was quite so close," Hannah said.

"What d'you think was here? Ipswich?" Dax snorted.

She smiled, irritated. "Well, no one would know how to get here, if they didn't live locally."

A woman walked in the distance with two kids. Dax turned down the radio and picked up his cigarettes. He offered her one and she declined.

"So how come," he said, lighting it, "how come you ain't got kids, with that big house?" He opened the window and chucked out the match.

Hannah turned, shocked. "Bloody hell, Dax! That's a bit rude."

"Ha! What are you, thirty-summat?" He dragged on his cigarette, a wicked glint in his blue eyes.

She laughed. "God, you say what you mean, don't you?"

He blew out smoke and tapped the ash. "Can't have 'em, I reckon. What is it? Your bloke shooting blanks?"

Hannah snorted indignantly. She opened the window to let out the smoke, not caring if he took offense. "No, he's bloody not, Dax. God, what are you like?"

"Ha-ha!" He guffawed again, showing surprisingly white teeth.

She sat back in the seat, watching the tide retreat, taking more snow with it. Oh, who cared any longer?

"Well, as you've asked so nicely, the reason I've been decorating is because we're waiting to adopt."

"Are ya? What, from China or someplace?"

"No . . ." she said. "From foster care. Here. Or from London anyway."

"Oh, right." He took another puff and blew it out with a whistle. "Someone what someone didn't want?"

She glared. "That makes it sound simple. No. Probably a child who's been removed from their family because the parents are struggling to look after them, or the child's at risk. Sometimes it's a child whose parents have died."

She watched the muddy sea, realizing she was speaking about the adoption as if it were still going ahead. As if Will had not declared his uncertainty to her.

Dax reached into the side pocket and pulled out a hip flask. He took a swig and offered it to her.

She sniffed. Whisky.

"Good for the cold, my old granddad used to say," he said with a grin.

She didn't know why, but she took it. It set her throat on fire, and she coughed and handed it back. Dax shook his head again, as if she was an idiot.

She wondered what she was doing, sitting in an oily van with a man with the manners of a wolf, drinking whisky.

"So that's why I've been decorating," she continued, even though he hadn't asked. "Social services are coming to make sure the house is suitable for a child, and to meet Will's family in Thurrup."

"What, they going give you a test or summat?"

"Yes, that's right—a sit-down exam in how to change nappies."

Dax stopped, mid-puff.

"I'm joking," she said. "No, we're approved to adopt—that doesn't change—they just need to check nothing's altered because we've moved. That's why we're trying to do it so quickly, in case a child comes up soon. We don't want to miss one."

Dax looked cynical. "That bloody house needs pulling apart, not painting."

"I know." She nodded. "I'm starting to realize that. And we will do it. It just needs to look good enough for now, when they come. Have you got kids, Dax?" she asked, to change the subject.

Dax's gaze settled on the woman and children disappearing around the headland. "Do I look bloody stupid?"

She found the door handle. "OK, well, thanks for the lift. And for yesterday."

Dax threw the butt out the window. "You can help me now, if you want."

"Doing what?" She let go.

Dax didn't reply. Instead he turned up the radio, slammed into gear, and accelerated onto the shingle beach.

"Where are we going?" Hannah asked, alarmed. The truck hit the shingle, listing at an angle, spraying snow as it raced along the beach. She grabbed the seat to stop herself falling sideways.

"Are you allowed on here?"

"By who?" Dax swerved around driftwood and rocks.

She was going to mention the council, but suspected he wouldn't care.

The truck sped along, stones skittering out of their way, the engine growling. A few seconds later they skidded around the headland and came to a stop outside a tin-roofed house on the marsh, right by the shore. The yard was full of old cars. An elderly man looked up. He was unusually tall, with long skinny legs and a red face and white hair. He wore a boiler suit like Dax's, a black hat, and gloves. He regarded Hannah with rheumy eyes, with an unnervingly still expression that made her look away.

Dax flung his door open. "Come on then."

She stepped out onto a slushy path.

The elderly man turned away. He pointed to a stack of tires and mumbled something indecipherable to Dax, before walking off on his long, spidery legs.

Dax picked up a tire. "Ten of these."

"Oh, OK," Hannah said, taken aback.

As Dax carried his to the truck and threw it onto the back, she tested the weight of the second one. She decided to roll it to the truck. Dax took it from her and threw it into the back as if it weighed the same as a loaf of bread. Without speaking, they carried on like this: her rolling, him lifting.

It wasn't what she'd expected to do this morning, but it took her mind off Will. It was good to be outside, too. The sea air blew away the effects of a bad night's sleep.

Dax threw the last tire in, then banged the tailgate shut. He climbed into the driver's seat, and she followed. To her surprise, he drove off without saying good-bye to the elderly man. Hannah watched the strange red-faced man in her wing mirror, as they took a different path off the beach, down the side of the shack. Maybe if you saw the same few people every day out here, there was no need for the kisses and bright hellos she was used to in the city, almost as if people were so pleased to find like-minded souls among eight million people that they celebrated every time they saw someone they knew.

"You done that all right," Dax said, sounding surprised.

"Thanks," Hannah said drily, wondering how Dax would cope with driving through a desolate stretch of desert, knowing gun-wielding militia were in the area.

Will's words returned. *I can't believe you gave up your job like that.*

A thought hit her. Her new neighbors in Tornley would never even know that side of her. It was over.

Dax raced up to a gate and stopped. Without being asked, Hannah jumped out and opened it, then shut it as he passed through and waited for her.

They continued on, speeding alongside the marshes, till they braked at a paved road. Hannah had absolutely no idea where they were.

Dax turned down the radio and motioned to the tires. "Got to drop these down to a fella in Snape, then do a pickup at Marshleton."

"I'll come," she said, playing him at his own game.

"Ha! Will you now?"

She nodded, and he accelerated off to the right. A second later he skidded to a stop at a T-junction with a three-pronged signpost. Hannah leaned forward to see if Tornley was on it, but the place names were all unfamiliar.

"I suppose no one ever comes to Tornley, do they?" she said. Dax turned right onto the road, then accelerated. "I mean, it's a dead end, isn't it? You wouldn't even know it was there, unless you knew someone there. Will and I only found it by accident while he was trying to show me the pub where he hung out as a teenager."

Dax turned. The first weak sunshine in days shone through the windshield, lighting the yellow around his irises. For the second time today Hannah thought of a wolf.

"That's how we like it, in't it?" he said. "Get up to what we want to get up to out here!"

Maybe it was the thought of the wolf, or the strange light, but for that second Dax's eyes seemed to devour her. Flushing, Hannah leaned forward to turn the radio back up and watched the fields and farms zoom by.

Will's words from last night repeated in her head, the implications deepening.

She had no idea where Dax was taking her. She just knew that, right now, she wanted to be anywhere but Tornley Hall.

20

In London that morning Will sent Matt out for coffee, food, and painkillers, while he cleaned up the bin, then left his nervous-looking assistant to load up the vocals, drums, bass, strings, and guitar for mixing, as he took a shower to try in vain to clear his head. He didn't care what Matt thought about the sight that had greeted him this morning—he'd seen a lot worse as an assistant. But he did care that Matt spoke to Hannah on the phone occasionally, and Matt was clearly wondering what Will was up to with Clare.

This had to be sorted.

When Will returned from the shower, he saw a light under her door. He thought about knocking, then hesitated. He'd speak to her when there was a better chance he wouldn't throw up.

In the studio Matt pointed to a second coffee he'd made Will.

Will took it, too hungover to thank him. For a while he watched, bleary-eyed, over Matt's shoulder, then lay back down on the sofa. "Wake me when you're ready," he said, shutting his eyes.

Matt shook him an hour later. Will pulled himself over to the Mac and stared at the tracks in front of him, already knowing it was useless. He couldn't mix a fucking cake today.

"Listen, mate, my stomach's not right. I've already done a couple of late nights this week, so let's call it a day. We'll come at it fresh on Monday."

He waited for his eager assistant to argue, to offer to stay on and make himself useful. But Matt's usual enthusiasm had vanished.

"Sure?" Matt said, avoiding Will's eye.

"Yup, sure." This was irritating. Matt needed to pull himself together. This was work.

• • •

Half an hour later, when Matt had left, Will checked his phone. Still no reply from Hannah.

He thought back over last night, shaking his head as more snatches of memory returned. He drank another coffee to steel himself, then knocked on Clare's door.

No answer.

His stomach rumbled. It was midday. He needed food. He threw on his jacket over the baggy clothes Clare had lent him, then walked to the King's Head and ordered food.

"And what can I get you to drink?" the barman asked.

The beer pumps were lined up in front of him. Despite the nausea of two hours ago, Will realized he wanted a beer. He pointed.

"Pint of that, mate."

As the barman poured, a movement caught Will's eye in the mirror.

His fingers were tapping on the bar. He realized he was still singing "Carrie" in his head.

Then, just like that, he remembered.

.   .   .

He'd been standing here when he met Hannah.

Exactly at this spot. Eight years ago. Tapping his fingers.

The pub had been packed. The lads had been here, a couple of them fresh off the train from Salford that Friday afternoon. He'd been waiting to order a round, pleased to have real money in his pocket for a change, after a week assisting a producer at SmartYak, and psyched that the guy had offered him another week's work.

In this mirror Will had seen the reflection of a woman, watching his hand, whispering to someone hidden by the throng. He'd turned.

"Oh! Sorry!" The woman laughed. She had short gray hair, and warm eyes with a black granite core, and small, tough lips, painted red.

"That's all right." He smiled.

She pointed at his fingers tapping on the bar.

"We were trying to guess. What is it? The song?" she asked flirtatiously.

He liked her cheek. "What do you think it is?"

"Right . . ." she said, screwing up her eyes. "Er . . . 'Wonderwall'?"

He shook his head. "Manchester accent, eh, and everyone thinks Oasis."

She laughed wickedly and leaned forward to grab a wine list, revealing the woman behind her. "Your turn, Hannah!"

This woman was younger, around his own age. She had the weirdest hair color he'd ever seen. Neither red nor blond, but a very pale golden-pink, pulled back into a scruffy ponytail. Her skin was almost translucent, too, apart from three sore-looking strips of sunburn across her forehead, nose, and chin, and oddly dark freckles that looked as if they'd been stamped on her nose. She had wide, flat cheekbones, small, slanting blue eyes, and a blunt upper lip that had a sexy quality about it that didn't fit in with the rest of her. He dropped his eyes casually. She was skinny like a boy, wearing scruffy jeans, a white T-shirt, and a blue scarf chucked around her neck, as if she couldn't be bothered. Her face broke into an easy smile that pulled the upper lip firmly out of its pout, as if she and it were constantly at odds.

"New Order. 'Blue Monday.'"

Will stopped tapping. "Fuckin' hell!"

The girl laughed, bunching the freckles.

"Oh, please, he's just saying that cos he fancies you," said the gray-haired woman, handing the girl a wine menu and giving Will a good-humored wink.

The girl looked startled. She mouthed "Sorry" at Will, then dropped her eyes to the menu. Behind it, he saw that the rest of her skin had flushed the same tone as her sunburn. He found himself wanting to tell her it was OK.

"You . . . you have a very interesting hair color. Where are you from?" he shouted over the music.

She looked up. "Nigeria."

He hesitated. Was she winding him up?

"You're from Nigeria?"

She reached up to hear him repeat it. "No!" she said, pointing to her suitcase. "Sorry, I thought you said where've I come from. No. I've just got back. From Nigeria." She turned to point out a bottle to her friend. The side angle hardened her soft cheekbones unexpectedly.

"Really?" Will said, trying and failing to think of a more intelligent reply.

He couldn't stop looking at her. Everything about her was unexpected. Nothing fitted together in a way that made sense.

She was small—maybe five foot two—but had a physical confidence about her, as if she could handle herself. And maybe it was his imagination, but she smelled a little of wee and day-old deodorant, and her hair looked greasy.

A word on her bag caught his eye: TEACHERSSPEAKOUT.

Her friend left the bar with glasses and a bottle, with a cheerful good-bye. The girl waved, with an embarrassed smile, and followed the woman to a high table with stools near the bar. He watched in the mirror. As her friend poured the wine, the girl's face turned more serious. She took a sheaf of pages and some photographs out of her bag. He saw the words ABUJA and CONFERENCE on the front. She and her friend knocked glasses, then bowed their heads over the material.

"Mate?" the barman said. "Do you want a drink or not?"

"Yeah. Sorry," Will said.

TeachersSpeakOUT. Where had he seen that name before? Outside an office somewhere—up by the Tube?

As the barman poured his round, Will checked on the lads in the mirror. It had been a while since they'd all spent a weekend together getting wasted. He realized he was the only one still doing music. The rest had long ago drifted into IT, and a college course, teaching, and a building site. Two were back home in Salford, one with a kid. If he wasn't careful, he knew he'd be next.

Will carried his tray from the bar. He saw that the three girls he and the lads had been chatting to earlier in the evening had moved their drinks over to their table. The one he'd thought was quite pretty glanced at him through thick eyelashes, hopeful. Unlike the freckled girl at the bar, this girl's skin was flaw-less, as if it had been airbrushed a deep tan. He suspected the effect had taken hours to achieve.

As he pushed through the throng, Will felt a shift inside him that was so powerful he couldn't identify it.

Maybe it was knowing that he'd blown it too many times, and that this chance to assist a producer he respected might be his last, or maybe it was because he'd just turned twenty-seven.

But suddenly, Will knew that it was time to stop fucking around.

The girl with the painted-on tan smiled at him with bleached teeth, and shifted to make room on the bench.

Stop fucking around, in more ways than one.

As he dodged the crowds, balancing his tray, he passed the girl with the sunburned face. She was scratching her head, looking as if she needed a wash. He wanted her to see him, so that he could speak to her again, or even offer to buy her and her friend a drink, but her gaze was fixed intently on her docu-ments. She was locked in a conversation that appeared to matter to her, like his week at Smart Yak had mattered to him.

Maybe it was the four pints and two shots he'd had since six o'clock, but right then Will had a crazy thought. He didn't want to buy the girl with the greasy hair a drink.

He wanted her to be his girlfriend.

•   •   •

"Here you go, pal."

Will paid for his pint.

In the mirror this lunchtime he saw a different man from the one he'd gone on to become with Hannah.

He saw his old man. Unshaven and hungover, in dirty clothes.

Drinking in the daytime, and messing around with other women. A knob who walked out on his wife when she got clinical depression, and left his kid to do his job for him.

Will looked at the beer. What the fuck was he doing?

He banged the glass down and walked out.

. . .

At Paddington Station every part of the forecourt was crowded with people like him, desperate to get home. He squatted against a wall, waiting for an announcement. When the trains to Suffolk finally started, half of London seemed to be trying to get there, and the service was painfully slow. There were no seats, so he leaned against the luggage rack for three and a half hours, budging aside every time someone went into the toilet.

Back at Woodbridge station the snow was melting. His car growled as he woke it from four days' hibernation. At the supermarket he stocked up, then headed off on the A12. It was only then that he saw the real effect of the weather out here. Abandoned cars littered the side of the road.

Hannah had been out here without food or transport. She'd tried to ring him.

He hadn't replied.

Will turned off the A12, speeding up. The B-roads were even worse. The snow was compacted, pushed to the sides like dirty ocean surf. It was 5:45 P.M. and the sun was starting to set. Will forced himself to concentrate on the new route he'd learned, to Snadesdon via Thurrup, then on past the village green. For the first time he didn't get lost. Three turns and he was back at the crooked iron gate with the red rope.

As he accelerated towards Tornley, he knew why he recognized that gate now.

They'd come here a few times, he and Laurie and a convoy of her young-farmer gang, after a night in the Fox's pub garden. He remembered now. There was a meadow hidden up the track beyond the gate, in a hollow of trees. They'd parked their old pickups and Minis in a circle, turned up the music loud, drunk cider, put on their hazard lights, and danced in the middle. One night, he recalled, he'd lain on the damp earth among the trees with a giggling posh girl called Phoebe, who lived in a vicarage and had smooth thighs. When she went home, he'd ended up in the back of a pickup with Laurie's best friend, Bex, a tough farm girl, all peroxide hair and chewing-gum kisses.

Oh, yeah, he'd thought he was the man that night.

Will banged the gear stick up into fourth as he hit the final straight. Last Saturday he'd hated being back on these roads. Maybe he just hated the dick he'd been then.

He drove through Tornley and around the bend, speeding up, needing to see Hannah.

When he turned up into the driveway, however, Tornley Hall lay in darkness.

He parked and opened the front door.

It was bloody freezing here. Hannah's words about the broken boiler came back to him. This was bad.

"Han?"

No answer.

The hall smelled of paint and wood smoke, and when he turned on the light he was amazed to see the hall not just clear, but the cracks filled and painted, too. In the fireplace there was evidence of a fire. How had she done all this?

"Han?" He tried the study and the sitting-room doors. Still locked.

Flicking on the lights, Will checked the kitchen.

"Han?"

A blast of cold air hit him. The big window above the sink in the scullery was wide open. He shut it, and went upstairs.

"Han?"

Each bedroom lay in darkness.

Where was she? She didn't have a car.

A new thought sent panic through him. Had she left him?

He went to check her clothes in the wardrobe, knowing it was his own bloody fault if she had.

Just as he opened the door there was the sound of a car outside. Will ran downstairs and out of the front door.

A red pickup with full-beam headlights skidded to a halt in the driveway, one foot from his car, scattering gravel everywhere, a radio blaring.

The passenger door opened and Hannah jumped out, looking at Will's car.

Their eyes met.

"Oh shit! Will."

In the truck headlights her cheeks were pink. Her eyes were that soft navy blue they used to be, before they hardened last summer.

"Where've you been?" he asked.

The driver's door opened and a cocky-looking geezer climbed out, a cigarette in his hand.

Instantly Will knew his type. He'd met enough of them, fronting bands.

Hannah stood in front of the man. Her voice sounded flat.

"Will. This is Dax. Our neighbor."

The tosser nodded. "Saw you in the Fox the other night."

Will avoided Hannah's quizzical look.

"Dax's been helping me with the house," she said.

I bet he has, Will thought. He regarded the guy.

"Right. You'll have to tell us how much we owe you."

The tosser waved and got back in the truck. "We'll sort it out." He shouted to Hannah, "Tell Jim: Dax says to get his arse down here tomorrow and sort that boiler out."

"I will, thanks."

The guy slammed the door and drove off.

Hannah glared at Will and put her hands on her hips. "That was necessary, was it? To speak to him like that?"

"Who the fuck is he?"

"Oh!" she growled. "Don't you dare!" She marched past him. "I don't know what the hell you think you're doing here anyway, after last night."

"Han." He put out his hand. She swerved, but he grabbed her coat and grappled her backwards.

"Get off me!" she shouted, pushing him away. This time, though, he didn't let go. He pulled her close as she struggled. He could feel that she'd lost weight around her waist and shoulders, even in a few days. Her hair smelled of paint and the sea.

He buried his nose in it.

"I was wasted," he said. "Sorry."

"Really?" she snapped. "I'd never have guessed."

She wriggled again, but he kept holding her tight, like he should have done a week ago, when he saw the fear on her face at the state of the house.

"After what we've been through," she said, "it's unbelievable. If that's what you want, Will—if you want to have your own kids—then fuck off! Go, now. I don't want you here."

He kept her tight in his arms. "I don't. I want a kid with you."

He felt the fight go out of her and realized in that moment

how much he'd scared her. He kissed her head. "I was being a dick. Sorry."

She shook her head. "You can't do that, Will."

"I know." He kissed the side of her face and held her for a moment. "Han?"

"Hmm?"

"You need a bath."

She shivered and to his happiness, he felt her arms creep around his back. "I'm so cold. The heating's not working."

They stood there, swaying, for a moment.

He kissed her strange-colored hair. "Han, it's not easy for me, either. The waiting."

She nodded. "I know." She pushed back from him, and he let her go this time. "Barbara says she has news. Can we go for it? Please." She pointed at the house. "I know it's a dump, but we're here now. Can we just do what it takes to make it work?"

He nodded, and put his arm around her shoulders.

They walked into the house, and he knew then that he couldn't tell her about Clare. Not now. Not till after Barbara's visit.

21

That evening was the first time Tornley Hall began to feel like home to Hannah.

She and Will made dinner together from the shopping he had brought, and she ate ravenously. He put on music and she lit candles.

Later she showed him the work she'd done in each room, and he made a good effort to look impressed. In the sitting room he glared at the Horseborrows' books, as she had done.

"Don't ask," she said. "It's getting sorted."

"OK." He threw a blanket on top of her head, which made her smile, then helped her pull the sofa to the fire, as she wrapped it around her shoulders.

"Do you want a coffee?"

"Please."

Hannah stretched out in front of the fire. With Will out of the room, she allowed herself to think about her strange afternoon with Dax.

This morning she'd been terrified that Will had flaked out on her. Now she knew it was going to be OK. He was back.

They'd just had a crisis. It happened.

What mattered was that they were going to move forward again.

Will returned with her coffee.

"Thanks," she said, lying back.

Will disappeared again, and she watched the flames flickering in the grand fireplace.

It was fine. Just a panic. They would carry on now. Put everything bad behind them.

She finished her coffee and watched the fire, thinking. Next thing, Will was back, looking down at her.

"What?" she said.

"Come on."

He led her upstairs.

She saw steam coming out the bathroom door. The kettle was outside.

"What have you done?"

The bath was full. In lieu of a bubble bath he'd used the lemon shower gel to create the illusion of bubbles, and had lit a red Christmas candle that he'd found in a box.

"Oh, God," she groaned. "I don't think I've ever wanted to get in a bath as much as I do now."

Will lifted up her arms and pulled off two sweaters, three layers of T-shirts, and a bra.

"Bloody hell, mate," he said, wrinkling his nose.

"Shut up."

She lifted her feet to help him remove the rest of her clothes, kissing his head as his hair brushed her breasts. Then he held her hand as she climbed in.

The sensation of warm water on her frozen bones was almost unbearable.

She lowered herself, eyes half-closed, and dipped her head under. When she sat back up, Will was putting a towel on the toilet seat.

"Are you coming in?"

"In a minute. I'm just going to turn everything off."

Hannah dipped under again and washed her face in the bath, forgetting about the shower gel.

Blinking as it went in her eyes, she felt for the towel and saw Will's outline in the doorway.

"I can't reach it. Can you pass it?" She held out her hand.

Will didn't speak. She washed her eyes with fresh water from the tap and rubbed them with clean fingers.

"Will? The towel?" Her eyes cleared.

The doorway was empty.

"Will?"

There was a distant clashing of pots, and then footsteps. "Yeah?" his voice came from downstairs.

Hannah sat up. Alarmed, she jumped out the bath, grabbed the towel, then peered down the corridor. Will appeared at the top of the stairs with a glass of wine.

"Why did you get out?"

"Were you just up here?" she asked.

"No."

She checked the hall again.

"What?"

"Nothing. The house has been creeping me out."

"That's not like you."

"Hmm. Well, talking of that, there's something I need to tell you."

"What?"

She reimmersed herself in the bath, trying to think how to say it in a way that wouldn't lead to more stress for either of them. She'd already decided not to tell him about Farmer Nasty, in case Will marched over there and started a neighbor dispute.

"OK, well, don't overreact," she said as Will put her wine by the tap, "but Dax thinks we've had visitors."

"Who?"

"Will, seriously. I don't want you telling anyone. Definitely not Barbara."

"OK."

"Somebody was sleeping here—casual workers. The ones who come for the season. Probably last summer. When I opened the sitting room, I found an old blanket and some food packets. And in the garage."

"Did you call the police?"

"No—Dax said there was no point. Apparently a few of them sleep in the sheds round here to save money, or because they're illegal. They're not criminals. They must have realized the house was empty and broken in."

Will frowned. "Lucky you weren't here."

"Hmm." She took the wine, avoiding his eye. Will pulled off a T-shirt she'd never seen before. "Where did you get that?" The tracksuit trousers were odd, too. They hung off his waist.

"Borrowed it."

"What, off the World's Biggest Man?"

When Will's face emerged from the T-shirt, he wasn't smiling. He was clearly still thinking about the intruder. It had been a while since she'd seen him naked. His shoulders were still naturally muscular, his torso lithe. She knew the effect he had on women. The irony of him being married to a woman who didn't want to have sex was not lost on her.

Will climbed in behind her. She leaned back into his warm, wet stomach, and his arms wrapped round her, resting across her breasts.

"Maybe we should get an alarm," he said, "if you're here on your own. We'll need one for the studio anyway."

"Maybe. Though it's not like they're here to steal stuff. They just need to sleep somewhere."

Will put handfuls of water on her hair and reached for the shampoo. "Where were you today then?" He poured shampoo on her head.

She stiffened as he washed it. "I needed to get out the house. I thought you'd flaked out on me."

He kissed her shoulder. Instinctively she jerked away.

Will sighed. "Han, I'm not doing anything."

She grabbed his hand and held it between hers. "I know. Sorry. I can't help it. I don't know why it's happening. It's just . . . all the treatment, and the social workers, and the waiting. I just feel like this . . ."

She clenched both fists and shook them in the air.

"It doesn't matter."

"No. It *does* matter. I know it does. I just don't know what to tell you. It will be OK. I promise. You're just going to have to be patient. You know, if I'd got pregnant, you'd have had to get used to it for a while."

He rinsed her hair with cupfuls of water. "I said it's fine."

"It doesn't mean I don't want to be here, though," she said, pushing back into him. She pulled his arms tightly around her. "Can you do that?"

"Hmm."

They lay in the hot water. The tap dripped in the sink.

She glanced at the doorway, glad that Will was here.

She wouldn't say it to anyone because it was stupid, but sometimes it almost felt as if Tornley Hall had a ghost.

22

Miraculously the sky was blue the next morning. After four days of heavy snow, spring appeared to be on its way.

"Where are they?" Hannah murmured, rooting around the sitting room.

"What?"

Will was at the window checking the radiator. Jim the plumber had arrived twenty minutes after they'd rung him this morning and had managed to fix the boiler, temporarily at least. Sunshine flooded through the windows. Within twenty-four hours Tornley Hall had transformed from bleak into a place full of warmth and light.

Hannah perused the bookshelves.

"You know those three photo albums I showed you last night in the bedroom?"

"Hmm."

"Have you seen the others? There were four more. I must have put them somewhere."

"No."

"That's annoying."

Hannah checked under the bottom shelf and behind the sofa cushions. Where were they?

She and Will had decided together, over breakfast, to trim down her manic schedule. She'd accepted his suggestion that their bedroom was fine, despite the shabby wallpaper. They'd leave it, and spend the weekend giving the upper and lower halls a quick coat of paint, and would bleach the floor tiles. Next Monday and Tuesday Hannah would pack up the books in the sitting room, while Will was finishing "Carrie" in London, and would make a start on painting it, which they'd finish together in the evenings.

They would also ring Laurie to see if she knew someone they could pay to cut the grass, and then use Wednesday evening to hang some pictures and tidy up. As for the second bedroom, they would be honest with Barbara. They would tell her how difficult it had felt to tempt fate, after last summer. They'd promise that the room would be decorated when they were definitely matched with a child.

Already Hannah felt less overwhelmed.

"Where did you find the key?" Will asked, nodding at the sitting-room door.

"In the scullery."

"Where's the one for the study?"

"It's the same one."

She removed it from the door and gave it to Will, then headed upstairs. The study door clicked open. She was on the top step when there was a commotion.

"What the fuck!"

"What?" she asked, running back down.

Will stood in the study doorway, looking stunned.

All four vinyl shelf units had fallen over and Will's precious vinyl collection had been catapulted around the room, as if there had been an earthquake. A thousand albums lay ten deep, many of the fragile black records ejected from their sleeves by the force of the fall.

"How did that happen?" Hannah groaned.

Will dropped down. The damage was visible, even from here. Dented sleeve covers and scratches on precious black grooves.

She knelt beside him, knowing what this collection meant to him. "How could that happen? How could they fall over like that?"

"Why were the shelves even up?" Will exclaimed. "I thought you'd just carried the shelves and boxes through here and left them for me to sort out."

"No," she said weakly. "Dax put them up. I just was trying to get on."

"Did he secure them to the wall?"

"No, was he supposed to?"

Will threw a broken record down on the ground. "For fuck's sake, Han!"

"I don't understand," she said miserably. "They were standing upright for days. Why would they all just fall over like this? Don't you think that's weird?"

Will didn't even look at her. She stood there, feeling terrible. The four brown patches of wallpaper had reappeared, and for some reason her clever shortcut now made her feel ashamed.

"Sorry," she tried. "But listen, it'll be insured."

Will remained silent.

They both knew it wasn't just about the insurance.

He'd been collecting vinyl since he was thirteen, and she

knew why. When she'd first visited his mother's oppressive, smoke-filled flat in Salford, she'd soon worked out for herself that music had been a teenage Will's only escape.

When he spoke she could hear the distress in his voice. "Why didn't you wait till I was back?"

"I don't know! I didn't even ask Dax, OK? He just did it. I think he was trying to help because you weren't here. I wanted to get on. Sorry."

"But, Jesus, you know that . . ."

A shriek cut across him. "Yoo-hoo!"

There was a rap on the door, then the bell rang.

They looked at each other.

. . .

"Well, for goodness' sake!"

A very short, very round woman stood on the doorstep. She had vivacious eyes and wide cheekbones and was carrying a huge bunch of flowers. Her hair was dyed an expensive raven shade, and was professionally set in a bouffant crown. The woman was flapping a chubby manicured hand in the air.

"For goodness' sake, we go to Spain for a week and get new next-door neighbors! How lovely. Welcome to Tornley!"

She grabbed Hannah and gave her a hearty kiss on the cheek. There was a waft of expensive perfume.

"Now . . . Tiggy!" she said, clutching her chest. "And that's Frank." A mild-looking gray-haired man came up behind her, a hand lifted in greeting. Without warning the woman reached up, took Will's face, and kissed him, too.

"Hello." Hannah laughed nervously, relieved to see Will attempt a smile.

Frank shook hands. "Frank Mortren."

"Hi. I'm Hannah . . ." She pointed. "Will."

"Oh, we know that!" Tiggy giggled. "We grilled your poor estate agent every time we saw him." She grabbed Hannah's hand. "See, Hannah, we had Olive and Peter here for forty years, so when Tornley Hall was up for sale, I'll admit we were in a bit of a tizzy that someone might turn it into a hotel or flats, or something. There was a developer. Very keen for a while. So we were very glad." She stood back to admire them. "A young couple—just like we were, when we came here, forty years ago!" Her eyes grew wider. "And a music studio?" Her expression changed dramatically to "serious," as if she were listening to an opera. "Wonderful. We love music."

Hannah wondered if they would like Will's music.

"So here we are," Tiggy continued. "And here's a little something to say 'Welcome to Tornley.'"

"Oh, that's so kind, thanks," Hannah said, taking the flowers.

"Thanks very much," Will said.

Hannah smiled. Grown-up Will was back. "Would you like to come in?"

She felt Will's hand arrive firmly on her waist.

"No, no," Tiggy said, the smile boomeranging back onto her face. "We won't disturb you. We just wanted to say we're here, and that if you need anything—*anything*," she trilled, as if about to burst into song.

"Well, it's nice to meet you. I'm just sorting out, um . . ." Will started, pointing behind him.

"No, you go!" Tiggy said. "We've caught you in the middle of things."

"OK, well—see you again." Will disappeared back into the study.

"So you've been in Spain?" asked Hannah politely, glaring at Will's back.

"We have, Hannah! We have a flat there. Pop over from Stansted—lucky we missed that snow." She swiped the air. "For goodness' sake, who knew we were coming back to that, eh?"

"And you grow the flowers, is that right? These are beautiful."

"Yes, that's right. Me and Frank, and our Elvie . . . We don't do as much as we used to, mind you. We're taking it easy now, huh, Frank?" She winked comically at her husband, as if they were doing the opposite.

Frank appeared to be pondering something serious, rocking on the doorstep, hands in his pockets. "How are you getting on with this grass?"

"Hmm, that's a sore point," Hannah said, pointing to weeds. "I think the estate agent must have paid someone to cut it whenever we came to see the house."

Tiggy made an embarrassed face. "Frank!"

"Oh, really?"

"Uh-huh. He used to ring, didn't he, Frank? Ask you to get it looking spruce for viewings the next day!"

"Really?"

"That's right—Frank offered, and Brian was delighted to take him up on it."

Frank pursed his lips. "Now, do you have a sit-on mower?"

"No, just a normal one," Hannah replied.

"Well, I tell you what. Let's give this snow another day or two, and I'll come and do it for you."

"Really? That would be amazing," Hannah replied.

"How does Monday suit you?" Frank asked.

Tiggy's mouth dropped open as if she'd just won the lottery. She put her hand onto Frank's chest. "Frank—Elvie."

Frank nodded. "Good idea, love. We'll send Elvie over."

"Now listen, you'll see Elvie around, probably feeding that donkey." Tiggy dropped her voice. "Just to warn you. Very shy."

"Elvie?" Hannah repeated. "That's so weird. I was just reading a list of Victorian girls' names before we came to Suffolk, and I saw 'Elvie.' I'd never heard it before. It's beautiful."

Tiggy glanced at Hannah's stomach briefly.

"What's it short for?" Hannah said, to distract her.

"Oh, Elvie's always been just Elvie!"

"Right," Frank said, clapping his hands together. "Let's leave these good people."

But now that she'd heard the donkey mentioned, Hannah couldn't help herself. "Actually, can I just ask you something, Tiggy, about the donkey? Do you know who owns it—I was a bit worried about it in the snow. . . ."

Tiggy shot Hannah a conspiratorial look, grabbed her arm, and pulled her close.

"Madeleine," she said in a stage whisper, her eye roving dramatically towards the farm. "Husband, Charlie. Shotgun accident. 1998. Took a piece of his head off shooting rabbits—never the same afterwards." She pointed to the side of her head and twirled her finger. "Then he disappears. Never seen again. So it's been a tough time, for our Madeleine. Her boys do their best, but it's not easy. Last year she gets herself talked into taking the donkey off a family from London, like yourselves—"

"Second home, up in Thurrup," interjected Frank.

"That's right, Frank, they had a weekend home in Thurrup, with a donkey in the field for the kids." Tiggy shook her head. "He lost his job. Sold up. Asked Madeleine to take the donkey—

because they couldn't take it to London, could they? Gives her some money for the keep." A look of mock-horror crossed her face, then melted back into a smile. "But Madeleine's not keen. So Elvie helps her out with it. So that's nice that you've been concerned, Hannah. I know Madeleine will appreciate that."

"Oh, I'm not sure she—" Hannah started.

"Now," Tiggy interjected, "you enjoy those flowers. And remember, we're just delighted to have you here. Anything you need, just ask!"

Then, with a flurry of good-byes, she and Frank walked past the sitting room. To Hannah's confusion, they didn't continue down the driveway, but turned right onto the side lawn and vanished. Hannah peeked around the corner a second later, to see Frank and Tiggy disappearing behind a bush into the wall.

There was a gate!

As she returned to the house to tell Will, she spotted the donkey in the far field, grazing on grass.

Oh well. At least now the snow was gone she wouldn't have to worry about it for a little while.

She thought about what Tiggy had said about Madeleine's husband and her struggling to cope. Maybe she needed to find out more about what was going on.

23

That weekend, after four days by herself, Tornley Hall felt like Piccadilly Circus to Hannah. As they cleared up Will's records and started to paint the upstairs hall, people came and went. After Jim the plumber, and Tiggy and Frank, a friendly postwoman called Gemma knocked to introduce herself and bring them their first mail. On Saturday afternoon Bill appeared with his golden retriever to check—in his slightly unnerving, monosyllabic manner—that they'd managed to get hold of Jim. On Sunday morning a dark-haired woman of about forty, whom Hannah suspected was Tiggy's daughter, Elvie, gave her a shy nod from the lane as Hannah fetched something from the car. Then on Sunday afternoon Laurie, Ian, and the kids came over, as planned.

Hannah steeled herself when she saw their blue station wagon pull up outside.

Laurie had been her one reservation about moving to Suffolk. Her manner had aggravated Hannah from the moment they met, but up till now at least that had only been once or twice a year. Her mind flew back to the number of times she'd sat, rubbing a finger along the squares on the plastic tablecloth in Nan Riley's kitchen, sipping her tea, while Laurie took center stage. If Laurie wasn't updating Will in tedious detail about the lives of people he'd once hung around with in Thurrup, she was recounting their wild youth together, with peals of hysterical laughter at Nan's horrified expression, and shorthand references that appeared specifically designed to leave Hannah out of the conversation.

And then there were Laurie's children. They were lovely kids, but there had been too many painful conversations about how much Daniel looked like "Uncle Will." How Sam had Will's musical talent and was already a whiz on the piano. Hannah had caught Nan Riley watching her a couple of times and, with gratitude, saw concern in her eyes. Nan was too sharp an old bird to be convinced by Will's mumbling about Hannah and himself being "too involved in their careers at the moment" to start a family.

The door slammed down below. A child yelled with excitement.

Hannah told herself to pull it together. She and Will were here now, in Suffolk, in Laurie's territory. She was their chosen "family support" for a future adopted child, and would therefore need to meet and impress Barbara next week.

Hannah headed downstairs, reminding herself to be polite.

By the time she made it down there the kids were running across the lawn and Will was at the front door.

"Hello!" Laurie called as she walked in and hugged Will. As usual Hannah waved from a distance, recalling the one time she'd kissed Laurie hello, causing her to jerk back, declaring:

"Oh, God, I never know what to do with you London types. What is it: one cheek or two?"

"The kids all right out there, Hannah?" Laurie asked.

"Course they are," Ian cut in, making a face at Hannah. "Why wouldn't they be?"

"It's Hannah's garden. I'm just asking." Laurie glared at him, her implication painfully clear to Hannah.

Laurie, of course, now knew the truth about Hannah's infertility, and with that had come a new patronizing approach to her cousin's wife.

Do you mind, as a childless woman, if my children play in your garden? Will it be too painful for you to see that?

"They're absolutely fine, it's wonderful to see it being used," Hannah said, overcompensating. "Do they want juice or something?"

"You can just ask them, Hannah," Laurie said. "They'll tell you themselves."

Hannah flushed.

An awkward silence filled in the hall.

"Well, look at this," Ian said, wandering into the decorated study to see Will's reerected—and secured—record shelves, the damaged vinyl now sitting in a woeful pile by the fireplace, ready for the call to the insurance company.

"So, did you find that toilet then?" Laurie asked Will. She shot him one of her meaningful looks.

Of course—the meaningful looks. Hannah had forgotten about them.

The meaningful looks were always used, along with Laurie's shorthand stories, to show Hannah how close she and Will were. Hannah might be Will's wife now, but she'd never break the special bond that he had with Laurie. Hannah would never understand a relationship built on the teenage escapades of so many wild, hot summers, and the shared genes of two useless dads.

"What toilet?" Hannah asked.

"The old Victorian one with blue flowers. Will? Did you not tell her?"

She could see the likeness between the cousins today. They both had their fathers' deep-brown eyes and dark hair, though Will's was curly, like Laurie's eldest, Daniel.

He glanced at her. "Laurie's convinced we came here when we were kids."

"We did, Will! With Nan, when we were about six or seven! I'm not imagining it," Laurie said, pointing at the peacock window. "I definitely remember that. And you wet yourself in there. . . ." She pointed at the kitchen floor.

"Here she goes. . . ." Will said.

Hannah smiled, pretending to enjoy their sibling-style jousting, when in truth, inside, she felt a stab of pain for six-year-old Will, far from home, wetting his pants, without his mother there to help.

"No, there's no toilet with flowers on—they were both put in recently," Hannah said.

To her irritation Laurie stuck her head in the downstairs cloakroom anyway, then came out, frowning.

"It was definitely this house. Because I remember the yellow wee running over those tiles and—"

"Oh, for fuck's sake," Will muttered.

Hannah forced a laugh.

"Will, you got the latest ZZ Top album?" Ian shouted from the study. Hannah liked Ian. He made her laugh. It was a point of great hilarity within the family that the only time the stocky nature-reserve warden ever went south of Ipswich was to see ZZ Top on a UK tour.

"No, mate."

". . . and the old man and lady who lived here gave you a toffee because you were crying," Laurie continued. "And Nan took you to the toilet."

Hannah grasped Will's hand, partly to show Laurie that she belonged here, too. "Seriously? Will, do you not remember?"

Laurie swung round. "Hmm. Was it not through . . . here?"

Off she strode. Hannah went after her.

Laurie pointed at the scullery. "There. It was in there maybe. The toilet."

"Well, I suppose it might have been. They redid the plumbing ten years ago," Hannah said. "Maybe they took the toilet out to make a laundry room."

Laurie ran a hand over the wall. "God, you've done loads since last week, Hannah. How have you managed it?"

"Oh, you know, painting all night," she half-joked.

She could hear Will discussing ZZ Top patiently with Ian in the study.

To her irritation, Laurie flung open the newly painted gray cupboards, revealing the scruffy insides. "And a guy in the village helped me move stuff around and filled the cracks in the hall," Hannah continued, not knowing what else to say to Laurie. She'd tried a few times to find something they had in common, but, beyond Will, she'd failed. "I have to say, it didn't help Will being stuck in London because of the snow, but now he's back I'm . . ." Hannah mimed cracking a whip. She didn't even know why she did it. It was not normally something she'd say.

A pained expression crossed Laurie's face. "I was going to

ask you about that. Do you think he's managing, Hannah? I mean, to do all this, and the commute. He looks exhausted."

Hannah turned and switched on the kettle, gritting her teeth. In eight years Laurie had never once visited Will in London. She knew nothing about his life there—*their* life there. The only way she seemed able to connect with her cousin was to drag him back into some 1990s time capsule.

"Well, we don't have a choice really," Hannah said, reminding herself that she would be relying on Laurie next week when Barbara came. "If we want things to go ahead quickly with social services, we need to be ready for Thursday. After that, our social worker is tied up for a month, and it delays everything. Talking of which, it might be good to go through what Barbara's going to ask you on Thursday, if that's OK?"

Laurie brought over four mugs from the cupboard. "Oh, don't worry, I won't tell her about Will's wild years." She raised her eyebrows. "I'm not telling anyone about those!"

Hannah ignored her. "No, but obviously—you know—there are things it would be better not to say."

Laurie walked to the fridge. "Like?"

Hannah picked her words carefully. "Well, I suppose what you just said: that Will's really tired from his commute, and we're spending all our time doing up the house. We don't want to give Barbara signals that we haven't got time for a child."

Laurie brought over the milk. "Well, I think that's a bit unrealistic, Hannah. I mean, who does have time for kids? Ian and I both work, but we still manage to juggle three of them. Everyone does."

Hannah put down the kettle, her hackles rising.

"It's different, Laurie."

"How?"

"It just is. You know what happened last summer. It might happen again. There might be other people interested in the next child, too, so we need to make everything appear as perfect as possible. It's not about lying; it's about showing them the best parts of us. That this is a nice, relaxed, safe home, and that we will be committed parents. That we have nice family living up the road." She smiled, trying to keep Laurie onside. "That we don't have other, bigger priorities. The thing is, if you only have one meeting with a child's social worker, you have to make it count."

Laurie poured the milk in, as Hannah found tea bags.

"Hannah, I'm just saying I'm not going to lie."

Hannah gulped. "But we're not asking you to, we're just—"

The men walked in, and she shot Will a panicked look.

"You know, it's weird, this," Ian said, his skin ruddy under his sandy hair from working outside all year. "I've lived round here my whole life and I'd never heard of Tornley. Not till we came to get the keys last week, eh, Lor? I've heard of Graysea, but not this place."

Laurie suddenly banged her hand down. She stood dramatically, clearly waiting for a reaction.

"What's wrong with you?" Ian said. "Got a wedgie?"

Hannah bit back a smile.

"Do you know, I just remembered something. About being here. In this room. There was an argument."

Hannah handed Ian a cup of tea. "I thought you said the old couple were nice to you?"

"No, they were. It was something else. Someone else. I remember Nan rushing us out to the car, and being cross. Do you not remember, Will?" She snapped her fingers.

Will rolled his eyes. "No—I was too traumatized about pissing myself, Lor."

Ian snorted. From outside came the shrieks of children.

Laurie walked to the kitchen window and regarded the high wall. Hannah took her tea over and, to her surprise, saw tears in Laurie's eyes.

"Are you OK?"

Laurie took the tea. "Thanks. Oh, you know. It just takes you by surprise sometimes. You think, 'I'll ask Nan, she'll remember' and then you realize she's not here."

Hannah glanced at Will.

He stared into his tea.

She wanted to hug him. She knew Will couldn't even talk about Nan Riley.

"Game of football?" Ian said, slamming down his cup.

"Yup." Will nodded, and they headed off to find the kids.

24

Laurie and Ian and the kids stayed for a while, playing football with Will on the forecourt in front of the house.

Hannah excused herself to carry on painting the hall up-stairs, watching through the window as Will dribbled the ball between Daniel and Sam, and threw Caitlin high in the air with a squeal when she saved Ian's goal, her blond hair snaking in the sunshine. Laurie knelt at the side, weeding a flower bed, taunting the men, and shouting encouragement to the kids.

If they were going to live here, she needed to find a way to get on with Laurie—but Laurie would have to accept her, too.

For a start, Hannah would have to break it to Laurie that her hints at Will's dark past were wasted on her. Hannah knew all about him—and about Laurie.

Will had told her everything.

He hadn't wanted to at first, but eight years ago, when they first started to bump into each other in the King's Head, she'd made it clear that she was in no rush. That she didn't respect the way Will lived his life, and that she wasn't interested in being another of his many girlfriends.

So they'd become friends first.

She'd seen how much Will drank. So while she continued to throw herself into the challenge of learning how to run complicated press trips and attend conferences abroad, in Jane's place, when she returned home she insisted they meet in a café instead of the pub, and talk, sober.

They had coffee after work, went to a few gigs, and sometimes had dinner at her flat—to which she always invited other people.

And during that time Will started to talk.

He told her about his dad leaving, and his mum's depression and having to look after her when he was so young. About his goal of working in music, but how he kept messing it up. Missing sessions. Sleeping in. Getting wasted. She told him she thought it must be difficult, if other people didn't expect things of you, to know where to set your own expectations.

Then he'd told her more. How his summers with Nan Riley had been the only time he was allowed to act like a child, and how he used to test the old lady to the limit. Nan, on the other hand, had seen both her own sons turn out to be losers, and was determined not to let him and Laurie go the same way. The night she found weed in the back of her old Ford Fiesta she'd threatened to take them to the police.

He told Hannah everything. About dragging a paralytic Laurie out of a party, aged fourteen, on the night her dad didn't turn up for a visit. About escaping to London, and the guilt at leaving his mum to carers back in Salford. The endless one-night stands on the London gig circuit. How he knew he was wasting his life.

In return, Hannah had told Will that she didn't care. She described to him the kind of officially sanctioned cruelty that she dealt with on a daily basis. In comparison, Will's debauched years paled into insignificance and were his own business. He'd hurt no one but himself—and the women who should have seen him coming.

She also made it clear, however, that she wasn't one of them.

Each time she came back from abroad, she saw a difference in him. He sobered up. Managed to hold on to his freelance assistant's job at SmartYak. He left his shared party house in Camden and moved in with another SmartYak assistant in Ealing. He worked long hours. Found his confidence. Discovered he was good at the technical stuff, and that people trusted his ear and his ideas. It was the night he got his first full-time assistant's job with a respected producer, and came round to see her—sober, his eyes alert with the possibilities of a new future—that she started to trust him.

Which was just as well.

Because the minute she'd seen him in the King's Head that first night with Jane, tapping on the bar with his long, tanned arm, eyes shut behind curly hair, mouthing the words to "Blue Monday," she'd known it had to be him.

25

It was difficult to let him go, but after the weekend in Tornley, Will went back to London early on Monday morning.

When she came downstairs, Hannah found a note in the kitchen. A smiley face and kisses.

She walked around with a coffee, her spirits raised. The difference in Tornley Hall was astounding. Even without fresh decoration, the sitting room had a comfortable feel, now that the spring light was bursting through the windows. The house felt solid and comfortable. She looked out through the trees to the houses of Tornley and miles of flat fields beyond.

This was a beautiful place. They could do this.

Just three more days.

A figure suddenly stepped onto the lawn, making Hannah start.

It was the Mortrens' daughter, Elvie, whom she'd seen in the lane. She was carrying what looked like an electric Weedwacker. Loud chatter drifted over, and Tiggy appeared beside her, holding a rake, pointing at the grass. She waved at Hannah.

Close-up, Elvie was much taller than Tiggy. She had Tiggy's dark hair, but her skin was pale and her jawline stronger. She wasn't as round as Tiggy, with long legs and arms and a thick middle, but everything about her appeared sloped. Sloped shoulders, heavy breasts. Even her eyes sloped downwards at the sides.

A motor started. Frank appeared on a large sit-on lawn mower. He gave Hannah a friendly salute.

A sense of well-being filled her. The upper and lower halls were painted, if you didn't look too closely. The grass would be cut today, with the help of their new neighbors. The little donkey was happily grazing in the field, so she could forget about Farmer Nasty for a while, at least.

Will would be back tonight.

Everything was fine.

She really could tell Barbara, with a clear conscience, that all was well.

. . .

A few minutes later Tiggy arrived at the door.

She wore black slacks and a snow-soft white jacket with a pink scarf. She held out an extension plug.

"Morning, Hannah! Have you got a place for this?"

"Hi, Tiggy. Yes," Hannah said, finding a socket for the Weedwacker. "Thanks so much for doing this." Frank waved at her. He was checking the wheels of the lawn mower. Elvie gave Hannah another shy glance. "It's really kind of you."

"Oh, you're welcome—and haven't you got on fantastically!" Tiggy effused, peering into the hall. "Olive and Peter tried, you know, Hannah, but it was getting difficult for them. Frank and I managed to make them get the plumbing sorted out, but after that, I'm afraid . . . Well, it's a big house. There was no family, of course."

The Weedwacker started up with a whine.

Hannah stood back. "Do you want to come in, Tiggy?"

Tiggy swatted the air. Gold bangles jangled. "No, thank you, Hannah. We're just heading off again. Down to Devon to pick up stock, so we'll leave you now with Elvie. And, Hannah, I'm only going to say this once, but you know where the gate is, in the wall? Hmm?"

"Oh, yes, I just saw that."

"Right. Well, in you go. Help yourself. No need to ask."

"Oh. Really?"

"Absolutely. It was one of Olive's favorite things, poor thing. Once a week she came in for her flowers. She'd bring a cake and we'd have a cup of tea and a chat. Once a week for nearly forty years, Hannah. And we miss her dreadfully—seeing her out there, with her basket. Loved her peonies and lupins."

"Ah," Hannah said sympathetically.

"At the end, Frank brought them in for her instead. Set them up in her bedroom by the window, and it would just light up her face. So sad, Hannah."

Hannah pictured Olive in their garden, her plaits on her head.

"Tiggy, I'd love to ask you more about the Horseborrows," she said. "It's been strange moving into their house without meeting them."

"Oh, yes. Anytime! Now, listen"—Tiggy pointed—"Elvie's here with you now. Just leave her to it. She's as happy as Larry on that thing. Just one more thing." She pulled Hannah close. "Now, I was telling you the other day that Elvie's shy—huh?"

Hannah nodded.

"Well, what can I say? It wasn't an easy birth, Hannah. So what we do, at this time of year when we're not as busy, is we find things for Elvie to do. It makes her feel useful. So when she's cut that grass, if there's anything else she can help with, just let her know. She was always over here, helping Olive and Peter in the garden, right from when she was a little girl, so it's just great for her to have this opportunity, OK?"

"OK, thanks," Hannah said uncertainly. Was Tiggy suggesting that Elvie work in the garden for money?

"Good. Right, we'll leave you to it. We'll be back on Friday. Bye!"

Hannah waved as Tiggy and Frank walked off.

She waited for them to say good-bye to Elvie, but their daughter was Weedwacking the weeds and long grass with her back to them, apparently oblivious to their departure.

• • •

That morning Hannah carried the empty vinyl boxes into the sitting room to pack the books. The Weedwacker continued to whine outside.

She packed shelf by shelf, lifting each fragile old volume down, careful not to damage its spine. The wooden shelves underneath were thick with two and a half years' worth of dust. She'd have to clean them thoroughly.

When she reached the fourth shelf, she pulled out a set of six brown leather-bound books from the far end. "Accounts," they said on the front.

"Wow!" Hannah muttered, flicking through. Each page was written by hand.

She realized, in astonishment, that she was looking at Tornley Hall's household accounts reaching back decades. This would

be a gold mine of information about the house. Each book held
ten years' worth of accounts. The writing was done in copperplate, with a page for each month. Household receipts were
stuck in the back. Outgoings were listed separately in various
columns:

April 1947

Suit, P.H.—£4
Groceries—3s 6d
Fishmonger—1s 2d
Beeswax—6d
Shoes, O.H.—22s

She sat down on the sofa. This was fascinating. A suit for
Peter, shoes for Olive? In the incoming column was one large
sum on the first of each month, which appeared to be some
sort of salary or income. She noticed, as she checked the later
decades, that the sum only increased by a tiny amount each
year. By the 1980s it looked quite paltry. That was interesting—
Peter and Olive must have been broke, by the end. There was no
evidence of any other money coming in.

Pleased to have more documents to add to her history of
Tornley House, Hannah stood up to make some tea.

Through the window she caught Elvie's eye and motioned
the offer of a drink, but Elvie shook her head. Her eyes had a
blankness in them. She was a few years older than Hannah, but
her skin was smooth like a child's, as if unmarked by time.

After her tea Hannah started packing again, and forgot about
Elvie as she became immersed in her own plans.

Only three more days now.

A frisson of excitement ran through her and she allowed

herself to enjoy the thought of what might come after Barbara's visit.

. . .

By midday Hannah had cleared out the right-hand bookshelf. It was as she was shutting the last box of books that she heard the noise outside change to a heavy growl.

Through the window she saw neat piles of cut long grass and raked leaves at the edge of the lawn. Elvie was now criss-crossing it on the sit-on mower. Strips of pale-green stubble appeared behind her. If she did have learning difficulties, as Tiggy had suggested, had she always lived here, with her parents?

At twelve o'clock Hannah took Elvie a cup of tea and a cheese sandwich.

"Thank you," Elvie said in a deep voice, her eyes on the ground. Both words were said in a monotone.

Half the lawn was now cut and tidied.

"Wow, you've done an amazing job—thanks, Elvie."

Elvie examined her sandwich with great interest.

"Is cheese OK? I'll see if Will bought any cookies later on."

At the word "cookie" Elvie glanced at Hannah, then quickly away.

It was only a second of eye contact, but it was enough.

"OK, see you later!" she said, walking off, wondering what had just happened.

Was she mistaken, or had Elvie's eyes been filled with absolute fury?

. . .

Before starting on the left-hand bookshelf, Hannah carried some of the packed boxes upstairs to the attic to store them till the bookshop clearance. It was hard work, so she had a rest on the landing. The lawn mower stopped outside. She watched Elvie shaking grass seed onto bare patches in the shorn lawn. Then she picked up a hose and watered it. It wasn't the right time to mow a lawn, with the snow just gone, but it was better than leaving it. The grass was green and muddy, but the shape was, at least, neat and defined. Elvie had done a great job.

After her breather, Hannah carried on up to the loft with one of the boxes.

There was a sound as she entered. Out of the skylight, she saw Frank and Tiggy driving away from their bungalow in a blue van that said MORTRENS' FLOWERS on the side, a trailer on the back. The metal gates scraped behind them. Hannah opened the window properly to see the homestead, now that the snow had gone. There was some machinery outside now, and some tools; and she could see the washed-out colors of flowers growing inside the polytunnels. She considered Tiggy's offer. She couldn't imagine walking in the gate and just taking flowers, as Olive had done. Olive had brought a cake each time. Maybe she should do the same. It would take some time to understand this countryside exchange of help and produce. But it was a kind offer. She must remember to mention it to Barbara.

Dust tickled her nose. She took her hand away from the open skylight to scratch it.

With a creak, the skylight fell shut heavily.

Hannah jerked back to avoid it trapping her hand, and tipped awkwardly against the wall. There was a sharp scratch on her back.

"Ow!" She touched it under her T-shirt and found blood on her finger. What was that?

A screw was sticking out of the wall. Below it was an empty screw hole, and on the floor beneath a plastic handle and an identical screw. Hannah now saw a rectangular line running around the wall panel. The handle must have been here at some point. Tentatively she pulled at the remaining screw.

The panel opened silently. It was a door.

A smell of damp and cold rushed out. Hannah peered in. Ahead of her were the sloped eaves. Through them she could see the lines of roof tiles. Light shone through the few loose ones that their surveyor had reported. Hannah stuck a hand into the loft space and fumbled for a switch.

A dim light came on.

She stuck her head in.

It was a cupboard, a big one. The space was very narrow—it was only three feet or so tall before it hit the sloped roof—but it appeared to run the whole length of the house. Each end vanished into darkness as the low-wattage light ran out.

This was useful. It would give them plenty of storage space, if they ever converted the loft into a room.

Hannah was about to turn out the light when she saw a large gray shape at the far end.

What was that?

Testing the joists first, she crawled carefully into the cupboard, spitting out the dust she disturbed from the eaves.

It was a mound covered by a gray blanket.

She touched the edge. Stiff.

Hannah gripped it with a thumb and forefinger and pulled a corner.

The face of a young boy appeared.

"Ooh," she said, trying to sit upright. It was a painting. Gently she lifted the blanket, blinking away more dust.

The portrait was the first of many unframed canvases. There were lots of them, all piled together.

Hannah took the painting of the boy and crawled out in reverse, to view it in daylight.

Although it was dirty, she could see that it had been painted in the vibrant colors of the Pre-Raphaelites. The boy was about eight years old with sad, soft eyes and dark hair. He looked Arabic. He wore a deep-ruby velvet hat with tassels, a billowing gold shirt, and bright-purple velvet pantaloons. In the background were pyramids and palm trees.

Who had painted these? Hannah returned to retrieve a few more.

They were all warped to some extent, presumably with age and damp, and had the same naive style. Some were portraits, others landscapes, but all were set in exotic locations: the Acropolis against a hill, with a sunset of deep scarlet and orange; a Turkish dancer throwing a turquoise veil in the air.

They weren't badly painted, but the leaden nature of the limbs suggested an amateur hand. In the corner of one Hannah found black squiggles, and held it to the light.

"Ol . . . ive . . . Horse . . . borrow," she mouthed. More faded squiggles on the back looked like dates—1945 in this case.

Olive! Hannah sat back. Had she done these on her travels? This was fascinating. She'd have to invite Tiggy for tea next week, to find out more.

The last painting in her retrieved pile was another portrait, this time of a woman's upper body. She had Mediterranean coloring, wore a Spanish headdress, and carried a fan.

Her red lace dress revealed a voluptuous cleavage. "Goodness me, Olive!" Hannah said quietly.

Like the other paintings, the image was sentimental, yet the woman's face was not idealized. Her brown eyes stood out, but not for their beauty; there was a wistfulness in them.

Hannah sat back. Olive looked cheerful and fun-loving in her photographs. Yet there was a sadness in the expressions on the faces of all these paintings. Nobody smiled.

Maybe a life of friends and family and travel had not been enough. Olive had been unmarried. In those days there would have been no other way to have a child. Maybe a life without children had been a sadness to her, as it had been to Hannah. She felt a connection with her predecessor across the decades.

She headed downstairs with a few paintings, making Olive a silent promise: one day Tornley Hall would hear a child's voice again.

• • •

Hannah propped up three of the paintings on the mantelpiece in her bedroom. There was something quite kitschy and cool about them. Perhaps when the studio was built, and the dining room was ready for Will's musician clients, they could have the best six cleaned, framed, and hung in there. They were part of the history of Tornley Hall, after all.

Hannah checked the clock. Half past one. It was time to box up the rest of the books.

Outside, she saw the lawn was finished. Thank God. It was done. Elvie had clearly been too shy to say good-bye.

A wisp of gray flew past the window.

Hannah watched it. Before she registered what it was, an acrid smell drifted into her nostrils.

Smoke.

"Oh, my God!"

She ran downstairs. A quick search revealed that the fire, at least, was not in the house.

Outside, the smoke was thicker. It billowed from the side of the house. She raced to the side lawn.

A bonfire was raging near the wall. Elvie stood next to it with a spade.

Beside it was a wheelbarrow of branches and rotten leaves. Hannah scanned the garden. Some of the bushes had been cut back.

"Elvie!" she called. "This is amazing, thank you."

Her neighbor regarded her briefly, expressionless over a mountain slope of shoulder. That look in her eye again. Her stillness was unnerving.

Elvie threw on more leaves and Hannah backed away, not wanting another awkward conversation.

She looked round the garden. It was completely transformed. Barbara was going to see an amazing space for a child on Thursday, not a forest of weeds.

Should she tell Elvie to stop?

Hannah turned. Bugger it. There were only three days left. Elvie seemed to be enjoying the work, anyway.

Hannah left her and went to pack more boxes of books.

26

In the end Elvie stayed till five thirty, and left just as it was getting dark. Without a word to Hannah, she vanished through the wall. Hannah's guilt had kicked in late afternoon when she'd caught Elvie pruning hedges at the far end of the lawn and realized that she had been working for eight hours straight.

She had brought more tea and sandwiches, but left them on the step, rather than walking over to Elvie.

Each time, they'd disappeared a minute later. She suspected she could leave twenty coffees and sandwiches, and they, too, would disappear.

What her neighbor had done was impressive. Clearly Frank and Tiggy's daughter was skilled in horticulture. She'd even weeded a flower bed near the house, next to the one Laurie had done.

Hannah strolled between the borders, reevaluating the space. This space at the far end of the front lawn would be perfect for a play area. Her parents had already offered to buy a trampoline and climbing frame out of their retirement pot. She'd begged them not to tempt fate, then felt bad as their faces fell, desperate as they were to know how to help their daughter with an experience so far removed from their own, of effortlessly producing Hannah and her two brothers in three successive years.

Deciding to go for a walk and ring Will before it got dark, Hannah took her phone down to the lane.

Dax entered her thoughts. She hadn't seen him since that weird day on the beach, when Will arrived back. Was he staying away on purpose?

Ten minutes later she reached Dax's terraced cottage. There was no sign of life, so she kept going, until the skinny hedgerows gave way to a barbed-wire fence around a field. There was a bray—and there across the field was the little donkey. Hannah checked her bearings. So, this must be Madeleine's farm. If she stood on tiptoe she could see the farmhouse across the field. A high-pitched squeal from the barn was just audible. One gable of Tornley House lay diagonally opposite, in the distance behind a tree.

The donkey certainly looked happier now anyway, its ears pointing forward. She picked some long grass and held it out at the fence.

"Hello," she called. "I'm sorry they took you back. I did try. Were you OK?"

The donkey came over, its head nodding.

She patted its velvety nose, sensing it was pleased to see her. It took the grass and she scratched his ears, then carried on down the lane till she reached the entrance to Madeleine's farm. The long driveway had no sign. It was just a functional, muddy working farm. She imagined Madeleine, who looked in her sixties, trying to run this alone. The screeching of machinery from the barn was much louder here.

Across the fields the sun was dipping into the horizon. Feeling better for the fresh air, and ready to do some painting, Hannah returned past the cottages. Their pink walls had turned a pretty burnished-rose color in the dying light. The door of the cottage next door to Dax's opened. A fit-looking woman in her late thirties walked out. She wore jeans and a white T-shirt, despite the cool evening air. Her peroxide hair was pulled back in a ponytail and she had hard-worn skin with premature lines. She started when she saw Hannah, then nodded hello and turned up the lane towards a car.

Hannah continued home, wondering if she'd ever befriend her new neighbors. Is that what happened in the countryside: you compromised? Made friends with whoever lived near you? It would certainly make friendships simpler here, rather than the endless promise in the city of meeting like-minded people.

It was on her way back in the dusk that Hannah saw a distant figure through the hedge, in a field, carrying a sack.

Despite the failing light she recognized the silhouette against the darkening sky. The long arms and legs, and the sloping middle.

She checked her watch and felt guilty when she saw the time.

Elvie must be helping Madeleine, too. That was a long day for her.

When Hannah arrived home a few minutes later, her step quickened as she saw their old gray station wagon parked by the front door.

"Hello!" she said.

"Hi," came a call from behind her.

Will was on the lawn. He'd found an outside light on the garage and was checking out Elvie's work.

"Bloody hell! Was this the people next door?"

Hannah was so pleased to see him that she ran across the lawn and hugged him.

"It's amazing, isn't it?"

"Are we paying them for it?"

"I don't know. People keep doing stuff for us, and I'm not sure what the deal is. Who cares? We'll find the money. And come and see this amazing stuff I found."

She led Will up to their bedroom and pushed him ahead, to see the paintings.

"Where did you find those?"

"In the attic. Olive did them." Hannah followed behind him.

"Oh, that's weird."

"What?"

"Honestly, don't laugh, but sometimes I think there's a ghost in this house."

On the mantelpiece one of the three paintings was turned towards the wall. "Or maybe I'm so tired I'm going insane."

She turned it round. The little Egyptian boy regarded her with his big brown eyes, full of distrust.

· · ·

That Monday evening, after they ate, Will carried the rest of the book boxes up to the loft. They agreed that he would return to London on Tuesday morning and sleep in the studio to finish "Carrie," then return on Wednesday afternoon to help Hannah finish the preparations for Barbara's visit on Thursday.

"How's the track going?" Hannah asked as they laid dust sheets in the sitting room.

"Yeah. Good."

"Really? Because you seemed weird that night you got back when Dax was here. I thought something had gone wrong."

He turned away. "No."

"What? Something's up, I can tell."

Will sighed. "Han, you just said you didn't want to talk about anything that's not to do with Barbara. Yes? Then let's do that."

"OK," she said uncertainly. "Now you're freaking me out. Tell me it's not about money? Are we going to be OK with the mortgage?"

"Yes," Will said, reaching up with the roller. "Right, come on—I need to be into bed by one, if I'm catching the train."

She waited for him to make eye contact to reassure her, and he didn't. She picked up the tin of duck-egg-blue emulsion for the walls and told herself this was not the time to worry about it.

27

Will left at quarter to seven the next morning, when it was still dark, trying not to wake Hannah.

His guilt gnawed at him as he drove away. Another day without telling her about Clare. The longer he left it, the worse it was going to be. Yet he knew, also, that Hannah would never forgive him for upsetting her when Barbara was coming.

He hit the lane and accelerated, promising himself that this was the last time he did something to fuck up his life. Ahead he saw a big bloke dressed in black carrying a sack on his shoulder, up the lane in the dark. The sack looked heavy.

As he drove past, he wound down the window and realized too late that he was mistaken.

A surly-looking woman stared down at him.

"That looks heavy. Can I give you a lift?"

The woman glared as if she wanted to punch his lights out, and kept on walking.

"So that's a 'No' then," he muttered, putting up the window.

He accelerated past the cottages and farm and drove off out of Tornley, his mind returning to what he'd done in London.

He had another tough conversation to deal with today, too.

. . .

Clare hadn't been at work yesterday. This morning, however, when Will arrived at SmartYak from the train station, he heard a metal grinding noise from her studio. Unusually, Matt was late, so Will took advantage and knocked.

Clare opened the door.

"Hi," she said, not looking surprised. "How are you?"

"Um, well. How are you?"

"OK. Do you want to come in?"

Clare's studio was much smaller than his. She leaned against her desk and motioned to the chair.

"Cheers."

"So . . ." she said, making an awkward face.

"So . . . Clare, I just wanted to apologize. About the other night. I was completely wasted, and it—it shouldn't have happened."

She dipped her head to one side. "That's OK. Are you all right? You look tired."

"Yeah. You know, there's been a lot going on. With everything. Not that that's an excuse . . ."

She held out her hand. Unsure, he took it. She shook it. The light had returned to her smile. "Friends?"

He felt relief. "Thanks. I didn't know if you'd be—"

"Listen, it's fine. And you know where I am, if you want to talk."

She stood up, and he took the cue to do the same.

"OK—well, thanks."

He walked into the corridor to see Matt walking towards them.

•   •   •

He and Matt spent the rest of the day on "Carrie," Will focusing intently on each element of the track, tightening up the flabby hi-hat and compressing the strings.

Matt said little. The atmosphere in the room was tense. This had to be nipped in the bud.

At lunchtime Will swung round. "What's up?"

"Nothing." Matt jerked back to life.

"Matt, mate, you need to focus. What goes on in here is work. It's got nothing to do with what goes on outside. I know you think that—"

Matt leaned forward. His face was white. "Emma's pregnant."

Will stopped. "Who's pregnant?"

"Emma. My girlfriend."

Will racked his brains. Matt had mentioned an Emma, but not in a way he'd thought was serious. Hadn't they met at a gig a few months ago?

"The one who's at uni?"

Matt nodded.

Will stared. Matt was twenty-two, fourteen years younger than Will, and going to be a father—by accident, by the look on his face. You couldn't get much more ironic than that.

"Oh, mate," he said, slapping Matt's back. "So is it congratulations?"

Matt's shoulders slumped. "Not sure about that."

He looked lost, like a teenager himself. Will remembered how he'd been at that age. Trying to be a man and failing, most days.

Will thought for a moment. "Right. Come on," he said, grabbing his coat. "You look like you need a drink."

Great boss he was. This had clearly been going on for days for Matt, and he'd been so caught up in his own mess that he hadn't even seen it.

They left Smart Yak, crossed the busy road, and entered the King's Head. Will ordered a whisky for Matt and an orange juice for himself.

"There you go."

Matt knocked it back in one, clearly in shock.

"So what happened?" Will asked.

"I don't know. Neither of us does."

Will tried not to think about the two years of test tubes and injections and broken eggs, and wanking in a hospital room, and the thousands of pounds he and Hannah had spent on a pregnancy that never happened.

An accident. You had to laugh.

Matt sighed. "Don't get me wrong. I like Emma—really like her—but she's nineteen. And I just got this job with you. And, you know, I live in a shared house with a student, a trainee accountant, and a lap dancer."

Will smiled. "Mate, you'll be fine. At least you are working. When I was your age, I was living in a squat in Camberwell, playing gigs in dodgy pubs for twenty quid a night."

Matt sighed. "Her parents have gone nuts. She was going to New York in the summer, to do a placement with her dad's law firm, and now . . . we've got to decide what to do."

What to do. The implication of the words hung in the air.

He glanced at Will anxiously. "Sorry, that must sound bad, with you waiting to . . ."

Will held up a hand. "Listen—it sounds like you need time

to sort it out. So take a couple of days. I'll finish up. You saved us time sorting those strings, so we're good."

"No!" Matt protested.

"It's not a decision you want to rush, mate."

Matt rubbed his cheeks, putting color back into the pallor. "What would you do?"

"If I was in your situation?"

Will recalled being twenty-two. If he'd known back then it was his only chance to have a biological child, he'd probably have taken it. But then he'd never have met Hannah, or found his career. He'd probably be back home, separated from a girl he didn't love, doing some shit job, hardly seeing the kid anyway.

A sudden sense of peace descended on Will about the way his life had worked out. His childhood had been shit—any way you looked at it. Now he had a chance to make it right for a child going through the same thing. And Hannah, with her good heart, would be able to be everything to that child that his mum hadn't been able to be for him.

For the first time since last summer, Will felt renewed optimism.

He shook his head. "I can't answer that for you, Matt. We've all got to find our own way."

28

Hannah spent all day Tuesday painting the sitting room, counting down the hours till she could throw the bloody roller in the bin.

Determined to pace herself this week, she stopped at four thirty to have a break before she started the evening shift. Upstairs, changing out of her painting clothes, she noticed the three photo albums on the floor, and brought them downstairs while she had a coffee and a sandwich.

The third album was the most interesting, with reference to what Laurie had said about her and Will visiting Tornley Hall as children. She guessed the images were from the 1970s. The photos were in color. Olive and Peter were older now, perhaps in their fifties. Olive's hair was dark gray, and Peter's white. Their clothes had not changed much, as if they'd committed themselves to a particular sartorial style early on and had stuck to it. Olive wore tweed skirts, cardigans, and walking shoes; Peter dark suit-trousers and shirts and a jacket or cardigan. He had put on weight as he aged, and his hair was combed over.

Hannah flicked through the album. Would the photos jog Laurie's memory?

Tornley Hall was definitely less grand in these later photos, as if the money had started running low. The 1920s and '40s photos had featured wisteria draped around the front door and pots of well-tended shrubs. In the '70s the paint was shabby, and a few weeds were discernible under the front window.

Hannah sat back, looking around. Where were the photo albums of the Horseborrows' travels? It would be fascinating to see if they contained images of the exotic locations from Peter and Olive's travel books, and from Olive's paintings.

Hannah pulled on her coat to go for a walk. A crunch of gravel outside took her to the upstairs window. Elvie was walking behind the garage to the farm. She wore a man-size red T-shirt with "Mortrens' Flowers" on the back.

Grateful though she was to Elvie, Hannah knew she must have entered through the wall gate into their garden and passed by their kitchen window. As with Dax, she and Will would have to lay down gentle boundaries, without causing offense.

This was their house now.

Hannah recalled the other keys in the scullery. Maybe one fitted the wall gate. She could start by locking it maybe, to make a polite point.

• • •

For her break, Hannah decided to see if she could find Graysea Bay again by foot.

First she fetched a carrot for the donkey, then she set off, trying to remember the route Dax had taken.

The air was even warmer than yesterday, and more infused with the smells of spring. She saw small buds on the cherry tree by the gate.

It was such a nice day as she walked up the lane past their garden that she allowed herself to imagine being here, teaching a child the names of the wildflowers, as Mum had done with her in Kent. She imagined the child on a bike, with Will and her walking behind.

The thought triggered a memory of that terrible moment three years ago.

.   .   .

The doctor's office. She could still remember the scent of something antiseptic covering the cloying smell of desperation. Sitting there, trying to shut out phrases she couldn't bear to hear: "eggs not fertilizing," "chromosome issues," "less than a five percent chance it will work next time." Stumbling out into the street afterwards.

Then, to her confusion, the horror of seeing Will check his watch.

"What are you doing? Why are you doing that?" she shrieked in a hormone-induced rage.

"I told you. I've got to see a client. At two."

She knew Will was miserable, too, but right then she didn't care.

"Go on then," she said bitterly, even though she knew he had to take the job to pay for the IVF. Will stood there, helpless.

"Han, I'm sorry, but I told you I'd have to go straight after. I'm already late." He tried to touch her, but she jerked back crossly. "How are you going to get home?" he tried. "Are you going to be all right?"

"Yeah, I'm going to be great," she spat. "I mean, I can't have kids, but you know . . ."

He reached out again. "Han, listen, it's not just you—"

She hit his hand away. "Yes, it *is*, Will. It is. It is me. You have no bloody idea." She flung her hand in the air. "Go on. I'll see you later." With that, she marched away, across Euston Road and up to Regent's Park. Then the tears came. Floods of tears. She saw pedestrians glance at her, but she didn't care. This was the worst thing that had ever happened to her in her life. It was over. After all these years of trying, she now knew that that child would never exist. Last week there had still been a chance. Now it had gone forever. *Result: negative.* And a suggestion from the doctor that IVF was very unlikely to ever work for them.

Then she heard a sound behind her. Pounding feet on the pavement. As she entered the rose gardens, she turned. Will grabbed her from behind and put her under his arm, supporting her as she stumbled, sobbing, into the park.

They walked fast, in no particular direction. "I can't believe it," she wailed.

He squeezed her tight. "It's OK."

"No. It's not."

Will guided her to a bench by a rose bush and sat her down. She fell against him, crying, neither of them speaking. They sat there for a while, as the implications started to hit her in waves. Her child would not inherit the strange-colored hair Hannah shared with her own mum, grandmother, and Danish great-grandmother. She would never look at her child's face and see Will's beautiful brown eyes. Everything would be lost—nothing passed on.

Then, from the hill behind a rose bush, there had been a rattle. A skitter of wheels. A girl appeared at great speed on a scooter, racing downhill. She was around nine years old. She wore a black leather jacket, bubblegum-pink leggings, stripy leg warmers, and a bobble hat. She scootered as if she was skiing, with grace and speed and extraordinary balance, bending her hips expertly to the side as she took each bend. As she whizzed towards them at an impossible-looking right angle, they both put out a hand to catch her, startled. She missed them by inches, came upright effortlessly, and chuckled, glancing back with mischievous eyes. She kicked a baseball boot on the ground and shot on by.

A teenage boy followed, a phone to his ear. "Leah!" he yelled at her, then returned to his phone conversation. "Nah, my sister, blood. She's doing my fucking head in!"

Hannah couldn't help it. She smiled through the tears.

Will pointed after the girl. "What a dude. I want one like that."

Hannah's smile slipped and she pulled away from him again, hurt. "Will! Why would you say that, when they've just told us that—"

He cut across her. "We'll adopt."

Hannah stared at him.

Adopt.

She'd never allowed herself even to go there. Not while the IVF treatment was happening.

"Would you even do that?" she asked, wiping away a tear.

"I said I would, right at the start."

She remembered. He had—and she hadn't listened. Hannah took Will's hand and pressed it against her cheek. She sighed a long sigh, and sat back against him.

"You know, it sounds mad, but there's part of me that's relieved," she said.

"About what?"

She pointed in the direction of the clinic. "Well, that all this is finally over. That we don't have to do this anymore. No more clinics and drugs and waiting for test results and spending huge amounts of money we haven't got."

Will punched the air. "Yes! We can eat again."

She smiled. "True."

"And you'll stop yelling at me."

She sniffed. "Sorry."

Will put his arms back around her. "I tell you what, if—no, when—we adopt, we'll come here one day. We'll bring the kid, and their scooter, and we'll sit here and watch them."

Hannah wiped her nose. "That's a nice idea."

Will held out his hand. "Deal?"

She shook it. "Deal."

"Good." He stood up. "Right, Han, I'm sorry but I've got to go."

She nodded. "I know." He leaned down and kissed her, then headed off.

She sat back on the bench, and watched the funny little girl with the scooter weaving through the rose bushes into the distance, realizing that for the first time in years of hoping for something that never happened, she might finally be able to see the future again.

•   •   •

And here they were. Three years later, and nearly there. They just had to hold their nerve for a couple of more days.

She carried on up the lane, imagining taking photographs of her own family, for their own Tornley albums.

Suddenly, to her left, there was a flash of red. On the other side of the hedge. Hannah peered through. It was Elvie again, walking along the field twenty yards ahead of her, carrying a huge sack, her head bent forward. It looked as if it weighed a ton.

Then, from a distance, Hannah saw another figure hurrying towards Elvie, across the field.

Farmer Nasty.

Oh no.

Hannah ducked down. She didn't want any trouble with her, certainly not this week, with Barbara coming.

Almost immediately shouting filled the air. Madeleine's arms flew up, aggressively.

Hannah frowned. Not again.

Madeleine flew up to Elvie, shouting. "What you doing . . . stupid . . . What . . . I tell you? In the barn, not out there . . . Lazy . . . fucking . . ."

Shocked, Hannah turned her phone to video mode. Personal problems or not, Madeleine couldn't behave like this. Apart from anything else, Elvie was clearly vulnerable.

She turned and started filming through the bushes. Someone needed to be a witness to this. What she did with the footage she'd have to decide later on, after Barbara had come.

Then, as Hannah watched in the viewfinder, Elvie dropped the sack.

From the momentum, Hannah knew that she'd tried to put it down, but let it go too fast. It slumped forward and down with a thump, and tipped sideways.

Elvie's eyes stayed on the ground, her shoulders slumped.

To Hannah's horror, Madeleine rushed at Elvie. Yet this time her leg shot out and she kicked her hard. Then, without a pause, her hand flew up and hit Elvie in the face.

Once, twice, three times.

Before Hannah could believe what she was seeing, the farmer grabbed Elvie's hair and pulled her close, talking intently in her ear.

Hannah sat on the verge, her mouth open, not believing what she was filming. This woman was a maniac.

But before Hannah could even think what to do, Elvie bent down to pick up the sack and its contents and walked back the way she had come.

Madeleine spun off in the other direction.

Hannah played back the footage to check she was not dreaming.

• • •

For five more minutes she sat by the side of the road, biting her thumbnail. Madeleine was clearly abusing Elvie when Tiggy and Frank weren't around.

Hannah watched the footage again and again, her stomach churning. Her instinct told her to run after the farmer and tell her that she'd been caught. To ring the police and act as a witness. Instead she stood up and forced herself on towards Graysea.

Barbara would be here in just two days.

She would do something, but not now. She couldn't.

Distracted, Hannah marched on for a mile down to the sea. She found the path Dax had shown her and walked quickly, hardly noticing the scenery. When she reached the shingle beach there was nothing there, apart from a large ship sitting far out on the horizon. She skimmed stones across the flat gray water, working out each permutation of the action that she could take right now.

The image of Elvie's bent head and shoulders returned to

her. The leg shooting out. The hand flying up. The menacing words in Elvie's ear.

An hour later she arrived back at Tornley Hall, just as the light was dying. There was no sign of Elvie's red shirt out in the fields now. Hannah started up the driveway towards home— then knew she couldn't do it. She couldn't ignore this. At the very least she needed to check Elvie was OK.

Turning back, she stood outside the electronic gate next door and pushed the intercom.

No answer.

Hannah took a closer look. At the bottom was a small glass circle.

A camera.

She pressed again and placed her ear at the speaker.

She heard the tiniest hint of a noise. A rustle.

"Elvie?" Hannah said, peering into the camera. "Are you there? Can you hear me? Could you just open the gate, or answer me?"

There was another rustle, then silence.

"Elvie, listen, I just wanted to check you're OK, with Frank and Tiggy being away?"

Nothing.

"OK, well, listen, I'm just next door. If you want a chat, come and find me through the gate in the wall. OK? Come for a cup of tea. And a cookie."

She walked away, working out dates—it was Tuesday; Frank and Tiggy wouldn't be back till Friday.

Three days. What if Madeleine assaulted Elvie again, and worse this time? How long had this been going on for?

Hannah thought for a second. Then it came to her. There was one other option.

As she reached her driveway, she walked past the bottom and continued towards Tornley.

.   .   .

For the second time she heard Dax before she saw him.

He was working on the motorbike again, in the shed behind his cottage, a giant spotlight on in the dark, a dirty rag in his hand.

He squinted to see who was coming.

"Aye-aye. Your husband know you're here?"

She arrived at the door. "Why?"

"Oh—he don't like me." He winked, and to her annoyance she blushed.

"He was just worried about where I was that day."

Dax threw the rag down. "So, what do you want then—not your bloody boiler again? Jim been up?"

"Yes, thanks." Hannah peered into the shed, to ensure it was empty. Lights were on in all the cottages behind them. A television was on in the window of one. To her surprise she saw the tall, red-faced man called Samuel, from the beach tire shed, walking around in the kitchen of the cottage on the left, next door to Dax's. He must live here, too.

"What's up then?"

She rolled her eyes. "Dax. This is awkward. Do you know that farmer?" She pointed towards Madeleine's field.

"Mad?" he said. "What's she been up to—spraying too close to your garden?"

"No." Hannah prayed she could trust him. "No. Actually, I'm not sure how to say this, but I think I've just seen her hit Elvie, the woman who lives next door to us. She has learning difficulties?"

She waited for Dax to make a smart-arse remark, but he didn't.

"What do you mean, hit her?"

Hannah swiped with an open palm. "Three times."

For the first time since she'd met him his face became serious. "That's no good. When's that happened?"

"A couple of hours ago. And she didn't just hit her—she kicked her, too. I mean, hard."

"Right." Dax blew out his cheeks. "Well, Mad's got a temper on her—you don't want to cross her on money—but I've never seen her hit no one. You sure?"

"Yes." Hannah sighed. "I wish I wasn't. The thing is, I just can't get involved, Dax. We've got the social worker I was telling you about coming on Thursday, and I can't get mixed up in neighbor disputes and police reports. She's coming to make sure this is a safe environment for a looked-after child, and if I tell her there's someone violent next door, she might have no choice but to halt everything, just in case. So what I really want to do is have a quiet word with Frank and Tiggy, and let them deal with it, but they're away till Friday. I'm concerned that Madeleine might be doing this regularly and Elvie's not telling them."

"Well, she's an odd one, that's for sure," Dax said.

"Elvie? In what way?"

"Difficult. Got a temper on her, herself."

"Elvie?"

"Oh, yes!" Dax snorted. "When that one goes, she goes. You want to stay out of her way."

"What—like tantrums?"

"Summat like that." Dax turned off the spotlight. "See, if you'd told me you'd seen Elvie kicking off, I'd have believed you. Maybe that's what you saw? Elvie kicking off, and Mad telling her to shut up."

"No, I definitely saw what I saw."

Dax scratched his black curls. "So?"

"So, I'm sorry to put this on you, but I wanted to ask if you knew how to get hold of Frank and Tiggy, and if you'd tell them what was going on. That way I can stay out of it—officially at least. Someone needs to tell them to come home and speak to Elvie."

Dax shut the garage door. He pointed to the other cottage, on the right. "Bill's got Frank's mobile number. We'll call him tomorrow."

"Really?" Hannah said, relieved. "You don't mind?"

He locked the garage door. "No. Now you go home to that husband of yours, before he thinks you and me's up to something. And get that baby of yours sorted out."

She smiled. "Thanks. And I'm sorry to put you in this situation." She walked backwards down the lane. "First new people in the house for a hundred years, and already we're creating trouble, eh?"

"Bloody Londoners!"

Hannah set off down the lane to go back to Tornley Hall, already feeling better.

29

Hannah finished up in the sitting room at midnight that night and went to bed. She lay in bed, going over the disturbing images she'd seen in the field, of Madeleine assaulting Elvie.

Now that the heating had been on, and turned off, the radiators creaked as they cooled.

With Will not here again, every noise made her sit up and check the room again, searching in the shadows.

She dropped off a few times, then woke up. Disoriented, she rolled over to see the clock: 3:11 A.M.

She adjusted her eyes. The room was dark. What had woken her?

In the corner there was a pale strip on the floor. Light was trickling under the bedroom door like rain.

Hannah's heart jolted against her ribs. She had definitely turned off all the lights tonight.

She took her phone from the bedside table and scrabbled for

Dax's number. Could she really call him in the middle of the night? She'd have to be sure something was wrong.

Then she saw that it didn't matter either way. The screen was dead.

"Idiot," she mouthed. The charger was in the hall.

Trying to put her sleep-addled brain into gear, she crept out of bed and tiptoed to the door, double-checking with a quiet turn of the handle that it was locked.

She put her ear to it, listening.

Earlier in the evening, on the phone, Will had told her he was making good progress on "Carrie." Maybe he'd finished and caught the midnight train from Paddington. If he'd rung to tell her, her phone would have been dead.

She shook her head, exhausted. She needed to sleep, and if she was scared like this, she never would. There was no point worrying all night, for no reason.

Hannah pulled on some clothes, then gently unlocked and opened the door, inch by inch to stop it creaking.

When it was half-ajar, she poked her head out.

The light came from downstairs.

The toolbox sat outside one of the guest bedrooms. She crept along to fetch a hammer, then tiptoed to the stairs. A hissing sound was coming from the kitchen. Her heart thumped so loud that she swore she could hear it in the corridor.

The hissing grew louder.

The kettle. *Someone was boiling the kettle.*

Then there was a soft, sucking noise—the fridge opening.

Will!

Hannah exhaled with relief. Burglars didn't make tea and toast. Dropping the hammer, she padded downstairs, ready to bollock him for frightening her. The lamp on the kitchen table was switched on. One of the old photo albums was on the table. There was a scuffle of shoes on tiles. Will was standing in the scullery, head in the fridge.

But something was wrong. Fragments of unexplained images flew at her.

The three photo albums were in her bedroom.

The big scullery window, to the left of Will's head, was wide open.

A jar of liquid with herbs in it sat on the table.

The odd, sloping shape of his shoulders. A flash of red T-shirt as he turned round.

"Oh, my God!"

Elvie stood there, a chicken leg in her hand, looking as stunned as Hannah felt.

"What are you doing?" Hannah gasped.

Elvie stood as still as a mountain. There was a dark bruise on her face. In this confined space she was so enormous that Hannah stepped back.

Elvie's expression changed.

Hannah knew then she had not imagined it the other day. In Elvie's eyes was pure, unbridled fury.

Suddenly, Elvie punched herself in the chest. Her mouth opened.

Out of it came a high-pitched whine, followed by a roar infused with more anger than Hannah had ever heard in her life.

"MYYY! HOOUUSE!"

30

On a hostile-environment training course for TeacherSpeak-OUT years ago, Hannah had been surprised in a corridor by a six-foot-four male training officer screaming in her face.

She had instinctively run, only to find herself trapped in a dead end.

He'd brought her back and taught her what she should have done.

If ever Hannah needed to remember what that officer had told her, it was right now.

She took three deep breaths to calm her racing heart.

Stay calm.

Stay in control.

Assess the situation.

She was alone in a house in the middle of nowhere with an emotionally or mentally disturbed, towering intruder who looked as if she wanted to kill her.

Show respect.

Engage her on a level where you can communicate.

As sweat broke out on her forehead, Hannah kept her arms by her sides to avoid a gesture that could be perceived as threatening.

"Elvie. Tell me how I can help you."

With another growl of anger, Elvie kicked a kitchen chair hard, as if trying to expel it from the house. It hit a cupboard and toppled over. Her body swayed with the aftershock.

Hannah tried not to flinch.

Assess the situation.

Elvie was angry. People stayed angry for a while. You couldn't rationalize with people while the chemicals that were created by anger raced through their bodies. She needed to let Elvie vent.

So Hannah waited, fighting the impulse to run out the front door into the dark and hide.

Elvie let out a frustrated howl, grabbed the photo album and flung it across the kitchen floor. It landed with a crack on the flagstone, the spine splitting into two.

Hannah blinked.

Having a strategy under attack will give you back a sense of control.

More seconds passed.

Then, to her relief, Elvie's shoulders slumped, and Hannah knew it was a sign.

She counted to thirty. The open fridge clicked as the temperature adjusted itself.

Now: engage her.

"Elvie. That's so interesting what you said. Would you tell me about the house?"

Elvie's mouth hung loose. Her eyes went slack.

"I'd like to hear more about it, and maybe help you fix this."

Then the unexpected happened.

A tear appeared in Elvie's eye and rolled down her long jaw.

Bewildered, Hannah slowly pulled out a kitchen chair.

"Elvie, what about a seat?" she said. "Shall we both sit down?"

She saw now that Elvie's trousers were stained and her fingernails filthy.

"I'd like to hear what you have to say. It's very important to me."

To Hannah's surprise, the woman looked utterly lost.

Hannah felt a stab of anger towards Frank and Tiggy. How could they leave her like this? Elvie was clearly vulnerable, unable to wash or feed herself properly.

She pulled out another chair more confidently and pointed towards it.

"Elvie, please sit."

And the young woman did. It was like a mighty tree collapsing. She bowed her head and placed her hands on the table.

Close up, they couldn't look more different from her face. Her hands were hard and calloused, the skin like leather—lined before her time.

Hannah guessed from experience that Elvie's anger was an expression of fear. She wasn't dangerous. She needed help.

"Elvie, it's very late and I am so tired. Are you tired?"

Elvie stared at the table.

"Listen," Hannah continued. "I'm on my own, too, tonight. Would you like to be my guest?"

Elvie didn't react.

Hannah stood up. "OK, I'll be back in a minute."

She walked upstairs, desperately hoping she was right, and ran a bath. As Will had done, she poured in shower gel to form bubbles and lit the Christmas candle, then returned.

Elvie was slumped at the table, the physical power of ten minutes ago extinguished.

Hannah held out a hand. "Do you want to come up, Elvie?" She didn't move.

"Elvie," she tried again, "can you come upstairs, please?"

The chair shot back and Elvie stood up. She thumped up the stairs behind Hannah.

"In here, Elvie," she said cheerfully. "I had a lovely bath this evening, and I thought you might like one before bed?"

Elvie surveyed the bath with utter amazement. She leaped forward and instinctively Hannah shut her eyes, waiting for a blow. There was a rush of air past her.

She opened them.

Elvie had sunk to her knees and was touching the bubbles. She dabbed some on her fingers and licked them.

"Elvie, would you like a cup of tea in your bath? I'm just making one."

When the woman didn't answer, Hannah motioned pulling off her clothes. Elvie stood up like a robot and did what she was asked, as if someone had pushed a button that said "remove clothes."

Hannah turned to give her privacy. There was a loud splash. She lifted Elvie's filthy clothes from the floor.

"Elvie, I'm going to find you something to wear."

She grabbed her phone from the bedroom, plugged it in downstairs, and checked the clock: 3:35 A.M. Jesus. She threw Elvie's clothes in the washing machine, returned upstairs with a cup of tea, and found a T-shirt and some pajama bottoms of Will's.

She knocked on the open door.

"Can I come in?"

No answer.

She entered cautiously. Elvie sat in the bath, holding her toes, her body rigid.

Hannah stared, unable to help herself. It was not just the bruises all over Elvie's arms, neck, and back, but the massive size of her arms. They were thick and well defined, like a rugby player's or a boxer's. Her back and shoulders were the same: heavy with muscle.

Elvie was sitting, mesmerized by the bubbles. She had some on her nose. Hannah lifted the shampoo and held it out. Elvie's gaze moved to the bottle, then up at Hannah. Her eyes looked childlike in the soft light. Hannah decided to tell her what was happening.

"Elvie, I'm going to wash your hair now."

Elvie bent her head down.

Hannah poured the gloopy shampoo onto her greasy hair and rubbed it gently. The hair loosened. Elvie scrutinized her knees.

"Mama," she said in her strange, deep voice as Hannah rinsed it off.

Hannah stopped. "Oh, Elvie, I'm sorry. She'll be back soon. She might even be on her way now."

To her shock, Elvie pulled away, nearly knocking the showerhead into her face. She jumped up, water tumbling off her long, naked limbs, stepped out the bath in one giant gallop and, naked, ran past Hannah.

"What are you . . . ?" she said.

She found Elvie at her bedroom window, pressing her face against it.

Hannah held up a towel, realizing the implication of her words.

"Oh, no, I'm sorry. That was a stupid thing to say. Not to-night, but she might be here tomorrow, OK? Elvie, turn round, please, you're cold."

Elvie did so. She seemed to respond best to direct commands.

"Right. I want you to go back to the bathroom and put on the clean clothes. Then I'm going to put you into this bedroom here," Hannah said, walking off with a giant soaking-wet Elvie behind her. "And tomorrow we'll try to find Frank and Tiggy, OK?"

She showed Elvie into the biggest guest bedroom and pulled back the made-up bed.

Elvie spoke again, in her strange, deep voice. "No flowers," she said.

"Oh. No, not yet, but Tiggy and Frank are bringing some back from Devon, aren't they? Do you like flowers?"

Elvie didn't respond.

"Right, sleep now, and I'll see you in the morning. Now lis-ten, you're safe here, OK? Don't worry."

Elvie pulled on the T-shirt. With no response from her, Han-nah went to let out the bath.

Will was not going to believe this.

When she came out, the guest bedroom door was open again.

Shit! Where was Elvie now?

There was a snore from the end of the corridor.

Hannah entered the smaller guest room. "Elvie?"

The young woman lay on the floor, asleep. Her thumb was in her mouth. In the beam of the hallway, her wet hair looked thick and lustrous, now that it was clean.

Shrugging, Hannah draped a blanket over her and placed a pillow by Elvie's head.

Then she locked her own bedroom door, pushed the door-stop under, just in case, and climbed back under her duvet.

Bloody hell.

How could Tiggy describe Elvie as "shy"? She clearly had learning difficulties and was unable to care for herself. Was Tiggy blind to Elvie's special needs, or just so protective of her that she'd kept her close to home for decades and had lost sight of what Elvie required?

Hannah thought about the high stone wall.

She recalled Tiggy's cheerful, manic banter and wondered if she used it to mask the difficulties of having a child who was so dependent upon her.

Hannah imagined Elvie hiding, scared, inside Tornley Hall when it was empty, to escape Madeleine's abuse, unable to tell her parents what was going on. She had come in the scullery window, and clearly knew how to loosen the catch.

Or, worse, maybe Tiggy and Frank were so grateful to Madeleine for giving Elvie work and keeping her occupied that they chose not to see what was happening.

Hannah wished Will was here, but knew also that if he had found Elvie wandering their house during the night, the police would be here right now.

"It's not our business," he would say. "Why do you think Barbara will care?"

Maybe she wouldn't. But it was a risk Hannah wasn't willing to take.

As she prepared to sleep, a faint beam shone on the tree outside her window, then disappeared. There was a low roar of an engine.

"What now?" she said to herself, getting up and going to the window.

A vehicle with headlights, maybe a small tractor, was driving slowly across the donkey's field. Behind it, two flashlight beams flickered back and forth.

Hannah yawned. Seriously—it was 4:14 A.M. Is that what time people started work on farms?

31

Two weeks had never passed so quickly in her life.

Hannah woke on Wednesday, realizing with a lurch in her stomach that Barbara's visit was nearly here.

One more day.

In just over twenty-four hours their social worker would be standing in this hall, deciding whether or not they could be parents.

She let Elvie sleep on, and texted Dax to find out if he'd heard from Frank and Tiggy.

Hannah had made a decision last night as she fell asleep. Elvie was in a state of emotional turmoil. The best thing was to keep her here, out of Madeleine's bullying path, for a few more hours today. She could easily do that, without having to tell Will or Barbara.

Elvie's snoring reverberated along the upstairs corridor. When Hannah peeked in, the pillow remained untouched, the blanket held tight in her hands.

Hannah sipped her tea, watching.

She didn't even want to think what would happen if Frank and Tiggy didn't return today.

Downstairs, Hannah retrieved Elvie's clothes from the machine and hung them out to dry. There was still so much to do today. She washed and dried the wooden bookshelves in the sitting room, before filling them with her own and Will's books, magazines, DVDs and CDs, souvenirs from her long-distance travels, and photos of them and their families. She spread it out to look homely, then polished the silver fireplace and hearth. The room was coming on. It looked clean and fresh. With the windows and door open, the petrol smell was starting to fade.

At eleven Hannah checked her mobile. Still nothing from Dax. Feeling nervous, she tried the Mortrens' Flowers number on the back of Elvie's T-shirt. An automated reply from Frank asked her to leave a message. She decided not to—not yet at least.

Instead she rang Dax and got his voice mail.

"Hi Dax, it's Hannah—can you ring me?"

• • •

Mid-morning the stairs creaked.

Hannah found Elvie halfway down, bewildered, her skin mottled with sleep, her short hair sticking up at a forty-five-degree angle, as if she'd dried it in front of a jet engine.

"Morning, Elvie," Hannah said brightly, hoping Elvie's mood was not going to deteriorate again. "Are you hungry?"

Elvie grasped the balustrade.

Hannah recalled her tactic from yesterday. "OK. Come on. Into the kitchen, please."

Elvie followed meekly. Hannah laid out tea, cereal, and toast.

"Sit down and eat, please."

Elvie gobbled the food so fast that Hannah put on more toast. She patted Elvie's shoulder and felt the solid muscles tense.

"Elvie, do you have a mobile number for Frank and Tiggy?"

Elvie chewed the toast, shaking her head.

Hannah checked the clock. She was running out of time.

"OK, Elvie, listen. This is what's going to happen. I want you to stay here with me, till Frank and Tiggy get back later. In the meantime you mustn't go outside, do you understand?"

A message beeped and Hannah rushed to her phone—a text from Will.

> Back at 5 x.

Damn. That was earlier than she was expecting.

Elvie was staring at the bread packet in Hannah's hand as if she wanted to eat it, plastic and all. Hannah put some fresh toast on her plate, and put on two more slices. Had Elvie even been able to feed herself this week?

Hannah sipped her tea and picked up the strange glass with herbs on the table. Holding it to the light, she realized that five grapes from the fridge were inside it.

"Elvie, what is that?"

Elvie stopped chewing. "Pea-cockle. Off the marsh."

"Pea-cockle. What it's for?"

Elvie dropped her eyes, guiltily.

Hannah looked back at the glass and suddenly knew. Elvie's words from last night returned to her: "My house!"

"Elvie, does it make people get a sore tummy?"

A defeated expression appeared on Elvie's face, reminiscent of the little donkey's.

Hannah picked her words carefully. "Elvie, have you been

trying to make me and Will go away? Because this is your special place? Your house."

Elvie's head dropped. Her shoulders shrank back, as if she was about to be beaten.

Hannah's mind flew to Will's toppled vinyl shelves.

Could Elvie have done that, when she returned from Spain and found them suddenly in Tornley Hall? Hannah recalled the fury in her eyes the day she'd cut the grass.

She regarded the young woman, astonished.

"Oh, God, Elvie! You are upset, aren't you? Listen, don't worry. I'm not angry. But Will and I are going to be living here now. It doesn't matter, though, because I'm going to help you. You won't need to hide here anymore. And we're going to be friends, so you can come and visit any time you want."

Elvie's eyes flicked up, then back.

"Listen. Tell me what work you do for Madeleine."

Elvie's lips parted uncertainly, revealing uneven teeth coated in wet toast. Four were missing, and the rest were discolored.

"Taters."

"Taters . . . potatoes? What—you plant them? Pick them?"

Elvie shook her head, wet crumbs falling on the table.

"Grow them?"

Elvie leaped up, knocking back the chair. Her big hands started to make circling motions, as if she were searching for a dropped object in a murky river.

"You sort them?"

Elvie's eye had roved to the fruit bowl behind Hannah. Hannah broke off a banana, held it out, and felt it tugged from her hand.

"Is that what you're carrying in those sacks?"

Elvie shrugged.

"OK. Well, Madeleine will have to manage without you today, until I've spoken to Tiggy. Now listen, I've got to clean the house for a visitor. Can you just sit here? Put the radio on if you like or . . ."

Elvie was chewing the banana with an ecstatic look on her face, already eyeing the bowl again. Hannah handed her a second. She turned on the digital radio, showed Elvie how to tune it, then took a bucket of bleach and hot water into the hall and started to mop the floor.

Will would be home in five hours.

She'd try Dax again in one hour.

She prayed that he had called Frank and Tiggy, and that they were nearly here.

· · ·

Hannah was down on her knees, scrubbing the tiles, when she heard the radio come on in the kitchen. Fragments of words and tunes flew around as Elvie flicked through the stations. Then it stopped. A classical aria drifted through.

That was interesting.

Another sound followed. Water pouring, and metal clanking.

Hannah poked her head round the door. Elvie was filling a bucket. She had their vinegar on the draining board, and a newspaper that Will had read on the train. Elvie tipped some vinegar into the bucket and threw sheets of newspaper in after it. She squeezed them, then rubbed the wet vinegary ball on the kitchen window.

"Oh, God, no," Hannah said. "Elvie, sorry, can you . . ."

Elvie hesitated. Hannah saw a streak of clean glass on the grubby window.

"Oh, OK. That's clever."

Elvie waited, hand on glass.

"Well, OK, if you don't mind, Elvie. That's kind, thanks," Hannah said. It would certainly help today, and would keep Elvie busy.

What was the harm?

. . .

And then Elvie wouldn't stop. She attacked the interior of Tornley Hall with the same zeal she'd demonstrated in the garden.

As Hannah scrubbed the hall floor, relieved to see the black-and-white tiles emerge in reasonable condition from beneath the grime, Elvie made the kitchen windows shine with her vinegary solution, inside and out. When Hannah's tiles were dry, Elvie started on the hall windows, while Hannah did the sitting-room ones with spray and paper towels.

Just in time, she caught Elvie heading into the garden to clean the outside of the windows. "I'll do those, thanks," she said. Madeleine could be roaming nearby.

At one point she and Elvie washed the same pane of glass, inside and out, their wiping hands chasing each other.

Hannah laughed.

Elvie didn't.

. . .

By 2:00 P.M. they had cleaned all the downstairs windows, and had swept and mopped the rest of the wooden floors.

Hannah was wiping the shutters, when Elvie went and stood at one end of the sofa and waited expectantly.

"Oh. Do you mind? Thank you."

Elvie lifted her end of the sofa effortlessly towards the wall, waiting patiently for Hannah to copy her. They moved the second sofa opposite it, then the cupboard, the two armchairs, and the side tables into place, too. Without asking, Elvie swept and mopped the last section of exposed sitting-room floor, then wordlessly they shook out the rug and lifted the coffee table on top of it. Hannah plugged in some lamps around the room and stood back.

The room wasn't ever going to feature in an interiors magazine, but it was ten times better than it had been. "Wow, this looks great," she said. "Thanks for your help."

But Elvie was already heading out the room. There was a clatter, then Hannah heard the growl of a vacuum cleaner. She found Elvie pushing the hose along the bottom stair.

"Oh, Elvie, no. You don't have to . . ."

Elvie ignored her.

Tiggy was right about one thing, at least. Elvie did look happier when she was busy. It gave a purpose to her slumped frame.

A new opera started on the radio in the kitchen.

Hannah slipped upstairs past Elvie, to start on the bedroom windows.

. . .

By late afternoon the transformation of Tornley House was nearly complete. Sun shone through the sparkling Victorian picture windows onto a neat garden. The hall tiles were clean, the cracks mostly covered by an Ikea rug. Just the pictures to put up on the walls tonight and they'd made it.

It looked good.

Hannah allowed herself one moment of excitement. Tomorrow they'd find out Barbara's news.

She checked her watch. Ten to four. Bloody hell—where were Tiggy and Frank? Will would be here in an hour. If they didn't come, she'd have to take Elvie home to the bungalow and just hope she kept out of Madeleine's way.

Upstairs, she checked on Elvie cleaning the bath, then slipped into the second bedroom.

The denim elephant lay on the floor. Hannah placed it on the mantelpiece. This wasn't tempting fate. This was being hopeful again about the future.

For a second, she let herself imagine this bedroom with a child in it. Toys in the corner. Books on a shelf for bedtime stories.

A screech of brakes and pounding music on the gravel shook her from her daydream.

Hannah went to the window, praying it was Frank and Tiggy.

Their own old gray station wagon was parked under the window. *Will?*

"Oh shit—Elvie!"

Will was early. Hannah ran to the bathroom.

It was empty.

"Elvie?"

Silence.

Where the hell was she?

32

Will turned off the car engine and regarded Tornley House.

Whatever Hannah had done since yesterday, for Barbara's visit, seemed to have transformed it. It looked cleaner somehow.

He didn't want to think what would happen if her efforts had all been for nothing.

He headed to the front door, still buoyed up with his success today.

"Carrie" was finished, and the record company was happy. This afternoon a newly inspired Jeremiah had e-mailed over the bones of another song that sounded promising.

Will pulled out his key.

Strangely, returning to Suffolk had been OK today. For a start, he'd found a seat on the train and had time to listen to a young Parisian singer-songwriter he'd been approached about. He'd scribbled down a few ideas for her. In the car, too, it had felt surprisingly relaxing to turn off the busy A12 onto a country road, with a clear reach ahead. He'd have to work harder to keep up his London contacts when the studio was built, but being out here might give him more space in his head to write.

It might yet all work.

As long as Barbara found them a child. As long as Hannah forgave him for Clare.

Will opened the front door, impressed at the sight of the revamped floor. Classical music was coming from the kitchen, which was odd for Hannah.

There was a rush of footsteps and Hannah came tearing out of the dining room.

"Hi. What's up?" he asked.

Her eyes searched behind him. "You're early."

"Nice to see you, too," he said. "House looks good."

"Did you just come in the front door?"

"No, I flew in a window."

"Did you see anyone?"

Why was she so jumpy? "Like who?"

Hannah headed into the kitchen. "Oh, nothing. Next door was helping out again—I just wondered if she'd finished."

He followed her in and changed the music on the radio. "So, they like 'Carrie'—which means I'll get paid soon."

"Great!" Hannah said. He saw her check the back-door bolt.

"What?"

She scratched her head. "It doesn't matter. Are you hungry?"

"Yeah, don't worry. I'll get something in a minute." He sat down.

"Don't get too comfortable." She nodded to a stack of twenty picture frames against the wall. "We need to put all these up tonight."

She seemed wired again.

"Tell you what—this had better be bloody worth it," Will said to make her smile. "Twins, at least."

But Hannah had gone to the scullery and was lifting and pushing the latch, frowning.

She didn't seem to have heard.

33

Hannah waited, biting her fingernails, until Will had eaten an early dinner and started putting up pictures with the drill in the sitting room. Then she continued her search for Elvie.

This was ridiculous. One second Elvie had been in the bathroom, and the next she was gone. How had she done it? The back door was bolted, and Will had been outside the front. The scullery window was still on the latch from when she'd closed it last night.

Hannah rechecked wardrobes and behind doors, then tried the attic and even the paintings cupboard.

What if Elvie was still here and appeared again, in the middle of the night, shouting?

Should she just tell Will now? Take the risk?

In the sitting room she found him measuring a drill hole, with a wall plug in his mouth. She surveyed the frames. There must be twenty more. It would take him hours.

No—no distractions. This house had to be ready tonight.

Barbara was nearly here.

She'd just have to assume Elvie had somehow left via the scullery window. When Will was busy, she'd pop next door and tell Elvie to stay in the bungalow till her parents returned.

. . .

Hannah was washing her paintbrush in the bathroom at around seven o'clock that evening when she heard a familiar noise on the gravel and a sharp rap at the door.

By the time she could reach the door, Will had opened it.

Dax stood on the doorstep in the dark, a cigarette in his hand.

"Aye-aye," he said to Will. "Your missus in?"

"Hi, Dax," she called.

Will's shoulders jarred. "What can we do for you?"

Dax looked past him to Hannah. "Bill rang Frank . . ."

No! She had to stop him.

"It's fine. I'll sort this," she said, walking in front of Will. "It's about the people next door."

Will didn't budge. She saw Dax's eyes on them.

"She's the boss round here, in't she?" Dax said with a smirk.

"No, really I'm not," Hannah said quickly.

She knew his remark would wind Will up.

"Honestly, Will, it's fine, I'll sort it out." She knew it would anger Will that she'd said that to him in front of Dax, but right now she had no choice. She waited till he'd gone back upstairs.

"What happened?" Hannah whispered, ignoring Dax's sly grin. "Did you find Frank and Tiggy?"

"No, I spoke to Mad. Told her what you told me."

Hannah did a double take. "Dax! I didn't want you to do that."

He drew on his cigarette and squinted through the smoke. "Well, see, I thought you might be jumping the gun, and I was right. Mad said Elvie had a right hump on, yesterday. Shouting and swinging her arms around. Mad was trying to stop her, she said—restraining her, Tiggy calls it. That's what her and Frank do."

How could he be that stupid? "No. Dax. That's not true. Madeleine whacked her. I've got it on video."

Dax's swagger dissolved in front of her. "You what?"

"I filmed it—on my phone. I've filmed her twice actually. The first time she was yelling at someone else, then I filmed her kicking Elvie, and hitting her three times in the face. I'm not making this up. There's no way you could call that self-defense, or restraining someone." She paused. "Oh, and I've also got photos of her leaving a donkey out in the snow all night. I don't think that was self-defense, either."

Dax sucked in more smoke. "Well, I don't know about that."

"Well, I do. And, Dax, I really wish you hadn't told her about me. It's put me in a difficult position." She sighed. "Listen, can you just text me Frank's number, and I'll ring him and Tiggy?"

Dax threw down his cigarette.

"All right—don't get yer knickers in a twist. Tell you what, if you're so sure, why don't we ask Elvie? Where is she anyway? Mad said she weren't around today."

Upstairs the drill stopped. Hannah motioned for Dax to be quiet. It started again.

"She was here earlier, but she's run off," Hannah owned up.

He motioned at the bungalow. "You been round?"

"Yes—I tried the intercom an hour ago. But she didn't answer. I thought I heard her listening, though."

"Come on, then," Dax said, walking off.

"Wait," Hannah called. She ran upstairs to the toolbox and found the flashlight, then tiptoed past their bedroom, where Will was drilling. When she returned, Dax was in the hall, examining her paintwork on the walls with a big, oily hand and an appalled expression.

"Don't say a word," she warned.

She followed him round to the side lawn and through the wall gate. A ghostly light shone through the peacock window onto the damp, shorn grass.

It was her first time in the homestead. Mist hung in the air. It was interesting to see Tornley Hall from this angle. Its roof rose above the Victorian wall. She could see now how the walled garden was designed to complement the house's setting.

There was a faint smell of manure, and solar lights illuminated their path to the bungalow. Dax banged on the front door, as Hannah stood back.

"You in there, girl?" Dax called.

It felt as if they were trespassing.

Dax peered in the unlit window.

Hannah leaned in to check the other window. Just at that moment Dax stood back and they careered into each other. Her hand shot out to steady herself and she felt the hard muscle of his arm, and smelled cigarette smoke and the now-familiar diesel smell.

"Oh, sorry."

"Aye-aye, five minutes on your own with me in the dark . . ." Dax teased.

"Han?"

A new flashlight beam shone out of the dark. She banged her leg into the lion statue by the door, startled.

It was Will. "What's going on?"

"Nothing." The word came out too fast. "We're just looking for Tiggy's daughter. Dax is helping"—Dax emerged from the shadows into Will's beam—"me to find her."

Will's eyes moved to Dax, then back to Hannah. "And why's this your problem?"

"It's not. It's just that Tiggy's away."

"And . . ."

Dax folded his arms. "Ooh, you're in trouble now, missy."

A look of menace appeared on Will's face that Hannah knew all too well. On the rare occasions a drunken moron had kicked her seat in the cinema, or bumped her on the Tube, she'd seen that same expression appear. It was usually followed by a murmured word, tight in the ear of her assailant, and then an apology to her.

"Dax, I'm not—really." She wished he would shut up. This was a nightmare. She had to get Will out of here. She took his arm. "Come on. It's fine."

Dax laughed. "Got you under the thumb, in't she?"

"Dax, please, shut up!"

Will pulled his arm away from her.

"Ignore him," she hissed, trying to take Will's hand instead. "Come on. I'll explain." But Will marched ahead of her back to the gate. "Wait," she said, running after him. At the peacock window she caught him up and yanked the back of his sweater. "Stop!"

He spun round. "What the fuck's going on?"

"Nothing! He's a wind-up merchant. He thinks everything's funny. Please. Don't get upset about it. Not now."

Will's fists clenched.

"Don't!" She touched his arm. "Look. There is weird stuff going on here, but I don't want to talk about it till Barbara's been. I will tell you, but right now it's too distracting. Please. Can we just concentrate on tomorrow?"

"Whatever." Will walked off into the house and she knew she was in for a massive sulk. "But I'm telling you, I don't want to see that wanker round here again."

"OK. Fine."

Seconds later the bedroom door slammed and the drill re-started.

Hannah sat on the hall stairs.

One more bloody day.

34

The next day it was almost as though the sun knew Barbara was coming.

It drenched the fields in a shimmering gold, as if it had been saving the best for today. The sky was a brilliant blue. A heron flew across the green sea of the marsh.

Hannah stood with a cup of tea, surveying the garden.

They'd made it. Not without complications, but they were there.

The pictures were almost all up.

Elvie had not appeared during the night.

Tornley Hall looked almost beautiful.

Barbara was on her way.

By the end of today there might even be news.

Inside, Will was drilling the last few holes. He'd been barely civil last night, using the drill to drown out any conversation. She prayed he'd warm up by eleven.

Hannah showered, then dressed in a summery dress she'd

bought for this occasion, a brand-new white cardigan, and sandals. She blow-dried her hair straight and pulled it back into a neat bun, applied makeup for the first time since her last meeting with Barbara, and powdered a sheen of nervous perspiration on her cheeks and forehead. She wondered if Barbara had ever visited the house of a potential adopter who did not dress as if they were about to attend a job interview. Did anyone ever dare to leave dirty dishes in the sink?

Will packed away the drill and went for his shower. When he returned, he'd pulled his jeans back on with the white shirt that she'd ironed.

She frowned. "Can't you wear your gray trousers? The smart ones?"

"Why?"

"Er—to humor me?"

Ignoring his eye-rolling, she remade the bed with the fresh white duvet cover, silk cushions, and coffee-colored cashmere and silk throws that she kept for Barbara's visits. *We are a sophisticated, measured, calm couple with time to enjoy life*, the bed was designed to say.

"Where's Laurie?" she asked. "I want to run through things with her—she was making me nervous the way she was talking at the weekend."

Will pulled on his gray trousers. "She knows what to say."

As if on cue, a car drew up below.

Hannah glanced out. "That's her."

She turned. There was a sadness in Will's eyes that she didn't understand.

"You look nice," he said quietly.

Hannah twirled. "Fragrant, maternal, trustworthy?"

"Nuts, obsessive, loon?" He dodged the pretend punch she threw at him.

On impulse, Hannah leaned down and kissed him, and saw the surprise on his face. It made her heart sore.

"I can't believe we've done it," she said, wiping lipstick off his upper lip. On impulse, she kissed him there again, for a second longer. A tiny jolt of forgotten desire flickered through her. She stood back. "Please, can this be it?"

"It's going to be fine," he said. "Don't worry."

They held each other's gaze—allies again.

"Can you let Laurie in, and I'll open the windows up here and see if I can get rid of more of the paint smell?" Hannah said.

As Will went downstairs, she reached up to the window catch as Laurie emerged from her car below. Thank goodness she'd made an effort. Beige linen skirt, white blouse, wedge sandals, subtle makeup. Touched, Hannah noticed that she'd put in rollers to give her hair "height," as if having hair that rose up like a cliff was a guaranteed way to added extra smartness. She looked perfect: like the professional village nursery teacher and respectable mother of three that she was.

"OK," Hannah muttered, scanning the bedroom. Laurie was fine. This room was fine. They were nearly there. She headed out to the hall, checking her lipstick.

A shape loomed out of the shadows to her right.

Hannah's hand flew up to stifle a scream.

Elvie stood at the door to the small bedroom.

"Elvie! What are you doing here?" she gasped. "How did you get in?"

Outside, the car door slammed. She heard Will and Laurie chatting on the forecourt.

"Elvie, you have to go. You can't be here," Hannah said, sweat breaking out on her forehead. "Come on, quickly." She motioned the young woman downstairs urgently. Hannah grasped her leathery hand and pulled, hardly able to breathe.

There was a burst of voices and the front door flew open. Hannah swerved backwards, pushing Elvie behind her. "No! Go!" She couldn't explain this to Will. Not now. Not with Laurie here.

She searched for an escape route and saw the attic stairs.

"Come on." Hannah pulled Elvie up the old stairs and shut the attic door, muttering. "Shit, shit, shit!"

It was stuffy up here. The spring air had risen and become trapped under the eaves. Hannah opened the skylight, trying not to creak the rafters.

"Elvie, what are you doing here? Are you OK?"

Elvie's eyes were fixed above Hannah's head. Her mouth dropped open and a low bellow started to emerge.

It was a spider.

"No! Shh!"

Hannah cupped it in her hands and chucked it out onto the roof tiles. "Look. Gone."

Elvie stuck out her bottom lip. Hannah watched in despair.

No. This was a disaster.

She tried to think.

"Listen, Elvie, you have to stay here. For a little while. You can't come downstairs. But you'll be safe up here, I promise you."

She took the woman's coarse hands in hers. "And you have to be quiet, or you'll get me into trouble. Please."

Elvie watched her blankly.

Hannah felt the panic rising in her chest. It was all going wrong. She was clearly never meant to be a mother.

"Are you hungry?" she asked desperately.

Elvie nodded.

"OK. Now, stay here. I'll see if I can find cookies."

Hannah rubbed the sheen of desperation from her upper lip and walked to the door.

From that angle, with the sun shining in, Elvie's brown eyes suddenly seemed familiar. But Hannah was too panicked to work out where she'd seen them before.

• • •

Nails digging into her palms, Hannah went to the kitchen, trying to appear normal.

Laurie carried in two baskets of lurid blue and pink petunias from the car.

"Hi, Hannah. Where do you want these?"

"Oh, thanks, just by the door," Hannah said, trying to compose herself.

"You look very tense," Laurie said, peering through her big glasses. "Listen, it'll be fine. I promise not to tell them about Will getting strip-searched by the police on his way to Glastonbury. Ha!" She reached up and ruffled Will's hair. Hannah forced a grin. Some things never changed.

She felt his eyes on her. "Lor's right, Han. You've gone white."

"I'm just nervous." In the kitchen she ripped open the posh cookies they'd bought for Barbara, took three, and found a bottle of water in the scullery. She crept back into the hall, terrified of finding Elvie on the stairs.

What if she just asked her to leave? She could see it now: Elvie shouting, "My house!" just as Barbara turned up, and refusing to go.

Where the hell were Frank and Tiggy? She looked on the hall table for her phone, to see if there was a message from Dax or

Barbara. Confused, she spun around. It wasn't there. Where was it? She looked around, then gave up and ran up the stairs. She had to keep Elvie hidden.

In the attic she gave Elvie her snack, and held her finger to her lip.

"You must be quiet. OK?"

Finally the woman spoke. "Yes."

"Good."

It was far from good. It was a disaster.

Downstairs, Hannah found Laurie banging a nail into the portico. Will was laying out plates.

"Have you seen my phone?" Hannah asked, checking the worktop.

"No. Han?"

She turned. "What?"

"Seriously," he said. "You look wired."

Suddenly it was all just too much. She bit her lip. "I am, a bit."

"What's up?"

She rolled her eyes, knowing she had to tell him. She checked that Laurie was out of earshot, then walked over to him. "I've done something really stupid."

"What?"

"I've got involved in something that—"

Laurie walked in. "Right, what's next?"

Hannah shook her head at Will. "I'll tell you in a minute."

Through the door Laurie had left open she saw Laurie's blue station wagon.

"Laurie, did you shut the gate on the driveway behind you?"

"Yes, was I not supposed . . . ?"

Hannah charged past her and down the driveway, ignoring Laurie's "God, what have I done now?"

She opened the black, rotten gate and shoved it far out of sight into the bushes, then held it in place with a rock.

· · ·

There was no time now.

Desperate as she was to tell Will about Elvie, it was ten to eleven. Barbara was due.

"What if she can't find the house?" Hannah wiped the kitchen worktop for the third time. "What if she gets lost, like we did, and gives up? Or tries to ring us and can't get a signal? Or what if she's trying to ring and I can't find my phone?"

Will read a newspaper, ignoring her.

Laurie fetched four mugs from the cupboard. As she filled the kettle, Hannah replaced them with matching white ones that she kept for Barbara. Laurie and Will exchanged amused glances. Hannah ignored it. They could fuck off, with their secret cousins' code.

"Listen, Laurie. Can we just go through it again? It's possible Barbara might invent a situation—say, I had food poisoning and was throwing up all day when Will was in London—and asks what you would do to help. Or if I had to go to hospital. Or Will was—"

"Han!" Will banged down his newspaper. "She knows. You get it, Lor—right?"

Laurie took a cookie, and Hannah had to stop herself from grabbing it and putting it back on the carefully arranged plate.

"Hannah, please, just let me speak. I'm a mum and a nursery teacher. I know the kind of things she'll want to know."

There was the crunch of a car on gravel outside.

Hannah gasped. "Oh, God!"

Barbara was here.

Laurie stood up, matter-of-factly. "Good. Now, listen, the house looks great. Everything's fine. Just relax."

"Will, you sure you haven't left anything stupid lying around?" Hannah asked.

She checked up the stairs, terrified of seeing Elvie at the top.

"Just a bit of porn and coke by the bed."

"OK," she said, distracted.

Will and Laurie laughed. Will took her shoulders and made her look at him.

"Han, it's going to be fine."

"Is it?"

"Yes."

"God, this is exciting!" Laurie said, moving the hall rug an inch to cover a crack in a tile. "I can't believe I'm going to help find my new niece or nephew!"

Will opened the front door, and Hannah followed.

Just one hour, that's all they needed. Then half an hour back at Laurie's house, and it would be over.

Will halted abruptly and Hannah nearly walked into his back.

She peered round, expecting to see Barbara's white hatchback.

Instead there was a mud-spattered Land Rover jammed carelessly across the forecourt.

An angry shout came from behind it.

"Oi. I want a word with you!"

Madeleine?

• • •

"No!" Hannah said.

She grabbed at Will.

"How dare you?" the farmer yelled, her boots hammering gravel in all directions as she strode towards Hannah.

"What's going on?" She heard confusion in Will's voice.

Madeleine's eyes flashed like an angry dog's. Up close, she was an inch taller than Will, and probably about thirty pounds heavier.

"You cheeky fucking cow!" The farmer poked a finger at Hannah's chest. "How dare you. You come here, and make accusations about me to my neighbors. After what you've been doing, you mucky bitch?"

Hannah stood, stunned, her eyes darting, checking for Barbara.

"What are you talking about?"

"You think you're going to report me? After what you did?"

"It's about the donkey," Hannah said to Will and Laurie. "Please. Can we please discuss this later? We're waiting for someone important. It involves a child. You need to go."

The farmer planted her strong legs on the gravel. Her elbows under the rolled-up shirtsleeves were red and raw.

"Tough! Now I'm going to tell you this once. You say another word about me to anyone and I'll report you." She turned to Will. "You know about this, do you—your wife shagging Dax in his truck down at the beach? Susan and her kids bloody saw you, as well. Kids! And Old Samuel."

Hannah stared. "What are you talking about?"

The words flew at her. *Shagging. Saw you. Kids.*

The farmer made an unconvinced face.

"I said, what are you talking about?" Hannah shouted.

Will wouldn't meet her eye. She grabbed his arm. "Will. Ignore her. She's only doing this because Dax told her I saw her assaulting the woman next door."

"I thought you said it was about a donkey," Laurie asked, confused.

"Dax, from last night?" Will cut in, ice in his voice.

She faltered and realized the implication. "No! No. That's what I was doing, in the garden with Dax. Looking for the daughter. She's gone missing. He was helping me find her. And I knew if I told you, you'd tell me to butt out and . . ."

The distant sound of a second car appeared in the distance. Hannah glanced, terrified, at the gate.

"Will. That's her. Oh, God." She looked at Madeleine beseechingly. "Please, you've got to go!"

There was disgust on the farmer's face. "I'm telling you. One more word and I'll have the police on you. Public indecency, they call it. Bloody cheek!"

She returned to her truck and reversed at speed down the driveway, gravel spraying everywhere.

Hannah watched in shock.

Will put his hands behind his head. She saw Laurie touch his arm, immediately taking his side.

"Oh, don't tell me you believe her, for God's sake!" Hannah yelled. "Will! Elvie—the daughter—is here, right now, in the house. That's what I was going to tell you. I'm hiding her because she's so scared—of that woman."

"What are you talking about . . . ?"

"She's in the house, now?" Laurie asked.

"Yes! That's what I was trying to tell you. Will?"

Will's eyes flashed. "Why didn't you tell me last night?"

"I don't know! I thought you'd make me ring the police. And she did run away yesterday. Then she appeared upstairs, literally ten minutes ago. I don't even know how she gets in."

He blew out his cheeks.

"OK. Where is she, Hannah?" Laurie asked.

"In the attic."

"Right—you two, stay there. I'll sort this out."

"Laurie, be careful, she's not very . . ." Hannah started, but Laurie was gone.

Hannah put her hands on Will's shoulders. "Will, please, come on—you don't seriously believe I had sex in a truck with that man, do you? Or with anyone, for that matter?"

He wouldn't meet her eye. "That was the day, wasn't it?"

"What day?"

"The day after we had that fight. When you thought I wasn't coming back. You said you'd been on the beach with him."

"No!"

"You did. You were upset. You said you thought I'd walked out on you, and on the adoption."

"No! Don't be stupid. Even if it was true, I wouldn't do that, would I?"

A sound of feet on the stairs. "There's nobody there," said Laurie.

"What?"

Hannah ran past her and took the stairs two at a time.

Laurie was right. The attic was empty, the skylight still open. Hannah cursed. How was Elvie doing this?

"There are cookie crumbs on the floor, and her water bottle is still here," she shouted, returning downstairs. "Elvie! Come out now, please."

Will wandered past her to the kitchen and slumped onto a chair.

"Will! Don't be ridiculous—why would I do that?"

Another car pulled up outside.

Hannah shrank back. "Will, please. Not now. She's here."

Laurie came out from behind Hannah and pushed her face into Will's. "Listen, I don't know what's going on here, but you are going to get up and do this. *Now!*"

She yanked him upright.

"Stop it, Lor," he said, shaking her off.

Laurie smoothed down her skirt. "Pull yourselves together, both of you. You can talk about it afterwards."

Laurie took Will's hand and dragged him to the door.

In shock, Hannah followed. Everything was spinning out of control, and she didn't know how to stop it.

$$\cdot \quad \cdot \quad \cdot$$

Barbara stayed for exactly an hour.

Despite every minute of the last two weeks having led to this precise moment, the details of her visit would remain patchy in Hannah's memory forever.

She would only recall managing to force a manic grin on her face, and glancing repeatedly at Will, willing him to speak.

"What a super house!" Barbara said. She'd straightened her black hair into a bob and wore her usual smart suit, with a chunky necklace. "Wow, there's so much space." She made suitably impressed noises about the garden, too.

Hannah filled in gaps in the conversation whenever Will said little.

Laurie helped, too—talking about her kids and Ian, and all the beaches, and trips to the circus at Great Yarmouth, and her nursery work. At one point Hannah and Will left Laurie and Barbara in the garden and went inside to make tea.

"She likes the house," Hannah said, her cheeks flushed.

Will put on the kettle, his back to her.

"Will. That farmer is nuts."

Barbara and Laurie walked into the house, chatting.

"Right, I'll head back, Barbara. Get the troops ready. See you in half an hour?" Laurie said. She shot Will and Hannah one of her meaningful looks.

Barbara waited till Laurie had gone, then sat down and opened her bag.

"Right. Now, I said I had some news."

Hannah nodded numbly and sat down, too.

Will stayed standing.

Barbara pulled out a file. "There's a little girl I want to talk to you about. She's three, and lives in east London. She's been in foster care for one . . ."

She began to talk, and Hannah willed Will to sit down.

Barbara gave her a photo as she continued talking.

Hannah blinked hard, praying that she would feel something, then opened her eyes.

She tried to focus.

A chubby white face with lips stretched in a shy grin, a missing tooth, deep-brown eyes. Red wavy hair, badly cut into a publicly funded fringe.

Everything around Hannah fell still.

Barbara's voice faded, and her movements froze.

There was something familiar about the child. A chemical connection that Hannah didn't understand. Physical elements of the child were like other people in both of their families. It was as if she already belonged here.

And her eyes. The photo had been taken in the sun, yet the little girl's eyes were in shadow. As if she was shy, and unsure about coming out.

Nothing in Hannah's life had been as certain as this moment.

She wanted to take the child's hand and lead her out of the shadow, and tell her it was OK.

This was her—this was Hannah's daughter.

Happy tears filled her eyes.

". . . and as far as I know," Barbara said, her voicing reentering Hannah's consciousness, "there are no other families in the picture."

Hannah showed the photo to Will.

"Oh, God—look, Will. She has brown eyes like you. And red hair, like me."

Barbara turned to watch Will's reaction. He smiled. "She's cute."

When Barbara turned back, Hannah saw him turn away, his smile fading.

35

Ten minutes later Barbara drove away.

Hannah waved from the doorstep, then spun round. "Will?"

Something about him had changed. He was rubbing his torso, as if he'd been punched. He sat down and put his head in his hands.

"Oh, Will." She put her arm round him and kissed the side of his head, and his cheek. "Don't be stupid. The farmer's just terrified I'm going to call the police on her."

He sounded shattered. "Han, you've got to be telling me the truth."

"Of course I am. And it's easy to prove. We can do it now. Come on." She grabbed the car keys from the hall, pulled him to the car, and started it. Wearily Will climbed in, and they headed down the driveway.

"Listen, I was in Dax's pickup on the beach, but I was helping him to move tires. I wanted to walk to the beach, and he

gave me a lift—then I didn't want to go back to the house because I was upset, so I stayed out all afternoon . . ."

"And . . . ?"

"That was it. It was boring. He delivered stuff all day and
hardly spoke to me, but I was lonely, so I went for the ride. And
I was upset with you—but that doesn't mean I had sex with
him."

They took the bend and pulled up outside Dax's cottage.

"Come on," Hannah repeated, touching his cheek. "Apart
from anything else, you know how I feel about sex at the moment. And why would I throw everything away for him? You
said yourself he's a tosser."

But Will wouldn't get out of the car.

"OK. Wait here," she said. She climbed out and marched up
to Dax's front door. She was so stunned by events that she didn't
register the objects around her.

A toy truck on the doorstep.

A skateboard on the lawn.

Ballet-dancer ornaments on the windowsill.

She banged on the door. To her relief, Dax opened it. For the
first time he was not wearing his boiler suit. His face was clean,
and his hair brushed down into a greasy side parting. He was
dressed in a green T-shirt and tracksuit trousers.

"Aye-aye. Thought you'd be round."

Women's shoes on the hall floor. Photos of children on the
wall.

A photo of an older man Hannah vaguely recognized, with
two blond women.

"*Have you got kids, Dax?*"

"*Do I look bloody stupid?*"

She brushed away an uneasy feeling.

"Hi, Dax. Listen, something really bad's happened. Could you come out and speak to Will?"

Dax peered at the car. "What's this about then?"

"Would you just come?"

"All right. Keep yer hair on."

He strolled down the path after her and she opened the car door. Dax leaned against the car in a way she knew would annoy Will.

"Dax, listen. Madeleine has just turned up at our house, screaming at me. She told Will that you and I—we . . ." Hannah sighed. "That we had sex in your truck on the beach. And that people saw us. And obviously that's not true, so can you please tell Will? And can you also explain that you told Madeleine that I saw her hitting Elvie."

Dax folded his arms. "Well, that's difficult, in't it?"

"Why?"

"Well, I don't want to get no one into trouble, but I don't want to lie, do I?"

Hannah blinked. "Dax, will you just tell him?"

Dax crouched down and looked in the car door. "Sorry, mate, but she was all over me. Once down the beach, once up in the meadow, once by Snadesdon. Summat you're not giving her at home?"

Hannah reeled. "Dax, stop it! This is not a joke. Can you please tell him?"

"She likes it up the arse, don't she?"

The passenger door flew open. Will shot out.

"No!" Hannah yelled. She ran and jammed her hands into his chest. His eyes above her were aflame. "Will, no. Dax? Why are you doing this?"

A woman emerged from Dax's cottage. It was the woman from next door who she'd seen on her walk the other day. Confused, Hannah realized it was this blond woman's photo that she'd just seen in Dax's hall.

"Is this her, is it?" the woman barked. "Your tart Mad was on about? Fucking cheek!"

Dax glowered. "Back inside, Carol. Now!"

A child's grubby face popped up at the window.

The woman ducked around Dax and jabbed her finger at Hannah.

"He's got kids, right? My girl's little mate and her mum saw you. You come near him again and I'll do you. You understand? And you, get your hands off me," she spat at Dax.

Bewildered, Hannah gestured helplessly to Will. "I have no idea why he's saying this." She turned back to Dax. "Please. I told you we're waiting to adopt. Why are you doing this? It's not funny."

"Emotional, in't she?" Dax said to Will.

"No, this is emotional, mate," Will said, pushing past Hannah again.

Dax laughed, squaring up to him. "What you going to do— sing me a nice song?"

Hannah shoved Will back again. "Will! Don't do it. He'll call the police, and we'll lose her."

Will ducked like a boxer out of her grasp. He kicked Dax's gate, shot her a furious look, then jumped in the driver's side of the car and slammed the door.

"Will!"

Hannah tried to grab the door handle, but he drove off, ripping it from her fingers.

"Will!"

Dax leaned over the gate and lit a cigarette.

Hannah spun round. "Why did you do that? Why would you do that to me?"

Dax blew out a relaxed puff of smoke.

"He believes you! It's not funny!"

"Hmm," Dax said, appearing to mull something over. "Tell you what. Wait there a minute."

He returned inside. The child watched her through the window. Why had he lied about having a family? Dax returned, thrust an envelope into her hand, and disappeared back into his front door.

Hannah opened it.

To Owner, Tornley Hall, the note said. *Work completed 2 x days @ £200 per day. Logs, £20. Glass plus installation, £50. Total: £470.00 plus 20% VAT.*

36

Will drove so fast out of Tornley that his wheels struggled to keep traction on the tarmac. He rammed the wheel down at the next bend, and the car bucked.

He wanted to smash that wanker's face. The image of him having sex with Hannah in the truck seared into his mind. He took another bend, faster. As one hand fought to keep the wheel down, he used the other to turn the music up.

There was a bump. The back wheel hit a low curb. The car swerved the opposite way.

He knew he'd fucked up, but right that minute he didn't care. *Hannah*.

Too late, Will saw a car turning into the junction thirty yards ahead.

His car hit a skid. He turned into it and came to a furious, screeching halt flat across the road.

The car in front slammed on its brakes, too. Laurie jumped out.

"What the hell are you doing! I've got kids, you arse."

Her face was beetroot. She looked like Nan Riley when she had found a condom in his pocket, aged fifteen. He felt ashamed then, and he did so again now.

He opened the door. "Sorry, Lor."

A 4x4 turned into the road behind Laurie. She held up a hand.

"What's happened?"

Will gripped the steering wheel. "She did it."

"Who?"

"Hannah."

Laurie's shoulders slumped. "No."

The 4x4 growled behind them.

"Shit! Who told you?"

"He did."

"Aw, Will." She waved a hand again at the driver. "OK. Come on, I'll help you reverse."

He did what she asked, even though what he wanted to do was ram the fucking car into a tree.

· · ·

Hannah walked way from Dax's cottage, gripping the invoice in trembling fingers. The last hour had been a waking nightmare.

Will had never talked to her like that in eight years. How could he drive off and leave her, like that—now?

She wanted to press "delete" and start again. Make it all go away, but she knew it wouldn't. It was happening again.

She was going to lose this child.

The photo of the little girl's face entered her mind.

Her heart opened up and swallowed her. This could not be happening.

A car pulled up to her right. "Hannah!" Laurie waved through the open window. "In."

Robotically Hannah did as she asked, and sat shivering with shock in the front seat.

"Will drove off really fast. I think he's going to crash."

Laurie drove towards Tornley Hall. "No, he's not. I've just seen him. I told him to slow down. He's gone on to ours. Ian's waiting. His mum's got the kids."

Hannah shook her head. "I didn't sleep with that man."

Laurie looked exasperated. "Well, he thinks you did. God, Hannah, why would they both say it?"

Hannah wound down the window, inexplicably hot. "I asked Dax for help and he turned on me. I can't believe Will believes him."

"He said the guy said something convincing."

Summat you're not giving her at home?

"No. That was a coincidence. That would wind anyone up." Hannah rested her head on the window, stunned. "What happened to Barbara?"

"Nothing," Laurie said. "It was fine. She stayed twenty minutes. Kids behaved. Ian behaved. I told her what a fine, upstanding couple you are." She rolled her eyes.

Hannah rifled in a box for a tissue as they approached Tornley Hall. "Laurie, why would I do all this, then throw everything away—now?"

Laurie bit her lip.

"What's Will said?"

"Nothing. I just get the feeling that things haven't been right for a while."

"From me?"

"From Will."

A chill ran through Hannah.

Laurie turned into the drive. "He seems all over the place, to me. He used to look like that when he came here in the summer. He hates change. And you're making him change everything. He can't deal with it, Hannah." She parked.

Hannah felt her frustration rising. Why didn't anyone ever understand?

Hannah turned to face her. "Laurie, listen—no offense, but you have no idea what it's like. No one does. I mean, you got pregnant, what, three times? It just happened for you. It didn't for us. This is it. Our only chance of becoming parents is if the social workers say we can. I'm just trying to make them choose us and"—she laughed—"it worked! Barbara loved the house! She likes you. She's found us a child. And all we had to do was meet the child's social workers and persuade them, and that would be it!" She flung open the car door. "And then Will strops off like a sulky teenager because he believes that guy, over me." She put her legs out the car. "You know, I'm starting to wonder if Will really wants to do this. Just last week he was talking about pulling out. I mean, he doesn't *need* to do this. He could go out tomorrow and shag someone—not something Will's ever found particularly difficult—and have a kid."

She drew a long breath, then looked up at the huge house with nobody in it.

Laurie picked up a packet of kids' sweets and offered her one. "OK, well, Will clearly does want to do it—he's just freaked out. What I don't understand is this woman, Elvie. What's she got to do with everything?"

Hannah took a sweet. "Oh, I really don't know. And I don't know how I've got involved with it. I just know she needs help. Her parents are away, and she's vulnerable."

"What's wrong with her?"

"I don't know. Her mother said she'd had a difficult birth. So brain damage, perhaps? Learning difficulties? That's why it's so bad. The farmer was hitting her. She must know that Elvie can't—or won't—tell anyone. I saw bruises. I mean, what would you do?"

"Call the police?"

Hannah laughed bitterly. "Oh, that would be great, wouldn't it. 'Hi, Barbara, welcome to our house; here's Elvie, she's being beaten up by the nutter next door, who has a rifle, but honestly it's a really safe place for you to bring a vulnerable foster child to.'" She imitated Barbara's voice. "'Er, OK. Well, let's just give it another six months, until it's sorted.' Or maybe never at all."

Laurie ate her sweet. "Barbara doesn't have a hotline to the Suffolk police."

"No, but if she found out later—say, if the case went to court and was in the papers—she might think we'd lied to her about our lives, and how we lived. You need to be completely transparent with social services. They're trusting you with a child."

Laurie shrugged. "Well then, maybe you should have just walked away from Elvie. Your kids have to be the priority. I'm not being funny, Hannah, but what is it with you, needing always to get involved in other people's problems?"

Hannah bristled. She remembered Laurie telling her that she hadn't voted because "politicians were all as bad as each other." "I don't know—if we all said that, Laurie, then nobody would help anyone."

"OK, but when it affects your own life this much, that's when I don't get it. Will used to get in a right state when you went off to those places for work."

Hannah frowned. "No, he didn't."

"He did!" Laurie pushed her glasses up her nose. "That time when you couldn't get home, because some soldiers had taken over the airport or something. He was going mental. I thought he was going to get on a plane over there."

"I didn't know that."

"But why do you do it?"

She realized Laurie was asking an honest question. "Well, why are any of us the way we are? I don't know—because of my parents probably. They always took us on marches: CND, and the miners . . . Dad was a union rep. I don't know—it's just the way we are. My brothers are the same. One works for a medical charity in Johannesburg, the other one's in politics."

Laurie chewed her sweet thoughtfully. "So where do you think this woman is now?"

"I don't know. She keeps getting into the house, but then she disappears."

Laurie nearly choked. "Getting into your house?"

Hannah nodded. "I don't think she can feed herself, so she's been stealing food. And I think she's been using the house as a place to hide from the farmer. It's sad—she's obviously confused about why Will and I are here at all, in 'her house.' She's been trying to scare us away."

"Really? And the parents have just left her on her own?"

"I think they're in denial. They just want to keep her busy. I'm pretty sure Elvie could be doing more than working for that abusive old cow, though. She's brilliant at gardening."

"And you definitely saw the farmer hitting her?"

"I filmed it."

Laurie threw her hands up. "You filmed it? For God's sake. Hannah, why didn't you say that—show Will!"

"He ran off!"

Laurie flung open her own door. "Right. Enough of this. Let's take the phone back and show him."

Hannah let them into Tornley Hall with her key and went to fetch her phone from the hall table. Too late, she remembered searching for it this morning.

"Oh, I forgot. It's not here," she said uneasily.

This time she searched for it carefully. The drawer of the hall table was empty, too, and nothing was plugged into any of the sockets they used to charge their phones. She widened her search to every room in the house: beside her bed, in her coat pocket, down the side of the sofa.

"It's really not here," Hannah said.

Laurie frowned. "Could Will have taken it?"

Hannah looked at the front door and her hand flew to her mouth.

"Oh, my God! No, but I found Dax in the hall last night. The phone was on the table."

"You think Dax took it?"

"I don't know!"

"Why?"

"He knew I'd videoed Madeleine—maybe she told him to take it."

"Because . . . ?"

"I don't know," Hannah replied, having to stop herself shouting in frustration at Laurie.

Laurie glanced around the big, echoing hall and up the stairs to the dark upstairs landing. She wrapped her arms around her chest and shivered. "You know, Hannah, it's just as well you're brave. I'd get the creeps out here. I know my house is the size of a cereal box, but at least I've got my neighbors through the wall."

"Well, I wasn't expecting to be out here without Will." The

thought of her old neighbors in the London flat made her miss her old life more than she could bear. When everything was normal with Will. When they were happy. The prospect of another restless night in the shadows without him, with the creaking walls and floors of Tornley Hall for company, was unbearable right now. Especially after Barbara's news.

A terror filled her that this had all been for nothing. That it had ruined everything it was supposed to fix.

"OK, well, listen—I've got to get back to the kids," Laurie said, opening the front door. "I'll get Ian to take Will to the pub and calm him down. Try and find the phone, then come over tomorrow and we'll bang your heads together."

Her eye fixed on the table in the kitchen. Hannah turned and saw the photo of the little girl.

"That's her." She went to fetch it and held it up.

"Aw, don't," Laurie said, following her. "You'll make me cry. Oh, look at her. She looks like both of you—little pumpkin." She touched Hannah's arm. "We'll sort it out."

She glanced around the kitchen.

"What?" Hannah asked.

"Every time I come here I remember that night with Nan. Someone was definitely shouting, and Nan was cross." She returned to the hall and opened the door. "Right, leave it to me. Get some rest."

Hannah said she would, but she didn't.

She knew if she sat down or went to bed, her mind would fill with images too awful to contemplate.

So when Laurie left, she spent the rest of the evening checking in every box and drawer in the house for her phone.

She had to find those photos to show Will.

She needed him back. This was their child.

37

As Laurie suggested, Ian did take Will to the pub that night, and when he woke on Laurie's sofa the following morning, his head was thick with a whisky fuzz. There was a heavy weight on his legs.

He pried his eyes open.

The image plowed back into his head of Hannah and that tosser in the truck.

He tried to sit up and found Daniel sitting on his legs, playing a video game. The TV clock said 6:15 A.M.

"What's your score?" Will croaked.

"Fifty-eight. Were you and Dad playing last night?"

Till about 2:00 A.M., if he remembered right. "Yup."

"Did you beat Dad?"

"We both won a couple."

Daniel nodded at an empty whisky bottle. "What does whisky taste like?"

Will eased out his back. "What food do you hate?"

"Zucchini."

"It tastes like zucchini."

Daniel bounced on his legs, making him groan.

"Can I try it? I'm eleven."

"Have you asked your mum?"

"No."

"Why not."

"Because she'd say no."

"There you go then."

Will watched Daniel for a while, remembering what he was like at that age.

The same, but not the same.

. . .

Will made himself and Daniel breakfast at 7:00 A.M., even though his stomach protested. He'd avoided Laurie the previous evening. He knew she wanted to force him back to Tornley to talk to Hannah, so he'd escaped to the pub with Ian. This morning he left Daniel to his game, then sat in the tiny back garden with a coffee, in a futile attempt to shake off his hangover. Laurie appeared at 7:30, wrapped in a purple bathrobe and slippers with puppies' heads on them. The top of her hair was sticking up at a right angle.

She sat beside him on the bench and laid her head on his shoulder. She smelled of sleep and toothpaste. "Did you sleep OK?"

"Yeah, thanks," he lied.

"How are you feeling?"

"Don't want to talk about it."

She sat up and sipped her tea. "You need to get back there and sort it out. There's a child involved now."

"No, there's not."

"Will!" She banged his arm. "She's so beautiful. It's weird—she's like a cross between the two of you."

He shook his head. He didn't want to know. The truth was that when Hannah had held up the photo in front of Barbara, he'd been so angry that he'd focused his eyes beyond it.

"Sometimes these things are not meant to be, Lor," he said.

"Don't be stupid."

"I'm not. It's not just what happened yesterday."

"What do you mean?"

"I did something last week."

"What?"

He checked to see that Daniel was out of earshot. "A girl at work."

Laurie slapped him across the head.

"Will Riley! What's wrong with you?"

He rubbed his cheek. "I didn't sleep with her."

"You didn't?"

He drank his coffee. "I nearly did. First time, since I've been with Hannah."

Laurie made a goofy face up at Caitlin looking out of the window in her pajamas. The little girl smiled shyly when Will waved at her.

"Oh, don't be an arse," Laurie said. "You're not going to mess this up with Hannah. She might be a bit up herself, but Nan thought she was the best thing that ever happened to you. Nan only stopped worrying about you when you met her."

That was unfair. Will threw back the rest of his coffee.

"And for what it's worth, I don't think Hannah's lying, but even if she was, there's a reason for it, so you still need to sort it out," Laurie finished. "She's had a difficult year, Will."

Sam and Daniel started fighting in the living room. The noise stabbed at Will's sore head. He needed to get out of here.

"I don't know, Lor, maybe I'm just like the old man."

She looked sad. "Don't say that. Not after what Nan did for us."

He stood up, realizing he couldn't deal with this. "Listen, thanks, but I'm going back to London."

She grabbed his arm. "No."

He pulled away. "It's fine. You lot have stuff to do."

She grabbed him again. "Please tell me you're not going to do what I think you're going to do."

He gently released her hand and pulled on his jacket. "Lor, it's not your problem. You need to worry about this lot. You're a great mum. Nan always said it. It's you that's the success in this bloody family."

He leaned down and gave her a quick hug, and she took his face in her hands. They looked at each other with the brown eyes they'd inherited from their useless dads. She kissed his cheek, then he left.

38

That same morning Hannah sat at the kitchen table in Will's T-shirt, her cheeks puffy from broken sleep.

She couldn't find her phone. She'd searched the whole house. The video she needed to show Will—and anybody else—were definitely gone.

The first thing she'd done when she woke was to check outside, to see if Will had returned last night. When the car wasn't there she checked the spare room, in case he'd taken a taxi. When she saw an empty bed, her fear returned. Where was he?

She needed to find Elvie, to prove to Will that Dax and Madeleine were lying.

Rubbing her eyes, Hannah walked up to the attic and peered out at the homestead to see if there was any sign of her.

Her heart leaped.

Frank and Tiggy's blue van was in the driveway.

They were back.

She took the stairs two at a time down to the bathroom,

washed and dressed, then walked out, entered through the wall gate, and passed the polytunnels. The curtains in the bungalow were open. She banged on the front door and heard the click of heels.

Tiggy flung open the door. The hall was white and tidy, with a laminate floor and a vase of flowers on the table. She looked worried.

"Oh, it's Hannah," she shouted back into the house.

"Tiggy, I'm so glad you're back. Is Elvie here?"

Tiggy frowned. "Why do you ask, Hannah?"

Hannah took a deep breath. "I'm really sorry, but something bad happened while you were away."

Tiggy's hands stayed firmly by her sides. She turned. "Frank!" she called. "Can you come here?"

Frank appeared wearing a yellow golfing sweater, his face equally serious.

"Hi, Frank. Listen, this is a horrible thing to have to tell you, but I am afraid when you were away I saw Madeleine hurting Elvie. She hit her across the face three times, and kicked her. I asked Dax to ring you, but for some reason he told Madeleine instead, and now she's gone mad at me. Is Elvie here? Is she OK?"

Tiggy's eyebrows remained flat, clearly trying to compute this unpleasant information. Frank's happy demeanor from last week was nowhere to be seen.

Hannah continued. "I just thought I should tell you she's been upset. And I need to get Will to speak to her. Madeleine's so angry that she's told him a ridiculous lie about me and . . ."

She stuttered to a halt. Frank and Tiggy exchanged a look.

"Hannah, I have to say that Frank and I are both very upset," Tiggy started. "We came home to some terrible news. Dax's wife, Carol, is a good friend of mine and, I have to tell you, she's in absolute bits about what you've done."

Hannah blinked in disbelief. "No. Tiggy, that's not true."

Tiggy's flying hands finally made an appearance.

"Dear, this is a very quiet little place. We've all lived peaceably beside each other for a very long time. The idea that Madeleine would hurt Elvie, or that Dax would lie like this, is preposterous. And as for Carol—well. I mean, for goodness' sake. You know she's just had a hysterectomy?"

Hannah couldn't help it. She snorted. "Tiggy. Frank. You're not listening to me. I've just told you that I saw Madeleine hitting Elvie. Why are you not reacting?"

Tiggy pursed her lips. "Hannah, Elvie's been helping Madeleine out since she was a little girl. She loves Madeleine. And Elvie's not easy, Hannah. She has her tantrums. Madeleine's one of the few people who keeps an eye out for her." She shook her head impatiently. "Honestly, I'm sorry, but you've been here five minutes and everyone in the whole village is upset. We were all dreading some new development next door, but honestly, now we're all wondering if that might have been a better option. I really can't hear any more of this."

Hannah laughed bitterly. "But I haven't done anything! I'm just trying to help your daughter."

Tiggy nodded sideways at Frank. He stepped onto the veranda.

"We'd like you to leave now, please, Hannah." He put out a hand.

Hannah stayed put.

"No, Frank. Please, I'm not lying. I filmed the farmer hitting Elvie."

"You filmed it?" Frank said. "We'd like to see that, please."

Hannah sighed. "Well, it's on my phone, and I think Dax stole it."

Tiggy let out a horrified laugh that creased her blue eyelids into sockets of shimmering silver. "Please, Frank, I can't listen to any more. . . ."

Frank tried to guide Hannah down the stairs. She didn't budge.

"No. This isn't right. You're not listening to me."

"And I'd appreciate it if you would stay away from our property," Tiggy said.

When Hannah didn't move, Frank took her elbow firmly. Realizing they were not going to listen, she shook him off and marched out through the gate.

There was a clang behind.

She turned to see Frank locking it and walking away.

Hannah threw her hands up in the air. "What the hell is going on here?"

.   .   .

The traffic on the A12 was clear, so Will arrived in London by Friday lunchtime. After a stop-off at the shopping center in Shepherd's Bush to buy clothes, a bag, and toiletries, he returned to their old road. As his parking permit was still valid for a while, he parked outside their former flat, before heading down to Grayson Road.

He found Arndale Road easily again.

It had emerged from hibernation since he was last there. It was busy with cars now. Kids circled on bikes, music came out of flats. A woman in a vivid yellow African headdress sat on a step, chatting to a white-haired elderly neighbor who was trimming a bush. Will climbed the stairs, knowing that once he did this there was no going back.

He heard laughter inside as he arrived at the door.

When Clare opened it, she saw his bag. "Oh. Will. Hi."

Behind her, a boy was playing on a Wii. A console was in Clare's hand, too.

He thought of trying to explain, but gave up and shook his head. "I need somewhere to crash on the sofa for a few days."

Clare didn't flinch. "Well, my friend, you are at that place," she said, motioning him in. She flashed him a sunny smile.

●　　●　　●

Hannah returned from her bizarre meeting with Frank and Tiggy and tried to take stock.

People—for some reason she couldn't understand—were telling lies about her. Why?

Her instinct was to ring Jane and ask her for advice, as she'd done so many times before. But her former boss was in the States, her mobile number lost on Hannah's missing phone.

She tried to think.

What would she do at work, if an imprisoned teacher's statement was being discredited?

Jane's voice entered her head.

Find the evidence.

What else could she do—without the photos—to prove the truth to Will?

And then she knew.

Madeleine said Samuel had seen her having sex in Dax's truck. That clearly wasn't true—and Samuel knew it.

Hannah leaped up.

In the dining room she found her TeachersSpeakOUT office box and searched until she found the voice recorder she used for witness statements. Fired up, she locked up, fetched her bike from the garage, and cycled down the driveway, remembering too late that the map book was in the car. Imagining herself lost deep in the Suffolk countryside tonight, she turned left towards Tornley. It was still worth the risk.

Checking from the bend that Dax and his wife weren't around, she rode along till she found the narrow road to the beach, and continued onto it. Anytime she heard even a hint of a car engine in the distance, she jumped off and pulled her bike through the hedge.

She didn't want to meet Dax or Madeleine today. She needed to speak to Samuel on her own.

Hannah reached the beach ten minutes later, her forehead covered in a light sweat and peppered in tiny flies. The beach was empty, too, despite the warmer weather. Keeping in the long grass, she pushed her bike over the shingle around the headland. When Samuel's shack came into sight, she dropped her bike down into the grass, lay down, and checked. Dax's red truck was nowhere to be seen, just a beaten-up mustard hatchback that she assumed was Samuel's. Without Dax there, she prayed there was a possibility the old man might speak to her.

She pressed the "record" button on the voice recorder and placed it in her shirt pocket.

A few minutes later there was a movement.

Samuel came out of the door, carrying a dustbin bag. He moved slowly on his gangly legs, as if something hurt. His height sat oddly on a man of his age, suggesting the energy of a much younger man. He put the bag in a big black bin, then returned inside.

The door lay open.

A smell of burning drifted out from inside, and a clang of metal.

Hannah walked over nervously. "Hello?"

Samuel appeared at the door.

Close-up, he was even older than she'd realized. His chin was unshaven, with a rash of weak white hair across it. His navy sweater was stained with oil.

"Samuel, hi. I'm Hannah. I was here the other day with Dax?"

The old man stared down at her. He didn't seem completely with it.

"I was helping with the tires. Dax, from Tornley?" she tried.

He peered over her head, as if trying to spot someone he recognized.

She raised her voice, in case he was deaf. "Dax. Carol's husband."

A flicker of movement in the rheumy eyes. "Carol. Bill's girl."

She shook her head. "No, Dax's girl. Dax's wife?"

"Bill's girl," he repeated.

She was about to contradict him when an image returned from yesterday. The photo in the hallway in Dax's house that she'd recognized. An older couple with a daughter. That woman had been Carol as a teenager. And now Hannah knew why the man's face was familiar. That big, fleshy face on the narrow shoulders. The pale-blue eyes.

Carol's father was Bill.

Bill was Dax's father-in-law.

Hannah stared.

That would explain why Carol was in Bill's house with the keys.

Samuel's face had clouded over. Then he turned, as if remembering what he'd been doing. He ran his fingers over the work counter behind him, as if he were searching for something.

"Samuel," she tried again. "Dax says that you saw me in a truck the other day. When the snow was here. Me and him. Doing something. Can I ask you what you remember, because he said you saw something?"

Behind her there was a roar of an engine.

Hannah spun around. She knew that sound. The growl of diesel. A gear being slammed into place.

Without a word she slipped away from the distracted old man, back to her bike. She jumped on and cycled straight down the back of Samuel's property onto the other lane, as Dax had done last week, through the gate she'd opened for him and into the trees.

At a safe distance, she threw her bike down behind the hedge again and watched. Dax's red pickup with its wide tires screeched to a halt by the shack.

He jumped out and strode into the hut, his greasy curls flying.

He did look like a wolf, she thought.

Hunting.

But there was nothing even faintly charming about that anymore.

. . .

Hannah picked up her bike and cycled off-road behind the hedge as fast as she could, listening for the engine.

Two minutes later she reached a paved road, and checked it was clear before turning right, following Dax's route from last week towards Snadesdon.

This was useless. She needed to find Will at Laurie's and persuade him to believe her.

She cycled fast, thinking about what she'd just learned.

Bill was Dax's father-in-law? Why had Dax not mentioned

that? Was this about him being married to Carol? Had Dax thought he'd a chance with Hannah, and tried to cover up that he was married till he'd got what he wanted?

Whenever Hannah heard a vehicle behind her, she jumped off, in case it was Dax, and hid behind a hedge or trees. The last thing she wanted was another conversation with him, not out here on an empty country road, alone. Before she reached Snadesdon she saw a signpost to Thurrup and took it, memorizing the return journey for later. Two miles on, she hit a busy A-road. Traffic appeared from nowhere. Trucks and RVs sped past her every minute or so, on their way to the shops at Thurrup and the coast. She was shocked at how happy she was to see the outside world again.

She cycled the rest of the nine miles on the flat East Anglian roads.

What had she been thinking, trusting Dax like that? Idiot. Loneliness and desperation to please Barbara had lowered her defenses and wiped out her normally good instincts about people.

When she reached Thurrup's old-fashioned main street, breathless and pink-cheeked, Hannah asked a dog walker for directions to the big new supermarket. She and Will had parked there to buy wine on the day of Nan Riley's funeral. Her memory told her it was a few minutes' walk from Laurie's cul-de-sac.

Outside the supermarket Hannah shut her eyes, recalling that day.

Left. Definitely, left.

She cycled on and saw a familiar row of higgledy-piggledy pink cottages up ahead.

There. That was it.

A lane led to a row of newly built redbrick houses. She

turned in and stopped. Disappointment punched her in the gut. Their old gray station wagon wasn't there.

A few kids cycled around her. She spotted the dark hair and eyes, like Will's.

"Hi, Daniel," she called.

Laurie's elder son nodded shyly.

"Is your mum in?"

"She's gone to the post office."

"Oh, OK. Do you know where Will is?"

His eyes shifted past her. She turned to see Laurie walking into the cul-de-sac with some shopping bags, and with Caitlin and Sam.

"Is he here?" Hannah asked, taking one bag off her.

Laurie's face fell. "He didn't come back then?"

"No." A new fear ran through Hannah. Where was he?

Laurie took out her key. "Come in." She motioned Hannah into the kitchen and shut the door.

· · ·

They waited until the kids were in the garden.

"Laurie, where is he?" Hannah asked.

Laurie put down her shopping bags. "He said he was going back to London this morning. I really hoped he was coming to see you first."

Stunned, Hannah sat up at the breakfast bar, which was covered in bowls of half-eaten kids' cereal and spilt milk. "I can't believe it. I can't believe he just took Dax's word over mine like that. He didn't even give me a chance to explain. He just stormed off!"

Laurie removed the bowls and wiped the counter. "Hannah, that's Will, though. The minute anyone hurts him, he's off. It's why he was always—you know—breaking hearts when he was young. . . ."

Hannah sighed. "You mean shagging around, Laurie?"

Laurie dumped the dishes in the sink. "You know then?"

"I know." Hannah put her head in her hands. "Shit! This is our daughter, Laurie, I'm sure of it. He can't do this, not now."

Laurie put on the kettle and lifted some laundry off the other stool and sat down. "Well, I don't know if this is going to help, Hannah, but Maureen at the post office told me something weird today. She was at the funeral—one of Nan's friends?"

"What did she say?"

"Well, I told her you'd moved into Tornley Hall. And that Ian was saying how it was weird that we'd never heard of it; and she said that she had, but only because she knew the family at Tornley Farm."

"Madeleine's farm?"

Laurie nodded. "Apparently the sons went to school with Maureen's grandson. She remembers them because there was a hoo-ha when the dad had a shotgun accident and went a bit bonkers. She said the boys had to leave school to help their mum and uncle keep the farm going. But this was the weird thing. Maureen said, 'My boy was friendly with the younger one, Craig, but not so much with the older one, Dax.' "

Hannah thought she'd misheard. "No. No, that can't be right. Dax lives in the cottages."

"Well, that's what she said."

"Seriously?" Hannah sat back. What the hell was going on here? "Oh, God! Well, if that was true, it would certainly explain why Dax told Madeleine. Of course he would." She hit herself on the side of the head. "I didn't even think they might be related."

"And you're sure Madeleine was hitting Elvie, not someone else?"

"Definitely—that day anyway. I saw her yelling at someone else another time, too. I filmed that, as well."

Laurie picked up a half-eaten satsuma from the worktop and ate a segment. "Who was that then? The other son? The uncle?"

"It might have been the other son. I haven't seen the uncle, though. He might have died by now, I suppose."

Laurie chewed thoughtfully. "Maureen told me his name. Something beginning with an S." She put down her cup. "Stephen . . . ? No. Samuel."

Hannah's mouth fell open. "Laurie—you are bloody joking."

"What?" Laurie asked.

Hannah thought for a moment. "Laurie, there is something seriously weird going on over there. Samuel's the one who 'saw' me having sex in the truck. I went to ask him about it today, and Dax turned up, as if he knew I was there, so I left. And that day on the beach, when it was supposed to have happened, there was a blond woman and kids in the distance, but now I'm wondering whether it was Carol and her kids, and that she lied that it was her friend. It's almost as if they're all working together to make Will believe Dax. Why would they do that?"

Laurie poured the tea. "What's Elvie's surname?"

"The flower place is called Mortrens', so Elvie Mortren, I suppose." Hannah rubbed her face. "Why?"

Laurie put a cup in front of her and took hers out through the kitchen door. "Right. I've got an idea."

. . .

Laurie was gone for twenty minutes.

Hannah sat, sipping her tea, wondering where Will could

be. All her numbers—for his mobile and the studio, as well as Mum and Dad's, Jane's, and everybody else's—were stored on her bloody phone.

There was a giggle, and Caitlin rushed in from the garden, asking shyly for a cookie.

Hannah found her one, then went to push her on the swings.

The little girl flew in the air, her blond hair flying. Hannah remembered Caitlin being born three years ago. The panic of picking up this tiny baby when they came to Thurrup, feeling the whole family's eyes on her. Desperately hoping that Nan Riley and Laurie wouldn't ask about her and Will starting a family—not when her belly was still sore from that morning's IVF injection.

She thought of the photo of the little red-haired girl back at Tornley, and her determination grew.

That was her baby, and she wasn't giving her up. She wanted this with her own child—now. She was ready.

Laurie rapped on the window and motioned Hannah back inside.

"Right, my mate Jonathan is a police officer on the coast. I've rung him and told him one of my dads at the nursery was driving past Tornley and saw a special-needs woman he thinks is called Elvie Mortren being assaulted on Tornley Farm by a tall woman in her sixties. I said the dad doesn't want to get involved, so he told me anonymously. Jonathan's going to ask around at the farm and at Tiggy's. They'll think it's a bloke who's reported it, not you. I mean, if that farmer hit Elvie outside, anyone could have seen it from the road. It'll put the wind up them anyway. Maybe they'll back off and leave you alone."

Hannah nodded. "Thanks. But how would this 'driver' know Elvie's name?"

"Well, people must know the Mortrens, if they have a business round here."

Hannah felt reassured. "And you don't think it'll come back to me. I can't have Barbara finding out about any of this."

"I didn't mention your name."

"Thanks, Laurie."

The boys ran into the garden, and Daniel took over pushing Caitlin on the swing. Hannah imagined the little red-haired girl in the middle of this happy throng. Three ready-made cousins.

The thought galvanized her. She jumped up. "Right. I better go, before it gets dark."

Laurie picked up her keys. "No. I'll give you a lift—and, by the way, take this."

She handed Hannah a small mobile.

"It's Daniel's one, for school. You need one out there."

"But . . ."

"It's fine. I'll give him mine."

Grateful, Hannah took it. They shouted good-bye to Ian and the kids, put Hannah's bike in the car, and drove out of Thurrup.

"Thanks for this," Hannah said, watching the light dying over the fields. She gave an awkward smile. "I always assumed you weren't very happy about me and Will. . . ."

Laurie glanced over. "Don't be daft—you're the best thing that's ever happened to him."

Hannah frowned, surprised. "Really?"

Laurie turned back onto the B-road. "Of course you are, silly. I wonder sometimes how much you know about our Will, and what he used to be like."

"Well, quite a bit."

"OK, well, he must have told you that his dad buggered off after poor Auntie Rita got ill. And he was a child carer—he used to have to do everything. I mean, everything. Shopping, sorting the food, washing her sometimes, getting her medicine."

Hannah nodded. She didn't say that when Will first told her, she almost didn't believe him.

"So Nan took him for the summer, to give him a break, and when he arrived he was always quiet for a few days. Then he'd go wild. Drove her insane."

Hannah shifted uncomfortably. "What, like criminal wild?"

Laurie turned into Snadesdon. "No, nothing really bad. More self-destructive. Like if we all went clubbing in Great Yarmouth, he'd always end up in a fight with the bouncers. And he was always causing problems between my friends. They all fancied him, of course, and he'd mess them about, then piss off back to Salford and nobody would talk to me for about three months."

"Oh, Laurie."

The marshes appeared to their right.

"But he stopped it when he met you. Although there was that one time he messed up, and you dumped him?"

Hannah stared, surprised. He'd told Laurie that?

"Yeah," she said uncertainly. "He did. He slept with an old girlfriend when we were starting to hang out together. He said that she was upset that he was starting to see me, and it just sort of happened. He was drunk."

Laurie took the turn out of Snadesdon, checking both ways on the empty road. "Well, he was cut up—he really thought he'd blown it with you. You were the first girl who'd ever told him to get lost."

Hannah tensed as they approached Tornley. Nothing felt good about coming back here. They passed the cottages and peered in.

"So they're all related? That's creepy," Laurie said.

"Hmm."

"You get that round here sometimes, in rural places—but we're not all like that."

"I know," Hannah said.

"Ian's from Woodbridge, you know."

Hannah smiled at her joke, and Laurie chuckled.

They pulled up in the driveway of Tornley Hall, Hannah praying that Will's car would miraculously be there, but it wasn't. Laurie turned off the engine and looked up. "Damn, I should have asked Maureen about the house, too, in case Nan ever told her why she was so cross that night."

They got out and lifted Hannah's bike out of the back.

Laurie pointed. "Now I remember standing here, getting into Nan's car, and she was furious. Somebody was shouting in the house, but it wasn't at us."

Hannah put the bike against the wall. "Probably Madeleine, telling lies and pissing Olive and Peter off, too. Listen, thanks for the lift. And for your help."

"No worries. Ring me on that mobile if you haven't heard from Will tonight. I'm under 'Mum.' And I'll text Daniel's number to Will, and tell him to call you."

Hannah gave her an awkward hug. "Thanks."

Laurie smiled and drove off with a wave.

Watching her, Hannah realized that if Will had actually left her, he'd still be close to Laurie the rest of his life. Laurie would always be family.

But not her.

Hannah went inside with a stab of pain at the thought of losing him.

She looked around. The hall was clean and tidy, ready for a family that was only going to exist if she made it happen.

39

Laurie texted Hannah later that evening, to say she'd sent Will Daniel's number and told him to ring her. But Will didn't call Hannah that night, or on Saturday, or on Sunday, either.

On Monday morning she was starting to despair.

Trying to stay positive, she rang the phone company and managed to get a rescheduled appointment tomorrow for the landline engineer.

As she put the phone down she saw Gemma waving on the driveway, and heard a letter fall on the mat.

She ran down, desperate for news. The name of Barbara's office was stamped on the front.

Hannah ripped it open:

Dear Will and Hannah,

Lovely to see you in Suffolk, and congratulations again on your new home. Just to let you know that X's social workers are very interested in meeting you. They've suggested this Friday, for a home visit. Please let me know if you can do it (I texted you, Hannah—not sure if you've received it?). I double-checked, and I was right: there is no other family involved.

Best wishes,
Barbara

Hannah read it again, a smile breaking through the misery of what was happening. If the little girl's social workers liked them, it could happen quickly. A matching panel, then two weeks at the child's foster home to acclimatize them all to each other, before bringing her back home.

They were so close. This was news that Will should be sharing.

She lifted Daniel's phone and tried Will, knowing he'd come home when he heard this.

"Will, it's me. Barbara has been in touch. I have amazing news. Please ring me back on Daniel's phone."

She sat on the hall stairs, holding the phone, willing it to ring.

She waited twenty minutes, then tried again.

"Will, please, this is stupid. How many times can I keep saying it: it didn't happen? You need to ring me and sort this out, or we're going to lose her."

When he didn't reply, she texted Laurie and asked her for another number. There was only one more place to try.

The number arrived a minute later, and she walked down to the lane for a better signal. She knew it was a fifty-fifty chance it would be answered.

"Hello," said a quiet, sad voice.

"Hi, Rita, it's Hannah."

"Hi, love." Will's mum always sounded as if she were stuck behind a high wall, unable to burst through.

"I was just looking for Will. He's not there, is he?"

"No, love. He rang me Saturday, to make sure my shopping got delivered. I thought he was with you, at the new house."

"Oh, don't worry, I must have got mixed up. He had loads of work to do, so he'll probably be at the studio."

She waited for Rita to ask how the move had gone. "Will you tell him, love, the chicken only had a day on it. If he tells them, they might send a new one next week. Save him a few pennies. They did last time."

Hannah's ache for Will grew. "I will, Rita. Listen, you'll have to come and see us. Stay for a few days."

"Thanks, love," Rita said, even though they both knew she wouldn't. She hadn't even managed to attend Nan Riley's funeral.

When they had said their good-byes, Hannah sat, not knowing what to do next.

In the scullery she saw the last can of paint for Tornley Hall.

It was not a cheap, DIY color-matched version, like the gray for the cupboards. It was expensive and carefully picked, the color of sunshine.

Hannah stood up.

Fuck Will. The social workers were coming on Friday.

She had to keep going. All she could do was pray that he would get her message and see sense.

• • •

Hannah spent the rest of the day preparing the second bedroom for decorating. The room, which had been Peter Horseborrow's, was a little smaller than theirs, but still a fantastic size for a child. It had a pretty window out onto the front lawn and a small Victorian fireplace, a built-in wooden wardrobe with shelves, and a stripped wooden floor. It was in fairly good condition. There was a faded rectangle of lighter wood on the floor, where Peter's single bed must have stood for many decades, and a similar one in the middle of the room that might have been under a rug. There were lots of small cracks in the ceiling, but only one large one on the white walls. Hannah went to examine it, hoping there was enough filler left.

As she crossed onto the faded area of wood, her foot hit a loose floorboard. It flipped up an inch and she stumbled.

That wasn't safe. She'd have to nail it down before the little girl's social workers came.

Every surface in here would have to be perfect.

.   .   .

An hour later Hannah was up a ladder filling the ceiling cracks when she saw a police car passing down the lane.

Blood rushed to her cheeks. That was it—there was no going back now.

She ran upstairs to spy through the attic skylight. Frank and Tiggy were on the veranda, looking agitated. Tiggy's hands swatted the air. The metal gates opened and the police car entered. Abruptly Tiggy and Frank's stance changed. They waved cheerfully.

The police officers got out. One was around Laurie's age— her school friend Jonathan, presumably. There was an intense discussion. Hannah creaked open the skylight to see if she could hear it, but then the police officers entered the bungalow and the door shut.

Hannah bit her fingernail. Would Tiggy and Frank believe it was a passing male driver from Thurrup who'd reported the assault on Elvie, and not her?

To occupy her mind, she continued filling the ceiling. Ten minutes later the police car passed her driveway again, going in the opposite direction, and appeared in the distance gliding up to Madeleine's farmyard.

Oh, God. The shit would hit the fan now.

She carried on working, trying not to think about the discussion taking place right now across the field.

It was an hour later, just as she was finishing on the last of the ceiling cracks, that a vehicle pulled up down below. It was Laurie's blue station wagon.

Maybe she had news.

Hannah went to let her in, expecting to see Laurie's cheerful expression from yesterday.

It had gone.

.   .   .

"Do you mind if I carry on upstairs while we talk, or the filler will dry wrong?" Hannah asked uncertainly.

Laurie followed her up to the child's bedroom. She said nothing as Hannah climbed back up the ladder.

"So what happened?" Hannah asked, flattening out the paste she'd just applied.

Laurie's eyes scanned the bedroom. Hannah saw her looking at the box of child-safe locks and felt strangely exposed—her hopes laid bare. Laurie put down her bag and settled on the floor. "Er, Jonathan's pissed off at me is what happened, Hannah."

"Why?" She realized Laurie was avoiding eye contact.

"Well, he went to see the Mortrens next door, and said that a man from Thurrup had reported seeing Elvie assaulted in Madeleine's field."

"And?"

Laurie picked at a knot in the floorboard. "They said they didn't know who he was talking about."

Hannah hesitated, her trowel midair. "What do you mean?"

"They said they didn't know who Elvie Mortren was."

Hannah put the trowel down. "Of course they know who she is!" she exclaimed. "Maybe her name's different. Tiggy said they'd always called her Elvie, but maybe her name's Elvira or something."

"No, Hannah. They didn't know her at all."

Hannah searched Laurie's face for the alliance of yesterday and couldn't find it. "Sorry, Laurie, but that's mad. They have a daughter. Did he ask them that?"

"They said they didn't."

The idea was so ridiculous that Hannah laughed. "But they do, Laurie! Why would they lie? Your friend's a police officer. That's stupid. He can easily check the records and see that she lives there."

Laurie nodded. "He did, and there's no other resident at that house. Just Margaret and Frances Mortren. He said they were trying to be helpful, but they had no idea who he was talking about. They don't even know anyone of that description."

Hannah climbed down, not believing what she was hearing. "But why would they say that? I met her."

Laurie's eyes flicked away. "Then he went to the farm, and the cottages in Tornley, and everyone said the same thing. Nobody knows her."

Hannah banged her trowel on the windowsill. "Laurie! This is crazy! Elvie was here. Tiggy and Frank sent her to cut the grass. I spoke to her. Will saw her."

"Will was here when she cut the grass?" Laurie said, surprised.

Hannah thought. "No, he was in London then. But he definitely saw her. He told me he offered a woman who sounded like Elvie a lift on his way to the station. She was carrying something heavy."

Laurie looked confused. "So he has spoken to her?"

Hannah put her hands on her forehead, frustrated. "Not really, no. He said she ignored him and kept walking."

"Why?"

"I don't know why! Because she has learning difficulties? Because she was scared of him? I have no idea. She hardly speaks to me."

Laurie scratched her head. "Hannah, is it possible you've got mixed up? One thing they all said is that farms around here employ foreign casual workers. Maybe you thought this woman had special needs, when actually she couldn't speak English? Maybe that's why she ignored Will? Maybe you misheard her name even?"

Hannah had to stop herself throwing the trowel at the wall. "Laurie, please! Her name is Elvie, and Tiggy sent her round here. Tiggy told me she'd had a difficult birth. I spoke to Elvie. She made a fire in my garden. She ate my sandwiches." She pointed to the windows. "She cleaned those. I gave her a bath, and she was covered in bruises. And what I said happened." She pointed. "In that field over there. I am not mad."

"You gave her a bath?"

"Yes, in the middle of the night. She was filthy. Why is this so difficult to believe?"

She saw that Laurie's legs were pointing towards the door.

"I'm just confused, Hannah. So, Frank and Tiggy said she was their daughter?"

"Yes, they—" Hannah stopped. Had they? "Oh. Or . . . Hang on. I suppose I assumed that she . . ."

Her mind whirred backwards. She had simply assumed Elvie was their daughter. That she'd been in Spain with them that first week. If that wasn't true, could Elvie have been here all the time? Images flew at Hannah: of Madeleine shouting at a dark figure in the snow that first week. Was that Elvie, too? And then of the looming figure in the sitting room under the blanket.

More things: the snow-penis meant to frighten her out of the house; the shadow at the window.

"Oh, my God! Of course. That makes complete sense," Hannah said, marching to the door. "Hang on."

She ran up to the attic and returned with a bin bag. She pulled out a dusty T-shirt and jogging trousers. A familiar sour smell rose up.

"These are hers—Elvie's. I've just realized. I found someone sleeping rough in the house when Will was in London, and I thought it was a man . . ." Her eyes opened wide. "No. Wait. Dax said it was a man. But I think it was Elvie. She escaped out of the window, and we nailed it shut."

Laurie looked pained. "Who nailed what shut?"

"Me and Dax. The side window."

"What did Will say?"

Hannah rubbed her face. "I didn't tell him. I thought he'd make me call the police and it would mess things up, with Barbara coming."

She saw the uncertainty on Laurie's face.

Hannah thought about all the people she and the charity had helped abroad, and who depended on Hannah, Jane, and the others believing their story. Now she finally knew—really knew, for the first time—how they felt.

She also knew how frantic people could become when no one believed them, and she forced herself to take a breath, trying to sound calm. "Laurie, I know this sounds mad, but everything I'm saying is true. And I need you and Will to believe me."

Laurie bit her lip.

Hannah continued. "Frank and Tiggy sent a woman they—not me—called Elvie to cut my grass. They know who she is. I saw Madeleine assaulting this same woman. And I woke up and found her wandering around the house. We spoke—in English—and she was very upset, and dirty and hungry, and I helped her. Dax knew who she was, too. He said Elvie had tantrums. Why they're all denying it, I don't know. Maybe she is Frank and Tiggy's daughter, and they're scared I'll tell social services that they left her alone, and that someone will put her in assisted housing. Maybe that's why they don't have her registered as living there. Maybe they're getting too old to cope with her, but don't want to lose her."

Laurie shifted on the floor. "Hannah."

"What?"

"It's not that I don't believe that's what you think happened. It's just . . ."

"What?"

She pointed at the walls of the bedroom. "I don't know. You're clearly under strain. Do you think, maybe, it's possible that you're just so anxious about the adoption you're . . ." She paused.

Please, Hannah thought, *don't say it*.

". . . I don't know—the mind does weird things. I know when I saw a bereavement counselor after Nan died, she said grief can be like a car crash to the brain. People muddle things up. And I know you didn't lose a baby last summer, Hannah—as in a baby died—but maybe losing that little boy, when you'd set your heart so much on adopting him, felt like a massive loss and . . ."

Hannah thought about the little red-haired girl in the photo. She was fading in front of her eyes.

She struggled to stay polite. "Laurie, listen, for my work I've sat and listened to people telling me incredible stories that are so unbelievable, even I didn't believe them at first. But I am telling you the truth. Tiggy and Frank are covering something up about Elvie, and Madeleine is hurting her. And Dax and the rest of Madeleine's family are lying about me, and what I did, to protect her. Can you please ask Jonathan to try again?"

Laurie got up off the floor. "Hannah, Jonathan wanted to know who the parent at the nursery was. I think he thought it was someone winding me up. I can't ask him again." She dusted herself off. "Right. Listen, I have to get back. If you want my advice, you need to forget about this woman for now. It's not your business. From what I can see, your business is talking to Will, and starting your family."

"She's called Elvie," Hannah said quietly.

Laurie sighed and walked out.

·   ·   ·

Hannah spent the rest of the afternoon sanding the ceiling cracks and the rough windowpane, her head buzzing.

She ran back over all of the details, checking that Laurie wasn't right.

Elvie definitely spoke English.

Tiggy and Frank were definitely lying.

She was so distracted that when the window was finished and she moved the ladder to fill the crack on the wall, she forgot about the loose floorboard from earlier on. As she climbed up, the ladder leg dipped down, nearly toppling her over.

"Great! That's just what you need now," she said out loud. "A broken neck." She went to fetch the hammer and nails from the toolbox by the window.

Outside, the light was starting to fade.

She stopped and stared at the garden below. The garage doors were wide open.

Her heart leaped. Was Will back?

Dropping the hammer, she ran down and flung open the front door.

Disappointed, she saw the driveway was empty. It could be Elvie, though. At least, if she found Elvie, that would be a start to Will and Laurie believing her.

"Elvie?" Hannah called, approaching the garage. She scanned the dusky shadows for the looming shape of her. It still smelled of the donkey.

She pressed the light switch, ready to peer up on the roof shelf. There was a click, but no light.

Too late, she saw glass on the ground under the light fitting and heard a scrape of metal.

Hannah turned.

Madeleine and Dax were pulling the garage doors shut behind them.

"What are you doing!" she yelled. She tried to push herself out of the gap between the closing doors, but Dax blocked her way.

"We's bringing you a welcome gift," Madeleine said, slamming them shut.

They towered over her in the dark garage.

She backed off, the threat clear. Her voice trembled. "Let me out now, or I'll call the police."

"Found your phone, have ya?" Dax asked.

Hannah touched the wall to steady herself. As her eye adjusted to the gloomy light, she could see the likeness now. The height and broad shoulders, and Madeleine's gray hair, which could once have been black, like Dax's.

"You need to keep your nose out of our business," Madeleine said, prodding at her.

Hannah glared. "Well, that won't be difficult, will it, as the person I saw you beating doesn't seem to exist, does she?"

"Who's that then?" Madeleine asked Dax.

"Some vagrant, I expect."

He stepped forward. Hannah tried not to flinch.

"How's that adoption of yours going?"

Why had she ever told him?

"How'd your social worker—Barbara, is it?—like to hear about our dirty little romance down on the beach, when she comes back with your little girl's social workers?"

Hannah froze. He *did* have her phone. And the new text message from Barbara about Friday's meeting that she'd never received.

"You know the police can trace where calls are received?" she said, ashamed at the tremor in her voice.

"Then I expect they'll find your phone on the beach, where you dropped it, then, won't they? Just before you and me had our special moment, eh?" Dax winked in a way that made her want to shower.

Hannah struggled to hold his gaze. "Nothing happened between you and me, and if you say again to anyone that it did,

I'll take legal action and you'll have to prove it. I know you're all related round here—so nothing would hold up in court."

Dax grinned. "Well, see, I don't think you will. Way I see it, you need to do what we say, or you don't get what you want."

He stepped closer again. This time she backed away, catching her shirt on the hook she'd used to tie the donkey up. She found herself becoming less certain about what Dax would be prepared to do.

He already knew nobody believed her.

"You know what I heard," Dax said. She could smell the oil, and the stale cigarette smoke on his breath, now. "That there's all these Londoners move to the countryside, then realize they've made a mistake. It's not for them, see? They go home."

The menace in his words hung in the air.

"Anyway, *honestly*," Dax said, turning without warning and opening the garage door again, "it's *actually* been very nice to see you."

"And you be careful out in those marshes," Madeleine said. "Shooting season soon. You don't want some old boy to get you mixed up with a wood pigeon."

As quickly as they came, they were gone.

Hannah stumbled out after them.

On the front doorstep was a wicker basket. She could smell its rancid stink before she reached it. A dead pheasant was squashed into it, its feathers and beak a muddy mess of matted scarlet, blue, and gray.

Maggots crawled in its feathers.

Retching, Hannah ran to the fence and threw the basket as hard as she could into Madeleine's field, then returned and double-locked the front door.

40

Hannah sat on the hall stairs, dazed. Something sinister was happening here in Tornley that she didn't understand.

Frank and Tiggy were lying to the police about Elvie.

Dax and Madeleine were trying to intimidate her into leaving.

Everyone in the village, in fact, was lying. Why?

Outside, the fledgling spring sun fell weakly from the sky. Shadows gathered on her newly painted walls.

Hannah tried to think. She knew from professional experience that tyrants usually won. TSO campaigned for people who were threatened for trying to speak and work freely as educators. Yet its success stories would always be in the minority. The tyrants had the power. She'd seen them threaten victims and witnesses, and their families. Chase them out of jobs and homes and into hiding. Discredit their stories and reputations. Hide the evidence.

She thumped her fists on her thighs.

But she *knew* these people in Tornley were lying.

She had photographed Madeleine hitting Elvie. Frank and Tiggy had lied to the authorities about the existence of a vulnerable woman that Hannah had met. Dax had told a shocking lie to Will, to discredit Hannah and shut her up.

Elvie is "not your business," Laurie had said.

But if Hannah didn't speak out for Elvie, who would?

"Your business is talking to Will, and starting your family," Laurie had said.

Yes, but what kind of person did Hannah want that little girl to see, when she arrived? A coward?

She stood up and returned upstairs to the child's bedroom with renewed determination. Dax and Madeleine were hiding something. They were possibly coercing people—including Frank and Tiggy—to do the same, and it had something to do with Elvie. She was going to discover the truth, get help for Elvie, and expose Dax's lies. Then she was going to persuade Will to come home.

Until then, she would carry on exactly as she'd planned.

She was going to adopt a child with Will, and bring her up in this home, where he was going to start his business. And nobody in bloody Tornley was going to stop them.

. . .

An hour later Hannah had painted the front wall by the window a pale yellow, and had formed a new plan.

First, she had to prove that Elvie existed. If the residents of Tornley were going to deny it, she had to inquire further afield, beyond the village. Elvie was so distinctive—someone must know her.

Then, as Hannah reached upwards to touch up the last patch, someone entered her mind.

Gemma—the postwoman. Perhaps the only person who came to Tornley regularly and who didn't live here. Gemma must have seen Elvie.

Hannah leaped down, checking her watch. It was nearly seven o'clock. Gemma delivered the mail around ten in the morning. Tomorrow, Hannah would be waiting for her by the gate.

Tonight, however, she'd get this room done.

She moved the ladder to the next wall, over the faded patch of wooden floor where Peter Horseborrow's bed had once been. She climbed up and yelped as the ladder listed to the right, remembering once again—too late—the loose floorboard.

Cursing, she fetched the hammer to secure it. She pushed one end of the yard-long floorboard, to see where nails were required. To her surprise, it see-sawed up at the other end. The whole board was clearly just resting on a joist below. This was dangerous. Presumably, if it had been hidden by a bed for a hundred years, nobody had ever noticed.

Hannah picked up the hammer. Just as well she'd noticed it, before a social worker stepped on it. She took a nail—then stopped.

Twenty small black nail holes ran along the edge of the floorboard. It wasn't one or two nails that were missing—it was every single one. Why?

Hannah lifted up the floorboard.

She stared at the sight that met her. A pile of postcards and letters was tucked against the joist.

. . .

Two minutes later Hannah was sitting, against the wall, with the secret stash spread out in front of her. Her face broke into a shocked grin as she flicked through a pile of sepia and black-and-white postcards. "Naughty Peter," she said out loud. It was an extensive collection of faded Victorian or Edwardian porn. Young women, either naked or semidressed in lace dress and petticoats, sat astride each other or on various well-to-do gentlemen sporting handlebar moustaches and black socks, and occasionally a birch stick. One of the oddest images was of an older man wearing a monocle, top hat, and morning coat, lying back on a chaise longue, his erection taking center stage. Hannah's mind flicked briefly to the snow-penis in the garden. Had Elvie seen this postcard?

She sat back. Peter had never married, by all accounts. This little hiding place under the floor had presumably been his only place of privacy from his sister.

She pushed the postcards aside and undid a bundle of three yellowed envelopes. What were these? Letters to a secret lover?

To her surprise, the letters were still sealed. They had never been opened. There was a blue stamp on each, with a photo of King George VI and a price of "2½d." "Air Mail" was written by hand on the left, yet there was no post-office stamp. The addresses made no sense, either:

D. Burstenstein
All The Kings Horses
And All The Kings Men
Couldn't Put Humpty
Together Again

Feeling strangely uncomfortable about invading the privacy of a man who had died, Hannah opened the first envelope and pulled out a letter. It was written in old-fashioned copperplate on two sheets, but again in the same gobbledygook verse of nursery rhymes. The date at the top was August 19, 1945. Who was D. Burstenstein? Had Peter Horseborrow's secret lover, in fact, been a man? It would have been difficult, she supposed, for him to have been openly gay back then.

She checked the envelope again and found a photo inside.

It immediately appeared to disprove her theory. The black-and-white image was of an unsmiling girl, around sixteen years old, standing against an ivy-strewn wall. There was something familiar about the girl, but it wasn't Olive. Olive had pale features and a round face. This girl's face was narrow, her eyes and hair dark. In the teenager's arms was a newborn baby. Hannah stuck out her bottom lip, surprised. She'd always assumed from what Brian, the estate agent, had said that Peter had been unmarried. Perhaps that wasn't true. Perhaps he'd had a family early on, then lost them and returned to live with Olive?

Hannah followed the handwriting to the bottom and saw a signature. It appeared to have been scrawled by a three-year-old: MaBeL vYnE.

"Hello, Mabel Vyne. Who were you then?" Hannah asked, opening the second envelope. The letter inside was almost identical: two pages of nursery rhymes with the same scrawled signature. In this one, however, the date was January 30, 1946, and Mabel Vyne—if that's who she was in the photo—stood against a tree holding the baby, who was now around six months. The baby shared the teenager's dark hair and eyes and unsmiling face.

Why was Mabel Vyne writing nursery rhymes and putting them in unopened envelopes? And why was Peter hiding them under his bed? Tornley was turning out to be a place of more than one secret. Hannah opened the third envelope.

The same two-page letter and a photo dropped out, this time

dated 15 August 1946. The baby wore a dress and had short hair brushed to the side in curls. Its gender still wasn't clear. Mother and child sat side by side, awkwardly. Mabel wore a plain dress and flat shoes. Her hair was now cut in a bob, pushed to the side with a pin. Within a year she'd transformed herself—to a grown woman. Hannah examined the photo closely. The young woman's face was even more familiar now.

Something was . . .

Hannah peered closer.

A stained glass curve of feathers was visible behind Mabel's shoulder. That was the peacock window. That was the hallway in Tornley Hall.

She dropped that photograph and checked the other two. The wall behind Mabel in the first shot: was that their Victorian garden wall, behind the kitchen? And in the distance behind the tree of the second image: was that a group of spiky cat's tails in the marsh across the lane?

Hannah frowned. This young woman, Mabel Vyne, had been standing here, downstairs in Tornley Hall, with a baby in the mid-1940s, nearly seventy years ago. Had she lived here with Peter and Olive? Who was she? And why were these letters sealed and never sent.

Hannah sat back, wishing she had the Internet to do a local-history search. Somebody, somewhere, had probably documented life around this area in the 1940s.

Then she remembered.

.   .   .

Five minutes later Hannah stood bent over in the attic, rummaging through the boxes of books from the sitting room. The idea had come as she'd rechecked the dates on the letters.

The old Tornley Hall household ledgers were in a book near the window. She yanked them out and sat on the dusty floor, searching for the 1940s domestic accounts.

Now she thought about it, skimming through them, there was something strange about these ledgers. Decades of household costs for Tornley Hall, yet no foreign-travel costs listed, anywhere. And neither was there a single week when groceries had not been purchased. It was almost as if Peter and Olive had never left Tornley, let alone visited the exotic foreign locations of their books and paintings.

The ledger she wanted finally appeared in the middle of the pile: 1940–1950: *Household Accounts*.

Hannah leaned against a rafter and began her search to see if Mabel Vyne had ever been listed as a householder.

•   •   •

She nearly missed it.

Twenty minutes later her eyes were starting to skim over the cost of butcher's sausages, candles, and vinegar, when two letters caught her eye: *Hat, M.V.*—2s.

"Yes!" she hissed. Mabel Vyne.

Now that she knew that the name was definitely listed, she double-checked the entries she'd already skimmed.

In 1945 there was another one she'd missed: *Dress, M.V.*—5s.

Five shillings? That was a lot less than the fifty-five shillings that Olive had spent on her dresses.

Hannah searched and found some more.

In total there were one or two entries each year, all through the 1940s. Whoever Mabel had been, she either had her own income or had only lived in Tornley Hall from time to time. On a whim, Hannah carried on into the 1950s: *Hat, M.V.*—1s. Mabel continued to appear a few times a year in the 1950s, and then in the 1960s and 1970s.

The last entry Hannah found was in 1986: *Shoes, M.V.—£4.*

This was interesting. Someone called Mabel Vyne had visited or lived in Tornley Hall, at least off and on, for around forty years.

So what had happened to her child?

· · ·

There was one more place to look. Downstairs, in the kitchen cupboard, Hannah found the photo album that Elvie had flung on the floor the other night.

Eagerly she flicked through it. The photos were again black-and-white ones. The fashions worn by Olive and Peter's friends suggested that it was now the 1960s. Peter certainly had more hair than he did in the images from the 1970s.

Once again the photos were located around Tornley Hall, and at what she now recognized as Graysea Bay, increasing her new suspicions that Peter and Olive rarely left home. There was one shot of a grinning Olive in the lane on a bike, the sun glinting on her plaits.

The photos were only four-by-four inches, and there were six on each page. She searched carefully. Finally, halfway through, she saw it.

In one set of images Olive, Peter, and their friends were eating a picnic on the shingle beach, sitting on rugs. Behind them a dark-haired woman leaned over a basket, in profile.

Hannah peered. Was that Mabel? She would be older now, of course, maybe in her mid-thirties, but the coloring was definitely familiar.

She flicked over to the next page, then the next—and stopped.

The dark-haired woman was standing up now, still in the distance, but closer and face-on to the camera, behind Olive and her friends. While they were laughing, she was not. Hannah was almost certain it was the sulky teenager of the earlier photo, twenty years on. She had the same dark eyes and hair, and the long, narrow jaw. There was that same dull gaze in her eyes. With other people to give perspective, Hannah now realized that Mabel Vyne—if it was indeed her—was very tall.

She held the book under the lamp to see better. Her breathing felt shallow. Goose pimples covered her arms.

She knew that sullen face. That's why it was so familiar in its teenage form.

"I am not seeing ghosts!" she whispered.

This photo was taken fifty years ago, yet she was looking straight at Elvie.

41

Despite being exhausted from the day's events, that night Hannah tossed and turned in bed. The curtains were once again closed against the black night. Disturbing images came at her from all angles. Every creak made her glance at the door.

Before she'd turned out the light she'd rung Will for the twentieth time, to find that his voice mail was now full. If he didn't call her tomorrow, then she was going to London.

Eventually she fell into an uneasy sleep, only to be jerked awake by images of Dax and Madeleine in the garage, towering above her. Twice she got up and double-checked the locks downstairs, put on another lamp, and then rejammed the wooden wedge underneath her bedroom door. To chase away the memory of the garage encounter, Hannah summoned the image of the little red-haired girl. Hard as she tried, however, she couldn't picture the two of them and Will at Tornley Hall. She tried to imagine a trampoline on the lawn, and swings, but could only see scrubby grass and piles of rotten leaves and the dead pheasant, its rotten stink back in her nostrils.

So, instead, she turned on the bedside light at 3:00 A.M. and, to distract herself, picked up the old letters from the floor and thought more about the mystery of Mabel Vyne, and her physical similarity to Elvie. How could they be related? Apart from the fact that Elvie might be Frank and Tiggy's daughter, the baby in the teenage Mabel's arms in 1945 would be almost seventy years old now. Elvie was forty at most.

At some point Hannah did fall asleep, jerking awake when the telephone engineer rang the doorbell at nine o'clock. She dressed and waited impatiently for him to install the phone, Internet, and television channels, checking out the window for Gemma.

As soon as the broadband was up, Hannah flung open her laptop and, joyful at being connected back to the outside world, checked a long list of new e-mails in her in-box. One in particular stood out. It was from Laurie and had arrived yesterday morning, a few hours before Laurie's talk with Jonathan and her visit to Tornley Hal. The tone was friendly and supportive—clearly written before Jonathan told Laurie off for sending him on a wild-goose chase:

> Hi Hannah, not getting through on the mobile, so
> e-mailing in case. Just to let you know that Jonathan
> is going over to Tornley this morning—you might see
> him around. And also I spoke to Maureen again. She
> did vaguely remember Nan being upset at a house over
> near Snadesdon. She thinks it was something to do with
> catching an old man shouting at a young woman in
> the house, and Nan telling him to lay off her. He didn't

like it, and she gave him hell, and that's probably why I
remember Nan rushing us out, cross.

Hannah read it again, confused. If Will had been six or seven
on his visit here with Nan Riley and Laurie, it would have been
around the early 1980s. Who was the young woman in Tornley
Hall at that time? It couldn't have been Mabel Vyne—she would
have been in her fifties. Olive would have been sixty-plus.

Intrigued, she waved off the engineer and sat back at her
computer. She might be isolated geographically out here, but
the screen gave her a renewed sense of empowerment. Dax, and
everyone else round here, said that Elvie didn't exist. Well, she
could now find proof by herself.

First she inserted "Elvie Mortren" into a search engine.
Nothing appeared. She tried possible variations and combina-
tions of Elvie's name, as well as the location and Frank and
Tiggy's names, but nothing came up. That was strange.

Next she tried "Elvie Vyne," in case the strange young
woman was related to Mabel. When nothing materialized for
that name, either, Hannah tried "Mabel Vyne, Suffolk."

This time there was a hit. She peered at the screen.

It was just one link, and a modern one at that. An Ipswich
newspaper cutting about a planning application refused in 2012
for a new hall. The photograph of a group of cross-looking pa-
rishioners accompanied the photograph. Mabel Vyne, a plump
woman with glasses and short gray hair, was their spokesper-
son. From here, Hannah could see no similarity between her
and the teenage Mabel in Peter's black-and-white photographs,
or indeed to Elvie. But surely there was some link? Mabel Vyne
could not be a very common name in Suffolk.

She stood up and walked to the window. Maybe the two Mabel Vynes were related, even distantly. It was certainly worth finding out if it explained why Frank and Tiggy were hiding Elvie from the authorities.

Outside there was a crunch of tires on gravel.

Hannah ran to the door.

Gemma.

42

Will woke that Tuesday morning and stretched out on Clare's sofa, his back muscles even tighter than yesterday. He surveyed the whisky glasses and ashtray from last night. His watch said half past nine. Sitting up, he squinted at Clare's and Jamie's bedroom doors. Both were open. They'd left quietly again, without waking him.

He eased his legs round off the sofa, and groaned with pain. He sat for a second, one hand on his back, the other on his forehead.

Last night he and Clare had talked for hours again, well into the middle of the night. He hadn't meant to tell her so much these past few days, but she had a way of making him talk. She was easy to be around. Jamie was like her, a nice lad who had invited him outside on Sunday to watch him and his mates from Arndale Road skateboarding and jumping over ramps on their bikes. Clare had brought Will out a coffee and they'd sat on the wall, watching the group show off, the shock of what had just happened with Hannah hitting him in waves.

He'd only been at Clare's a few days, but a pattern had formed. Each evening Jamie went to bed at nine. Clare made food, then brought out the whisky and weed, and put on quiet music, and they talked. He'd told her everything. About his childhood, about meeting Hannah, about how much last summer's incident had changed her, and about that tosser she'd slept with in Suffolk. (He didn't tell her, however, that the image made him feel sick and full of rage every time he thought about it.) He'd told her about the little girl, and how he purposely hadn't looked at the photo Barbara had brought, because he knew that would complicate what he was going to do.

Clare was sympathetic. She told him not to feel bad. The little girl wasn't his child yet. They'd never met each other. And, anyway, she needed a stable home. From what Will was saying, he and Hannah would be no good to her—not anymore.

She reminded him that there would be other people out there desperate to adopt her. He had to look after himself right now, after what Hannah had done to him. The child would find another family, and would be fine. In the meantime, Clare would be here for him, as a friend.

Each night they'd ended up sitting on the same sofa, Clare's soft blankets thrown over them. He knew the danger. Clare had given him clear enough signals about where her interests lay, but since that first time they'd kissed, she'd backed off and, right now, he didn't have the energy to find somewhere else to stay.

No. He'd only known Clare a short time, but she was nice. Easy to be around. She wasn't Hannah; but then again, neither was Hannah these days. There was no rush. No need to leave straightaway.

Will thought about finding breakfast and having a shower, then going in to work. Then he decided to lie back on the sofa for five more minutes. He pulled one of Clare's throws over him. Matt would be all right on his own for another hour. He'd go in later.

He shut his eyes, and went back to sleep.

43

"Gemma!"

Hannah chased out of the front door of Tornley Hall with the utilities letter that Gemma had just delivered, and caught the startled postwoman in the drive.

"Sorry, Hannah—that's it today," Gemma said. "You waiting on something?"

She had a jolly face, round and pleasant, with large, innocent blue eyes like a three-year-old, despite being in her forties. Crinkled blond hair was crammed under a cap.

"No," Hannah said. She was about to explain, then saw a tractor traversing Madeleine's field. "Actually, Gemma, do you have a minute? Would you mind . . ." She gestured into the house.

Gemma nodded and came with her.

"Listen," Hannah said, shutting the front door. "I wanted to ask you something. It's a bit sensitive, though."

"Oh, gosh—you've done well," said Gemma, examining the walls.

"Thanks. Listen, it's about Elvie, the woman who lives next door? The Mortrens' daughter."

Gemma looked as if she'd swallowed a hot chilli. "Frank and Tiggy have got a daughter?" she yelped.

"Oh," Hannah replied, disappointed. "You didn't know." She lifted her hand above her head. "Tall, well built, brown eyes, looks a little sulky."

Gemma looked blank.

"No? Honestly, Gemma, she's been here since we moved in."

"Gosh, that's odd," Gemma said. "I've done Frank and Tiggy's mail for twenty years and they've never mentioned her to me. Are you sure?"

Hannah sighed. "Maybe not. Listen, don't worry . . ." She went to open the door, defeated.

"I tell you what, though—that girl sounds like the one who stayed here with Peter and Olive sometimes," Gemma said behind her.

Hannah spun round. "In Tornley Hall?"

"Yeah, a big girl, long face, very shy?"

"Yes," Hannah whispered.

"Oh, yeah, I know her. I used to see her in the hall or the kitchen, when Olive opened the door for a parcel. Always scooted away when she saw me. I don't think she lived here, though. I only saw her a few times. Is that the one?"

Hannah clapped her hands. "Yes! Elvie. So you *do* know who she is?"

"Well, no. I never worked it out, to be honest. She didn't live here. I mean, there was no post for her or anything. I think

Olive said she was family. Didn't she visit in the holidays, or something?"

Hannah stared. "Family? Did Olive actually say that? Not 'family friend'?"

"Ooh, I don't think so."

This was becoming even odder, not clearer. Hannah tried again. "But, Gemma, Elvie was here last week. Why would she still come, if Olive and Peter are no longer here? Sorry, I'm just confused."

Gemma went to speak, then stopped.

"What?"

"Well, I don't know. You've got me thinking now. Actually, I have seen her a couple of times since they died. In the lane. I just thought she was here with the rest of the family, packing up the house?"

"The rest of what family?"

Uncertainty entered Gemma's voice. "Peter and Olive's?"

Hannah took a breath. None of this made sense. "Gemma, we were told that Peter and Olive didn't have any family. We thought it was why the Horseborrows' solicitor accepted such a low offer on the house. They knew there was no one to inherit the money, so they decided to take our offer because it was the only one that was slightly more than the property developer's offer. I mean, did you know Olive? Did she talk about family?"

Gemma crinkled her eyes, concentrating. "Um, well, we did have a chat now and then. I remember her saying that her father had built Tornley Hall. Some big, rich Suffolk shipbuilder, wasn't he?"

A shipbuilder? Hannah thought about the library. Had the travel books actually belonged to the father, not to Peter and Olive?

"But nothing else—not that I can remember," Gemma continued. "But I definitely saw people up here. So you're saying they weren't family?"

Hannah shook her head. "Do you know what they were doing?"

"Well, there were lights on. And the front door was open. The garage was open a few times—there was machinery in there. Farm stuff." Gemma's mouth fell open. "Oh, and then a few months ago I came up here with a letter, and those shutters were open." She pointed at the sitting room. "I remember thinking that was odd—there was machinery in there, too."

"Machinery?" Hannah said, incredulous, suddenly remembering the diesel smell.

"Yes. It was a circular that I had to deliver. They still send them after you die, you know. It's terrible. I always think it must be upsetting for bereaved people when they see a letter with the name of—"

Hannah interrupted. "Gemma, why would someone store machinery in this house?"

Gemma scratched her head. "Oh, gawd! I should have probably called the police, shouldn't I? I didn't think. I thought it was the family. Should we ring them now?"

"No!" Hannah exclaimed, louder than she meant to. "No. Not, yet. There's probably an explanation for it." She blew out her cheeks. "Listen, can I ask you a favor: not to mention this to anyone? Not until I've found out who Elvie is. I really thought she was Frank and Tiggy's daughter. But if there's any chance she's related to the Horseborrows, there might be legal implications about the house sale. So . . ."

"Oh, OK. No worries." Gemma pointed at her own head. "Listen, I don't want to be cruel, but she did seem a little . . ." Gemma made a face.

"No, you're right. She definitely does have some sort of learning difficulties. I mean, it's not impossible—now I think about it—that she might have lived in a care home, and stayed with Peter and Olive for holidays, if they were her family. What I don't understand is what she was doing here last week."

And why had Frank and Tiggy denied that they knew her?

Gemma headed out the front door. "Well, let me know. I'll be wondering all day now!"

As an afterthought, Hannah scribbled down her new mobile number and handed it to the postwoman, asking her to ring immediately if she saw Elvie. Gemma headed back to her postal van with a friendly wave.

Hannah's eyes drifted over to the field.

The tractor had stopped.

It was parked, with its cab facing her.

"Oh, go to hell," Hannah said, slamming the front door behind her.

· · ·

Ten minutes later she had written down everything she'd just learned from Gemma, and realized she was none the wiser than she had been an hour ago. Was Elvie related to Frank and Tiggy, or not? Was she actually a Horseborrow? And why was everyone else in Tornley lying about Elvie's existence, and trying to scare Hannah and Will away?

She stood up. The little girl's social workers would be here on Friday, and she needed Will back. This had to be sorted, for her own sake as well as Elvie's.

She was running out of time. She needed more information.

She phoned a taxi, and quickly grabbed what she needed.

An hour later Hannah arrived in Woodbridge and caught the train to Ipswich.

There was one thing that she could at least try to find out today: who was the pregnant Mabel Vyne?

•   •   •

After two weeks in a rural hamlet, Ipswich was a shock to Hannah, even if it was a fraction of the size of London. Petrol fumes from the busy road made her feel queasy. She'd already forgotten the art of dodging around people on the busy pavement, and banged arms more than once.

Hannah arrived at the Records Office just after two. If Mabel Vyne had lived at Tornley Hall, she guessed this was the best place to start. At the desk she explained her task. The office searched the documents archive and the old *Kelly's Directory* listings of business addresses, and came up with three Mabel Vynes who had lived in Suffolk in the past hundred years.

Hopeful, Hannah scanned the list. One Mabel Veronica Vyne was the lady in the newspaper cutting, and lived in a village on the outskirts of Ipswich. The second, Mabel Katherine Vyne, had died in 1923. Hannah struck her off the list. The third looked most interesting: Mabel Anne Vyne, born on 4 March 1930. She would have been a teenager in 1945–6 and would now be in her mid-eighties.

"Wow. That might be her," Hannah said to the woman on the desk.

She arrived at the Registrar's Office at lunchtime, to see if the trail continued there. To her disappointment, it dried up immediately.

The first and last record of Mabel Anne Vyne was her birth

certificate. After that, there was nothing. No marriage or death certificate, or any birth certificate for the child she bore. There was no record of her even on a census. The house on Star Street where she'd been born had long been demolished.

Mabel Anne Vyne had simply disappeared.

. . .

Hannah sat on the wall outside the library and ate a sandwich. She knew Mabel had not actually disappeared. If this was the right Mabel, she had remained in Suffolk, at Tornley Hall, for forty years. So why was there no listing of her in the official Suffolk records after her birth?

She wandered to the local library and found a friendly local historian in a tweed jacket and cane, with sharp blue eyes, who directed her back to the Records Office to look at the microfilm of local newspapers.

"You could look for a mention of her, or her family, or even of Star Street. If their house was bombed in the war, that might explain why she disappeared from the records, for a while at least," he said.

Sighing, Hannah stared at the screen, not knowing where to start. It was nearly three o'clock. She wanted to get back to Tornley Hall and turn on the lights before dark.

She forced herself to look at the evidence. The first proof she had that Mabel Vyne existed was a photo dated August 1945, at the end of the war.

Knowing now that she was clutching at straws, Hannah started earlier, with newspapers from January 1, 1945.

The search quickly became tedious. There were endless reports of Allied victories and local church fairs, and of lost dogs, and building work. This was pointless. She still had so much to do, back at Tornley Hall, before the social workers came. She'd give it an hour, then that was it.

Forty minutes later she was slumped forward, head in her hands, when a name finally jumped out at her from the screen. The story was from February 6, 1945:

MISSING WOMAN

> Information is desired by the police con-
> cerning the whereabouts of Miss Mabel
> Anne Vyne, aged 15 years, of 43 Star Street.
> She has not been seen since about 2:30 P.M.
> on Tuesday, when she was last seen at the
> corner of Bullgate Street.

Hannah had to stop herself whooping in the quiet office. Instinctively she knew she was a step closer to the mystery of who Elvie was.

Fired up, she searched on. Yet the story did not reappear. Had Mabel been found? Who would know?

Remembering the Mabel Veronica Vyne who was in her fifties, Hannah decided to give her a shot. She searched the local phone listings in the library for the woman's number and, as an afterthought, picked out the only other three listings for people with the surname of Vyne in the Ipswich area. Tentatively she rang each number.

The man who answered Mabel Veronica Vyne's number told Hannah that he and his wife had moved here from Nottingham three years ago, and had no relatives in the area. She crossed her name off the list.

The second Vyne didn't answer. The third was a friendly woman called Jean Vyne. She told Hannah to ring her husband Mark, at his shop. Vyne was his family name, not hers.

The March light was now starting to dim, and she had to get home. She walked towards the bus station, ringing Mark Vyne's number. If this came to nothing, she was giving up for today.

"Vyne Plumbing," said an equally pleasant voice when the phone was answered.

"Oh, hi, is that Mark?" Hannah asked.

"It is."

She suddenly felt worn-out. She was cold and tired, and she wanted Will. What was she doing, spending all this time in Ipswich on some ridiculous trail of a woman she didn't know? The missing Mabel Vyne from the newspaper might have nothing to do with the girl in Peter's photo. And it might be pure coincidence that Peter's Mabel and Elvie shared the same physical features.

"Listen, I'm sorry to bother you," she continued. "Your wife said it would be OK to call. This is going to sound crazy, but I live over near Thurrup, and I'm trying to track down a woman from this area called Mabel Vyne, who'd be in her eighties now. I know it's unlikely, but I'm just ringing people with the same surname to see if anyone knows what happened to her, and . . ."

She stopped, hit by a wave of exhaustion. She needed to go home. Stop this, now.

There was a silence at the other end.

"Auntie Mabel?" Mark Vyne exclaimed. "Good God! Now there's a name I never thought I'd hear again."

· · ·

A reinvigorated Hannah arrived twenty minutes later in a taxi. Vyne Plumbing was located on the outskirts of the city. A white van was pulling away as she climbed out.

"Mark?" she asked nervously, walking in. The shop was long and narrow, lined with floor-to-ceiling shelves packed with cardboard boxes and silver valves and piping.

A cheerful-looking man glanced up from the counter.

"Hello! Hannah." He held out a hand.

Instantly she felt disappointed. He was nothing like the tall, dark-haired woman in Peter and Olive's photos. He was of normal height, for a start, with gray-blond hair and curious pale-green eyes.

"Well, this is exciting, isn't it?" he said with a grin. "Very intriguing. Can I get you a cup of tea?" He pointed at his Ipswich Football Club mug.

Hannah held up a hand. "No, thanks. Listen, I know this sounds mad, but I'm trying to track down someone who I think used to live in my new house. I won't explain why, because it's boring and complicated, but you said you might know her—Mabel Vyne?"

The door tinkled and a large man came in behind her. "All right, Danny." Mark swung up the counter and the man went into the back. "Well, I might do," he said. "Not personally. But my dad did have an Auntie Mabel. I'll have to ring him and ask. Always been a bit of a family mystery."

Hannah felt hope return. "In what way?"

Mark checked behind him and lowered his voice. "Well, the story was that she ran off, when Dad was a baby. There were nine of them—she was the youngest, and his dad was the oldest."

"And when was that?" Hannah mentally crossed her fingers.

"Hmm . . . during the war? End of the war?"

"Really? And you say, 'ran off'?"

"That's right."

Hannah frowned. "Right. It's just that I found a newspaper report about a Mabel Vyne, which made it sound as if she disappeared—as if the police were involved. So I'm curious that you say 'ran off.' "

Mark winked. "Yeah, but that's what they all said back then, didn't they? Didn't want a scandal. No, the way I always understood it, old Mabel ran off with one of those American GIs, from the station out near Sudbury. Not that you'd blame her. Florida or Ipswich? I know which I'd choose."

Hannah stared. "She married an American?"

"Well, I don't know about married, but she certainly got knocked up by one. That was what my dad told me."

A frisson of excitement ran through her. "Mabel was pregnant?"

"Yes, it was all a bit of a scandal, I think. Stupid really, if you think what teenagers get up to these days. No, that was the story. That she got knocked up and did a runner with the GI, back to America. My Uncle Stan tried to find her once. He did our family tree in the eighties, but he couldn't find any record of her. Probably changed her name over there, he said."

Hannah nodded. "Wow. Do you happen to know the name of the GI?"

"No, sorry. Stan might, though. I'll give him a ring."

Hannah remembered the old green photo album from the 1970s. She pulled it out.

"Actually, Mark, can I show you something? In case you spot a family resemblance."

"Ooh, this is her, is it?" Mark put on his glasses and peered at the dark-haired woman, in her thirties, on the beach. He looked

uncertain. "I don't know. My gran's side were dark, I suppose."
Mark pushed his glasses back. "Tell you what: I've got a scanner
on my printer. Why don't I e-mail it to Dad, see if he knows?" He
lifted the book, smiling. "This is fun, isn't it—like that program
on television. She wasn't rich, was she, Auntie Mabel? We're not
coming into a fortune, are we?"

Hannah smiled as he walked off, grateful for his good humor.

This was becoming weirder and weirder.

If this was the right Mabel Vyne, how had she ended up living in Tornley Hall when everyone thought she was in America
with a GI? And what was her relation to Elvie?

Mark brought the album back. "So where was this place you
thought old Auntie Mabel might have been living?"

"Oh, it's by the coast," Hannah said, taking it back. "It's a
tiny hamlet, near Snadesdon, called Tornley. I think this woman
lived at Tornley Hall, for a while at least."

The smile slid from Mark's face. "Tornley Hall?"

"Why?"

He shouted to the man working in the back. "Danny, didn't
we do the plumbing out at Tornley, few years back? Big old
house, out by Snadesdon?"

"Yeah . . . That's right." Danny laughed. "Mr. Toffee, wasn't it?"

Hannah stared. "You *are* joking."

"Ha!" Mark grinned. "That's right! I remember it because
the old bloke wanted me to come out with Danny, even though
I run the shop side of things now. Wanted two of us. He was a
strange old bloke. Hung around, chatting, when we were working. Kept offering us toffees. Like we were kids. Mr. Toffee, we
called him."

Hannah put the album back on the counter. "But that's my
house."

"Is it?" Mark exclaimed. "Lovely old place. Hope the plumbing's still working!"

Hannah shook her head. "Mark. This is quite strange. I mean, why would Peter Horseborrow want you to go over there, rather than use a local plumber? That was only about ten years ago, wasn't it? If he did know Mabel, and he knew you were a Vyne, why ask you to go there, but not tell you that she used to live there? The last mention I found of her was in 1986 anyway—almost twenty years before you went out there."

Mark laughed again. "Well, this is interesting. A family mystery. Dad and Uncle Stan are going to love this."

. . .

Hannah managed to arrive back in Tornley at sunset in a taxi. The sky was violet above the marsh, the cat's tails a field of black spikes. She brought with her a promise from Mark Vyne that he would e-mail her when he'd heard from his father.

Each time she came home and found Will's car not there, her disappointment at his behavior turned more to fear.

Not once, after that first regretful mistake with his old girlfriend, had she ever doubted Will's commitment to her. And yet now, three days before the social workers were due to visit, he'd still not come home.

The new landline sat on the hall table next to her laptop. It was a welcome sight.

At least now she could e-mail Jane and tell her what was going on. Jane would believe her, even if no one else did. But first, Will.

She threw off her coat and googled the Smart Yak number. "He-llo," said a mockney voice when she rang it on the landline, cheering silently at the unbroken line.

"Hi, Matt, it's Hannah. Is Will there?"

"Oh. Hannah. Hi!" From the way he shouted, she guessed Will was sitting beside him. "Sorry. Yeah. He's just gone out, actually. A meeting." His tone was bright and forced. She waited for him to ask her to leave a message, or promise to get Will to call back. He didn't.

She resisted the urge to ask Matt who Will was meeting and where. It wasn't his assistant's fault.

"Matt, listen, I need Will to ring me. It's really urgent. Can you tell him that he needs to be here in Suffolk on Friday first thing, for a meeting? And if he doesn't ring me tonight to discuss it, I'm coming to London tomorrow."

"Oh. Yeah. Sure. Um. It's just, I'm just not sure what time he's coming in tomorrow, because . . ." Matt started pathetically.

"Just tell him. Please."

Hannah put down the phone.

.   .   .

Hannah shivered in the hall. The temperature had dropped again after a few days of spring sunshine. She went to find a sweater.

The minute she arrived upstairs, she smelled it: that familiar sour odor.

"Elvie?" Hannah yelled, switching on the lights. "Are you here?"

She searched the bedrooms, and the attic. She listened. Nothing.

"Please, Elvie, can you come out? I just want to help you."

She searched the downstairs rooms, discovering the sour smell in the kitchen. She saw that a new packet of bread had been opened and two apples had gone.

Yes! Elvie had definitely been here.

She was not going mad.

She checked the latch on the scullery window. How did Elvie open it from the outside—did she jiggle it till it came loose?

"Elvie, please, come out!"

There was a tiny scrabbling sound. Hannah spun round.

Her eyes roamed the kitchen cupboards, and the bolted back door. "Where are you?"

Nothing.

Just that same odd feeling that she was being watched.

•   •   •

It was when Hannah returned to her bedroom to find the sweater that she noticed the painting on the mantelpiece. It had been turned inwards again. Why did Elvie keep doing that?

She examined it again, and the sad face of the little boy.

She lifted down the other two as well. As she did so, she spotted one of Olive's small black squiggles on the back of one. She placed it under the light.

M.V. it said in tiny letters, in black paint, in the bottom right-hand corner.

Feeling a rush of blood, Hannah turned it. The dark face of the Spanish señorita stared back at her.

"Mabel?"

Initially she wasn't recognizable. The skin was more Mediterranean in tone, the eyes larger than in real life, but now Hannah saw that the features and expression were definitely her.

So, Olive had painted Mabel?

On a whim, she ran upstairs and pulled all the other canvases out of the attic cupboard.

There were more than she realized: thirty-six in total. White

mold obscured many of the images, although others were almost clean. She sorted them into two piles—moldy and those
in good condition—spotting the Acropolis, Machu Picchu, and
the Italian Lakes as she went.

All these exotic locations, which Olive apparently had not
visited after all. Had she painted them from her imagination, or
from the travel books her father had left her?

The more Hannah learned about Olive and Peter, the more
she began to suspect that they were the idle children of a rich
father. She wondered if they'd sat around in the grand house
that he'd left them, playing with their rich friends, painting
badly, and achieving nothing in life, apart from spending their
inheritance—or investing it badly perhaps—and letting their
father's hard work and house fall into ruin.

As Hannah laid the Acropolis painting down on its front,
another black mark became visible on the rear: M.V.

"Yes!" Hannah said, turning it round. The subject was a
young woman, dressed as a Greek goddess. She wiped away the
dust.

A familiar pair of sulky eyes stared back.

So, Mabel had been Olive's muse? Was that why she'd come
here? Perhaps she'd lived quietly in a coastal town with her
baby, and had come here to work as an artist's model. Clearly
Olive had no better way to spend her time. Hannah's sympathy
for Olive, with her private income and posh friends, was starting to fade.

She carried on, holding each painting under the light. She
found more and more of Mabel, her skin painted various
shades—both darker and lighter than it was in real life, her hair
longer or shorter to suit the classical theme, her body ranging
from voluptuous to boyish.

She started on the moldy pile next, and saw more initials and, this time, a date: 1952.

One painting made her stop. The black squiggle looked different. Not M.V., for Mabel Vyne, but . . .

". . . C.V.?" Hannah mouthed. Who was "C"?

She turned it over. Behind the white film of mold she made out the image of a child dancing under a tree, waving a fan. There was a swan in the background.

From what she could see, the child had lighter coloring than Mabel.

She stared. Was this the child Mabel had been pregnant with? The date suggested it could be.

She turned over more of the moldy paintings. There were three more of the same child, at different ages. On others, the black initials had worn off in the damp, or were so moldy that they were unreadable.

Tired now, Hannah put the last one down and decided to go and do some more painting. She was running out of time to finish the child's bedroom.

In her own bedroom she changed back into her painting clothes, regarding the image of the Egyptian boy. Was "C" Mabel's child, too?

On impulse, she held the painting up to the lightbulb. The white mold had marked most of the back. Yet there at the bottom, behind the mold, she saw a dark squiggle, with another date. To her surprise it said "1982." Mabel's daughter would have been in her late thirties by now. Who was this new child?

Two initials, so worn out they'd practically disappeared, sat next to the date. Yet they were not M.V. or C.V. This time. Hannah screwed up her eyes. An "L"?

"L.V.," Hannah read out loud.

It was as she was putting the painting down on the mantelpiece that she heard what she'd just said.

.   .   .

Long shadows danced in the bedroom under the lightbulb.

Hannah sat looking at the child's face. She could see it now. The blank, brown eyes. The anger. The tufty hair shorn tight.

My house!

Elvie as a child. *L.V.*

No wonder she looked like Mabel. If C.V. was Mabel's daughter, then that made Elvie what—C.V.'s child. Mabel's grandchild?

This was exciting.

Then Elvie was Mabel's granddaughter, not Frank and Tiggy's child. Somehow Hannah knew she was getting closer to the truth.

Her phone buzzed with a text message. She picked it up, desperately hoping it was Will. *Have e-mailed you! Mark.*

Rushing downstairs, she opened her laptop and found a message.

> Hi, Hannah, Nice to meet you today. Dad's been in touch this evening, and Uncle Stan, who did the family tree. They were very surprised at your news, and hoping to speak to you! Dad thinks the photo could be Aunt Mabel. He's curious to know where you found it. Can you let him and Stan have any information, on the above e-mail addresses? I've CC'd them in.
>
> Stan knows a bit more (he interviewed Mabel's oldest sister, Gertrude, for the family history before she passed

away in 1981). Gertrude told him—her words—that Mabel was a bit of a "flibbertigibbet" and that their mum wasn't surprised she got into trouble! Said she was sickly as a child, and missed a lot of school. He got the impression she was illiterate and a wee bit vulnerable—she probably got into trouble with the GI because she didn't know any better. (Stan was told the GI's name was Burstein, but never found him.) Anyway, looks like we could be talking about the same Mabel! Dad and Stan would like to talk more. Thanks for getting in contact.

All the best, Mark Vyne

Burstein?

Hannah grabbed the old letters from the mantelpiece. D. Burstenstein.

There was no doubt now.

Somebody—she now suspected Peter—had written non-sensical letters to the GI who got Mabel pregnant in 1945, then hid them, instead of sending them. Mabel was illiterate, so it wasn't her. Had Mabel believed the letters had gone to her lover? Had she been waiting for a reply? Hannah thought of the dull gaze in the young woman's eyes, and knew that she'd been unhappy. Waiting for the father of her child to come and take her away.

On the contrary, it seemed he had never come. And instead Mabel had lived in Tornley Hall her whole life, and possibly had a child, C.V., and even a grandchild, Elvie, here.

Yet the families who lived in Tornley denied that Elvie existed.

Why?

．　．　．

Hannah thought of Laurie's cynical, concerned face the last time they met, yet knew she had no choice. She'd have to beg her to help again.

She rang Laurie's phone. It went straight to voice mail.

Sighing, she called up Laurie's e-mail address and, for good measure, CC'd in Jane. Jane wouldn't doubt her. Hannah needed to tell someone what was going on. The rest could make up their own minds.

She began to write an e-mail that listed everything that had happened since she'd arrived in Tornley. It took ten minutes, and she included as much detail as possible. She reminded Laurie that she had to keep the police out of this because of the adoption, but Hannah needed Laurie to persuade her police officer friend, Jonathan, to look further into the truth about Tornley; into an old missing-persons case involving a woman called Mabel Vyne from Ipswich; and the vulnerable woman who, Hannah suspected, was her granddaughter, Elvie—all without involving Hannah directly. She also told Laurie about the strange, and possibly illegal, activity that had been going on in the house before they moved in.

Then Hannah pressed "send."

Nothing happened.

She tried again. She checked the Wi-Fi signal on her screen. It was gone.

How had—?

The bedroom light clicked off.

Hannah's stomach lurched.

The whole house fell silent, as if everything electrical had been turned off.

She tried the bedroom light switch, then the one in the dark hall. Nothing. It was a complete power cut.

Hannah stood in the pitch-black house, knowing that her nerves couldn't take any more. She'd tried, but the dream of Tornley Hall was dying. This place, with its long corridors and creaking floors, was starting to scare her.

It was bad enough being out here on her own, with the hostile force of Dax, and Madeleine next door, and Elvie wandering around at night scaring her. She couldn't possibly sleep here without lights.

She tiptoed down the corridor to fetch the flashlight from the toolbox. Then, with the beam in front of her, she made her way downstairs. The fuse box was in the scullery. If this wasn't just a simple tripped switch—if it was a real power cut—then she was ordering a taxi right now and staying in a hotel in Thurrup, bugger the money. In fact she'd stay there every night till Will came home.

Hannah reached the downstairs hall.

Shadows disappeared into black corners. She flinched as a branch waved outside the hall window.

No, she was done now. Her bravado had gone. She didn't want to be out here alone any longer. Sadly, Hannah realized she was starting to want not to live in Tornley Hall, full stop.

The dream was over.

Fumbling her way into the scullery, she found the fuse box next to the sink. The cover was lying open.

Behind her was a rustle.

"Elvie?" she whispered, her heart thumping hard.

No reply.

Trying to control the shaking that was starting in her legs, she tiptoed back into the kitchen. In fact she had to get out of here—right now. Her nerves were shot. She'd ring a taxi from the hall phone, then lock herself in the sitting room until it arrived.

Hannah tiptoed towards the hall table. Suddenly a shape in the hall moved in front of her.

She gasped and jerked back.

"Elvie?" she whispered.

No reply. The shape moved again. A chorus of breathing in the hall.

Then she knew.

This was not one person. This was people.

People were standing in the hallway. Lots of them.

For a second, Hannah felt a hopeless sense of relief. Crowds were safe. Then her flashlight picked out a face.

Dax.

"Oh!" she shrieked before she could stop herself. Her knees began to buckle. The beam jerked around, as she tried to make sense of this group. Faces peered into her flashlight beam. Madeleine, Carol, Frank, Bill, Tiggy, and a younger man who looked like Dax.

"Who let you in my house? You need to get out of my house," she said, breathlessly, desperately trying to sound calm. Authoritative. "Get out now, or I'll call the police."

Dax walked towards her. In his hand she saw the rifle.

"Stop it!" was all she could say, her hand jerking out in front of her. Her beam flicked desperately again at Tiggy and Frank. Frank's eyes were fixed on the ground. Tiggy's makeup seemed to be melting down her cheeks. She dabbed at herself, blue eye shadow smudged on the sides of her face. Bill stood at the door, frowning, a hand on his fleshy jaw.

A hand reached out and, before she knew it, Hannah was

being propelled fast back into the wall. She hit it at speed and yelped, as a sharp pain shot through her shoulder. Tears sprang into her eyes. The young man's face was close to hers.

"Hold her, Craig," Dax growled. He pushed his face into the same position. "Where is she?"

"Who?"

"You know who. Elvie."

Her eyes met his, defiant. "I don't know who you're talking about."

A hand came out of the dark and slapped her so hard across the face that she cried out. Carol's face appeared in the beam.

"Get off me!" Hannah shouted, trying to hit her away. Craig pushed her arm behind her back, making her scream, "Get off me!"

But he held her arms so tightly she thought they'd snap.

"Why are you doing this?" she said, gulping back tears.

There was no reply. Something black rose above her head and came down over it.

"No!" she screamed, struggling. Then someone kicked her in the leg, and she buckled over.

"Shut up! Use that one—the landline, Carol," she heard Dax say.

"Who are we ringing? Thurrup Taxis?"

"Yeah. Tell 'em Woodbridge station, and he needs to hurry up, cos you're catching the seven forty-nine to London. Make sure you say London."

They were putting her on a train back to London, to make her go away? Hannah nearly laughed through her tears. They were mad. This had all gone too far. The blanket on her head pushed into her nostrils.

"I can't breathe. Tiggy, please," she pleaded.

She heard a small whimper.

"Leave it, Tig," Dax grunted.

"Dax, please don't—" Frank started.

"And you, too, Frank. Shut it! Too late now."

There was a loud "Shhh" and Hannah heard Carol putting on a voice that was presumably supposed to sound like hers. "Woodbridge station from Tornley Hall in Tornley, please. I'm catching the London train—the name's Hannah. Thanks."

"No!" Hannah shouted.

A punch came on the side of her head and knocked her sideways.

Dazed, she half-fell to the floor.

"You were told to shut up." This time the voice was Madeleine's.

"Madeleine, come on, there's no need for—" Frank started again.

"Frank, I said don't bloody start," Dax replied. "Or you'll be going in there with her."

There was a small gasp.

"And you, too, Tig. Pull yourself together. Bill, get the door."

Bewildered, Hannah felt rough hands start to drag her across the tiles.

44

The darkness was disorienting.

At one point Hannah passed out from the blow. When she came to, she was lying on something hard and metal, feeling dizzy. She tried to move her arms and realized they were pinned behind her back, with something tight and sore cutting into her wrists.

Her jaw ached, and there was a metallic taste of blood in her mouth. She groaned and tried to move.

Terror gripped her. They were taking her somewhere, and she was pretty sure it wasn't the train station. She tried in vain to remember her kidnap training, but it was a desperate thought, and she knew it. This was not a kidnap.

This was not part of a training course, with a chance of a good outcome if she did the right thing. This was an act of madness, perpetrated by desperate people. The punch had told her that.

The stink of diesel entered her nose now, and the ground below her moved. Then she knew where she was.

Dax's truck.

There was a screech and it raced along, making her head bang in hard little bounces on the metal truckbed. A foot pressed down hard on her back, expelling the air from her lungs.

Will appeared in her mind.

Tears started to fall down her cheeks. Her head ached. She wanted Will.

He hadn't believed her. If something happened to her and he found out the truth, he would never forgive himself. He would find that message on her laptop and know he'd let her down. And, because of that, this had happened to her.

Her tears mixed with sweat inside the suffocating hood.

The truck bumped and banged over the ground, then she felt a kick below her as it jumped, and knew where she was.

She could hear the sea.

The truck swerved, and she banged into the side as it hit the shingle below.

There was another vehicle behind. Then a screech of wheels on loose stones, a skid, and a stop. Engines cutting out.

Metal chinked, then hands were wrenching her from the truck and carrying her like a sack.

A door slammed. A stink of hot iron.

Samuel's shack.

She was thrown onto the floor on her front.

. . .

Hannah lay on her stomach, motionless, too scared to move.

No, this was not a kidnap or abduction. She could tell by their voices.

Dax, Carol, and Madeleine were barking commands at the others. Tiggy was sniffing and Frank kept coughing, as if trying to clear his throat.

She could smell someone's nervous sweat as they leaned down and roughly tugged at her hands. Something was pushed in between them, shooting pain up her wrists and arms, then they were tugged to the left.

"Right, ten o'clock, meet back here. Bill, watch her. Samuel? Samuel! Look at me. You watch her, too. Do what Bill tells you."

Hannah heard a chair being kicked, and flinched. Dax was yelling now.

"Samuel! Listen to me. You *watch* her, when Bill gets the boat ready. And don't speak to her. Everyone else—move it! Carol—me and you will go over to the Fox, with Mum and Craig. Tig, you and Frank go late-night shopping in Thurrup. Make sure you buy something on a credit card. When's that taxi coming, Carol?"

"Half an hour."

"I don't understand," Hannah heard Tiggy wail, hysteria in her voice. "Why are you ordering a taxi, Dax? What's happening?"

"Oh, for fuck's sake!" Dax yelled. "Will you shut her up, Frank?"

"Tig," Carol said. "Look at me. She won't be there, will she? The driver goes back to Thurrup and then tomorrow, when nobody can find her, they'll finger 'im."

"That's a point. You got her phone, Carol?" Dax said. "Wipe it, then chuck it in a field out by Snadesdon. Ring nine-nine-nine on it or summat, then turn it off. They'll think he took her out there."

Sweat trickled down inside the hood. Hannah tried to shake it away, but it ran into her eyes, making her blink. Dax's voice faded, as if he'd moved away. "Tig, Frank, sort yourselves out. I'm not saying it again. You're in this, same as the rest of us. Too late for whining now."

Then there was a creak of floorboards. Stale cigarette breath blasted through the hood. She flinched, but there was nowhere to go.

Dax's voice appeared right in her ear. "You've seen Samuel's soldering iron. Lie there quiet, or him and Bill will take your eye out."

She bit back a scream.

The doors crashed, and the voices stopped.

. . .

Hannah didn't move.

She tried to hear where Samuel and Bill were—anticipating a burn on her body at any time.

She heard murmuring, doors bashing. Somebody moving something behind her head, and a diesel smell that made her push herself inches closer to the wall, terrified.

Then, gradually, her pulse started to slow. Nothing was happening. Not yet.

"Right. I'll be at the boat. Keep her there," Bill said.

The door slammed again. Bill had said he was going to a boat. A boat for her?

A new dread filled Hannah. She could hear Samuel working at the bench, mumbling to himself. Did he even know she was here?

Even though her head was dizzy, she told herself she had to take a risk. This could be her only chance, while Bill was out of the shack.

"Samuel," she tried quietly, "I have a little girl. I need to get home for her."

Metal clanked and then hissed.

"Samuel?"

She couldn't move her hands. Dax had tied them to something. So instead she pressed her forehead on the ground and tried to drag the hood off her face. It came in three moves, almost all the way to her eyes.

There was a scrape and she tried to turn her head.

Samuel stood above her with a chisel, staring down through milky eyes.

"No!" she shouted, flinching.

"Who are you?" he said.

"Hannah," she replied, terrified.

Samuel glazed over again. He walked back to the bench and continued with his soldering.

At least she could see something now, even if she was still trussed like an animal. She tried to move and couldn't and, strangely, felt ashamed.

"Samuel," she called into the floor. "What are they going to do to me?"

A clink and a hiss. "Put ya down."

She thought she'd misheard him. The words entered her head one by one. "Put," "you," "down." A chill ran through her as she connected them.

"Put me down? Like an animal? What do you mean?"

"Drown ya. With Bill's boat. That's what they do."

Hannah struggled to find words. "Who do they do it to, Samuel?"

"The farm girls," Samuel said. "When they're old and sick."

Hannah stared. "Farm girls. You mean Mabel. Mabel, and her daughter, C.V.?"

She was starting to feel nauseous, and tried to move her stomach off the floor.

"That's right. Elvie, too, now, when they get her. They told her to be quiet when you lot come, and she wasn't. Dax said it wouldn't work."

Dax and Madeleine were hunting Elvie now, too?

"Samuel. Why do L.V. and C.V. just have initials, and not names?" she said, looking around for anything to help her. On the floor was an iron bar. If she could untie her hands and—

Something banged down on a table beside her, making her jerk away. "Don't need them."

"Why?"

Samuel's head came down close to hers again. His rheumy eyes were staring, trying to make sense of his confused mind.

"Got no use, but do stuff. Work on the farm. Don't give cows names, do thee?"

Samuel went back to his soldering.

Hannah lay in shock, trying to understand. What was he saying? That Dax and Madeleine had killed Mabel and her daughter, C.V.—or let them die, at least, because they'd become old and sick—then put their bodies in the sea?

From the sound of it, they were now hunting Mabel's granddaughter, Elvie, too. Destroying the evidence, perhaps, now that outsiders had come to the village and realized that something strange had been going on there.

And she—because she couldn't keep her nose out of other people's business—had got in the way.

Hannah lay on the floor, the horror of it washing through her, with the realization that she, too, was going to die.

Her eyes roamed the dirty shack, with its clumps of mud and oil, the iron bar too far out of reach. Was this the last thing she would see, before they came to get her?

She thought again of the unsent e-mail on her laptop, and wondered if Dax had found and stolen the computer. If he had, nobody would ever know the truth.

She thought about the report in the newspaper about Mabel Vyne. *Police are searching for Hannah Riley, 36, a charity publicist who disappeared on Tuesday evening in Suffolk. A taxi driver from Thurrup is currently being questioned.*

Her parents and Will would spend the rest of their lives wondering what had happened to her.

The grief and the pain and the dizziness threatened to send her into hysteria, and she knew she had to stop it.

Bill was still outside on the beach. She had to persuade Samuel to let her go. He was so confused that she might have a chance.

As she tried to think how to make him listen to her, she felt a quiver in the floor under her body. An aftershock of movement— once, then again, but stronger. The third time it was a palpable thump under the floor.

Behind her, Hannah heard the door crash open.

"No," she whispered.

It was too late. Bill was back. Or, worse, Dax.

She shut her eyes helplessly, waiting for a blow. But instead she heard a grunt.

She tried to turn her head, and saw feet in their big boots. Dirty, leathery hands shot out, and then her own hands were being pulled.

"Elvie?"

Pain shot up her arm. There was another twist and then, to her astonishment, her hands fell free behind her back. She tried to get up on her knees, but the huge hands were round her, lifting her right up.

"Thank you," she said, staggering to her feet.

Elvie was filthy. Her hair was matted, and on her face was

that same expression of fury. Hannah realized that Elvie was glaring at Samuel, who sat at his bench looking confused.

"Oh, God—no, Elvie," Hannah said.

But it was too late. Elvie flew at Samuel so fast that he didn't even flinch. She punched the old man on the jaw. He fell to the floor, and she picked up a chair.

"No!" Hannah shouted. "Put it down, Elvie."

Elvie dropped it. Her hands shot out and grabbed Hannah. Before she could speak again, Elvie half-lifted, half-dragged her out through the door of the shack into the dark, and then into the long grass.

There was a distant yell through the wind from down at the shore.

Bill had seen them.

"Run, Elvie!" Hannah shouted.

· · ·

Hannah was so sore, frightened, and disoriented that she had no idea where they were going. She just knew that it would be seconds before Bill rang Dax and he'd be on his way back from Snadesdon. They had to disappear into the dark and hide.

It was only when Hannah saw the marsh under the moonlight that she realized Elvie was taking them home.

"No!" Hannah called, twisting away. "No, Elvie! We need to go to the main road and get help. The other way."

But Elvie was having none of it. She practically lifted Hannah off the ground, under her arm, and pulled her on. Her strength was unbelievable.

"No, please! We need to stay and hide behind the hedges, and then find our way to Snadesdon."

Elvie ignored her. She pulled and yanked Hannah, until she

gave up and ran with her, her feet skipping along the ground.

Halfway down the track Elvie pulled her unexpectedly into the marsh and they crossed through the long grass. Soon Hannah saw where they were. It was a shortcut. They were almost back at Tornley Hall.

Hannah grabbed a branch and tried to hold on. "No, Elvie, please! Listen to me. We can't go in there, Dax is going to—"

It was too late.

As they reached the end of Tornley Hall's driveway the sound of engines appeared in the distance.

"Shit! That's him coming back. We have to hide."

But Elvie dragged her on. She pulled Hannah up the driveway and in through the front door, which still lay open. The lights of three vehicles shone through the hedges as they came round the bend. Desperate, Hannah kicked out. Elvie was going to get them killed.

"No, Elvie. We need the phone!"

Hannah tried to shut and lock the front door, but Elvie kept dragging her into the kitchen.

"No, stop it—they'll find us in here and . . ."

Elvie pulled Hannah into the scullery. What was she doing? They were going to be trapped!

The giant woman grabbed the fridge and started to pull. It moved with a screech across the floor. Elvie grabbed Hannah and pushed her down the side of it. To her surprise, Hannah flew through an opening into a dark space. Elvie came behind her and, grabbing the electric elements at the back of the fridge, pulled it back into place.

Hannah held the wall, her chest heaving, trying to catch her breath as silently as she could.

Where the hell were they?

45

From the vehicle sounds outside, the people in the cars were definitely here to find them. Doors slammed, and there was shouting. Engines restarted, and cars drove off.

Behind her, Hannah felt Elvie bend over. There was a click and a flashlight came on.

She peered, bewildered. They were in a small room with no windows. Pressing into her leg was a Victorian toilet covered in blue flowers.

There were blankets on the tiled floor, and food scattered around. The missing photo albums lay in the corner.

Elvie's hiding place.

Elvie went to the doorway, which was now blocked by the fridge, and turned off the flashlight.

A tiny slice of light appeared on the wall to the right. There was a crack. A piece of brick was missing, Hannah guessed, under one of the scullery shelves.

Elvie stood back to let her see.

Stunned, Hannah saw Dax on the other side of the wall. He'd put the electricity back on.

"Where the fuck are they?" Carol was yelling in the kitchen. "What if they're on the Snadesdon road?"

Dax shook his head. "Nah. Elvie's never been out of the bloody village. Not in forty years. You'd have to sedate that fat cow to move her. She's 'ere."

He turned back to Carol. This close up, Hannah saw that his face was murderous.

"Bill's on the marsh with Craig. Tig and Frank are looking next door. We'll find 'em. Tonight, or tomorrow. Don't matter. Elvie won't leave."

Hannah turned. Elvie sat, motionless, on the toilet seat.

Doors slammed around the house.

Frank and Tiggy appeared in the kitchen, now even more agitated than before. "They're not next door."

Tiggy's hands swatted an invisible battalion of wasps. "You have to find them, Dax. Or they'll know. They'll find out. About everything!"

"Oh, shut up, Tig! Always the same with you. Fine when it suits you having them working your bloody flowers all hours, while you're swanning off to Spain, and then shouting your mouth off when it doesn't."

Tiggy's face was puce, her voice hysterical. "Oh, don't you blame me, Dax. It was like this when we got here. Olive and Peter started it, long before we were here. . . . Do you remember?" Frank tried to calm her, but she pulled away. "No, Frank! I told you all to get a doctor for Mabel, and for C.V. I was never happy letting those poor women pass away like that. I was never happy using those girls. Never. You just go too far, Dax. And I told you—I told you—about storing that damn stolen farm machinery in here. Poor Frank, having to offer to cut that bloody grass every time the estate agent did a viewing, just to give you time to get it out. Ten times it must have happened. He nearly burst a blood vessel. I warned you that you'd get caught. I told you outsiders were on their way. I told you people would ask questions." She put her fists to her face and groaned. "And now—Hannah! We won't get away with it. We won't, Frank." Frank patted her back.

There was a sound outside. Another car was drawing up outside. Hannah saw them all glance nervously at the front door.

"The taxi!" Carol hissed.

"Fuck!" Dax grunted. "Get rid of 'im. Say you're her, and you've changed your mind."

Tiggy squealed and ran out the back door, followed by Frank. Hannah watched as Dax stomped out of the kitchen.

The taxi.

Hannah turned in the dark and whispered, "Elvie, the taxi's here. That's our chance. We have to go . . ."

Elvie shook her head.

"Please?"

Hannah knelt down and took Elvie's hands. "Elvie, it's OK. Come on, I'll be with you."

There was a look of complete terror on the woman's face. "Not allowed to go Ipswich."

"Elvie, that's not true. You *can* go there. I'll look after you."

Elvie stood up, checked the crack, and pushed the fridge quietly. She disappeared and the light turned off in the scullery. A second later a long arm came back into the dark and pulled Hannah out.

The scullery window was open.

Elvie pointed to the sink and Hannah knelt on the worktop,

holding her shoulder. She turned sideways through the gap, rested her foot on the windowsill, then jumped down onto the bench.

"Come on," she whispered.

But Elvie shook her head through the window.

"Please, Elvie—quick!"

There was a sadness in Elvie's eyes.

She couldn't leave, Hannah realized with a jolt. She didn't know how.

"OK, I'll come back for you," she whispered. "Hide!"

Then she ducked down and crawled to the side of the alcove. The taxi was parked, lights blazing, by the trees.

She heard voices at the front door. Carol was saying it had been a mistake, and the driver was arguing, saying that she'd need to pay anyway. Carol was shouting in her grating voice for someone to fetch some money from inside.

It was now or never.

Hannah moved on her hands and knees through the flower beds until she reached the sitting-room window. She poked her head round it and saw Carol furiously counting money.

The taxi was five yards away. A radio blared from inside. Its headlights were pointing towards Carol and the driver.

Knowing she only had seconds, Hannah continued on her knees along the edge of the side lawn towards the dark shadows of the oak trees, then doubled back up behind the taxi. The front door of Tornley Hall was slamming as Carol got rid of the driver.

Now!

Hannah dived down the side of the taxi and opened the back passenger door quietly, hoping the blaring radio would cover the noise.

Gravel crunched as the driver walked past the sitting-room windows.

Hannah eased herself in, hoping his headlights would also blind him to her movement, and pulled the door gently closed. She lay flat across the footwell.

The driver opened his door, shut it, turned down the radio, shouted something rude about Carol into his taxi radio, then swung round and headed out of the driveway.

He turned up the radio again and sang along tunelessly.

Hannah lay still. The dark tops of the trees whipped past the window. She sensed the fork in the road by the three cottages, and then the right turn at the T-junction towards Thurrup.

The driver accelerated.

She wondered at what point to tell him she was here.

46

The next day the snow was long gone. The rivers were full. The grass was a vivid green among the puddles of mud. It was a fertile land, unfrozen.

Signposts pointed down leafy roads to places most people would never go. To houses, hidden up isolated lanes. To suburbs, with bolted doors and drawn curtains.

Hannah leaned her head against the train window to cool the thump of her headache.

It was time to tell the truth.

• • •

One hour to London.

She rubbed the bruise on her cheek. In her hand sat Daniel's phone and a scribbled number.

A sign for Essex appeared ahead, and the future she'd dreamed of in Suffolk dropped behind, and then away.

She rang the number, knowing there was no choice. Not

because of what was about to happen later today, but because it was the right thing to do and, for a while, she'd lost sight of what that was.

A voice answered six rings later. Hannah hoped she hadn't pulled her from a meeting.

"Barbara, it's Hannah."

There was a tentative tone in her social worker's voice. Her instincts were probably finely tuned. "Hi, Hannah, how is everything?"

"Actually, that's why I'm ringing you . . ."

And then Hannah started. She told Barbara everything. She told her about Tornley Hall and the mess she'd got into, and about Will walking out. Her lie about him being in Thurrup, when he was actually in London. And how she had been so desperate to be matched that she'd ripped apart their carefully built lives in London, without making sure it was what Will wanted, too. And now she didn't know where he was.

Barbara listened, then related her own shock and sympathy for Hannah, at what had happened in Tornley.

There was a pause, and then Hannah made herself say it, even though she didn't want to hear the answer. "Barbara, are we going to lose her?"

"Hannah," she replied, "listen. Go and find Will, and sort things out. I'll ring her social workers and explain what a mess you've been thrown into, and why. And I'll ask them to give you a couple of weeks to sort out what's happening with the house. But try not to worry. Right now, I promise you, she's not going anywhere. They're very keen."

Hannah watched a dad farther up the carriage, with a toddler asleep on his chest, face sweetly squashed to the side, as he read a book. "The thing is, I know it's her, Barbara—I don't know why. But I think it's why it didn't work out last summer. Because we were waiting for her, and we didn't know it." Tears came into her eyes as she watched the scatter of houses start to gather together and build into towns. "God, I've messed up, haven't I?"

Barbara sighed. "Hannah, listen. I haven't mentioned this before, but I'm an adoptive parent, too. Trust me, we all want to be perfect."

• • •

Hannah arrived at Paddington just before six. Her stomach rumbled painfully, and she realized she hadn't eaten for twelve hours, apart from a cup of tea and a cookie at the police station this morning. She entered the first place she saw, a bar serving food, and ordered at the counter.

Even though the police had warned her it was going to happen, it was surreal to see Tornley Hall appear on the television screen at the end of the bar. A customer with a beer looked up to watch it.

She took her drink over and sat on the next seat. A reporter stood at the end of the driveway. He was speaking to an anchorwoman back in the studio, on the six o'clock news. The house looked shabby and rundown, the driveway unwelcoming.

"Yes, Alice, it's strange, this one. We understand that police raided a number of properties in this quiet corner of Suffolk last night, after a tip-off that a woman has been living in domestic servitude in this hamlet. Even more extraordinary, allegations are also emerging that the woman's mother and grandmother may have been kept here, too, by three local families, and that this crime may reach back many, many decades. Police are questioning eight people, and are investigating reports that a recently deceased brother and sister, Peter and Olive Horseborrow—the former owners of this house behind me, which was built by their father, the Suffolk shipbuilder John Horseborrow—were also involved."

Hannah sipped her wine as the anchorwoman asked the reporter for more details. The man at the bar shook his head at her.

"Strange world," he said.

"Yes, it is," she replied.

The reporter was speaking again.

"Well, it's early days, Alice, but we understand the woman the police discovered was found hiding in a bathroom. This is the extraordinary thing. We understand this woman may be as old as forty, yet she has never left Tornley. Let me be clear, however. There is no suggestion that she was physically held here. This appears to be a case of vulnerable women being coerced into doing free labor, under psychological duress. I should be clear, too, that this story is just breaking. We understand that a second local woman was abducted and escaped last night, and that tomorrow police divers are starting a search around Graysea Bay. I'll keep you updated as we receive more news."

•   •   •

Hannah finished her food and made her way to the Tube. She got off at Shepherd's Bush, and put her head down as she made her way through the early crowds arriving for a gig at the Empire.

Although it was dark, the air was balmy with the promise of spring. She walked the route home, which she'd walked hundreds of times, towards Will, not knowing what she would find this time.

The receptionist of Smart Yak, Aleisha, was packing up for

the evening when Hannah arrived. They had met a few times, but Aleisha shifted uncomfortably today, as if she didn't know what to say.

Hannah walked up the stairs, then checked behind her. As she suspected, Aleisha was phoning ahead.

At Will's door she didn't hesitate. She turned the handle and walked in.

Will was at the desk, replacing the receiver.

On the sofa was a woman she didn't recognize. She had a fake bohemian look that Hannah hated. Long bleached hair. A maxi-dress with a whimsical cardigan. Boots. She was lying on Hannah's parents' couch, checking her mobile.

She and Will looked good together. Arty, cool. Laid-back.

Hannah's heart broke in two.

"Hi," Will said. She saw it now, in his eyes. The hard shell of deep brown that melted like chocolate when he was hurt, just like Daniel. He could never hide it from her.

"Hi."

The woman raised her eyebrows at Will and stood up, with a languorous uncurling of her limbs. She was taller than Hannah and wore an expression of disdain. Hannah knew what she wanted.

"I'll leave you to it." The blond woman winked at Will, walking out.

To it.

Hannah stayed standing. "Have you seen the news?"

Anger simmered in his voice. "No."

She looked at the familiar shape of the chest she could always fall into, the arms that always came round her, and the hair that brushed her cheek, and realized she didn't know if they were hers any longer.

"Well, you need to watch it. It's about Tornley."

A ripple of curiosity. "OK."

She fought back tears. "Will, I'm sorry I made you move there, without asking if it's what you wanted, but I did it because I wanted to have a baby for you. Because I couldn't give you one. And I wanted to make it right."

He picked up a pen and drummed it on the desk. "When did I ever say that's what I wanted, Han? I didn't ask you to do that. I just wanted things to be like they were."

"Yes, and I understand that, but I was panicking—we could have discussed it. But you won't discuss things. You just sulk and walk off. You can't bear me needing something from you, but I'm not your mum, Will. You left me out there on my own because of that," she said. "You didn't believe me, because you were angry. And when you see the news, you need to think about why."

Silence filled the room.

Will turned the pen upright and clicked it on and off, on the desk. She knew he wanted to ask what had happened, but couldn't.

Hannah smelled the woman's perfume in the room. A cloying, sexy scent.

She nodded towards the door. "She likes you."

His voice was dry. "Don't they always."

Hannah took out a folded sheet from her bag. "Barbara says I can start again, and apply to adopt her by myself. So you need to decide what you want to do."

She placed the photocopied picture of the little girl on his desk.

"But if you want to do it with me, you and I have to be solid. No cracks. It's not fair on her. What this little girl has been through is worse than you, Will, and she'd need us both to be strong. If you want to do this with me, then you need to really grow up."

She opened the door and, although it made her heart break, she walked out.

The blond woman sat in her studio at the end of the corridor, watching her, unsmiling.

47

Hannah arrived back at the clinic in Ipswich the next morning and was directed to Dr. Barton's office. She put down the bag of items that she'd brought, which contained clues to help the team now in charge of Elvie's welfare piece her life together.

"Hi. How is she?" she asked, when Elvie's psychologist bounded in with a cheery hello and shut the door. He was in his late fifties, with thick gray hair and a beard. He wore a sleeveless cardigan over a shirt and tie, and held a sheaf of notes. The spark in his eyes told Hannah this was a thrilling moment in his career.

"Well, she keeps surprising us!" He laughed, taking a seat opposite Hannah.

"Really?"

"Oh, yes." He opened his folder. "First of all, thank you for your offer to help. Normally I'd be speaking to family, but clearly these are special circumstances. Now, can you tell me again: when we spoke on Tuesday, you said Elvie had learning difficulties? Someone had suggested a loss of oxygen at birth?"

"That's right—Tiggy." Hannah recalled her first meeting with the Mortrens. She'd thought a lot about this. Whose decision had it been to pretend that Elvie was their daughter? How much time had the Mortrens and the others spent trying to decide how to explain Elvie's identity to the first newcomers to Tornley in eighty years? "But Tiggy's one of the ones who've been arrested. So I wouldn't trust that."

"OK." He sat back. "Well, we've done some tests, and Elvie is illiterate. And I suspect, if the domestic-servitude theory is correct, that would have been done on purpose. No knowledge, no escape. Hmm?" Dr. Barton placed his folder on the desk. "But, so far, no evidence of birth-related learning difficulties, or a clinical disorder."

Hannah watched, surprised. "Really?"

"No. In fact, we've already seen a slight improvement in her language use, as the staff talk to her. I wanted to ask you—you thought she'd spent time with her mother and grandmother, as a child?"

"Yes, I found photos of her grandmother Mabel up till the 1980s, and then apparently the police found more photo albums in the bathroom . . ."

"Where Elvie was hiding?"

"Yes. One album had photos of her mother, C.V. They think C.V. might have died—or disappeared—around 2000. Here."

She pulled out a photo of C.V. that she'd been allowed to bring. As in Olive's oil painting, C.V. was different from Mabel and Elvie—much slighter of frame, with lighter, curly hair. Only the long jaw and the flat expression in her eyes were familiar.

Dr. Barton scribbled on his notes. "Right. Well, yes, that might explain it. If Mabel and C.V. were around during the crucial developmental phases, Elvie would have developed normally, as far as attachments and language skills and socialization are concerned. Elvie mentioned a bedroom to one of the staff— is it possible she could have shared it with her grandmother and mother? Maybe one with flowers on the wall?"

A memory returned of the night Hannah put Elvie to bed in Tornley Hall. "No flowers . . ." Elvie had said in her strange, low voice. She hadn't been talking about Tiggy's homestead. It was a reference to the flowers that Hannah had painted away, on the wall of the only home Elvie had ever known.

"Yes! Wow, that makes sense. I mean, it's pretty clever what she did—making that secret room after the Horseborrows died, in a place where nobody would notice. Even our surveyor missed it. But why does she appear so . . . well, slow?"

Dr. Barton jiggled restlessly. "Well, environment is our best bet right now. Twenty-five years with very little stimulus and no education; nobody to speak to but Mabel and C.V.—and who knows what emotional state they were in? Depression, self-harm, suicidal thoughts perhaps. No children to play with. Then another fifteen years alone, surrounded by people who emotionally and physically abused her. Two and a half years of that, possibly sleeping in the garage, and on the sitting-room floor, you thought?"

"Yes," Hannah replied. "It was like Elvie couldn't understand why we were there. She said it was her house. I think that's why Dax and the others got spooked and decided to get rid of her. It was too risky that we'd find out. They told her to stay away from me, and not to speak, but she kept coming into the house."

She looked at the closed folder of notes about Elvie.

"I have to ask: were there any signs of . . ."

He shook his head. "Bruises, historical small bone fractures in her hands. No signs of sexual abuse."

Hannah blew her cheeks out, relieved. "It's bothering me that somebody must have got her mother, C.V., pregnant, though. Maybe Peter? Or one of the others?"

"Well, it's a grim thought, but if it was Peter, that would at least put Elvie in a position to contest the proceeds of Tornley Hall. Talking of which . . ."

"Oh, yes." Hannah opened her bag and took out the letters. "This is what I wanted to show you. I think Peter Horseborrow wrote these to the American GI who got Mabel pregnant with C.V. But he didn't send them. And they're written in gobbledy-gook. Do you have any idea what he might have been doing?"

Dr. Barton took the faded reams of nursery rhymes, clearly fascinated. "Goodness! Well, he was clearly trying to control the situation, wasn't he? Increasing his efforts to coerce poor Mabel, perhaps." The psychologist broke into the impression of a posh Peter talking to the pregnant teenager. "'He doesn't answer the letters, dear, he doesn't want you and the baby. Your family doesn't want you, either. No, you're better off with us.'"

Hannah regarded the neat, copperplate writing of the ar-rogant, idle Peter Horseborrow and imagined him plotting to keep Mabel at Tornley Hall. How clever he must have thought himself, to find this vulnerable, working-class teenager. How perfect a plan to use her as free domestic help, to replace the servants that he and his lazy sister Olive could no longer afford, now that their father's hard-earned estate had been lost.

The thought of Mabel's family reminded her of the plumber Mark Vyne. Mabel's nephew.

"Oh, and you met Mark Vyne?"

Dr. Barton dragged his eyes from the letters. "Yes, I did. DNA results are due back next week."

"And he told you that Peter Horseborrow called him to

Tornley Hall about ten years ago, on a pretext? I just wondered: why do you think Peter did that? Do you think he felt guilty?"

"What—did he have a moment of conscience towards the end of his life?" Dr. Barton sat back and folded his arms. "Who knows? Perhaps Peter thought he'd been very clever. Perhaps he wanted to gloat. He'd not only managed to find one young woman to do his dirty work, but two more—born in Tornley—to carry on after Mabel. As you said, they almost bred the girls like farm animals."

Hannah nodded. "I keep wondering how Peter met Mabel. Mark said his uncle Stan thought she'd hitched a lift to Sudbury to find the GI on the day she went missing. Peter and Olive definitely had a car. I saw one in the photos. I keep imagining them pulling over on the road and finding her in tears, because the GI had told her to get lost, or had gone back to the States. And Mabel being too scared to go home, because her mother was so angry at her for getting pregnant."

"What—and they offer to take her home and look after her? Offer her free board and food, in return for a little domestic work till the baby is born?" Dr. Barton interlinked his fingers and pushed them behind his head. "Makes you wonder, doesn't it? At what point does a bit of free help around the house become seventy years of group abuse by a whole farming community? And at what point does it become serious enough that they decide to let Mabel and C.V. die—or even bring about their demise—instead of calling a doctor and risking some busybody asking questions about who the women were, and what they were doing there?"

Hannah recalled, with a shudder of terror, her night in Samuel's shack. "Samuel used the phrase 'put down.' I believe they were going to get rid of me, and Elvie."

Dr. Barton sighed. "Well, they must have known that if you spilt the beans, they'd be charged over the deaths of Mabel and C.V., at the very least, to say nothing of coercing her into free labor. I imagine they were panicking, and blaming each other. This type of group abuse can be incremental, of course. One person's act is built upon another's. The Horseborrows use a vulnerable teenager for free domestic help. The farmer next door gets suspicious, so they lend her to him to work during the harvest, to shut him up, and he enjoys the profit he gets from the free labor. Then the Mortrens move in, to start their flower business in the 1970s. They ask questions, and the girls are 'lent' to them, too. If Mabel wants to leave Tornley with C.V., how does she do so? She's illiterate, has no money, no way to communicate, no transport. Even if she could walk out of there, the Horseborrows tell her that she's shamed her family and nobody wants her. She'll end up on the streets. She'll go to prison, for wasting police time searching for her. She can't leave. Anyway she owes them now for all that food and accommodation, and there's the baby, too. She's better off at Tornley." He shook his head. "It really is astonishing. It could only happen in a closed community. Think about it. There are no outsiders to condemn the group behavior. And it becomes worse. Mabel loses the will and confidence to leave. The abusive use of her labor becomes so entrenched within the community that nobody can remember who started it. When C.V. and later Elvie are born, it carries on."

Hannah frowned. "But to cause a death—somebody must have been responsible for that. Surely one of them must have had less of a conscience than the others?"

Dr. Barton nodded. "Quite possibly. It is certainly a serious development within the group."

Hannah thought of Dax, and of those cold wolf eyes. "I can guess." She shuddered.

• • •

After her meeting with Dr. Barton, Hannah visited Elvie. Elvie sat opposite a member of staff, who held up cards with pictures on them. She regarded Hannah with the usual blank eyes.

She was clean and wore a bright-pink tracksuit, which the nurse said she'd chosen herself and would not be dissuaded from. Her black hair was brushed to the side, and on her feet she wore large, furry slippers.

"Hi, Elvie," Hannah said, walking over. "You look lovely."

Elvie smiled shyly.

Hannah took her big, rough hand, and Elvie let her. "Thank you for helping me the other night. You did a very brave thing."

Elvie kept smiling.

The therapist kept her eyes trained on her. "Elvie's been telling me one of the nursery rhymes her grandmother Mabel taught her and her mother, C.V."

"Wow, I'd like to hear that," Hannah said.

Elvie opened her mouth and started to speak. It was a shock to hear so many words come out in her deep, flat voice:

The apples fall down one by one
And with a crack they hit the ground
And with one chop, a head falls free
Under the rotten apple tree

The apples fall down two by two
And roll under my leather shoe
And with one chop, a head falls free
Under the rotten apple tree

The nursery rhyme continued till Elvie reached verse ten.

"Thank you, Elvie," the therapist said. "I wonder what that nursery rhyme is about?"

Hannah knew the woman was testing the responses from Elvie, but she couldn't help herself. She squeezed Elvie's hand in hers.

"It's about waiting, isn't it, Elvie? Killing time," Hannah said. "Counting the days till something happens, even when you don't know if it ever will."

She thought of Will.

· · ·

Back in London, Will finally turned over the photo of the little girl on his desk. Her eyes met his, from within the shadows.

He stared. She was amazing. She was everything he'd ever imagined. Her eyes seemed to be asking him what he was waiting for.

48

THREE MONTHS LATER

The sun was out in London. It was July and the city appeared to have emptied out for the summer.

Even though it was half-past nine on a Monday morning the North Circular route around London was quiet. They turned off onto a road into east London, then took various turns, still following the GPS. For the second time this morning it lost its way, due to a new road layout.

"No!" Hannah cried. "It's gone again."

"Why haven't we updated it?" Will said.

"I don't know. Why *haven't* we updated it?"

"Where's the map?"

"Why are you asking me? I'm not the bloody First Officer."

And so it went on for two more minutes, until Hannah spotted the main road they were meant to turn right at, and shouted for Will to brake.

He reversed and they pulled into a long road of neat terraces.

"OK, we're five minutes early," Hannah said. "Where's Barbara's car?"

"Can't see it," Will said, turning off the engine.

Hannah sat back and stared at the house.

They were here.

A familiar white hatchback drew up and parked in front of them. Barbara climbed out and waved.

Will wound down the window.

"Right. Give me a few minutes," Barbara said. "I'll tell you when to come." She laughed. "I love this bit!"

She walked into the gate of the house two doors along.

Hannah and Will fell into silence.

"Oh, my God! This is it," Hannah said. "What if, after all this, I'm crap at it? What if I'm a terrible mother?"

Will leaned over and brushed a stray hair back from her face. "It'll be fine."

Barbara emerged from the house and waved them in.

They got out of the car and walked up the driveway towards the door, the photo in Hannah's pocket, where it had been for the past three months, welded to her skin.

They walked through the doorway into a hall and saw a woman in shadow at the end, with a little figure held high in her solid, safe arms.

A flash of sunlight on red curls.

A finger in a mouth.

A child hoping that everyone was telling the truth, and knowing that she had no choice but to trust them.

Hannah walked in, Will walked in, and the child's eyes flicked between them.

The front door closed.

Acknowledgments

Many thanks to Emily Bestler, and all the team at Emily Bestler Books/Atria in New York. Also, to Trisha Jackson, Harriet Sanders, Lizzy Kremer, and Harriet Moore in London.

A further thanks to Nick Southwood for talking me through studio production, and to my family for accommodating me on writing trips to the very beautiful county of Suffolk, England.

Pick up or download Louise Millar's gripping novels wherever books are sold.